L.B. DUNBAR

www.lbdunbar.com

Cover Design: Lori Jackson
Cover Photographer: Golden Czermak/Furious Fotog
Cover Model: Sean Michael Rae
Editor: Nicole McCurdy/Emerald Edits
Editor: Gemma Brocato

Other Books by L.B. Dunbar

<u>Sterling Falls</u>
Sterling Heat
Sterling Brick
Sterling Streak

Parentmoon (standalone)

<u>Holiday Hotties (novellas)</u>
Scrooge-ish
Naughty-ish

<u>Road Trips & Romance</u>
Hauling Ashe
Merging Wright
Rhode Trip

<u>Lakeside Cottage</u>
Living at 40
Loving at 40
Learning at 40
Letting Go at 40

<u>The Silver Foxes of Blue Ridge</u>
Silver Brewer
Silver Player
Silver Mayor
Silver Biker

<u>Sexy Silver Fox Collection</u>
After Care
Midlife Crisis
Restored Dreams
Second Chance
Wine&Dine

<u>Collision novellas</u>
Collide
Caught

Rom-com for the over 40 (standalone)
The Sex Education of M.E.

The Heart Collection
Speak from the Heart
Read with your Heart
Look with your Heart
Fight from the Heart
View with your Heart

A Heart Collection Spin-off
The Heart Remembers

BOOKS IN OTHER AUTHOR WORLDS
Smartypants Romance (an imprint of Penny Reid)
Love in Due Time
Love in Deed
Love in a Pickle

The World of True North (an imprint of Sarina Bowen)
Cowboy
Studfinder

THE EARLY YEARS
The Legendary Rock Star Series

Paradise Stories

The Island Duet

Modern Descendants – writing as elda lore

Dedication

For E. You gave us a little scare entering this world, but our lives are forever richer with you here.

Thank you to authors willing to support other authors, like Skye Warren.

The first two chapters, in part, appeared in *Nightingale*, a USA TODAY Bestselling Collaboration.
I was honored to be part of that collection.
The proceeds were donated to a worthy cause.

Kindness should be without end;
cyclical like the shape of a donut . . .
or a baby-Bundt cake.

Chapter 1

October

[Enya]

Falling on my backside in front of a handsome man was the last thing I expected to happen today.

Then again, the day has been full of surprises.

After leaving the small-town bakery with only minutes to spare before it closed, a torrential downpour came out of nowhere as I stood on the shop's stoop. Balancing my tote and a paper bag containing one of the most delicious-looking baby-Bundt cakes, I snapped open the travel umbrella I'd found in the bottom of my oversized purse and risked the deluge.

However, when stepping onto the sidewalk, a gust of wind careened along the storefronts on the quaint main street and jacked my umbrella. The flimsy thing snapped backward to look like an art deco buttercup flower, offering no protection from the cold, pelting rain which rode the wind and came at me sideways. In an effort to right my worthless umbrella, I spun on my heels in hopes the gusts of the gale would snap the thing back into its proper position. The wind took me as well, forcing me backward when the umbrella momentarily expanded. As I tried to maintain my balance, the heel of my over-priced stiletto slipped into a grate in the sidewalk. Struck by the ridiculous physics of a thin spike wedging into an even slimmer slat opening, my ankle gave way and I collapsed onto my ass.

"Miss, are you alright?" The broad and slightly rebellious-looking man from the bakery I just left asked me.

Perfect. Just perfect.

For a moment, I sit on the rain-drenched sidewalk, allowing the chilly drops to batter me, plastering my hair to my face and further drenching my already soaked dress.

This is what I get for wanting to celebrate.

For wishing for something more in my life. For grasping at something I never thought I'd have.

I almost laugh until the concern in the dark blue eyes of the large man standing over me has me swallowing instead. His jeans are saturated at his ankles, above a pair of solid biker boots. His white T-shirt is plastered to his body, the opaque material accentuating dark hairs on his chest and the solid muscles of his upper arms. He's thick in the midsection. Firm might be a better description. A paw of a hand extends toward me and slowly I lift mine to accept his help.

My umbrella is nowhere in sight. The bag containing my miniature cake tragically sits in a shallow puddle on the sidewalk. My foot has slipped out of my shoe. My wounded pride is the only thing present. I've never been so embarrassed. And my backside uncomfortably aches.

"Let's get inside, yeah?" he yells over the torrent of rain, swiping at his face to clear the drops. His eyes are kind. His voice rough. A sprinkling of silver peppers among his temple and over his ears.

I nod and accept his assistance, as he holds my hand and gathers up the remains of a soggy paper bag. Once we enter the cool breeze of the bakery, he tosses the waterlogged sack on the counter and turns to face me. The thickness of his hand is a comfort as he pushes back my hair, effectively exposing my mortified blush. His gentle fingers glide through the wet strands, tucking an errant lock behind my ear. His thumb trails a blaze of warmth down my cheek. Heat infuses my whole body, from my frozen toes to the tips of my ears. It's a welcome sensation beneath the cool air-conditioning.

I shiver. Teeth chattering. Tailbone throbbing. I'm off-balance wearing only one shoe.

"We should probably get you out of those clothes." The depth of his voice has my body humming in a new way, but I still choke around my next word.

"What?"

"Got a change of clothes in that bag?" He nods at my tote which surprisingly remained looped over my arm; however, water drips through the seams. I'm certain everything inside is as soaked as the leather. Why do bag companies make totes without closures? And why did I own something that couldn't protect my belongings?

Oh right, it matched my now-ruined shoes.

"No." I can't hold my teeth still.

"Only speak one word at a time?" His rugged tenor matches the hitch on one corner of his lips, suggesting a smile is hard won from him. Still, the expression is doing strange things to my lower belly.

Or maybe that's something else inside me fluttering.

Don't be ridiculous. I only took a test this morning. Surely, I can't feel anything yet. Although I'd read home-tests are ninety-nine percent correct, I won't know anything with certainty until I see my doctor.

"I-I'm sorry. I ruined the cake." Hopefully, he can't decipher between welling tears and water on my face as I'm on the verge of crying over a silly lemon cake. Then again, maybe it's simply my emotions which have been pinging all over the place since this morning.

"No worries." He pauses, stepping back to size me up while tipping his head. His hand still holds mine or maybe mine is clinging to his. I don't want to let go. His palm is so warm. His fingers strong. "I have a T-shirt that might fit you more like a dress, but it'd be warmer than what you are wearing."

At thirty-eight, everything in me should clang like warning bells. I don't know him. I'm not from this town. No one knows I made this stop. But while his sapphire eyes could be interpreted as dangerous, the heat in them glides over me like a protective blanket.

I nod, blindly following him to the back of the bakery, limping on my one heel.

When we step inside the office, he releases my hand. Rummaging through some boxes, he pulls out a large T-shirt with Curmudgeon Bakery on the back. He scowls at the shirt before handing it over to me.

"It's going to be loose on you, but it will be dry. I'll step out while you change, but if you hand me your things, I'll toss them in the dryer."

I weakly smile. "It's dry clean only." A tumble in a dryer would ruin the material of my dress. If it isn't already destroyed.

His eyes roam my soaked outfit, like a physical caress. From the collar of my dress, trailing right down to the saturated hem plastered to my thighs, those warm eyes peruse every inch of me. He takes a deep inhale through his nose, his wide chest puffing out with the movement, before pausing a second. Then he turns his head to the side. Without a word, he slips around me and softly closes the door.

Once he leaves, I glance down at my dress, suctioned to every curve and dip of my figure. My nipples are protruding peaks giving away how cold I am. Or is it something else? My body reacting to the way he was looking at me. The heat in his gaze. Warmth fills my cheeks once again. I shiver at the possibility he might have liked what he saw.

Shaking my head, I dismiss crazy thoughts. He wasn't looking at me in any way other than he might stare at a drowned rat. With shaky fingers and chilled limbs, I work to remove my clothing. Deciding my bra and underwear will only cause discomfort under the dryness of a fresh shirt, I remove them as well. With the oversized T-shirt on, I run my hand over my backside, confirming the length covers my butt. Every attempt to bend forward forces me to catch my breath and wince at the pain in my tailbone.

Glancing around the office, it's an accountant's nightmare. Papers stacked like lopsided pancakes on the floor. A box brimming with receipts rests on a file cabinet. The desktop is covered in haphazard piles. But the thing that attracts my gaze the most is a large zipper sweatshirt draped over the back of the desk chair. Taking the liberty, I swipe up the soft cotton and wrap myself in another layer for warmth. The collar smells like vanilla and motor oil, which is a strange yet surprisingly refreshing combination. I smile to myself as I inhale what I assume is the scent of the curmudgeon baker himself.

A soft knock comes to the door, but it opens before I answer. "I figured you might want these. I don't have shoes that would fit you." That crook of his lips happens again. He's making a joke. He's also holding out a pair of socks when he glances at my feet. His feet must be four sizes bigger than mine. "Or you can keep hobbling on one foot."

When he looks up, the flame in his eyes flares. His gaze lowers from my face to the sweatshirt dangling too long on my arms and the T-shirt that hits just above my knees.

"Thank you." My voice is still unsteady but I'm not certain it's the cold making my throat rumble. I shrug and smooth my fingers down one side of the open zipper. "I hope you don't mind."

He shakes his head, and I take the socks from him, wincing as I bend forward to slip them on.

"Are you hurt?"

"Besides my pride?" I joke then reality hits me. Am I hurt? Did I do any internal damage? Is everything still good in there? "My backside is killing me."

At the mention of my ass, he chokes, and I glance up to find him swiping his thick fingers around his mouth, stroking at the bristly hairs on his chin. He looks more like a biker than a baker but he's the man who filled my cake order. He has swapped his wet clothes for a dry pair of jeans and a light gray Henley shirt. His close-cropped hair is damp. A towel hangs over his shoulder.

"Are you the curmudgeon baker?" I ask, righting myself and wincing again as pain shoots up my spine.

"A joke from my family," he mocks.

"But are you the owner of Curmudgeon Bakery?" I tip my head. He's solid brawn, and I can't imagine his hefty fingers delicately decorating baby-Bundt cakes, but the judgement is unfair.

"Yeah." His gaze lowers to the floor and the corner of his mouth tips up again. Pride fills his voice while his cheeks pinken the slightest bit.

"What? Only answer one word at a time?" I tease.

His head pops up and those dark eyes dance with mischief. He stares at my saturated hair. "I brought you this." Dragging a towel off his shoulder, he hands it to me and arches a brow. "And that was four words."

With a cheeky smile, I mutter, "Thanks," and rub the material over my face, inhaling a stronger blend of vanilla mixed with laundry detergent. My makeup must be a frightful mess.

He tilts his head toward the storefront, "How about some coffee?"

With a nod, I finger comb my long hair as best I can. Following him into the bakery while wearing his socks, I twist my hair around itself, forming a messy bun. He points to a long wooden bench, and gingerly I sit, wincing before trying to balance on one cheek.

The sexy baker rounds the display counter, and I take the opportunity to glance at his well-sculpted backside. *Nice.*

He pours two mugs of coffee, and then comes to the table, setting down each steaming container. "I'll be right back."

Disappearing through a door marked Private, he quickly returns and holds out a bed pillow. "For your ass."

I laugh as he takes a seat across from me in a chair. "I'm Enya, by the way. Enya Calloway."

"Nice to meet you, Enya Calloway." He lifts his mug, watching me over the rim. In typical conversation this is where he should tell me his name, but he doesn't offer, and I don't ask.

There's something very unconventional about this man.

As silence grows, I glance around the bakery. Display cases line one side while the long, wooden, booth bench where I sit, and a scattering of tables line the opposite wall. The floor is giant black and white squares while subway tiles decorate the wall giving the place an old-world-bakery atmosphere. Or maybe it's New Age as the stark white, clean lines have made a resurgence. With the hum of the air conditioner no longer buzzing, music can be heard.

"Imagine" by John Lennon fills the space.

"Beatles fan?" I hitch a brow, glancing at him over the rim of my mug. He shrugs, all casual coolness across from me, watching me drink my coffee. One arm rests against the back of the chair beside him; the other hand cups his mug. Silence has never been so comfortable, but I can't keep quiet for long. I glance up at a quote on the wall.

There is NO HOLE in Kindness.

The capitalized Os are shaped like donuts.

"Strange quote."

"This location used to be a donut shop." He offers, as if that explains everything.

"Donuts have holes."

He shrugs. His smirk matches my smile. "Bundt cakes do as well." He tips his head to read the quote himself. "It was here when I bought the place. Figured it brought the previous owners thirty-two years of business luck. I left it on the wall."

Taking a second glance, a faint outline surrounds the quote, as if fresh paint didn't match the original color.

"Maybe it's a metaphor. Like kindness is cyclical."

He shrugs again and scoffs while lifting his mug. "Maybe it was a nicer way of saying don't be an asshole."

Glancing back at the quote, I mutter, "Maybe." Unfortunately, I've known a few assholes in my thirty-eight years. Lowering my gaze, I look at him again. "Got any other quotes for good luck?"

His lip quirks up on one side and he tips his chin. "What do you need luck for?" Those heavy blue eyes scan my face.

Do I need luck? I should already feel like the luckiest woman in the world. But my eyes instantly well. Damn my emotions.

"I'm pregnant." Saying the words aloud for the first time feels strange. A little unreal. A lot exciting.

His arm along the back of the chair slips to the seat. His hand on the handle of his mug flattens on the tabletop. His entire demeanor shifts, and that hint of danger becomes more apparent. An invisible wall goes up around him. He leans forward.

"Husband must be happy." His rugged tone, which once sounded friendly, is now jagged.

"No husband." With my gaze aimed at the table, the wood surface blurs from the threat of tears.

"Boyfriend, then?" His voice croaks on the term.

I shake my head. How do I explain my situation to a stranger?

"You're the first person I've told." A sour lump fills my throat when I'm actually ecstatic deep down.

"Shit." The gruffness filters into my ears, but all I really hear is the pulsing of my own heart.

I'm going to have a baby.

Suddenly, I'm hefted off the bench and wrapped in thick arms. My head is pressed to his chest where the rapid rhythm of his heart is a steady song. Thrown off guard at first, my arms are trapped between us, but slowly, I loosen them and circle his waist. Tears slip down my nose.

I don't know why I'm crying. This is what I wanted.

Still, I'm scared . . . and his simple questions remind me I'm doing this alone.

"Want me to kill the bastard? I know people." The ferocity in his question tells me he isn't joking but there's no one to harm.

I shake my head against his solid pecs, anxiously giggling despite the flow of tears. "I'm good."

His hand glides down my back, pausing just above my ass. His other hand cups my head, holding me against him. I close my eyes, inhaling the vanilla and motor oil scent of him. We stand like this for long enough the awkwardness of hugging a stranger should settle in, but I don't want to move.

And I don't know why I told him this monumental truth.

As I pull back, his hand at the base of my spine keeps me close to him. His eyes search mine and I wish I could read his thoughts. I wish I could tell this stranger all of mine.

Wishing is what got me where I am, though. Pregnant and alone at thirty-eight.

"I was here to buy a Bundt cake. A little celebration of sorts." The explanation sounds even odder than telling him I'm pregnant. While some might pop champagne, I can't. A *baby* Bundt cake felt appropriate for a future birth. In roughly eight months, I'll have a birthday to commemorate.

He huffs, swiping back at the hair coming loose from my makeshift bun. Abruptly, he releases me, and the reality of standing in borrowed socks and a stolen sweatshirt hits me. He must think I'm a nut.

As he walks away, I shamelessly check out his backside, rounded and firm in tight-fitting jeans. He circles the counter once more but quickly returns to where I stand. A baby-Bundt cake sits on a small plate and two forks are in his hand. He nudges me to return to my seat and he slides into the chair across from me again.

Placing the plate between us, he holds up a fork and nods for me to do the same.

"To babies and Bundt cakes." His tone rings slightly somber. He taps my fork like we are clinking glasses of champagne and then he pushes the plate in my direction, suggesting I take the first bite.

The moist lemon cake perfectly balanced with a rich buttercream frosting melts in my mouth. As I close my eyes, I moan, not even exaggerating the orgasm on my tongue. The texture. The flavor. Chef's kiss.

When I open my lids, his eyes smolder at me, and the strangest fantasy fills my head.

He's the father of my baby and he's so excited by my announcement he wants to take me on this table to commemorate the good news.

My eyes widen. Horror fills my face in a heated rush. My imagination would only complicate matters.

Softly, he chuckles, pulls the plate closer to him and fills his fork. As I watch him take a bite, he sucks at the utensil, taking his time to savor the experience within his mouth. A place on me that has no business beating, pulses like a kitchen mixer, strong and fierce. Slowly, he removes the tines, taking his time to release the fork, now clean of cake. My mouth dries, curious about the mystery of his tongue. Wondering what his lips might feel like clamping onto parts of me. How firmly does he suck? How roughly does he kiss?

My body heats but shivers return with the carnal need to ask these questions.

I still don't even know his name.

However, as we share this piece of cake, and the silence between us fills with another Beatles tune, I fight back my lust and come to a decision.

A simple act of kindness might be more seductive than spreading me on this table.

No holes *is* a metaphor. Kindness goes around and around in quiet gestures, like fresh socks, a warm sweatshirt, a celebratory piece of cake, and a secretive smile.

And one day, I hope to repay the curmudgeon baker for his generosity in a grand way.

Chapter 2

[Sebastian]

I want to kiss her and that just makes me an asshole.

She's fucking gorgeous. That had been my first thought when I saw her on the other side of the counter, ordering a miniature lemon cake. In her skin-toned dress, hugging her curves, and wearing high heels that should be a sin, she didn't belong in my small-town bakery. Still, I wanted to sample all her goods.

However, I had a shit-ton of orders to fill. The day had been slow. Business tapers down a little in late afternoon which is why sometimes I close shop around three to tackle special orders and next-day deliveries.

She entered five minutes before I was ready to lock the door.

When I rang up her small purchase, a strange sense of longing overcame me. As in, I didn't want her to leave my bakery, which was ridiculous.

She was out of my league.

However, I watched her out the front window overlooking Corner Street. In slow motion, she wrestled with her umbrella before she fell on her ass. Her firm, tight ass without a panty line in sight.

Jesus. I was just happy she hadn't fallen backward and hit her head. The wind was wicked fierce.

When I'd helped her up, the weirdest thing happened when our hands connected. Like thunder exploding and lightning striking, which was probably only because thunder did rumble overhead, and the sky filled with a bright flash. An early fall thunderstorm was upon us as summer tried to hang on, but autumn wanted its season.

Thankfully, she followed me back into the bakery.

I knew seeing her in that T-shirt was going to be difficult. Fuck, I was hard just thinking about her in my clothes as I rushed up to my apartment and quickly changed into drier things for myself. But when I saw her in that sweatshirt, draping over her limbs, open at the front giving me a peek of the shortness of my tee and the length of her legs, I wasn't certain I could be a gentleman.

However, I contained myself.

I gave her coffee and watched her lips as she sipped.

I listened as she told me her good news.

I pulled her to me when she looked like she could use a hug.

I didn't want to let her go. But I did.

She is pregnant with another guy's baby. And I didn't do babies, or women that belonged to other men. I wasn't ever going to be a father.

So, I offered her cake and struggled as she moaned in pleasure around the moisture in her mouth.

We sat in silence, while John Lennon sang around us. Questions whirled around in my head about the bomb she dropped. However, as I wasn't willing to offer much of myself, I didn't ask about her.

It hadn't been a slip to not mention my name.

I just didn't see the point. She was going to finish her cake, leave my bakery, and never see me again. I've lived in Sterling Falls my entire life except for a seven-year stint I don't like to think about anymore. I knew everyone who lived here. Hell, I knew most people who lived in Milton County, named for the mountain this town sat on. Milton Peak was mountain country, and she was not a local. She had city-slick, business chick written all over her.

Comfortable with quiet myself, I could tell she was getting anxious to leave. I still didn't want her to go but I didn't have a reason for her to stay.

She was having a baby.

No husband and no boyfriend.

Where my thoughts went next weren't pretty, but she tried to assure me she was okay in her condition. The anger that felt like a constant hum inside me vibrated strongly beneath my skin. I'd hurt anyone who hurt her. Which was an unsettling thought about a stranger.

"I should probably go," she finally says when the plate between us is clean of every crumb of cake and dollop of frosting. Our coffee mugs are empty, and I have orders to fill. Yet, I don't want her to leave.

There's something about the rain hitting the bakery window, loud enough it almost ripples in beat with John Lennon's soothing voice. The darkness of the afternoon sky and the soft lighting of the shop make the atmosphere of the bakery cozy, almost intimate, and heavy with something thick, sweet, and tempting. When another loud clap of thunder strikes and Enya jumps in her seat, the illusion of what her and me as anything other than two people sharing a Bundt cake collides with things I can never have.

"I'll just collect my things." She slips from the booth bench, leaving behind the pillow that cushioned her fine ass. Without shame, I'm going to bury my head in that thing tonight. I'm going to inhale the down like she's on my face, riding my tongue and letting me eat her whole.

Jesus. I swipe a hand over my face as she glides past me toward the office. Looking over my shoulder, I watch her move. My sweatshirt is so large it covers all her curves, but I still sense the sway of her hips. Her hair has slowly been slipping out of the twist at her nape and long, loose, dark waves dangle down her back. Her calves are toned. She's cute in my oversized socks. I want to see her in all my things and then nothing at all.

Fuck. I stand and snatch up the two mugs along with the plate and forks. Rounding the counter, I set the things in a bin for the dishwasher. Too quickly, she's standing in the bakery with her bag over her shoulder. She's no longer wearing my socks.

"I'll just drive barefoot," she says, noticing me staring at her toes.

"That isn't safe." I don't like the idea. I don't like her leaving while it's still raining. I don't want her to go.

But I tamp down my desire and circle the counter once more. With a hand at her elbow, I guide her to the door. We seem to move in labored steps when the distance isn't far. Maybe she doesn't want to go any more than I want her to leave.

It's a silly thought.

When we're a foot from the front door, she spins to face me. Her dark eyes are wide and bright. The perfect blend of coffee with a touch of cream. My sweatshirt still covers her shoulders, and the deep navy highlights her skin. Unable to help myself, I reach for her hair again, swiping the still damp pieces framing her face over her ear.

"I promise I'll return your things. Clean, of course."

"Keep 'em." I don't need them back. I like that she'll have a piece of me wherever she'll be going.

"Thank you." She pauses, placing her hand on my bicep. "For everything."

She lifts up on her toes and leans in for my cheek. The softest touch lingers against the bristly hairs before she pulls back.

However, the gentleman in me snaps. I follow her retreat, chasing her mouth until mine meets hers. Like the final spread of icing on a cake, one finished with a flourish, proud of the perfection, I sweep against her lips. Once. Twice.

She doesn't respond at first. I'd overstepped. I need to get a grip on myself.

As I pull away no more than an inch, her hand cups my nape, and my head is tugged forward. Our mouths come together once more, eager for another sample. More than a simple taste this time, but the entire cake. One eaten with open lips and seeking tongues.

Fuck. She tastes like lemon and sugar and she's melting in my mouth. We move and her back lands on the sliver of wall between the front door and the large picture window. Her body presses against mine and the thinness of our T-shirts tells me she's naked underneath. Her firm swells flatten against my chest and my fingers twitch with the desire to explore.

"You aren't wearing a bra," I mutter at her mouth before delving back in for another taste of her.

Against my lips, she mumbles, "It was wet."

I bet she's drenched in other ways than a damn rain-soaked dress.

"Next you're going to tell me you don't have on underwear." I swallow her answer with another searing kiss, but she breaks for air and speaks against my lips.

"I'm not."

The words vibrate straight to my hard-as-a-knife dick.

My hands had been in her hair, digging into the thickness despite the damp waves, but I release her head and slip my fingers inside my sweatshirt on her. Outlining her waist, I lower, eager for the hem of the shirt she wears. My palms are my guide, searching for panty lines. Slowly, I clutch the hem of the tee. I want to touch her. Like a kid told not to reach for the flame on a stove, I'm tempted despite the warning sizzling through me.

This woman could burn me.

I dip underneath the shirt, tickling along the outer side of her upper thighs, cautiously climbing her curves while my fingertips scorch from the heat of her skin.

Fuck, I want her. I want to shuck my jeans and set my dick free to slam into her warmth.

A question douses my desire. Do I really want to take her against the wall of my bakery?

A resounding yes fills my head.

But would she want *me*?

My mouth stills on her lips. *What am I doing?* This isn't what *I* want from her. She might be a stranger, and while that should be the wrong part, the part that doesn't feel right is how much I'd like to know her. Be someone to her before I enter her body.

I'm the first person she told she was pregnant.

For a second, the most bizarre thought occurs. I could fuck her, fill her with my seed, and pretend that baby inside her is mine. Logistically, it wouldn't make sense. Someone else's sperm has already done the deed.

The thought freezes everything. Time. My breath. My desires.

I'd be a shit dad anyway, and a kid is the last thing I want.

Abruptly, I pull away from her and lower the edge of the shirt without glancing down at her naked center. The struggle is real, but the truth is harsher. She isn't mine.

My forehead rests on hers and her breath comes heavy and sweet over my face.

"You should go," I grunt while it's the opposite of what I want.

Her hands catch my wrists and hold. "Please don't say this was a mistake." Her voice breaks. Her eyes are bright. Her lips swollen.

Fuck, I want her mouth again and those lips around my dick. I want to suck and sip at her as well, but she isn't for me.

She's a coveted cookie in the jar before dinner. She'll spoil me, and I wouldn't be satisfied with only one nibble.

I shake my head, dismissing the idea of that kiss being a mistake. I'm never going to make lemon cake again without thinking of her.

"Maybe you could tell me—"

I cover her lips with a finger then skim over the sweet swell of the lower curve.

There's nothing to say.

This wasn't a mistake, but she'll eventually forget me. I'm forgettable.

On that thought, I press back from her and reach for the door at her side. Tugging it open, I hold it by my outstretched arm.

"Goodbye, Enya."

Her name is a song as sweet as a Beatles' tune.

"Goodbye curmudgeon." She slips to the side and gives me her back. As soon as she crosses the threshold, I close the door and lock it. Then I fall against that sliver of space and swipe both hands over my face. My palms smell like her. Rainwater and sugar. I crane my neck to sneak a peek out the front window, but she's already gone.

With the table clear of our plate and mugs, and the air conditioning humming along with the somber music, this afternoon feels like a dream.

Maybe she wasn't really here.

Then I return to my office where Enya's presence haunts me by her dress over a chair and her singular shoe on my floor.

The reality of her absence burns a small hole in my chest.

Chapter 3

The following May

[Enya]

I probably shouldn't be here. I'd done everything in my power to avoid the Curmudgeon Bakery since that embarrassing moment months ago when I fell on my ass outside the shop and then kissed the baker.

My emotions had been all over the place that day. They've only gotten worse over the past several months. I've never been an emotional woman. I'm someone who thrives on structure. Numbers are my thing. As an accountant, I work best with digits and derivatives.

At thirty-four weeks pregnant, the other thing that's changed is my body. My cheeks have a permanent ruddiness to them. My fingers are thick like sausages. My ankles have disappeared. I should have never worn these shoes today, but I had a meeting just outside of town. I'd made it through another tax season, but I had clients who needed additional accounting services. The forty-minute drive from my hometown of Huntington became a necessity today.

And while I told myself I wouldn't return to the scene of my crime—kissing the curmudgeon baker—the craving for one of his lemon baby-Bundt cakes is too great today. I'm so desperate I'm willing to face the possibility of running into my kissing victim.

Despite the unsettling pain in my belly.

"Come on, Cookie. Behave for mommy," I mumble to myself as I enter the bakery, holding my breath, hoping that the kissable baker won't be present, and gritting my teeth through the pain.

Since early this morning, the tightening of my belly and the pressure in my lower back has been building, but I'm not due for another six weeks.

Braxton-Hicks contractions. I can work my way through them.

Still, I falter in my steps once I enter the bakery. The gripping ache is like a vice, squeezing my belly. My hand protectively covers the stretched skin while I wait out the clenching. As the tension subsides, I glance up to find the curmudgeon himself behind the counter in what looks like an argument with a woman on the customer side.

"Sebastian," she groans. Finally, I have a name for him. *Sebastian.* Tilting my head, I puzzle over how the name strangely fits him. He reminds me a little bit of a historical romance rogue. Someone dashing with a hint of rebel inside him.

The woman's voice interrupts my thoughts. "It's only for a night. Why can't you take him?"

"Because I've told you, *Vale.*" He draws out her name. "I'm not good with kids. And I'd make a shit babysitter."

"He isn't a baby. He's almost nine."

"Ask Stone or Clay," he grumbles.

"You know I hate asking Stone for things and Clay is busy."

"What about Knox or Judd?" he suggests, ducking behind the counter where his body is distorted by the display case. He pulls a tray of brownies in a variety of chocolate, blonde, and something with coconut on top out of the case.

My, she certainly has a lot of men in her life. Provided all those names correlate to men.

"I can't. You're the only one available."

"How do you know I'm available?" He jolts uprights, setting down the tray with a heavy thud on the counter lining the back wall. Efficiently, he works at picking up the brownies and placing a few in a bag. He still hasn't glanced up at me which gives me another minute to check him out.

Those strong biceps. Those thick forearms. That fine ass. He's a vision of strength.

But I heard what he said about babies and kids. While I can appreciate his outer appearance of compelling strength, something lurks beneath my stubble-jawed baker.

Well, not *my* baker. He's not my anything.

On that note, my belly squeezes again, the force enough to double me forward and my palm lands on the glass display case at my side. A squeaking streak resonates as my sweaty hand glides along the glass while I bend forward, cupping my stomach.

Shit, this freaking hurts.

"Are you alright?" The woman standing at the counter offers concern as she addresses me, but it takes me a second before I can catch my breath and stand upright to answer her.

With a shaky hand, I swipe at my forehead, brushing back hairs that have come loose from the tight bun at the base of my neck.

"I'm good," I lie, as my teeth unclench. My jaw is tight. Maybe I should call the doctor.

After I get my lemon baby-Bundt cake.

The woman staring at me has dirty blonde hair and deep brown eyes. She's roughly my height which is simply average for a woman but she's thin and fit, and I want to hate her because I'm bloated like a blow-up costume one wears on Halloween. I feel like Tweedle Dee without his brother.

My gaze shifts from her to the man standing behind the counter who is struck dumb as he stares at me. Maybe he's upset that I never returned his sweatshirt and tee. He'd told me I could keep them when I'd truly intended to return his things, but I didn't know how to face him again.

I'd taken advantage of his sweet kiss and turned it into a mini-make-out session, eager for him to take things further. *Hormones.* On that day, they were already out of whack and making me have crazy thoughts, like him sliding his fingers the remainder of the way up my thigh and between my legs. Then, he'd slip into me, and I could pretend *he'd* been the one to impregnate me.

The idea was selfish and ridiculous, and completely unrealistic.

"Hi." Gingerly, I lift my sweaty palm like he'll remember me, and wave at the man I now know as Sebastian.

The shocked expression on his face and eventual crinkle of his forehead suggests he either doesn't remember me, or he's pissed that he does.

He promised it wasn't a mistake to kiss me.

I shake off the sudden wave of melancholy that ripples down my spine. Then again, that shiver is another back-curving piercing-sensation that has me leaning forward, clutching my lower belly once more.

"Enya?"

As I huff through the tightening, Sebastian moves around the counter. Suddenly, he's at my side. A soothing hand swipes down my spine.

"Just wanted to order a lemon baby-Bundt cake," I wheeze through the toe-curling ache. Huffing out a deep breath, I inhale the strong scent of vanilla and motor oil. Why does he smell like this combination and why is it so mouthwatering?

"Honey," the woman—Vale—addresses me. "How far along are you?"

As the contradiction subsides, I slowly straighten, rubbing a hand over my belly, mentally soothing the bun in my oven and cursing the jabbing pain. "I'm thirty-four weeks. I have six weeks to go."

"You don't look so good," Sebastian mutters beside me and I turn my head to meet his eyes.

"Sebastian," Vale chastises. "Be nice."

"I'm always nice," he snaps at her rather sharply before glancing back at me. "But you look a little ashen."

He presses a hand to my forehead, taking the liberty to touch me. His palm feels cool against my hot skin, and I want him to keep it there for all of eternity. I might have even hummed at the soothing touch.

Then I'm clutched again, forcing me to lurch forward and grip my belly with two hands. "Fuck."

A hand rubs down my back again while the bark, "Call 9-1-1, Rena" drifts over my head. Sebastian's commanding tone sends a tremor through my body or maybe that's the aftereffects of the wallop I just took from my little one.

"Cookie," I groan.

"I don't think she should have anything to eat," Vale says as I'm being ushered to the long wooden bench, where I sat that first time. When I sit all unladylike with my legs spread to accommodate the swell of my belly, I lose a shoe despite the tightness of these heels. Why did I think I could make it through the day wearing them?

I'm set between two tables because I won't be able to sit behind one. When my stomach clenches again, I grip the edge of a table, holding on for dear life as I feel like my body is being ripped in half.

"Seb, she's in labor," Vale warns.

"I can't be," I grind through gritted teeth. *I have one month to go.* I'm not ready. I will be moving in two weeks, and I wasn't fully packed. The house hasn't been finished yet and I was on my way there next after I got my damn lemon cake.

But as the pain rips through me, wetness leaks between my legs. *Did I just pee myself?* Could this get any more embarrassing?

"Shit," I grouse.

"Sugar, I think you peed yourself."

"Seb." Vale smacks the man's chest.

His eyes are wide, taking in the mess I've made on his tile floor. The same floor I wish would open up and swallow me.

"Honey." Vale leans toward me. "I think your water broke."

"What?" My eyes fill with their own liquid, and I rapidly blink, determined not to cry in front of this man again. Determined I won't continue to humiliate myself before him. "My water can't break." I suck in air to will away tears. "Too soon. Six more weeks. Not ready."

Vale softly smiles at me, her pretty face meant to soothe. "When the baby's ready, the baby's ready."

"What?" Sebastian asks, glaring at her.

"This bun is ready to leave the oven." Vale pats his arm as a chuckle fills her voice.

"Here's some water." A second woman with red hair and emerald-green eyes sets the glass on the table I'd pushed out of my way.

"Forget the water. Where the fuck is an ambulance?"

"No ambulance," I mutter, attempting to push myself from my seat but another contraction hits and I'm curling forward, trying to fold into myself.

"Sebastian, do something," Vale cries.

"You do something," he mocks, only he gently presses me to my side, so I'm lying on the bench.

"How close are they coming?" Vale asks me.

"How close are what coming?" Sebastian asks.

"Her contractions."

"I don't know," I huff, breathing through the pain. "I haven't been counting." Which is so stupid of me. I live to count numbers. Why hadn't I been timing the minutes?

"Vale, take a look," Sebastian growls, tension rising in his tone. From his perspective, I've made a mess on his floor, probably violating at least seventy-two health codes, and to make matters worse I'm about to have a baby in his bakery. My baby bun wants out of the oven.

"Okay, honey. I'm not a doctor. I don't even play one on television."

I get the joke, but I don't have the energy to laugh.

"Valentine," Sebastian groans.

She clears her throat. "But I am a mother, so I'm going to take a peek. See if I see anything."

I nod, unable to move any other part of me. Vale lifts my feet to the bench, and I shift to my back as best I can.

"Whoa." The space is narrow, and Sebastian is quick to move the tables out of the way.

The bell above the entrance door tinkles. "We're closed," he barks. "Get out." The doorbell *ting-a-lings* again as whoever entered races away.

"I'm sorry," I mumble, clenching my teeth as another contraction begins.

"Do not apologize," Vale warns. "This is nature at her best."

"Shouldn't nature happen in a hospital?" Sebastian strains.

"Shut up, Seb." Vale pauses.

The loose shift dress I am wearing has fallen to my hips and Vale gingerly removes my soaked underwear. She lifts the skirt of the dress, draping it over my bent knees for some privacy but all decency has gone out the door along with the frightened-off customer.

Vale's eyes meet mine. "Do you need to push?"

"No," Sebastian growls.

"I think so," I say as my body does what it needs to do, contracting again. I try to lift my upper half, but I don't have the strength. Sebastian slips behind me, setting my shoulder blades to rest against him. From behind me, he swipes a hand over my forehead. A kiss comes to the top of my head.

Vale and I catch gazes. Her eyes widen while I'm simply stunned by the tenderness.

"She's going to have the baby right here," she warns the man behind me.

"No," he grits out.

"Yes." She narrows her eyes back at him.

My jaw locks. My molars grind. I hiss as another wave of pain clenches my center.

"I can see the head," Vale announces.

"You're doing good, Enya. Great job." Sebastian's encouragement is a little stiff, but I don't need a cheerleader. I need my baby out of me.

"Rena, bring me some hand sanitizer." A moment pauses. Vale shifts on the bench. "Where did she go?"

"Dammit." Vale stands. "I need to wash my hands." She rushes toward the back of the bakery.

I hunch forward again, moaning like an animal.

"Are you pushing?" Sebastian strains behind me.

"I can't help it. She wants out."

"She?" he whispers.

Through gritted teeth, I grunt, "I'm having a girl."

"Vale," Sebastian yells.

"Something's happening," I stress.

"Fuck." Sebastian lowers me to my back and scoots around me. With my feet on the bench, knees spread wide, and my dress at my hips, he sits in a precarious position, but his eyes stay focused on my face. "I won't look."

"I'm not certain how that will help." My intention is to tease him, lighten the moment as best I can, but another wallop of pain rushes up my center.

"You're doing great, beautiful." His voice is full of strain despite the compliment.

I huff as beautiful does not describe my current situation.

Then he yells over his shoulder, "Vale!"

"I'm coming." The call echoes back to us and I hear shoes tapping on the tile. "Can you see the head?"

Sebastian and I lock gazes. "You need to look," I snap.

"Do you trust me?"

Did I? I didn't know him, but I needed him. And something told me he'd never harm me or my baby.

"Yes," I whisper, confident while quiet.

He nods once, lowering his gaze. His eyes narrow then widen. "The baby's coming." His hushed whisper is awe and stress.

Vale falls against the bench behind my head and lifts my upper body. Sebastian's head snaps up. "Trade places."

"You got this," she says to him over me.

"I can't do this," he grouses. Panic fills those brilliant blue eyes.

"You can."

There's a battle of wills while they shoot dagger eyes at one another over me that I don't have the bandwidth to interpret right now. "I'm pushing." It's the only warning I give before I press forward, gripping my bent knees while Vale holds my back upright.

With a sluice and a rush, my body releases my little wonder, and I can only hope Sebastian caught her.

"Put her on Enya's chest," Vale says, but Sebastian is staring down at his hands.

"Let me see her," I beg, my body shuddering with the aftershock of expelling a tiny human.

Slowly, he lifts her, and a quiet cry escapes the smallest body. Everything blurs in my vision— Sebastian's look of shock, the baby being lifted over my chest, the bakery around us.

Relief washes over me as I sob at the miracle laying on my breasts and the reality that my future begins right now on a bakery bench.

Chapter 4

[Sebastian]

Holy fuck, that was intense.

As Enya is wheeled out of the bakery on a stretcher with the baby swaddled against her in another Curmudgeon Bakery t-shirt, I stare after them through the front window.

Go with them, something inside me screams.

I just held a baby in my hands. A baby I delivered when I'm the last man who should touch a new life.

Pinned in place, I'm not ready to turn and face the scene of the crime. The place where a miracle just made a gigantic mess of my bakery. I'm not ready to release them from my sight, which is ridiculous.

Enya doesn't belong to me. The baby isn't mine.

"How do you know her?" Vale says beside me, wiping off her hands. I never even got mine washed or sanitized before touching that innocent little babe covered in muck.

"I don't."

"But you knew her name."

"She was in here once. A long time ago."

Vale watches me but I can't take my eyes off the ambulance with its back doors now shut and the lights on.

"Is there something you want to tell me?" Her salacious tone turns my head, and her expression is a cross between a scowl and a smirk.

"You're such a pain in my ass."

"Well?" My younger sister glares at me.

"There's nothing to tell. She came in here once, last fall, and I haven't seen her again."

Vale continues staring, like she doesn't believe me. She resembles the pictures I've seen of our mother with her dark blonde hair and big brown eyes. She's everything opposite the rest of us, besides the obvious that she's female. She's the youngest of seven. Our mother really wanted a girl.

I turn my gaze toward the street, the ambulance now gone. In its place is a sheriff's vehicle.

"Shit. Here comes Stone."

Our eldest sibling is about to enter my bakery and I brace for the interrogation. Stone will only be doing his job as head of public defense but just once I'd like him to cut me some slack as the youngest brother in our clan. Somehow, this is going to be my fault.

"Did I just hear that our baby brother delivered a baby?" Stone's tall stature and broad shoulders fill the entrance. The tinkle of a bell over his head is a dichotomy. He's no angel but he isn't the devil either. He's done what he could to keep this family together. I'm the only stray arrow.

"I'm not a baby," I mock, sounding like one.

"You still look like one, even at thirty-five," he jests. With his mostly silver, thick beard, I appear much younger than him as my hair retains the jet-black trademark of the Sylver men. Only specks of white freckle my temples, near my ears. I'll never look as old as Stone, though. He's wiser than all of us, having to grow up faster in many ways. I might be a little shorter than him, but I'd still take him to the floor if I needed to prove myself.

Speaking of floors, I need to clean up a mess. The paramedics gave me something to soak up the blood and liquid splattered here and there. Then it will be bleach city, and some heavy duty wood cleanser for the bench.

Fuck. I still can't believe I delivered a baby in my bakery.

"So, what happened?"

"Woman had a baby, officer," I snipe.

His responding chuckle is stiff. He's a tense man.

"It was so beautiful, Stone," Vale says to our eldest brother with hero worship in her eyes. Stone is like a father figure to her, especially as our old man turned out to be a piece of shit. "You should have seen Seb. He was so calm." She rolls her eyes.

"I was calm."

"You screamed for me like that time you got your finger caught in the stable door."

"You closed it on me," I remind her.

"And you squealed like a pig."

I lift my finger. "And I still have a scar." The mark remains from where I dragged my finger free of a closed barn door, pulling off a layer of skin over the joint. It's a reminder that Vale has been my best friend most of our lives and I failed her when we were younger.

I failed most of my family when I was a kid, so the fact I just delivered one isn't lost on me. I have no business handling a child, especially a newborn.

Vale wraps her hand around my finger and shoves at me, sticking out her tongue like we're still those kids running around our land just outside of town. Back when we didn't understand yet our dad was a dick.

"Alright you two," Stone interjects, causing another flashback from our younger years. "Do you happen to know the woman's name?"

"Enya," Vale says. "Isn't that beautiful?" Her eyes focus on me, watching me.

"Yeah." My response is a little too wistful and I clear my throat. The pretty name suits the freaking gorgeous woman. Although I'd done a double take at her rounded shape as she stood here clenching her midsection. Her face was ashen. Her brow sweaty. Her fingers and ankles were swollen. Her belly was huge, but she practically glowed and I don't think I'd ever seen anyone so beautiful in my life.

"That's it? That's all you've got?" Stone's gone into interrogation mode, but I don't know what more he wants.

"You should head to the hospital. You can interview her there."

"But I'm asking you," Stone levels me with that stern glare I've seen too often in my life.

"Am I under arrest?" Old defenses fill my voice. No matter what I've done to redeem myself, I'll always be paying for the wrong I'd done. The hurt I caused my family. The shit I did. A stigma constantly hovers over me, like a dark shadow.

Only I haven't done anything wrong here today. This isn't a crime scene. However, the last time I asked Stone this question, I found myself cuffed and hauled off in the backseat of a sheriff's car.

"Dammit, Seb." Stone swipes a hand over his head before twirling his hat in his other hand as if he isn't already blaming me somehow, someway, for what happened in my bakery.

"Stone," Vale intercedes like she always has between us, placing a hand on my brother's forearm. "This was an incredible but stressful moment. Maybe you could find out more from the lady herself and let Seb and I clean up this place."

"You don't have to do that." Vale doesn't need to help me. In fact, I might find the mundane process of mopping my floor a relief. A moment to catch my breath and right my thoughts because I'm still reeling from Enya looking at me in her vulnerable position of knees bent and spread, and a baby coming out of her.

Do you trust me?

She didn't hesitate. While the response was quiet, she had given me her confidence.

I wouldn't harm her or her kid.

And fuck, if that didn't make my chest expand and the pressure not to disappoint her build. When I looked at the wonder of a baby leaving her body, shock and awe hit me at the miracle of what a woman's body can do and Enya was handling it like a champ without proper medical care or meds.

She was a fighter, like me.

"I got it." Vale pats my arm and heads toward my office in the back of the bakery, and the closet where cleaning supplies are kept.

Speaking of cleaning, I need to have a tough talk with Rena. Taking a fucking smoke-break during that little scene was unacceptable. While the feisty redhead has been my employee for roughly a year, she doesn't think sometimes. Did she not see the stress we were under? Did she not see the trooper Enya had been? Rena told me the scene made her anxious. However, *Rena's* anxiety could kiss my ass.

I'm only grateful my part-time help Barnett wasn't present. The high school teen would have been scarred. Then again, witnessing a birth would be a good lesson in safe sex.

"Any more questions, officer," I mock Stone while I really do admire him. He is only doing his job. He'd also taken on the role of raising his youngest siblings, which never should have fallen on someone so young at the time.

"You did good here." Stone nods at the mess behind me. His compliments are few and I hate the rush of giddy gratitude that ripples through me.

"Yeah, thanks."

Stone awkwardly pats my shoulder. And not for the first time do I wonder how he ever gets laid. He's like a wall. His name is appropriate. Affection isn't one of his traits.

I watch as he exits, the tinkling bell over the door a sound that's always annoyed me. However, the bell was a gift from Vale when I opened my business. She said every small-town shop needs the noisemaker.

For me, the sound will forever be synonymous with Enya scrunched up on the long bench giving birth to a kid that I strangely wish was mine.

Chapter 5

[Enya]

The past twenty-four hours have been hell.

Not only did I have my little angel in a bakery, but she went to the NICU unit upon our admission, and I've been sequestered in a separate hospital room because of blood pressure issues. As in, my blood pressure is too high, and I'm being monitored every fifteen minutes.

The pregnancy swelling had become a growing concern with my doctors. Being that I'm over thirty-five, I was already considered a high-risk patient. Another doctor's appointment was scheduled for today, only I'd gone into labor yesterday morning.

Sebastian Sylver had been my hero again, and I'd finally learned his full name.

I'd really wanted him to ride in the ambulance with us. Or maybe follow me to the hospital. But he was under no obligation to my little cookie and me. We were our own team of two.

I needed to continually face the fact I was on my own with her.

Tears fill my eyes again. The shock of yesterday. The separation from my baby. Other than holding her briefly to my chest, she's been removed from me for her care while my body tries to recover.

I just want this damn blood pressure to regulate. And as I don't have someone who can wheel me down to see her in the NICU unit, I'm stuck.

More tears flow, silently slipping along my nose.

My hospital room door opens, and I keep my eyes closed, assuming it's a nurse. I'm due for a blood pressure check soon and the nurses are used to the tears that keep leaking at random.

Hormones, one said, patting my arm in sympathy.

The crinkle of plastic has my eyes shooting open.

"Hey."

"Sebastian?"

Standing at the end of the bed is the curmudgeon baker himself with a beautiful bouquet of flowers. The plastic around them crinkles again as he shifts them to his other hand and swipes fingers through his hair. Sheepish eyes meet mine.

"How are you feeling?"

"Okay." I shift, pressing into the mattress to lift myself a little higher. Hastily, I swipe at my cheeks, brushing away the tears.

"But you're crying."

The tears continue despite my effort to erase them. "I can't see her yet. She's in the NICU which means we're separated, and I can't leave my room until my damn blood pressure goes down." I glance at a machine that's monitoring my heart, but the BP cuff needs to be manually wrapped around my arm. My other arm is still hooked to the IV apparatus where blood pressure medication drips in hopes of reducing the elevated rhythm.

As for the baby, she's beautiful but too small, weighing just over four pounds. The doctors are running a battery of tests on her. Her lungs were not fully developed, she really needed those six extra weeks to grow, and the medical team is worried about her current oxygen levels. She's also on a feeding tube.

"Do you have other family that could go in and see her for you?"

I shake my head before tipping it back and blinking up at the ceiling. "There's no one but me." My parents have not been supportive and the scorn that came from them caused me to keep my distance. I tried to call my younger sister who is overseas, but I only got her voicemail. She'd planned to be present for the birth and be my plus-one for a while after the baby was born. With my precious girl arriving weeks early, I don't foresee my sister getting here sooner due to her packed schedule.

Lowering my head, I look at him. He looks good. Rested. Fresh. Attractive. "Besides only mothers and fathers are allowed in the unit. Helps keep germ exposure to a minimum."

Sebastian nods. "I get that." Then his eyes narrow. "Where *is* the father?" The hard features of his face tighten. His cheekbones are almost elegant. His eyes are suddenly fierce. He can shift from dapper to dangerous in a blink.

"No dad," I remind him since he clearly forgot the day I told him I was pregnant. When I also told him there wasn't a husband or a boyfriend. My situation was too complicated to explain to a stranger, and I didn't want to tell him anyway.

We stare at one another for a long minute before he holds up the flowers. "I brought you these."

"They're beautiful." The vibrant combination of wildflowers is lovely. "A nurse should be in here any minute to take my blood pressure, so I can ask her if she has a vase when she gets here."

Sebastian looks at the collection in his hands. "I should have thought of that." He glances around the room, squints at the beeping monitor, and then gazes down at the floor. "I can go when the nurse gets here."

"Or you could stay?" I'd love the company. "I owe you a huge thank you."

His head lifts. "You don't owe me a thing."

"At the very least, I owe you a business cleaning service. I'm so sorry about the mess I made of your place."

Sebastian sets the flowers on the moveable table beside my bed and rounds it to stand closer to me. "It was nothing."

"You're my hero." I observe him as he nears me. A disgruntled expression tightens his face at my words. "That's twice now you've come to my rescue."

He snorts, swiping anxiously over his hair again. "I'm hardly a hero. Most people might say I'm the villain in a story."

"I don't believe that." But his brows crease and his eyes shift. Without thinking I reach out for his hand and squeeze. "Thank you. For everything."

Our gazes lock, and I recall saying something similar to him the first time we met. When he innocently kissed me and I went in for the kill, demanding he give me more of his mouth. I was so stupid.

When the door opens, Sebastian drops my hand and steps away from the bed, like he doesn't want to be caught touching me. A cheery nurse walks in. I haven't seen this one yet and she's telling me her name when her eyes catch on the man who has moved to the end of my bed.

"Sebastian?" Her cheerful tone rises an octave in surprise. She stops in her tracks, noting his position, which is ram-rod stiff. My head pings back and forth between them.

"It's great to see you again." Her shocked tone turns seductive, almost lusty. She's familiar with him and something inside me aches. My blood pressure check is going to be too high again.

"Good to see you too." He anxiously swipes at his hair again, glancing away from her and purposely not looking at me.

"I didn't know you two knew one another?" The friendliness in this brunette beauty's voice drops a little, probing for an answer to an unasked question. *Who are we to each other?*

Sedona is her name and she's beautiful with exotic eyes and waves of dark hair. I'm reminded of the pretty woman who helped me yesterday. Vale. Then my thoughts recall the striking redhead working at the bakery with Sebastian. He's a man surrounded by attractive women. And I don't know why I'm concerned about any of this. I'm a brand-new mother, with a postpartum body, layered with exhaustion and wacky hormones. I don't need to be thinking about him in any capacity other than as the man who delivered my baby.

Frustrated, I sigh.

Sedona wraps the blood pressure cuff around my upper arm—a little too snuggly—she leans over the machine and types in what she needs to collect the response. The cuff tightens.

"We—"

"I delivered the baby." Sebastian interjects before I explain that we don't really know one another.

Sedona's head lifts, enticing eyes wide. "I heard she had the baby in your bakery. I didn't know you were the one everyone is hailing as a hero."

She is right here, feeling like all the circulation has gone out of my arm as the cuff squeezes and then the machine beeps.

"Yeah." Sebastian looks down at me, the corner of his mouth hesitating to curl. I remember that look and thinking, at the time, how smiles from him must be a gift.

"He's my hero." My tone overshadows the truth in the statement. He really had been a lifesaver yesterday for both me and the baby.

Sedona's head turns toward me as if finally remembering I'm in the room and the purpose for her being here. She checks the machine which has beeped a second time.

"Too high." She gives me a sympathetic smile. "Another fifteen minutes?"

"Yeah," I weakly state, deflated like the cuff on my bicep. I still can't see my baby.

"Have you decided on a name yet?" Her tone returns to the pleasantry of her entrance.

I shake my head. I had two names in mind and planned to name my baby when she arrived, giving me a chance to see her and sense which name worked best but I hardly held her yesterday before she was whisked away from me.

"You don't have a name yet?" Sebastian's tone rings incredulous and the hit hurts.

"No," I snap, harsher than I should. He doesn't deserve my irritation. Between the separation anxiety and the hormones, he isn't to blame for anything, including the lack of naming my child.

"What is your mother's name?" I ask him, hoping to sound calmer.

"It was Violet." As his voice cracks over the name, sorrow fills his blue eyes.

The nurse gives him a sympathetic look as well and I sense a story here, but I don't ask.

"That's a beautiful name."

"Well, I'm all done here," Sedona gleefully stresses. She gazes at Sebastian. "Maybe you could stop at the nurse's station before you leave?" Her question is hopeful, eager for his attention.

"Actually," he says, and I swear she lets out a little gasp of anticipation. "Could you find us a vase or a container for the flowers I brought Enya?" His mouth curls a tiny bit more, giving her more of a smirk than a smile. I see how this goes for him. A little charm and women are putty in his hands. I'd certainly been in that position. He'd almost touched me as we kissed in his bakery, and I would have let him.

A complete stranger.

Isn't that a little bit like how I got where I am?

I lay back my head and let Sebastian and the nurse flirt. What do I care if *they* know one another? He helped me in a rainstorm once. He freakin' delivered my baby. He brought me flowers, but that doesn't mean I know him. I'll probably never see him again after today.

"Sure. I'll be back in a few minutes." Sedona's eagerness causes her to nearly bounce on her toes as she turns toward the door, happy to do Sebastian's bidding.

Once she leaves, I narrow my eyes at him. "Well, she's pretty and helpful."

He bitterly chuckles. "I don't remember her name."

"Her name tag said Sedona."

"Yeah, but I still don't remember her."

"That's really awful," I scold at his indifference to the nurse and any memory of them together.

His gaze lifts, holding on my eyes. "I'm a bad man."

Why would he say such a thing? It's shitty that he doesn't remember some woman he clearly shared a moment with, but he's not a bad guy. Not at his core. I don't believe he's a terrible person, despite his defensive tone, like he wants me to think poorly of him when I can't.

He clears his throat. "So, you really don't have a name for the baby?"

"I was torn between Adara and Ember."

He hums. "Do they mean something special?"

My head tilts, surprised by the question.

"My mother gave us all names that mean something. Stone. Clayton." Sebastian watches me. "Those are my two oldest brothers, and the names are obvious. Stone and clay. Then Knox which means hill and

Ford which means water." His mouth curls slightly. "Only Judd and I have ambiguous names. We joke that Judd rhymes with mud."

"And what does Sebastian mean?"

"Earth." He shrugs. "So pretty much dirt as well."

I smile, doubtful his mother considered him dirt.

"Then Vale, is short for Valentine, but fits the whole nature-scape thing."

"Vale is your sister?" Slowly things click into place. Her whining at him. His insistent rejection. Their overall banter, like they were siblings, which they are.

"Didn't we mention that yesterday?" He slips his hands in his back pockets.

"I was a little preoccupied." I give him another soft smile.

"So, baby names? Ember seems obvious to me. But Adara?"

"My name means flame. Both baby names mean fire. She's my candlelight in dark times." I swallow and clear my throat as I've said too much. "Anyway, I've been calling her Cookie since I found out I was pregnant and it's kind of sticking with me as well."

"Why Cookie?" he chuckles, the sound rough as if from disuse.

"The first person I told I was pregnant was this guy in a bakery and the nickname came to me there."

His shoulders relax and I hadn't realized he'd been so tense. His expression shifts. The edginess softens to something smoother, something gentler. His mouth curls more than I've ever seen. Is that a smile? If he lets those lips curve to full wattage, he might blind me with a grin.

"Yeah?" he whispers.

"Yeah."

The door to my room opens with a rush and Sedona looks almost harried. "I'm back," she announces breathlessly, holding up a green plastic container. Her gaze falls to the bouquet. "This is the best I could find for the flowers."

"Thanks." Sebastian rounds the bed and heads to the bathroom for water.

Sedona follows his retreat with longing in her eyes before turning back to me. Sheepishly, she lowers her voice and inquires. "So, is he the father?"

The question feels rather personal, intrusive even, however, I have already been asked about the father's name for the birth certificate. I've been tight-lipped about the paternity of my baby and specifically stated to leave that line blank.

Before I answer with an irritated, "That's none of your business," Sebastian returns and rounds the bed again, peeling the plastic from the flowers and setting the arrangement in the container. He sets the collection on a ledge by the window.

"Sedona," Sebastian announces her name like he's calling roll in a classroom. "We have a name for the baby. Adara." He glances at me for approval.

Adara it is, then.

"Violet will be her middle name," I add because I want to honor this man in some way. He helped bring my little candlelight into the world.

His brows lift at the mention of his mother before he rolls his lips and turns his head to the side. He blinks once. Twice.

I'm stunned by the effect such a simple gesture has on him. Then again, giving Adara such a name makes a statement. My little girl will always be a reminder of the miracle that happened in a bakery.

"Okay. Adara Violet," Sedona repeats.

"Oh, and Sedona? Can you get me one of those hospital bands?" He points to the one around my wrist. "I'm the father. I want to visit my daughter."

My jaw drops. *What is he doing?* But Sebastian isn't looking at me. His smile is aimed at Sedona, using his charm to get what he wants from her.

Crestfallen, she glances from me to him and back. "Of course. You're a lucky woman." A congratulatory note is missing in her tone, though.

"*I'm* a lucky man," Sebastian states, drawing her attention back to him. Then he taps his wrist as awkwardness fills the room. "The band?"

"Right. I'll be back again. And it will time for another blood pressure check." Sedona scampers from the room, definitively less energetic than her previous movements.

Once the door closes, I turn to Sebastian. "What are you doing?"

"I don't like Adara alone in there and you're not able to go to her. Give me your phone number. I'll go in, and Facetime you so you can see her."

Instantly, my eyes fill with tears again. "You'd do that?"

"Sure." He shrugs, casual and nonchalant like he didn't just offer me a gift through a phone camera lens.

I'm going to get to see my little girl while Sebastian pretends to be her dad.

Chapter 6

[Sebastian]

What the hell was I thinking?

Enya had looked so sad when I walked into her room. Those quiet tears rolling over her cheeks had my chest cracking open a bit, wanting to do anything to make her smile.

And fuck, that was embarrassing with Sedona. After seven years in the slammer, I went a little wild when I was first released. I've slowed down quite a bit since that time.

My brother Knox would joke that the reckless encounters have diminished because there wasn't anyone left for me to sleep with in this small town. He wasn't exactly wrong, but I also no longer like sleeping with women who only want a brief walk on the wild side with the town troublemaker.

Then again, I am the least likely to be tied down to any woman for more than a night. Building a relationship involves commitment and I lack dedication. Or maybe it's that I don't trust anyone anymore. Either way, I can't imagine a woman wanting to be saddled long-term to me with my past.

On that note, I have no idea why I'm in Milton County General in the next town over from Sterling Falls which only has a medical center. Or standing outside the neo-natal intensive care unit, waiting to be buzzed in by the receptionist who directed me to pod four.

As the doors close behind me, I count each room number as I pass.

What am I doing? Four words. Every step seems to further emphasize the question. What. Am. I. Doing?

When I near room four, I finally understand the pod thing. A large room, containing six baby beds, curtained off individually for privacy, surrounds a nurses' station. The soft sound of monitors beeping echoes in the space. The nurses speak in hushed tones.

A blond-haired woman stands. "Sebastian Sylver?"

I blink as I try to recognize her. Fuck, please don't be another woman I can't remember.

"Trinity Haven." She flattens a hand on her chest, reminding me who she is.

I'm slightly relieved as I slowly recognize her. A little older. A little bolder in her professional uniform.

Between the Sylvers and the Havens, our families have quite a history. Now, an unspoken vow hangs between the families, one that involves us never speaking to them and them equally ignoring us. Trinity falls somewhere around Judd-Knox-Ford's age. I can't remember exactly who. The youngest Haven, Clint, had once been my best friend. His mom was the one who taught me to bake. Telling me I'd stay out of trouble if I could keep my hands busy. Too bad it hadn't worked out that way for me when I was younger.

"Hey, Trinity." Being that I need to talk to her to see the baby, I hold up my wrist like I'm wearing a superheroes amulet. "I'm here to see Adara."

Her brows pinch. "Who?"

"The baby girl born to Enya Calloway." Given my track record so far today with women's names, first Sedona and now Trinity, I'm one for three.

"Oh." Trinity's forehead furrows. "We didn't know she had a da—" Her demeanor shifts. Her hip hitches to one side and she places her fist on it. "Well, it took you long enough to get here."

The censure in her tone is because she *thinks* I'm the father. The absentee man who should be accountable for these two flames. Who the hell gets a woman like Enya pregnant and doesn't step up to support her? Who doesn't want to be present for that sweet baby girl?

Not that I think babies are sweet. I don't know anything about babies.

Still, I'm standing in a room with a cluster of machinery and the sudden quiet cry of a tiny being.

"Let's get you over to your little girl," Trinity directs. She points to one of the clear plastic rectangles filled with a bundle of blankets.

"How is she doing?" I ask as I follow Trinity.

"She's feeding through a tube and her oxygen levels are still being monitored, but all her vitals are looking better. She still needs more tests, but in a few weeks, she should be good to go home."

As I draw closer to the newborn crib, the smallest human being in only a diaper and an array of cords all over her lays within.

"Why isn't she dressed?" I snap, glaring at Trinity.

"She's under a heat lamp." Trinity waves a hand beneath a machine that arches over Adara. "She's toasty underneath here."

I stare down at Adara. *Candlelight.* Tiny fire. She certainly glows pink and bright, and I can't seem to take my eyes off her.

"I want to Facetime Enya. I mean, her mom so she can see her."

"Poor woman. Heard she had this little one in your bakery. And to think she was at risk herself with pre-eclampsia."

"Pre-what?" My head shoots up, watching Trinity work, moving cords, and pressing buttons.

"Pre-eclampsia." She glances at me, scowling like I should already know this . . . as the father of the baby. "Some women get it when they're pregnant, especially women over thirty-five. It's dangerous. She should have already been in a hospital to be monitored. She could have seized out."

"Seized out?" I question.

"Had a seizure while going into labor."

Trinity doesn't need to further spell it out. If a seizure had happened, I wouldn't have known how to save Enya. She could have died in my bakery.

The thought suddenly makes me ill and I swipe a hand around my lips. My mouth has too much saliva in it. Bile tickles my throat.

I could have lost her. Before I ever even knew Enya, I could have lost her.

Without a father, what would become of this baby if something had happened to her mother? My heart races with the thought, especially since I hadn't had a mother and my father fell apart with her loss. I know what became of me.

"Okay, take your shirt off."

"Excuse me?" I blink, pulled from my tragic thoughts. This is hardly the time or the place for flirtation. Not that I'd flirt with a Haven, but—

"Your shirt. Skin to skin bonding is good for the baby. So, take off your shirt, Dad."

"Oh, I'm—" I cut myself off before blowing my cover.

Trinity points at an ugly turquoise recliner before reaching into the bassinet. "I'll bring her over to you."

Enya might not be happy about this, but I don't know what else to do. Swiftly, I slip off my jacket and tug off my tee. The coolness of the room hits me hard, making my skin pebble. Still, I fold onto the pleather-covered seat. My hands sweat. My brow does as well. I reach for my phone and set it on the thick wooden armrest.

"Hold her head and her bottom," Trinity explains.

My arms seem to have a will of their own, lifting and taking the baby now bundled in a blanket. I'm fighting a steady tremor in my limbs, telling myself to hold still while Adara is placed in my hands again.

The moment she was born comes back to me. Covered in slime and thick with gunk and still so . . . precious.

Her entire head fits in the palm of my hand. Her bottom is buried beneath the blanket Trinity wrapped around her.

And I can do nothing other than stare down at her. I need to Facetime Enya but there's no way I can move. Both my hands are full, and I'm mesmerized by the tiny thing before me.

She's . . . perfect.

"Let's move her up to your chest." Trinity starts unwrapping the bundle while adjusting the tubes and wires attached to Adara. "Sit back. Relax a little. Keep a hand on her head."

I don't know how to relax. I don't know how to move. I'm frozen in this position of bent arms and spread hands holding a tiny gem, afraid I'll jostle her breathing tube or jiggle her feeding one.

Trinity guides my arm upward, and I bring Adara to my chest. Her little belly hits my left pec and I gasp at the contact. She's so warm against me and my heart expands, like it's growing inside my chest, stretching like it can hardly fit behind my ribs. I can't breathe and yet I'm not gasping for air. I'm already . . . full.

What the hell is happening to me?

Adara makes a soft grunt.

"What was that?" My gaze leaps to Trinity. She needs to do something. Something is wrong. The baby made a noise.

"She's listening to your heartbeat and saying hello to her daddy," Trinity coos while smiling at Adara.

Daddy. My throat closes. I'm not her father. Some other man made this little thing. Some other man gave Enya this gift.

I'm ready to beg Trinity to take the baby back when little fingers expand and contract over my skin and curl into a tiny fist near my sternum. Sharp fingernails scratch my skin.

"What's she doing?" I try to glance down at her as best I can.

"She's giving you a hug."

There isn't any chance this gem-of-a-human is hugging me, but my eyes suddenly sting. My nose prickles. "I need to call Enya." I need to get this over with and get the hell out of here. I'm in over my head.

"I can hold the phone up for you, or you can hold it. Just keep a firm grip on her middle now, more toward the base of her head."

I nod like a freaking bobblehead. "Okay. Head. Hold. Got it."

Hesitantly, I release Adara's bottom, finding she doesn't even move. With one hand, I thumb over my contacts. I need to put Enya in my favorites in order to find her quicker. After pressing the Facetime button, the phone rings.

"Shit," I murmur, afraid it will disturb Adara. Then cursing again as I just swore over a baby's head.

"Hey," Enya greets me.

"Hey," I whisper. "Here she is." I hold the phone in a way that Adara is the focus. Trinity steps back allowing us some privacy.

"Hey, Cookie," Enya coos through the speaker, her voice drizzling like icing over lemon cake. "I can't wait to see you in person. To hold you."

Sniffles come through the video. She's crying again.

"Don't cry, sugar." She can't see me as the phone is directed toward Adara.

"She's so sweet." *More sniffing*. "And I already love her so much." *Full sob*.

"Oh, baby." Her tears are killing me. "The nurse says she's doing really well." I hope it's true.

"She's still on a breathing tube. And I can't nurse her yet while she has the feeding tube."

Instantly, I picture Adara cuddled against Enya, tucked into her mother's loving arms. Enya would offer a soft smile of contentment while watching her daughter breastfeed.

How would it feel to bask in something so unconditional as the love between mother and child? I'd never know as I never knew my mother.

"Where is your shirt?" Enya's surprise brings me back to the moment.

"Oh, uhm . . . the nurse said skin to skin contact was good for Adara." Guilt hits me. I shouldn't be the one holding the baby like this. Adara needs Enya's skin, her mother's comforting touch. "Did you do this with her?"

Her head sadly shakes. "If I can at least go an hour without a high blood pressure reading, I can be wheeled to the NICU."

"How is the blood pressure?"

"Still not great."

"I wish there was something I could do." I really do wish there was a way to calm her down, or make her feel better, or fix the pressure she's under.

"You are. Thank you for going in there, Sebastian. I know the situation is a little strange, but I appreciate you holding her. She looks so comfy." Her voice softens and I glance down again at Adara's tiny, closed lids, and her sweet open mouth. Her peanut-sized fist is still against my chest. She's so small. So fragile.

And I'm holding her like I have a right when there's blood on my hands and regret on my skin.

"I should probably put her back."

"Already?" The hitch in Enya's voice has me staying put.

Or maybe it's my fear that I'll drop her daughter if I try to move.

Or maybe it's that I'm a little *comfy* myself, with this warm body against mine, breathing in my scent as I breathe in hers.

"I guess can sit here a little longer." I steady the phone, aiming it toward the baby. Another soft grunt comes from Adara. "Sorry about the skin-to-skin thing. The nurse thinks I'm the dad, and I didn't know what to do anything to mess this up, so—"

"Sebastian." The quiet whisper of appreciation in my name should not stir something inside me. My emotions are like a kitchen mixer on full blend, scrambling everything together. Hope. Fear. Confusion at both.

"You really are my hero."

I close my eyes. I've never been a hero. I don't deserve to be called one, but I wish I could be.

For Enya.

For Adara.

For both my flames.

Chapter 7

[Enya]

The past five days have been torture.

The blood pressure bullshit. The struggle to pump my breasts. The limited trips to see Adara.

Thankfully, Sebastian has come to see me every day and he visits Adara, too, sharing videos of him shirtless and holding my child.

I should not like the tattoos over his shoulders and across his chest or the way he speaks to my little one, soothing her grunts and making her smile at the sound of his voice. She isn't really smiling yet, but it's still sweet to consider she's responding to him. He's so good with her.

If my hormones weren't already in upheaval, I'd be pregnant just looking at that man handling my child.

Fortunately, I'm preoccupied with the blood pressure medication I now need to take and the freedom I've suddenly been given to leave the hospital. I'm being discharged, but Adara needs to stay. And we've had another failed breastfeeding attempt. Tears fill my eyes as I rock my baby in my arms.

My life is a mess. I'm a mess. Damn these hormones.

"What's wrong?"

Sebastian's sudden appearance startles me, and I glance up, no longer concerned that this man continually sees me at my worst. Kissing him months ago. Having a baby in his bakery. Crying constantly, giving me swollen eyes and perpetually splotchy cheeks.

"I'm finally going to be discharged but I don't have a way to get out of here. My car has been parked in the public lot for five days, which means it's probably been impounded. Which also means I'll need to find out where it was towed and pay all the parking tickets to get it back. But I can't drive myself anyway. I need family or a friend to pick me up when I don't have either present." I quickly catch my breath before continuing.

"I'm moving to Sterling Falls. Well, I'll soon be living here, but my house won't be ready for another two weeks. The plan had been to move *before* Adara's birth." I give my little bundle a squeeze. "And I've contacted three short-term rentals in the area, but none of them have a last minute, two-week stay available." Taking another deep breath, I add, "And Adara won't nurse." A sob rips through my throat.

"Let's back up." Sebastian pulls another chair up to Adara's curtained area and takes a seat. Leaning forward, he rubs his hand over the back of her head. "How is she today, other than the breastfeeding thing?"

I glance down at her, sweet and quiet in my arms. "Every day I marvel at the miracle she is. The fact she came early was a wrench in my plan, but I'm so happy she's here. So grateful for her." I look at Sebastian, silently imparting additional gratitude for him. He begged me to stop calling him a hero and to quit thanking him for everything he's done, but I can't help it.

He's too humble. However, something tells me, there's a little more to his humility. I don't have him figured out yet as I'm too much of a mess myself, but I'd like to know him better. I'll always be gratefully indebted to him.

He glances at Adara, awed and a bit mystified. He's held her so he's felt the power she wields being so precious. One time I caught him kissing her little head when he video-called me, and then pulling back like he surprised himself he did such a thing. He's so sweet.

Adara is going to know this man whose hands brought her into this world.

"So, tell me more about needing a rental. Where do you live?"

The question is a reminder that we don't really know each other. He's been coming to the hospital for five days, and we only discuss Adara or my condition.

"I live in Huntington, but I've been coming to this area for months, and I fell in love with the quaintness of Sterling Falls." The small town is named for a set of falls I haven't been able to visit yet but is on my list of adventures to take once Adara is a little older.

Sebastian sits upright, his hands clasping his thighs. His brows crease. "For months? You've been coming to Sterling Falls for months?"

"I have a client in the area and—"

"Which client?" His sharp tone startles me.

"Sylver Seed and Soil. They're a big—"

"I know who they are." He cuts me off again.

"Why do you sound angry?"

"Because that's my family's business. The manager, Clay, is one of my brothers."

"Clayton is your brother?" I'm stunned. But upon further inspection, I see some resemblance. However, Clayton is jovial and flirty with dimples in his cheeks and a permanent smile on his face. He also has a head of silvery hair. He's opposite the curmudgeon baker sitting across from me with a huge scowl on his face.

"Did he flirt with you?" Sebastian turns his head. Squinting his eyes at the wall, he mutters, "I bet he flirted with you. I'm going to kill him."

A little tickled by his unnecessary jealousy, I release a soft laugh. "He was always a gentleman."

Sebastian turns back to me. "What do you do, that they are your client? Are you into seed sales or soil fertilizer or farming equipment?"

"None of that." I chuckle. "I'm an accountant."

"Judd is the family's accountant." Surprise rings in his voice.

Another overly attractive brother who is a little uptight while mischief twinkles in his eyes. If I were a betting woman, I'd gamble he has a secret wild streak. While he doesn't share the nearly solid silver hair of Clay, his hair isn't as dark as Sebastian's either. Still, he's handsome in his own right. He's also very good with numbers. "Your family's business was being audited, and a non-family member was required to go through the paperwork." I tilt my head. "I thought the bakery was your business."

Sebastian swipes a hand through his hair, slipping it to the back of his neck. "It is. I don't have much to do with the Seed and Soil, other than collect some measly dividends."

"That explains why I've never seen you there."

"Why didn't you ever come back into the bakery?" His expression tightens. His question sounds almost like he's hurt.

"I was embarrassed." I glance down at Adara, although I don't fully focus on her. My mind flips back to the soft kiss he gave me and the powerful urge I had to take more from him.

"Why?"

My head snaps up. "Because I kissed you." *Because I wanted you to touch me.* Naked beneath his shirt, prancing around without underwear when I've never done anything like that in my life, and he was so close . . .

"*I* kissed *you*," he counters, like he wants the credit for doing it first.

"Either way. . ." I dismiss before I do something foolish like ask him if he would like to kiss again. "I just haven't been back to the bakery." My defense is weak.

Sebastian watches me, puzzled, wounded even, although I don't know why he's so upset.

"Anyway, I need to find my car and find a place to live until my house is ready. And I need to get out of here." I glance down at Adara. "When I don't want to leave."

"I can help you with your car."

I look up again as Sebastian starts typing into his phone. "My oldest brother Stone is the county sheriff. He'll get you out of any parking tickets." He glances up and gives me a wink. "It's probably been towed to Perry's."

I swear my ovaries do a little flip. As messed up as they are, they are suddenly dancing a giddy jig over a simple eye-twitch. I feel like Sedona, the nurse he couldn't remember who floated out of my room upon first seeing him, and whose breath still hitched every time she re-entered, and Sebastian was present.

"You don't have to do that." He's already done so much. "But I'd appreciate knowing where my car is, if it's been impounded."

Sebastian exhales. "Okay, that solves your car issue. So, you need a way out of here and a place to stay? How long until your place is ready?"

"About two weeks." I jiggle Adara in my arms, and I swear she smiles, when I know it's probably only gas in her belly. As she came early, my tightly scheduled plan to finish the house and move in before her birth was foiled.

When I gaze back at Sebastian, he's watching Adara again. His brows pinch, a deep crease forming between them. Finally, he lets out a breath, and his shoulders fall. He lowers one arm to his thigh and reaches forward to stroke a finger over Adara's head.

"You can stay with me."

"What?" My gaze snaps up from watching his finger sweetly stroke my daughter.

He shrugs. "My place isn't big, but I have an extra bedroom. It's over the bakery, so it's an easy commute to the hospital."

"I can't ask you to do that."

"You didn't ask. I'm offering."

"That's so sweet of you, but I can't encroach on you. You've already been so generous"—I lower my voice, eyes shifting to make certain no one else is close enough to hear me—"Pretending to be Adara's dad so you can send me videos of her has been more than I could have ever hoped for."

"Yeah, pretending." His voice is tight, deep and hollow. He swallows and sits upright again. "Well, at the very least, I can be the friend that springs you from this place." His eyes never leave Adara as he offers me one more olive branch of assistance.

"I do consider you a friend." I never want to lose touch with this man who has done so much for Adara and me. I might have a flickering desire for more kisses and him to hold me to that strong naked chest of his like he cuddles my baby, but I can tamp down my fantasies in favor of his friendship. I don't know anyone else in Sterling Falls.

"Friends," Sebastian mumbles, like the word tastes bitter on his tongue.

"You know what?" Unhappy with his tone, I counter. "You've done a lot for me, and I'll always be grateful, but I can figure out how to get out of here on my own." I glance down at Adara, shifting her a little against me. "I'm going to be going it alone anyway. I need to start right now."

Seated in a recliner, I struggle to push my legs against the extension that supports my feet but eventually the chair abruptly snaps closed. Shuffling to the edge, my feet hit the floor and I stand in a rush, swaying a bit from the suddenness.

"Whoa." Sebastian catches me at the waist, steadying me. "Are you lightheaded?"

"It's nothing."

"Isn't that a side effect of the blood pressure medication you're taking?"

"I . . ." How does he know that? "It passes."

"What do you mean 'it passes'?"

"Just that." While the medications settle into my system, I can experience dizziness and headaches. I've only had a few incidents, but I'd self-diagnosed the lightheadedness from exhaustion and my out-of-whack emotions. Thankfully, the medication is safe for breast milk.

"No," he growls at my ear, standing close enough my body leans into his. His fingers tighten on my waist. "You're going home with me. You need someone to look out for you because Adara is counting on you to be here for her."

The ferocity in his demand has me catching my breath. I should be upset that he's commanding that I go with him, but instead, a rush of comfort and relief ripples through me. No one has ever taken care of me.

Plus, he's right. I shouldn't be unsupervised until the medicine regulates. "But I need to do things, like breast pumping and—"

Sebastian groans beside me while his fingers dig into my sides. "We'll figure it out. You'll have privacy with your own bedroom, and I'll be down in the bakery most days. Plus, you'll be coming here. We'll hardly cross paths."

The thought saddens me. I've enjoyed his visits to my room and his video calls with Adara. He's been a pleasant distraction during long, mundane days and I've looked forward to seeing him. That's dangerous. Because I don't want to become attached to him. He doesn't need a single, new mom, and her baby to muddle up his life.

The nurses here are ga-ga about him and I don't want to be in the way of . . . whatever he does with women. Not to mention, I have my limits. Picturing him with another woman is difficult enough. Sharing space with him, and hearing him or seeing him with someone else would be too much. I'm not strong enough to tackle that because I already have a little crush on him myself.

"What about a girlfriend? Or a lady friend?" *Friend with benefits?* Or even just a random hookup. "I don't want to cramp your style."

"What style?" He chuckles, shifting me so I face him better, but I peer down at Adara.

"You know what I mean." He can't be oblivious to his good looks and brooding charm.

Two strong fingers tip up my chin. "Explain it to me."

My eyes close. I can't look at him, but envy has no place here. I just called him my friend. "I don't want to be in your way . . . with women."

"Sugar, there's only two women in my life right now. You and her." He nods down at Adara. "And the two of you are more than I can handle."

His tone is teasing, but I'm still uncertain. "I still don't want to be a nuisance."

"You won't be." His blue eyes narrow, the heat in them like a low-lit flame. Watching me, it's like he's almost begging me to stay with him. *Yeah, I'm definitely imagining that.*

"Only for a couple of weeks?"

"Only for a couple of weeks." Then one of those hard-won smiles slowly curls his lip a little more than I'm used to seeing and a different organ in me somersaults.

I'm not certain my heart can continue to take the kindness of Sebastian Sylver without fully falling in love with him.

Chapter 8

[Sebastian]

Here I am again, all wrapped up in Enya like one of those blankets swaddled around Adara.

I'm learning the baby lingo.

And I'm a fucking moron because I just suggested she come home with me. Only for a few weeks, my ass. For five days, I've struggled—and failed—to stay away from her and the baby, and now I'm offering her weeks in my place.

But Enya has so much going on. She's kind of a hot mess for an accountant. Not that I know anything about bookkeeping, other than I'd assumed it's a structured, organized profession. With his glasses and his array of calculators, Judd is my money guy and a complete nerd, so that's my experience with people who get jazzed over digits.

Enya certainly doesn't look like a bookkeeper with her hair in a messy bun at the nape of her neck and a flannel shirt plus a pair of black leggings on her hot body. She looks . . . pretty and frustrated.

"Where did you get the clothes?" Her dress was wrecked during her delivery and unless she had a bag in her car, which she hasn't been able to return to, I don't know where she got these new items. She just told me she didn't have anyone to help her.

"Oh." She looks down at the flannel that's a little too big on her. "Your sister came to see me. She knew I'd need something to wear to leave the hospital."

Vale. She's always swooping in. I could have suggested Vale take Enya in for a few weeks, but I didn't want to put that on my sister. She's a single mom herself and has enough going on with Hudson. My nephew can be a handful. I'll be watching him the rest of my life to make certain he's good to his mother and doesn't become his father.

Standing in Enya's presence where she's still radiant despite unwashed hair and the purple smudges of exhaustion beneath her eyes, I worry once more that she'd been in a similar situation as my sister. A worthless man impregnated her, leaving her to raise her kid on her own. *Or worse.* However, I don't let my thoughts drift to visions of the horrific. The idea of someone hurting Enya makes my blood boil.

A visceral desire to protect Enya . . .and Adara . . . fills me. No one will ever lay a hand on either of my girls while I'm around.

Enya sets Adara in the hospital bassinet. After a long stare and more tears, she finally parts from the baby.

"The nurses told me it's okay to leave her here. I should go home, take a shower, and get some rest."

Exactly as I thought. She needs to take care of herself because Adara needs her.

Enya is discharged from the hospital with a breast pump and a packet of instructions. The flowers I'd given her have seen better days and I toss the lot. She doesn't have anything else to take with her. She lost another shoe in my bakery when she went into labor and she's only wearing socks again.

After wheeling her out of the hospital and helping her into my truck, we sit in the cab.

"Where to? Do we head to Huntington to pick up your things or hit a local store for some fresh clothing?" Huntington is a good forty-five-minutes away. "Or do you want to go to my place for a shower first?"

From her seat, Enya sighs. "I should probably go to my place and pack up a few things. All my baby stuff is there." She turns to look at me. "Are you sure about this? Babies have a lot of . . . stuff."

"Positive." I meet her eyes, dark and so sad looking. That look alone makes me want to take care of everything for her. "It's only for a few weeks. And then your new home will be ready, right? Where is your new house?"

"It's the Wallace farmhouse. Have you heard of it? I got the place for a steal, but it needed a lot of work."

Of all the places she could have purchased, she bought that house? I bet it was a steal. A crime happened there. Some people claim the place is haunted. That ghost can fucking rot in hell for all I care.

"How'd you decide on that place?" I stare out the windshield, lost in my memories. A rundown room. The stench of drug-laced sweat. A fucking coward hiding in the shadows.

"Something just drew me to the place. It had character and charm, although it looked a little sad. Unloved. It's improving nicely, though." Optimism and hope fill her voice and I don't have the heart to tell her the place holds a host of bad history and dark days. Glancing back at her, she's watching me, eyes bright despite the faint signs of exhaustion beneath them. I want to reach across the seat and swipe her cheeks as if I can erase how tired she is. She's still so gorgeous.

Then I remember that my hands are soiled and all the scrubbing in the world isn't going to cleanse them enough to warrant touching a woman like Enya. A woman surviving on her own, on her terms. She's going to rock the single-mom thing.

"You didn't tell me you had pre-eclampsia."

"I didn't know until I was in the ambulance. I had an appointment to see my doctor on the day Adara was born. They'd been concerned about the unusual swelling in my hands and feet. The EMT told me I was lucky." Her gaze holds on me. "I was lucky I had you."

I snort. "Me? I didn't do anything. I wouldn't have been able to help you had something gone wrong." Had she had a seizure or worse, I'm not medically trained in any way, and my throat thickens at the thought I could have lost her. I would never have gotten the time I've had to learn more about her if things had gone poorly in my bakery. "But I never would have let you go without a fight."

Her eyes widen.

"Or Adara. I would have given her my last breath if I had to."

"Sebastian." Enya reaches across the console and squeezes my wrist. Her eyes fill with tears again. Every time she cries, it fucking shreds my heart.

Swiftly, I swipe at the first loose one with my thumb and catch another on her other cheek.

"I can't seem to help them," she says, explaining the waterworks. "I'm not typically so emotional, but with Adara . . ."

"I get it." I'd never admit that seeing that baby girl has brought some unrecognizable emotions to me as well. A hint of hope. A dash of anticipation. Maybe a pinch of love when I have no right to love her. She isn't mine and neither is this woman.

With that thought, I pull back my hand and press the ignition button. My truck roars to life. "To Huntington we go."

Enya's eyes are on me, but I don't acknowledge them as I reverse out of the hospital lot and start the trek to her place, helping her move into mine, because I can't seem to let her go.

Like I've said, I'm an idiot.

+ + +

Four hours later, my apartment above the bakery is an explosion of baby things. Not knowing when Adara would be released from the NICU, we grabbed all the essentials for a newborn. A bassinet. The baby car seat. A stroller. Some kind of bouncy seat slash swing combination. A suitcase of clothes for Adara and another two for Enya.

And when I say *we*, I mean *me* because Enya shouldn't be lifting anything heavy, and her first wince was my hint she was doing too much.

My apartment sanctuary was a labor of love. I really needed my own space when I returned to Sterling Falls. And when I decided to buy the bakery, the second floor was a mess. I ripped out everything, including most walls. Only the two bedrooms and the bathroom are enclosed and even there, the walls don't reach the full height of the twelve-foot ceiling. I never wanted to feel caged in again. The living room and kitchen are one open space with a large island that has four stools for seating. As I don't entertain and I eat alone, I didn't need a dining table. The living space consists of a leather couch with an extended side perfect for full-body lounging, and a fifty-five inch, high-definition television with a gaming system below it.

The tall, arched windows offer tons of natural light and the exposed brick on the walls gives this place character. Charm, like Enya said of the old Wallace place.

Despite the sudden mess, Enya looks at me all exhausted and asks, "May I take a shower?"

"Sugar, you don't need to ask for a thing. Make this place your home for a few weeks."

Personally, I have no idea how I'll survive the time. Thinking of her, naked, and underneath the spray of my shower, water sluicing down her lush body, with those heavy breasts and the slight curve to her hips, and my dick is hard. I need to get out of here.

"I have a thing to do. Take your shower. Catch a nap. Let me find your car."

"You don't need—"

"Just stop," I snap a little harsher than necessary while holding up a hand. "You *don't need* to thank me, or apologize, or continually tell me I don't need to do things for you. I know I don't." Again, a little too firm, so I take a deep breath and swipe my hand through my hair. "I want to."

Her eyes widen at the admission, and even I'm a little shocked by what I've said. But I really do want to help her, and that scares the fuck out of me, which is why I need to get out of here for a bit.

"So." I swallow around the thickness in my throat. "You shower. Me go." I hitch my thumb toward the door and decide this caveman needs to get gone and quickly.

+ + +

Once inside Milton's Roadhouse with a non-alcoholic beer and a helluva burger before me, I feel a little more like myself. With the western saloon atmosphere, including rooms to rent on the second floor, this place is a Sterling Falls icon on one of the four corners of Corner Street and Main.

With a hardy sip of beer, I work to suppress my concerns for Enya and the ache of leaving Adara at the hospital. She's in good hands there. Enya and I talked about her care while we drove to Huntington. Being premature, the baby needs to be in the hospital for now.

I'm lifting my beer again, almost to my mouth, when a strong smack on my back forces me forward and my teeth collide with the heavy glass mug.

"What the fuck?" I grumble as my brothers Stone and Knox round the high-top table. Despite all the silver in Stone's hair, Knox is the opposite, like me, with jet black hair. His once military buzz has grown out to a floppy top with sheared sides. The thickness of his beard nearly matches Stone's.

"Well, look who it is?" Knox teases helping himself to a stool. "Daddy Warbucks."

"Who?"

"The rich guy in *Annie* who takes in a little girl." Stone explains. "Or are you Sir Lancelot, helping a damsel in distress?" His dark eyes narrow at me, filled with the same question I've been asking myself.

What the fuck am I doing with this woman?

"She's not a damsel in distress." Despite the emotional tears, Enya has a strength and determination to her that I admire. She wants to do things on her own, and she's frustrated that her body isn't allowing that to happen. Her misfortune is my good luck, which is a terrible way to think of her situation.

But I'm strangely relieved she's in my home where I can keep my eyes on her.

"No? I heard she's your baby mama," Knox teases again before holding up his hand and pointing at my beer then signaling for two from the bartender.

"She's what?" Stone chokes, full on glaring at me with the disapproval I've often seen from him in my life.

"She's not my baby mama," I chortle.

"But you're playing daddy to her baby," Knox continues.

"Who told you that?" As if there isn't enough gossip in a small town, nothing is sacred from Knox.

"Vale."

Of course.

"How do you know this and I don't?" Stone questions, glancing at our brother.

"Guess she just loves me more than you." Knox is full on poking at Stone, as we all know Vale has hero-worship of our oldest brother. He practically raised her. Hell, he raised Ford, Vale, and me, and we weren't easy. Stone was too young to be our father, but he was all we had at vulnerable ages. He gave up a lot to be present for us.

I'm the one who fucked it up the most.

Knox squeezes Stone's broad shoulder, playfully joking with him, who swats at Knox's arm. Knox only laughs harder.

"Can I get you anything else?" Eleanor Milton asks, after delivering their beers.

The Milton family is like town royalty, unlike the Sylvers or the Havens, and I'm surprised the youngest daughter doesn't have a more prestigious job in government. Her oldest sister is the town mayor and Stone's friend with benefits. However, rumor has it Eleanor quit law school and recently returned home. Not that I give any credit to gossip, though.

"I'll have a pub burger. Put it on his bill," Knox points at me.

"I'm good." Stone lifts his beer.

Eleanor walks away.

"Speaking of Enya, I need to find her car. Did you have Perry tow it?"

"Yes, let's talk about Enya." Knox sets his elbows on the table and places his chin in his hands, batting his eyes at me like he's settled in for girl-time.

"Can we get back to the playing daddy part?" Stone sets his beer down after a sip and crosses his arms on the table.

I glance around us before leaning forward. "Look, after Enya had the baby, she couldn't get into the NICU to see Adara because Enya's blood pressure was too high. She had to be monitored, which meant sticking to her hospital room, and being separated from her new baby. I said I was the dad so I could get in and video call Enya, so she could see Adara."

Stone and Knox stare at me.

"Is she okay?" Knox asks, sobering a bit.

"Why did she have high blood pressure?" Stone questions.

"Something called pre-eclampsia or some shit like that."

Knox sits back and peers at Stone.

Stone scrubs a hand down his face.

"What?" I glance back and forth between them.

"You know that's how Mom died, right?" Stone states, his voice heavy with regret.

I actually hadn't remembered. When our mother passed away, I was only two. She was pregnant with Vale and died while in labor. A fluke, everyone said. For the longest time, I thought that was an actual condition. *She had the fluke.* When people talked about the flu, I often thought they meant the fluke.

Now, I know better, and pre-eclampsia wasn't a joke.

"Fuck," I mutter, thinking once again about how I could have lost Enya.

"So you aren't really the father?" Stone glances at my wrist where the hospital band remains.

"Of course not," I argue, straightening on my stool.

"Do you want to be?" Knox asks.

"What kind of question is that? You both know I'd be a shit dad."

Knox looks at Stone again. Stone's brows crease. I swear he could hold a quarter in the divot made between those bushy things.

"That isn't true," Stone states, like he doesn't know I'd make a terrible father.

Stone was twelve when our mom died, and our dad disappeared into alcohol. My brother was off at college when everything really turned to hell.

"So you're playing *pretend* daddy," Knox confirms. "But she moved in with you."

"She did what?" Stone's voice rises as his shoulders stiffen.

"How do you know this?" I ask Knox.

He shrugs. "Rena told me."

Knox is certainly making the rounds for information.

"You got a thing for my employee?" Knox isn't really one to sniff around. I'm not certain if he even has sex. His ex-wife did a number on him, and he's been a lone sailor for a while. Plus, his heart once belonged to someone else, and I don't think he's ever gotten over her.

"I stopped in for a coffee and she told me you were getting a roommate. And no, I don't have a thing for Rena. She has the hots for her boss."

"I'm her boss," I retort.

"You can't really be that dense, can you?" Stone scoffs.

I hate when he puts me down. He doesn't outright call me stupid, he just says I don't have common sense. Or at least, he used to say that to me when I was younger. I was a reactor. I wanted to get shit done.

It's how I ended up selling drugs.

It's how I ended up using them.

It's how I killed a man.

"Rena doesn't have a crush on me." Rena and I have shared stories but that doesn't make us a private Narcotics Anonymous team, where confessions occurred, and encouragement reigned. I don't even consider her a friend but a colleague. I'd given her a second chance because she'd been honest with me. She is a recovering addict. There's nothing else between us.

"It's more than a crush. It's like you are peanut butter and she wants to be the two pieces of bread smooshing you together." Knox presses his hands together like he's mashing something between them.

"That's . . . graphic," Stone chokes before sipping his beer.

"You're nuts." I toss a French fry at him. He laughs as it hits his chest.

"So, she . . . Enya . . . is living with you now," Stone's serious tone brings us back to my situation.

"She's just staying for a little while. Two weeks. Then she's moving into a house she bought on outskirts of town." I hold my breath knowing what question is coming next.

"Which house?"

"The old Wallace place."

Knox's forehead lifts so high his baseball cap shifts. "I'm doing a brick patio at that house. I didn't know it belonged to her." Knox is a fireman first; bricklayer second.

Stone remains eerily quiet, knowing what happened in that house. "Have you seen the place?"

I lower my head, shaking it. "You know I try to avoid going in that direction if I can."

"Gonna get real hard to avoid when your girl lives there," Knox says, softening his teasing tone.

"She's not my girl." Defensive, almost angry, I glare at Knox. Even if she was my girl, I couldn't visit that house.

Stone holds up a hand. "Okay. So, Enya . . ." He looks at me. "Her car was towed to Perry's."

"Can you get it out?" I ask.

"She has three parking tickets."

"She had a baby, Stone. In my bakery," I remind him.

"Yeah, okay. Let me see what I can do. In the meantime, call Perry and tell him I said to let the car go. He owes me from poker the other night. I can call it even by him releasing her car."

When Stone shows he has a shred of humanity in him, it can really irk me. But despite his scowls and glares, he really is a good guy.

Chapter 9

[Enya]

By the time Sebastian returns to his place, I feel a little more like myself. His shower is luxurious, and I stood beneath the spray until my fingers shriveled.

I'd just finished a phone call to my sister who can't get away until the time we agreed she'd come to stay. I could really use her support right now. I'm out of my element living in the apartment of a man I've only known a week.

As I step out of the bedroom, he graciously designated as mine, he's entering his apartment. He abruptly halts at the top of the stairs that lead into his place. Our eyes meet before his gaze scans my body.

"You're wearing my shirt."

"Oh. This." I glance down at the Curmudgeon Bakery T-shirt he'd given me that first time. The one I promised to wash and return. A promise I never followed through on. I've worn it often in the past months, especially as my belly grew. Since I'm still not down to my original size, I slipped it on for its comfort. "I'm sorry I never brought it back to you."

He steps toward me, but stops short, keeping distance between us. "No. I told you to keep it. It looks good on you."

Heat creeps up my neck and flushes my cheeks.

Sebastian glances around his place. "What happened to all the boxes?"

"I put everything in my room. Like I told you, I don't want to be in the way, and I don't need to assemble half those items until Adara can come home."

Home. Right now, I'm a little homeless, living in this man's apartment while my condo is on the market, and my house isn't finished yet.

Sebastian had a strange reaction when I told him I'd bought the Wallace farmhouse. Does it have some sentimental value to him? I've heard the rumors it is haunted but Trudy Wallace, the woman who sold the place to me, assured me she didn't believe the gossip. Just in case, though, she brought in a Wiccan friend to burn sage or something.

Old spirits be damned.

With all the updates I've done, I don't see how a ghost would recognize the place.

"Enya, you shouldn't be lifting anything." Sebastian scowls. He's kind of cute when he's acting like he's angry but he's more irritated. Very curmudgeon.

"I didn't. I placed a box on a towel and then kind of pushed it, so I didn't scratch your floors." His apartment is amazing with hardwood flooring and exposed brick walls, plus the natural light is incredible. He doesn't have any window treatments.

"I want to head back to the hospital." I hate to ask, but I need to know. "Were you able to find my car?"

"It's downstairs."

"That was fast. But you didn't have my keys?"

"Oh, yeah." He sheepishly looks to the side. "I have my ways." I don't ask for an explanation. He offers, "If you give me ten minutes, I can go with you."

"Are you sure you want to go back to the hospital?" He's already been there so often.

Sebastian closes the space between us. "Stop asking, sugar." He reaches out for my hair and scoops a section behind my ear. His hand lingers along my neck.

His touch is tender, and it's been so long I've almost forgotten how sweet human contact with another *adult* person can be. He was the last man I kissed. As for sex, I can't even count backward that far, which is saying a lot as I'm into counting.

I bite my lip and meet his gaze. The blue in his heats.

"Ten minutes."

I nod, unable to speak when he looks at me like that. Like he's warmth on a summer day and heat in the dead of winter. It's how he looked at me when we first kissed, and I was foolish enough to think it was anything other than a friendly meeting of lips. I'm the one who turned it into something more.

Sebastian walks toward his bathroom, and I head to my temporary room to change. As I rummage through my suitcase, Sebastian appears in my doorway.

"What's this?" His jaw clenches as he holds up a bottle of pills and shakes them.

"It's an opioid. The hospital prescribed it for pain." I actually feel pretty good, despite today's physical exertion. I didn't do as much laboring as Sebastian, who hardly let me lift a finger. I might be sore later, but nothing a few ibuprofens can't handle.

Slowly, Sebastian lowers the bottle, gaze still fixated on the brown cylinder.

"Enya, I probably should have told you this before, but I'm a recovering drug addict." His head lifts, eyes meeting mine, while his shoulders remain tense like he's prepared to defend himself. "I've been clean for ten years, but I never want to tempt myself."

He lifts the bottle. His hand shakes enough that the pills rattle within the container. "I can't have these here."

Holy shit. "Of course." Without thinking, I rush to him and take the bottle from his fingers which are clamped tightly around it. "I'm so sorry. I didn't know."

"You couldn't have. You shouldn't know." His voice thickens. "And stop apologizing."

I have so much more I *should* say to him. Tell him I'm proud of him for getting clean, staying clean. Hell, even proud of him for telling me the truth about this sliver of his past. But I also can't believe I didn't know. Didn't even suspect. Then again, why would I? He seems so put together with the bakery and this beautiful apartment. Plus, he's still a relative stranger to me. However, I should know better about facades and false natures. I'd been with a man for eleven years who gave promises with a smile and declarations with sincerity, and never meant a single word he'd uttered to me.

With the pills in my hand, I brush past Sebastian for the bathroom. Dumping the lot in the toilet, I flush twice to make certain all the pills disappear. Then I peel the label from the bottle, fold the sticky sides together and tear it into small pieces, dumping it in the toilet next.

When I stand upright, Sebastian is at the bathroom door, hands on either side of the jamb. His expression is pinched, his jaw tight. With his head bowed, he appears bewildered. He doesn't look at me when he says, "You didn't have to do that."

"I don't need them," I quickly explain. "A few ibuprofens will be good enough, but I'm not really sore." I wave at my lower region, causing Sebastian's gaze to fall there, but that's the last place he'd want to go right now because I'm still recovering from labor.

That doesn't mean I don't fantasize about kissing him or him holding me, but he isn't going to want anything to do with me, even if I was healed.

Slowly, he looks up, eyes meeting mine. The blue of his eyes is like a soft flame, full of shame, regret, and something more. Confusion, maybe? Like he's trying to work something out about me but can't.

As I stand inside the bathroom, I don't feel trapped, but something swirls between us, like the beginning of a summer storm, when hot air meets rain-heavy clouds.

I lick my lips. Sebastian's nostrils flare.

His chest heaves.

My heart hammers.

"Shower?" My voice squeaks on a question that sounds like an invitation when I only intended to reiterate why he needs the bathroom.

"Why aren't you reacting to what I told you? I'm a drug addict." His expression hardens, eyes narrowing.

Should I be overreacting? I'm staying with a man I hardly know but have so many reasons to trust. He delivered my baby. He came to visit both of us. He's pretending to be her father. And he kissed me once like I was precious.

"Because you told me it was a long time ago and you are currently recovering. I get that it's a continual process. And I don't want to do anything to jeopardize your success. Thank you for being honest with me. I trust you."

"Sugar." His voice cracks. His hands tighten on the jamb like he's holding himself back when I wouldn't mind him leaning forward and letting me hug him.

And I would hug him. I'm proud of him for his recovery. It's a difficult path.

"Baby, you need to get out of that bathroom before I show you how little you should trust me." There he goes warning me again, like he's a bad man. Like he could frighten me. He'd never hurt me. I know it down to my bones.

Instead, seduction underlies his tone and warmth rushes through me. He couldn't possibly be attracted to me. Not in comparison to the other women I've seen in his life. Sedona. Rena. Still, my breasts feel even heavier and my pulse beats faster. Maybe? Or maybe, I'm the one who can't be trusted as my hormones wreak havoc and my imagination runs wild.

With a heavy push against the jamb, Sebastian forces himself backward, but he only turns sideways, pressing his back to the jamb next. The position offers me the opportunity to escape but only a sliver of space. There's enough room for me to get through the doorway, but not without our bodies sliding against each other. This is a dangerous game, but I make my move. I maneuver myself, squeezing between Sebastian and the door frame, relishing every second of my weighted breasts brushing against his firm chest. My nipples are painfully sensitive beneath my thin shirt as they sweep against the rough fabric of his. Sebastian hisses and I soak up the sound of him sucking in air through his teeth. A sizzling sound like I've burned him, scorched him through layers of fabric. I'm hyperaware of every point of contact. My nipples erect. My hand brushing against his. My nose almost meets his neck, inhaling him. My eyes remain focused and wide on the expanse of his chest as sparks crackle along my overstimulated skin.

As soon as I'm free from the doorway, the connection fizzles and Sebastian has given me his back, closing the door behind me. Despite the soft flirtation in what he said, there's no apparent effect on him.

With a shaky hand, I swipe at my forehead, wiping away an image of him taking me against the bathroom sink. *Silly woman.*

With a clearer head, I return to my room to dress for a hospital visit.

I'm going to see my baby again.

+ + +

At first, our drive to the hospital is silent. I've had time to digest what Sebastian told me and gather questions about his past. Questions I should have asked before deciding to stay with him.

"Just ask me." He's read my mind and flexes his hand over the steering wheel before tightening it again.

"I don't want to pry." What's happened in the past really isn't my business, but I'm still curious. I'm always fascinated that some people can get clean while others can never stop using. Where is that fine line? What finally wakes someone up to their addiction while for someone else, he only slips into oblivion?

"Then I'll speak." Sebastian swipes his finger and thumb around his lips. "It's complicated. But the short version is, I did stupid things as a kid. Even stupider things as an adult. And I used drugs."

Not exactly a full explanation, but there's only one present concern for me. "But now you're clean?"

"Now I'm clean."

There's definitely more to his story, but I don't push. We've all made unfortunate choices in our past and I'm not here to be his judge and jury. His brief explanation hints that he's reconciled with what he's done and admits he had an issue. Admitting a problem is half the battle.

"Now I have a question for you."

"Okay," I hesitate.

"How did you know what to do with the pills?"

Some would say common sense said flush them away, but there's more to my story, as well. "My brother was an addict." I swallow around the sadness that always swells when I think of Seamus. "He was a few years older than me, and he just . . . got in with the wrong crowd, I guess."

My family will never have answers. While loving at times, my parents were also conservative and opinionated. The effect was triple-fold. Seamus did drugs. Cadence tried to get as far away as she could. And I did what I did, resulting in Adara. Of the three, my decision was not the worst.

"I'm sorry about your brother." Sincerity fills Sebastian's voice.

"Thank you. He wasn't as fortunate as you."

Sebastian scoffs before shifting a glance at me. "What do you mean?"

"He's dead because of his addiction."

"Shit. I'm so sorry Enya."

Not knowing how to respond, I stay quiet, clutching my hands together. Apologies for death are always awkward condolences when someone doesn't know what to say to such news. I'm sorry my brother is gone as well, but when it happened, I was angry. My parents didn't want to claim his body. My father simply identified him. They were silent about details pertaining to his death. Drugs. That was the culprit in their eyes. He'd made his choices and he died from them.

Why didn't my parents do more? Why hadn't Seamus been strong enough to seek help? How had this happened to him?

Again, answers I'll never have.

Sebastian clears his throat. "You said he was older than you. How old are you?"

"I'm thirty-eight."

The corner of his mouth cricks upward. "Thirty-five." He points at himself.

I would have guessed him a little older from the hardness around his mouth and the weary light in his eyes, but age is relative. Experience is what ages us and I'd bet Sebastian Sylver has lived more than one lifetime in his thirty-five years.

"Any other siblings?"

"Just a younger sister. Cadence is her name. She's your age." Sebastian was Cadence's type. She liked bad boys in school, while I tried to stay on the straight and narrow path, never wanting to disappoint my parents like Seamus had. The biggest deviation I made was an eleven-year relationship that led nowhere.

"She's in London right now for work."

"Speaking of work." He side-eyes me. "How did you become an accountant?"

"What's wrong with accounting?" I defend.

"Nothing." His brows lift. "But most accountants wear classes and have a collection of calculators like my brother Judd."

"What's wrong with glasses?" I snap, defensive again. "I wear them on occasion." My eyes are getting older, and sometimes columns of figures blur together by the end of a long day.

"I'd like to see that," he mutters, biting the corner of his lip and slowly shaking his head.

"What about you? How did you become a baker? If we're going to be stereotyping, you hardly seem like a sugar and spice guy. What made you fall in love with baking?"

Sebastian shrugs. "When I was a kid, my best friend's mom taught me to bake. Said idle hands would get me in trouble." He bitterly chuckles. "She was wrong. Like butter adheres to bread, trouble always found me."

I smile. "And you've been baking ever since?"

He shifts as if he's uncomfortable with the question. "Actually, I've only owned the place for three years."

Puzzled by the sudden unease in his tone, I don't press for more. "Well, your lemon baby-Bundt cakes are the best I've ever had. They became a craving during my pregnancy."

He snorts. "Too bad it took you like seven months to come in to buy another one."

"Oh, I didn't wait seven months."

His head sharply turns. "What do you mean?" Then his eyes narrow as he focuses forward again. "Were you cheating on my lemon cakes?"

I laugh. "Cheating?"

"Buying them from another bakery."

I laugh harder. "No. When I came to town, various clients knew how much I liked your baby-Bundt cakes, and they'd always have one or two available for me."

"What various clients?"

"Okay, only one client."

His mouth falls open. "Are you saying my brother was feeding your lemon cake obsession?"

I bite my lower lip. Again, his irritation is so cute. Like he wishes he'd been the one feeding me his delicacy.

"I might have seen your bakery bag at Sylver Seed and Soil once or twice. And happened to mention how much I enjoyed the lemon dream." Glossing over how I'd kissed the baker and enjoyed him as well. "And then one or two magically appeared every time I visited."

"Clay is such a fucking brown-noser," Sebastian grumbles.

"Actually, Judd bought them. He's very sweet."

"Yeah, sweet." His hand flexes on the steering wheel again but his sarcasm relaxes his shoulders.

On that note, we pull into the hospital parking lot.

Chapter 10

[Sebastian]

After a few hours at the hospital, Enya needs to breast pump, and God forgive me, but every time she says *breast* the twelve-year-old inside me fights the urge to envision her supple breasts. Are her nipples rosy and bright or dark and husky like her eyes?

She asks for privacy, which I respect by stepping out of Adara's pod. I make a quick call to check in on my part-time employee Barnett. He's a good kid and I wish I could have given him the raise he asked for last summer. Instead, I hired Rena because I needed a full-time employee.

When I return to Adara's pod, there are tears in Enya's eyes and frustration on her brow.

"What's wrong?" I ask.

"I think I just need some time alone here. The pumping. And Adara."

The updates on Adara's progress have been good but she'll be here until she's considered full-term. Enya's stressed by the nurses' talk about milliliters of milk and grams of weight gain for Adara, plus sleeping patterns and how to hold her premature baby.

"How will you get back home?" *Home*. My place.

"I'll just call an Uber."

"Not certain you'll find many of those around here." This area is remote, and not for the first time do I wonder if the Sterling Falls community will make Enya happy. Her apartment was sleek while a bit cold with floor to ceiling windows, stark white tiled floors, and modern flat paneled cabinetry in her kitchen. She didn't have any art on the walls, and she didn't have much food in her fridge, which led me to believe she doesn't cook for herself. Her bedroom wasn't more than a bed and a nightstand. She lived like a minimalist.

"When will you eat?"

"Later." She avoids eye contact with me. The strain of the situation rests on her trim shoulders.

Shaking my head, I make a suggestion., "I'll go down to the cafeteria and get you a sandwich." Then I offer one final request. "Call me when you're ready to come home. I'll come back for you."

Her mouth opens like she's about to protest but I lift a hand, stopping her. "No argument."

I have no idea why I keep tossing out support for this woman I hardly know, but when she told me *again* that she trusted me, after I told her about a sliver of my past, the hold she has on me is like a warm hug, something I haven't felt in decades.

No one has ever trusted me. Not in the unconditional way Enya does.

Hours later, she finally calls me, and when I pick her up, she looks exhausted.

"Sugar, you need rest."

Her head tips back on the seat. "I need a lemon cake."

"I can do that. But did you eat dinner? You need something healthier first."

"Okay, Dad." Everything about her mockery is a joke and yet my heart hammers. *Dad*. I'm not Adara's dad. Still, hearing Enya call me such a term, has my belly twisted up.

"I don't see myself ever becoming a dad," I admit as we drive back to my place.

"Really?" Her head lifts. "But you're so good at it."

I snort. "What have I done to make you say that?" I've held Adara. Even learned how to change a diaper. But that's nothing compared to what dads need to do. *Who* one needs to be.

"You're sweet with Adara."

"How?" I honestly don't know what she's talking about.

A soft smile curls her mouth. "I've seen you kiss her head and heard the way you coo at her, calling her pretty girl and sweetheart."

Heat warms my cheeks. "That's not being a dad." That's just . . . I don't know what those actions are. Dads should be loyal, supportive, present. Not lost in a bottle. Not cursing his children for their existence like mine had done.

"It's a start. Every little girl needs a daddy." Enya rolls her lips inward. "Well, at least, it's a nice thought."

Little boys need dads, too.

"Where is the father?" Is some man going to come looking for Enya and Adara? Some guy going to threaten to beat my ass for pretending to be Adara's dad? Some dude going to come begging for Enya to return to him?

"Nonexistent." Her tone demands finality on the subject.

Got it. "Are you close with your parents?"

"Let's just say they didn't exactly agree with how I had Adara."

"Meaning?"

"Being single."

"Ah. My dad kind of sucked and my mom died when I was two."

"Sebastian." Enya twists in her seat, easily reaching for my forearm. "I'm so sorry."

"It happens." But it really did suck. I don't recall my mother, other than the stories my older siblings tell about her, and my dad turned into an ass after the love of his life died in childbirth. The thought of how I could have lost Enya in that same way makes my blood run cold, and I'm not even in love with her.

I doubt I'll ever love anyone because I'd want them to love me back and I don't see myself as loveable.

I clear my throat. "So, dinner?"

"Just pull through a drive-thru. I don't even care where at this point. I just need to eat something."

"Shouldn't you be on some kind of healthy meal plan? For breast feeding purposes?"

Her mouth falls open. "Are you implying I'm fat?"

"Not at all." I gape in response.

"Because I'm not fat." She practically breathes fire. "I was pregnant. I just had a baby. It took months to get to this point." She takes a breath while waving at her lap. "Thirty-four weeks to be exact, and it's going to take time to get back to my pre-pregnancy weight."

"Enya," I groan, gripping the steering wheel harder.

"And just because you hang out with women who are supermodel-worthy doesn't mean every woman is."

"What the fuck?" I snap, momentarily gazing at her. "Are you kidding me right now?"

Her mouth falls open, ready to spew more flames but I cut her off.

"You're fucking perfect, Enya. A total smokeshow with your beautiful curves and those lush breasts. You're right, you just delivered a baby, and you freakin' glow from it. Like I've literally never seen anything, *anyone*, so more lit up in my life. And I saw you before you had Adara, so I know firsthand how beautiful you were then and how incredible you look now. You're like a walking dream and if I was the settling down type, I'd lock you down with a ring so quickly, your head would spin."

"I—"

"Do not give me more bullshit," I continue before she can speak. "You don't need to be pre-pregnancy, pre-anything. You're stunning exactly as you are."

Her mouth pops open but then she's leaning forward and pointing out my window as I gas it past a burger place. She falls back against the seat, crossing her arms, and glaring out the front window.

"I didn't mean anything personal by mentioning a healthy diet. I read about it online. About mothers and nursing babies."

The weight of her gaze caresses the side of my face and I risk a glance at her before looking back through the windshield. "I'll take care of dinner."

"Sebastian," she groans, but the sound is a soften growl. More grizzly cub than mama bear. "I haven't had time to go to the grocery store."

"I did, so don't worry about it." When we pull into the lot behind the bakery, I quickly exit my truck and circle around the hood to help Enya with her door, but she's already opening it herself. I want to tell her to wait for me the next time. Then I want to grab her hand to lead her up to my place, but I don't.

Instead, I wave outward for her to lead the way up the back staircase and I fight the pull to look at her ass. Having changed out of my tee earlier, which almost gave me a heart attack to see her wearing, she now wears a loose top and leggings. The soft material outlines her legs and backside, highlighting how firm they are.

Like I told her, she's a fucking wet dream. What she doesn't need to know, though, is that I'll shamelessly be jacking off to visions of her again tonight. Like I've been doing nearly every night since she's stumbled back into my life.

When we reach the landing, she pauses and turns to face me. "Is that how you knew about the blood pressure medication and its side effects? Are you . . . have you been researching about new mothers and babies?"

I don't answer. Instead, I slot the key into the lock and open my apartment door.

Once inside my place, I cross to the fridge and open the door, feeling her questioning gaze still on me. "I have chicken. Steak. Pork chops. I can make something quick, like spaghetti or fajitas."

"Sebastian, if you tell me you can cook, as well as you bake, I might fall in love with you."

With my back to her, my hand clenches around the fridge handle. Cool air hits my face while the rest of my body heats. *She's only teasing.* A woman like her would never love a man with a past like mine.

"Baking is a science. Cooking is a crapshoot. *Top Chef* isn't going to be calling me anytime soon, but I'm decent in the kitchen." After years of eating off a tray, I swore I'd never take a homecooked meal for granted again.

Behind me, she clears her throat. "Spaghetti sounds good."

An alarm rings on her phone.

"What's that?" I close the fridge door and turn to face her.

"A reminder that it's time to pump."

Awkwardness floats between us. It's difficult to think about her hooking something up to her body and doing what comes naturally to any woman after having a baby. The immature side of me is thinking about the swell of her breasts again and the fact I'll never know if her nipples are large and dusty or tight and rosy, or some other combination.

"Why don't you . . . do what you need to do." I swallow, pointing toward her room. "And I'll make you dinner."

"You're too good to me, Sebastian. But thank you."

Enough with the gratitude already. But I don't argue with her. I simply shake my head before she heads to her room.

Twenty minutes later, she reappears. Dinner is almost ready, and I offer her a glass of wine.

"I probably shouldn't."

"Right." The baby. I bought the bottle for Enya without thinking.

"I hope I don't disturb you during the night. I need to wake up every three hours and express."

"Express?" I reach for low bowls to serve the pasta in.

"I feel weird saying pump around you."

Spinning with the bowls in hand, I say. "I don't want you to feel uncomfortable about anything with me. I know this isn't conventional but—"

"Hardly conventional," she interjects.

"But we agreed to be friends. I'm . . . comfortable with you here. Do what you need to do."

A light flush of pink races over her skin and her eyelids lower while she bites that damn lip. The one I want to suck on and run my tongue over.

"I'm comfortable with you, too." She slowly lifts her head. Warmth fills those dark eyes and my heart thumps once. Twice.

"I trust you." The statement is said like she can't believe it herself, but it's the third time she's said it to me. I want to believe her. I want to be trustworthy. I want her to find comfort in me.

We stare at one another for a long minute before the timer goes off for the garlic bread.

"Anyway," I say, reaching for the oven. "I remember you said you need to wake up every three hours. That's brutal."

"I need to work on my supply . . . for Adara."

"Ah." I nod while lifting the baking sheet with the bread and setting it on the stove. "I'm a heavy sleeper so I doubt you'll disturb me."

Only, hours later, her alarm goes off after I've been tossing and turning in bed, knowing someone else is sleeping in my place. Someone beautiful and surprisingly funny, and so fucking appreciative of everything I do for her, when I don't think anyone's ever been thankful for anything I've done.

The soft hum of a pulsing machine beats through the quiet, and God forgive me, but for half a second, I imagine it's something else.

Visions of Enya using a little handheld device, pleasuring herself with something thick and long, enters my head, and I cannot fight the desire to grip my dick. Lying flat on my back, with the rhythmic sound in the background, I stare up at the ceiling. With my imagination running wild, I picture Enya's almond-brown hair spread over a pillow. Her head tipped back. Her mouth slightly open. Her breath heavy and clipped. And her hands between her thighs, toying with a vibrator at her clit. Maybe it's one of those bunny-eared ones, that hits a sensitive nub and enters her at the same time, and now I'm thinking about her pussy and how sweet it might be.

She's all sugar. A perfect layer of buttercream frosting over lemony moist cake.

My mouth waters. My fist moves faster. Then the base of my spine tweaks and my balls tighten. I come, digging my teeth into my lower lip and holding back the cry of her name.

Enya. Sweet fucking Enya.

With a heavy sigh, I drape my other arm over my face, closing my eyes, ashamed of myself.

But not that ashamed.

Only once has guilt truly consumed me. That was ten years ago in a dark room, with the stench of heroin, and a coward quivering in a corner of an abandoned farmhouse.

The memory pulls me from my momentary pleasure, and I roll off my bed, swiping a dirty tee from my hamper to clean off my hand before heading to the bathroom to wash up the rest of me.

If only I could wash away my past.

+ + +

In the morning, I slip out early. I woke up minutes before my alarm at four a.m.

Leaving Enya a note, I tell her to come down to the bakery for breakfast.

When she finally appears, light purple smudges beneath her eyes are a stark reminder of her exhaustion. She didn't sleep any better than me, but she had a better excuse than my horniness.

"Hey," I greet her.

"Good morning. Did I wake you last night?"

"Nah," I lie. "What can I get you for breakfast? Muffin? Protein square? Lemon cake?" I wiggle my brows, pleased that she told me yesterday how much she loves my cakes. I'm still a little irked that my brothers have been feeding her a steady supply and I had no idea she'd been around town for months.

Months where I could have gotten to know her better, sooner.

"I'll take one of those protein squares and a decaf, black please."

"On it." I rush around Barnett who is ringing up a customer. Kid is tall with long limbs. He never gives me trouble and works hard. He takes care of his aunt, which is admirable since his mother dumped him with Bernadette, her sister. He's also seventeen, which means he's probably horny-as-fuck and can't take his eyes off Enya.

"Barnett," I snap, watching teenage hormones play out in his boyish face.

"Yeah." He closes his gaping mouth and turns toward me.

"This is Enya. Enya, Barnett Matthews."

"Nice to meet you, Barnett."

I swear the kid who looks like a rock star blushes under Enya's attention.

I get it, kid. I fucking get it.

I collect breakfast for my new favorite customer, handing over a medium coffee and the bakery bag. Enya offers me a warm smile and a twenty.

I scowl at her and push her hand holding the money away from me. I'm not taking a thing from her.

"I'll see you later," she eventually says, almost asking me, like she wants affirmation that I'll be here for her. It's a silly thought.

"I'll be here." I have work to make up for the hours I missed yesterday. Paperwork and supply orders, plus employee scheduling and managing special orders. But I deserve a day off now and again, although I don't often take time for myself. There were years I selfishly spent on me and then more years behind bars where my only concern was myself. Work is my priority now.

Watching Enya slip toward the back door for her Honda Passport parked beside my truck, I wonder what it would be like to have other priorities in life.

When I quickly turn back to the work at hand, I collide with Rena.

"Oops." An over-the-top giggle escapes her mouth as she covers her lips with her hand. I glance down to see my T-shirt covered in flour. Rena holds the bag in one hand. She drops the hand over her mouth and swipes it down my tee, at first hastily brushing off the white powder but eventually her hand slows and she's spreading it more than removing it. Her palm presses more firmly at my pecs, stroking down my sternum to my waist and—

"Whoa," I snap, stepping back from her and brusquely brushing at my tee with my knuckles. "Watch where you're going," I add. *As well as watch your fucking hands.*

With my eyes narrowed on Rena, her gaze hasn't left my chest, where white speckles streak my dark shirt. She blatantly licks her lips before meeting my eyes. "You look like a tasty treat, boss."

Is she kidding me with this shit? Is she . . . flirting with me? Since when? And why?

Suddenly, I'm cursing my brothers for all their teasing about my employee. There's nothing between us. Not a whisper of attraction. But I'm suddenly questioning that thought as Rena continues to hungrily stare at me. I know that look. I've seen it, acted on it, used it to my advantage in the past.

This is now, though.

"Let's keep our hands to ourselves," I state, standing taller despite the display of flour all over my tee.

Rena's deep-green eyes snap up to mine. She chews at her lower lip but not a hint of remorse or apology comes from her. If I could read her mind, I bet she's telling me we don't need our hands for what she wants from me.

Fuck. I swipe a flour covered hand through my hair. I do not need these kinds of disturbing thoughts in my head. I don't want any issue with my *employee*.

"I need a minute to clean up," I mutter.

Rena doesn't respond as I round the front counter and glare at the door Enya just exited, almost willing her to return.

Then, I remind myself the bakery is my *only* priority.

Along with keeping myself out of the kind of trouble that comes from having wishful thoughts about a woman and her kid.

Chapter 11

[Enya]

For days, Sebastian and I flow around each other. He's up early. I rise shortly after him and 'do what I need to do' as he calls it. Then I shower, head down to the bakery for breakfast-on-the-go and leave for another day at the hospital. Sebastian often shows up in the late afternoons.

The hours are consumed with concerns about Adara. Her breathing tube has been removed but the feeding tube remains to assist her weight gain. The doctors would like her to be at least double her birth weight before she can be discharged. Either that, or Adara removes the feeding tube herself, which is a clear sign she's ready to feed on her own. I still can't nurse her; forced to bottle feed her instead. The nurses warn me not to be upset if Adara never takes to breastfeeding because of her current situation.

In most respects, I'm fortunate. My little cookie only needs to grow before she can leave the hospital. Some of the sorrowful tales I hear floating around me in the NICU remind me to be grateful. Be patient. My daughter will come home with me soon enough.

Guilt over leaving Adara hits me every time I exit the NICU, but the nurses and a social worker have told me I need the break. Time outside of the hospital. Outside of thoughts about Adara. I don't have much else going for me, though, as I'm on twelve-weeks of maternity leave and without my new home.

When I checked in with my contractor earlier today, he told me he wanted an additional week, but I'm done waiting for my house.

"I needed to be in there, like a week ago," I argued. Initially, I was promised the construction would be complete two months before Adara's due date. When that didn't happen, I still thought I'd have time to be settled before her arrival. *Best laid plans and all.* With her early birth, I'd given the contractor two weeks to finalize my house.

Strangely, I've become accustomed to calling Sebastian's place home and I'm a little uneasy about leaving his apartment. There's a subtle comfort being in his place. The way we move about, like we're in tune with one another, like we've been together for a while.

He cooks. I do dishes.

He watches television. I read on the couch.

One night, Sebastian suggests we watch a movie together. I quickly warn him I can't watch anything that involves rape or pillaging, or kidnapping.

We are flopped on his couch. He sits in the section that has an extension piece, stretching his legs out and crossing them at his ankles. Opposite him, I curl against the thick and supportive armrest.

As the television warms up, Sebastian turns his head toward me. "I'd never let that happen."

"What?" I say, craning my neck to look at him over my shoulder.

"Any of those things. I'll always be here for you and Adara."

"That's so sweet, but you can't protect us every second of every day." Wouldn't that be nice, but it's just not humanly possible. Besides, Sebastian has a life outside of Adara and me. He isn't beholden to us. We're only temporary in his life, but I can't help hoping he'll permanently be in ours as the friend I need.

"Enya. I'd never let anything happen to either of you. Ever." As he stares at me, I stare back, slowly accepting he means every word.

He's so different from Lance. It's been a while since I've thought of my ex. Being around Sebastian, who is truly giving of his time as well as open with his living space, I have a new impression of the ideal man compared to the man I once thought was infallible.

"I know," I whisper, surprised by an overwhelming desire for him to be that person in my life. *The* person who wants to look out for me and my little girl. Love us. Protect us. I'd do the same for him.

However, we're friends and I'm not in a position for more. For romance and rustling around a bed. I have Adara to think about and my own heart to consider. I've already taken the route of pretty words, which led to unfilled promises. I won't be on that road trip again, nor will I bring my daughter along for such a ride.

Any man who wants into our lives must accept we are a package deal, and that deal demands loyalty and commitment. The desire for family and marriage. *Love.*

Sebastian has been abundantly clear on his stance. He doesn't see himself ever being a father. Which is too bad because his acting skills—pretending he's Adara's dad—are even fooling me.

He's so sweet with her. The way he speaks to her, calling her name with such tender emotion in his rugged voice. The way he holds her to his chest. Unfortunately, there are no longer displays of his naked skin and Adara swaddled against him. Not even in his apartment do I see him shirtless as he wakes early and leaves before me. I don't need to see him without a shirt, though. It's probably better that I don't, but it's still been a shame not to get an up close and in the flesh view of him.

Even if we are only friends.

On that note, his phone rings, and he quickly answers.

"Hey." His greeting sounds agitated, hesitant even. He side-eyes me and I'm wondering if I should give him privacy when he presses off the couch.

"Just about to watch a movie." He rounds the couch, holds up a finger to me and heads toward his bedroom.

For some reason, his explanation to whomever he's speaking with stings. There's no clarification that he's with me, not that he needs to quantify that he's watching a movie *with me,* but it feels dismissive. I also don't like that finger hold, putting me on pause.

The motion is very reminiscent of Lance, a man who put me on hold for eleven years.

Shaking my head, I will away all negative thoughts about a man I don't want to think about. For too many years, I was a presence in someone's life but not his priority. I promised myself I'd never live without being acknowledged again. If I'm going to be in someone's life, I need to be *in* it. Not a bystander. Not a minor character. Not second to everything else.

Sebastian has put my needs first in many regards. However, I'm not a priority for him, as I shouldn't be. Our living together is temporary. His daily existence in mine and Adara's life is only momentary.

Quickly, he returns to the couch.

"If you want to go out, you can." My haughty tone is unwarranted and I clear my throat. "I mean, don't let me hold you back if you have friends . . . or someone . . . wanting to see you."

"Enya." Sebastian has already tossed himself back into position in his corner. He reaches for the remote, settling back into position with outstretched legs and crossed ankles.

"I told you when I moved in, I don't want to cramp your style."

"You're not cramping anything. I don't have a style." He hitches his arm on the rest beside him and tilts his head toward me.

"You're an attractive man and I'm sure ladies line up for a sample."

He scrunches up his nose. "Did you just call me attractive? Why does that word feel icky?"

"What's wrong with the word attractive?"

"It makes me feel old. Like saying I have a nice personality."

"You do have a nice personality."

"Ugh." He tips his head back before springing it upward and turning it toward me. "I'm not nice."

"You're super nice," I counter, surprised that he thinks he's not.

"I am not."

"You are, too." I shift in a way my entire body faces him. With my legs crisscrossed, the armrest supports my back.

"Sugar," he growls as we stare at one another.

"What?" Our eyes lock. Suddenly, I see the not-so-nice part of him. Not menacing. Not mean. Just flames of temptation that I want to incinerate me.

"Don't say I'm nice." His voice drops deep and demanding. So cute when he's all scowling and irritated.

And I'm not good at being told what to do as I age. Chewing at my lower lip, I mutter. "You're so nice." All day. Every day. The husky sound of my voice isn't one I recognize but I like it.

He springs like a lion, startling me as I'm suddenly caged in with his arms balanced on the rest behind me. He towers over my body, hovering, heaving. His face is so close to mine I breathe in each exaggerated breath he takes. With my back arched, my breasts brush against his chest, the tease is torture to my sensitive nipples, which peak within my bra.

"I am not nice." His mouth cricks up in the corner, fighting a grin while he peers down at me. His biceps flinch in my peripheral view. His thick arms cage me in, and I want him to close the distance, lower over me, cover me with the blanket of his body.

"Hmm." I disagree. He's so very nice with that vanilla and motor oil scent and a hint of cinnamon on his breath. His eyes are the color of cool flames, sparked to life and on the brink of boiling over.

Slowly, that grin he's fighting grows larger and I'm stunned. A spell is cast, although there's not a single thing I fear from this man. But that smile is deadly. Wide mouth. White teeth. *I* want a taste of him, and I lick my lips, eager for my own sample. A second helping I didn't get when I left his bakery the first time.

Brusquely, he presses off the armrest and falls back to his haunches, digging his knees into the cushion before my crisscrossed legs. He swipes a hand down his face, like pulling down a shade, and then scrambles back to his corner of the couch.

I gingerly push myself upright, tucking my legs back to my middle and leaning into the armrest at my side.

What just happened here?

My heart hammers. My mouth goes dry.

Sebastian might be attracted to me, but he isn't interested in what I represent. Single mom. Commitment. And I'm sadly disappointed when I shouldn't be.

He grips the remote like it's the last rung of a fire escape ladder dangling a few feet above solid ground. He aims it at the television, and aggressively taps the device with his thumb like it's a magic wand that can make the past few minutes disappear.

I almost wish he would go out so I can retreat to my room and let the tears of rejection fall.

"That phone call was my sister." He stares at the television as he explains. "She was giving me a hard time for missing our weekly family dinner."

"You have weekly family dinners?" I turn only my head while my voice squeaks because my throat is still thick.

"Every Sunday."

He's missed the last two because of me.

"You're lucky to have family. You shouldn't miss meals with them." My family doesn't do anything collectively. Since Seamus's death, and Cadence and my distance from our parents, a weekly dinner isn't a thought.

"They're only going to harass me about you."

I subtly shift on the couch again. "Sebastian, I don't want to—"

"You aren't, okay?" His voice is harsh as he cuts me off. "You aren't a nuisance, or in the way, or cramping my style. They're just being fucking nosy, and we are none of their business."

"Nothing's going on here," I state.

"I know that." He snaps even harsher and then turns away from me, putting up an invisible wall between us.

He clicks the remote again, and a movie roars to life. For the next two hours, we blindly watch motion on the screen, but I have no idea what the show is about.

+ + +

As soon as the movie is over, I hop off the couch, eager for my room and some space from Sebastian. Certain he'd kiss me one minute, he was as cold as frozen cookie dough the next. I quickly use the bathroom and shut myself inside my space.

When I finish a pumping session, I need to put what I've collected in the refrigerator, but I don't want to encounter Sebastian again tonight. For now, I set the small bottles in a travel cooler in my room. Movement happens outside my door and then a presence comes to rest. From the shadow interrupting a sliver of light beneath the door, I know Sebastian is outside my room.

I don't want to fight with him. I don't want to push him into any situation that makes him uncomfortable, like explaining me to his family. He's already been overly kind, and I don't know what I've done to earn his generosity. And I'm a coward for hiding out in my room, hoping tonight he'll just walk away.

"Enya." My name is a soft plea.

I close my eyes and will my feet to remain still. We don't need to talk. Maybe it's better that we don't. My emotions are raw and rambling. I shouldn't be upset that we didn't kiss. He doesn't owe me kisses even if I'd like to give them to him. Kissing would only complicate our lives and I want him as my friend.

A soft *thunk* rattles the door. His quiet voice travels through the solid surface. "There isn't anywhere else I'd rather be than sitting on my couch watching a movie with you."

He speaks as if he is thinking out loud, speaking softly to himself, because I'm not listening, which I totally am.

"My family can be a lot and Vale wants me to bring you to the next dinner, but it's too much. They're going to scare you away. *I'm* going to scare you away. And I just want you to myself a little longer."

My brows lift. Eyes widen. I creep closer to the door, eager to hear what else he has to say when he thinks I'm not listening.

"You aren't a nuisance." A choked, bitter guffaw happens. "You've become a necessity."

How am I a necessity?

Another light tap hits the door, like the tender lift and loll of his head. "I don't want you to go."

He doesn't want me to go to the family dinner? Or he doesn't want me to move out of his place?

Because I'm going to leave soon.

Suddenly, I'm at the door with a hand on the knob and my forehead against the barrier. My heart is shattering, torn between hope that he wants me to stay and fear that he wants me to go away. However, he can't possibly scare me, like he said. The only thing I'm afraid of are my feelings for him.

As a man who has been charitable and compassionate, he's more dangerous for my heart's health than sugar-rich lemon cake every day of the week. Because I'm convinced a loving man stands behind this door and I want him to love me.

Love both Adara and me.

Chapter 12

[Sebastian]

The night after the movie mishap, I can't sleep and wander down to the bakery close to midnight.

I break out the good stuff—the high-quality dark chocolate—chopping it into small chunks before mixing it with butter and placing the combination in the microwave to melt. Next, I separate yolks from egg whites, setting the whites aside before adding the yolks to the melted chocolate mixture. As I concentrate on the measurements of additional ingredients and the skill of folding for the right consistency, my mind empties of the near kiss last night and the things I said to a silent door.

I meant what I said. She isn't a nuisance in my life. She's become this strange necessity. Like I need to see her every day for some reason. Watch her read in the corner of my couch. Or hear her laugh while we share dinner on the stools in my kitchen. Or witness the unconditional love she has for her daughter.

I hadn't seen Enya this morning because I was out with an order when she left. When I'd gone to the hospital in the late afternoon, I'd missed her again. A quick text message told me she was meeting with her contractor to go over the final specs for her house.

I fear she suddenly can't get away from me fast enough.

I hadn't missed how quickly she jumped from the couch last night, using her pumping schedule as an excuse to avoid me. With the open concept of each bedroom, I'd heard when the machine stopped, and she was free to talk to me. Or listen. Sadly, she hadn't acknowledged that she heard me at her door.

Distractedly, I whip the egg whites until they peak like miniature mountains. Then in three separate additions, I fold the chocolate mixture with the whipped whites. When the combination is just right, I set the mix in the refrigerator, allowing it to thicken as the oven pre-heats.

When I spin away from the oven, I freeze. "Enya?"

"I heard the kitchen mixer up the staircase." The door to the stairwell is open.

"Did I wake you?" She always looks so tired. I hate that I've disturbed what little sleep she gets.

"I was up from my alarm and headed for the refrigerator when I heard the noise. What are you doing awake?"

"I couldn't sleep." Because a certain someone is on my mind. And the desire to kiss her is haunting me. We promised we'd be friends. I can't risk fucking that up by telling her all my fantasies. Of bending her over the armrest of my couch and taking her from behind. Or laying her flat on her back and falling into her, pinning her ankles to my shoulders. My imagination is growing heavier, darker, desperate to have her and yet for once, I'm not impulsively reacting for fear I'll lose her . . . and Adara.

I lower my gaze and rub my fingers along the counter's edge. I hadn't bothered getting dressed, so I'm wearing only a pair of gray sweatpants and sport slides on my feet.

"Did I wake *you*?" The concern in her voice is genuine. She's just as worried about disturbing me during the night.

I shake my head. "Stress baking."

"What exactly are you making?" Her dark eyes meet mine, reminding me of the treat almost ready to be baked.

"How about if I surprise you?" I tilt my head, hopeful she'll join me since we're both awake in the middle of the night. "Although, you should probably go back to sleep."

"I'd like to wait until I see what you make." Her eyes spark with a bit of mischief.

I have employees who love to bake, and my family loves my creations. Even customers rave about what I make, but I want this woman's approval most of all. A real five-star review. And that scares me.

When the oven beeps, that's my cue to slip back into baker mode, and the distraction I need from what she's wearing, which is my Curmudgeon Bakery tee and a pair of silk pajama shorts. Her breasts are heavy and her nipples pert despite a bra.

Bringing my attention back to task, I quickly coat the ramekins I'd set out earlier with softened butter and granular sugar to help the dessert rise straight upward and give it a perfect crust. Taking the slightly solidified chocolate mixture from the fridge, I scoop enough into each ramekin to fill it, then level it off with a knife and run the tip around the edge, carving a channel.

"Just watching you work is making my mouth water." Enya's low voice interrupts my process and sends warmth straight to my dick which doesn't have much protection in these thin sweats with nothing underneath.

"Wait until you taste this." I'd love to have her salivating over the chocolate perfection. I'd also love to swipe it over her nipples and lick it off her but squash that thought as I set the tray into the oven to bake.

"May I come to that side of the counter?" she asks.

Only, I hear *may I come on the counter,* and I'd like nothing more than to spread her thighs and sample what's between them. She isn't in a position for that, though, and it's almost a godsend, like a natural intervention to what I'd like to do to her.

"Permission granted," I tease, tipping up my chin.

She nearly skips around the counter. Holding out her hands at her sides like she's balancing on a tightrope, she whispers as she draws closer to me. "I feel like I've entered your sacred domain."

In many ways, she has. I've let her into my home, my bakery, and my heart which doesn't offer much room. Just a corner, like the spot on my couch I will forever brand as hers. Because if my heart were to open its entire capacity to her, letting her fully reside in there, that would be the worst idea. If she loved me, she'd eat me alive. I'd be consumed by something I've only heard about and never believed I deserved.

An addict with a new addiction.

Thankfully, I still don't believe in love. I don't allow myself to dream of it.

"This *is* my domain." I glance up and around the bakery. "I worked hard to get here." I point at the floor, emphasizing this spot. This place. This moment.

"Recovering from drugs?" Her question draws my attention back to her. We haven't spoken again about my former habits.

"Among a few things." I turn my head, anxiously scrubbing the back of my neck.

Should I tell her? Does she need to know the details? Strangely, a desire to give her more heats my insides. I can do this. I can trust her. Thinking back on her reaction to my admission that I'd done drugs, Enya proved she'd be compassionate, maybe even understanding. She'd accepted me almost instantly.

Did I need more of her acceptance?

"I was in prison." Quickly glancing back at her, I hold my breath, waiting for her reaction.

Her lips clamp together, and she takes a moment to absorb what I just said. She slowly nods as if she's accepted the truth. "For what?"

"Voluntary manslaughter. I hadn't intended to kill someone, but that's not how the state saw it." I certainly meant to beat him. I'd intended to teach him a lesson but kill him . . . that hadn't been the plan.

I wait for Enya to take a step back in disgust and then bolt from the bakery. She might even skip returning to the apartment for her things and just race right out the back door, never to return.

Instead, she surprises me, holding still and watching me. My hand still cups the back of my neck. I hadn't expected to tell her like this. With us in the quiet of my bakery, in the middle of the night, when we both need sleep and can't seem to find it. Hell, I'm not certain I ever wanted to tell her.

"What happened?" The softness in her eyes along with quiet curiosity forces my tongue to move.

"He'd gone after Vale." I hate to think about what might have happened if Vale hadn't gotten away. If she hadn't somehow fled from him at a party in the woods where she shouldn't have ever been present. Vale had been too naïve, seeking love and acceptance, like me when we were younger. Thankfully, I'd been at the party, for all the wrong reasons, and I chased that fucker until he was trapped.

"We got into an altercation." That was putting it mildly. I'd hunted him down and cornered him. The judge pinned intent on me. Only, I hadn't had a plan. I'd simply wanted to confront him. Warn him with my fists to never look at my sister again. Not come near her. Not breathe her air.

"There was a time I was constantly angry. At my family. At my life. And I went too far that night." Being high can give you unparalleled strength. It can also inhibit your physical reaction. I was on one side of that equation. My opponent on the other. The frustration of years had flowed down my arm and into my fists, landing on him over and over again.

Stone thought it was possible the man had a heart attack in the middle of the fight. His heart giving out because of excessive drug use. However, the bruises on his body framed my guilt.

He'd tried to touch my sister, who had already been inappropriately touched once. I wouldn't let anyone disgrace her again.

Sparing Enya the gory details, I state, "I've told you I'm not a good man. And I'm no fucking hero."

"I don't believe that." Enya steps closer to me, crowding my space. Her clean scent of rain showers in autumn hits me like a balm. The crisp fragrance burned into my nose when we met and didn't leave for weeks after she'd disappeared.

"And I don't need you to be a hero to everyone. You're a hero to me. To Adara. And you're kind to both of us." She inhales sharply, closing her eyes a second before opening them. "And frankly, it's refreshing."

"Who hurt you?" I grip her shoulders, gently shaking her to tell me who was unkind. *Who touched her?* I'll kill him and not think twice about it.

"No one important." Her hands lift to my bare chest. The heat of her palms sears my skin, branding me. I'll wear the imprint for an eternity because I'd do anything for her.

My apartment. My bakery. My heart. *Take it all. Heart be damned.*

Leaning forward my mouth waters for hers. Her lips are the color of fresh-picked raspberries. The hue of her eyes is more tempting than chocolate. I'm fighting the desire to devour her when the timer on the oven buzzes.

Quickly, I step back, foolish to think I could kiss her after the confession that just left my lips.

"Hang on." Releasing her, I turn toward the oven. Retrieving the tray with a mitt, I set it on the counter to cool before reaching for the fridge door. I pull out whipped cream and fresh raspberries.

When I turn around, Enya has stepped closer to the hot tray.

"Did you make chocolate soufflé?" Her head lifts. "A master of tangy lemon wonders and now melt-in-your-mouth sweetness?" A dreamy glaze covers her eyes.

She's melt-in-your-mouth goodness.

With a smirk, I step to the counter and set down the additional ingredients. Generously, I cover a souffle with a dollop of whipped cream and several fresh raspberries.

"I never understand why bakers only give you one piece of fruit. You need a raspberry for every bite."

The simplicity is for presentation, but I agree with her assessment, thus the additional smattering of berries.

Reaching for two spoons, I hold one out for her, reminding me of the day we met and shared a celebratory cake.

She takes hers and taps mine like we did that day.

"What are we toasting to?" I ask.

"You," she whispers.

"Sugar," I groan, catching on her gaze and staring at her, momentarily recalling the memory of her stepping into my bakery and letting me kiss her. If I only ever have that one kiss, I'm a fortunate man.

"To you," she says again, stepping closer to me, mesmerizing me with those eyes, rich and chocolaty, and full of warmth. How would it feel to have a woman like her heat my body?

"Shall we?" I say before I do something stupid, like drop the spoon, skip the soufflé, and simply taste her.

We dip into the soufflé at the same time, and I watch with bated breath as she lifts the spoonful of chocolate, whipped cream, and one raspberry to her mouth. Wrapping those lips around the utensil, she closes her eyes and hums in appreciation.

She whimpers as she drags the spoon out of her mouth. "Oh my God. It's so good." Her lips purse, savoring each flavor bursting on her tongue. Eventually, she swallows. When her eyes slowly open, she licks the well of the spoon free of any remaining chocolate.

"Dammit, Enya," I groan, watching her tongue like I'm one of those *Bridgerton* fans drooling over some dude nearly French kissing a silver spoon.

"What?" The innocence in her voice playfully contradicts the flirtation in her eyes. Does she want me to kiss her? Is she provoking me?

To tease her in return, I lift my sample and swipe my lips over the decadent treat, holding it on my tongue before allowing myself to swallow. The flavors are exquisite. The combination of warm chocolate, cool crème, and a burst of fruity sugar is perfection. This treat defines Enya.

I lap at my spoon like she did, allowing the flat of my tongue to take its time to swipe up the last streaks of chocolate.

Enya watches me. Her eyes mesmerized. Her mouth slightly open. Her spoon softly thuds to the countertop.

"Kiss me," she whispers.

"We both know that's not a good idea."

"We won't do anything more than kiss." Enya has already told me that she'll meet with her doctor in a few weeks to ensure everything *down there* is healed. Tonight doesn't need to lead to sex. Just a kiss.

I cup the back of her neck and lower my forehead to hers. "Won't ever be enough." Because one kiss would lead me to wanting more kisses. Like more raspberries on a soufflé. One is never enough.

"You're too good of a man," Enya whispers as her forehead holds on mine.

"I'm not." Closing my eyes, I gently roll my forehead against hers, wanting to be a better man while also wanting to be so, so bad with her. I run my nose along the side of hers, swiping it over the tip and breathing her in.

"Let me show you"—she whispers, her voice breathy—"how good we can be." She has no idea how much I want to take her up on that offer. For her to gift me her goodness. Share with me her purity. How I want her to show me what love is. Or at least, what it might look like for others as I don't expect to fully have it for myself.

"I—" I pause, swallowing around the chocolate in my throat and the desire to ravish that mouth of hers. "I can't."

With an abrupt release of her nape and a large step backward, I pull away and hold up the ramekin like a shield between us. Like a simple circular ceramic can protect me from doing something stupid with someone so enticing. Guilt is on my dirty hands. Guilt, and blood, and shame at who I was despite where I am.

Enya stares at me, hurt filling her eyes. The rejection might sting but it's so much better than how much I could really hurt someone like her.

And the type of pain she'd inflict on me.

If only I could kiss her one more time and never again, but I know that would never be enough. The addictive trait in me would crave more and more of her, and that's just dangerous for both of us.

Chapter 13

[Sebastian]

On Sunday, there is no way Vale will let me miss another family dinner, so I head to the old farmhouse. When our father died, Stone moved in to raise Knox, Ford, Vale, and me. However, Knox was on the cusp of eighteen and pretty much a legal adult. He was headed for the military back then.

In many ways, I'm surprised that Vale didn't want to burn the house to the ground. Instead, the place has slowly been remodeled to what it is today. A picture-perfect home with a deep-green tin roof and shutters around each window, making it look like the goddamn Waltons lived here instead of the Sylvers—a clan of burly boys with one sacred daughter.

When I learned to bake, my father would tease me about it, stereotyping the skill as feminine. My fists proved otherwise. I was always a fighter. And dear ol' Dad never had a problem eating what I made.

The gravel space in front of the old house is full of cars, telling me who is present. Taking the front steps two at a time, I cross the wide porch and enter the house through the open screen door. After setting a plate of brownies on the kitchen counter, I head to the backyard where everyone gathers on such a warm day.

"Well, look who decided to grace us with his presence. Daddy Warbucks," Knox teases, calling me the rich dude once again when I live a conservative life. An honest life, making a legal wage, and running a legitimate business.

Knox pulls me into a hug, clapping my back hard enough to piss me off. I'm on edge and have been since that night in the bakery with Enya. I seem to be measuring every day by her. The day she moved in. The night I almost kissed her. The bakery incident. She's consuming me, and perhaps some family time is the distraction I need.

They'll irritate me just enough I won't think about her for at least five minutes.

"Where's your date?" Clay asks me next and there goes my willpower to stop thinking about Enya.

"She went to see the baby."

I didn't invite her to attend dinner. I'd meant what I said to her silent bedroom door the other night. These guys would scare her off.

"Ah, right. The baby." Clay winks at me. "Never pictured you as a dad." His smile says he's poking fun at me, but there is truth beneath the jest.

"I'm not a dad."

"But you're playing one. And you're not even a decent actor," Knox jibes, wiggling his brows.

"It's only for a little while." Realistically, I could pull the hospital band from my wrist and quit the farce. There isn't any reason to continue seeing Adara now that Enya is free to come and go from the hospital. Enya's even been taken off her blood pressure medication, which was the original reason I asked her to stay with me. She's doing so well.

"Hmm." Vale greets me next. "Typically, fatherhood is for life."

We all know that isn't true. Our own father stepped out of his role. He wasn't good to his kids and got progressively worse the younger down the line we were. With Stone in college, and Clay at the Seed and Soil, then Judd off to college and Knox heading for the military, there was some real fear in Ford, Vale, and me to remain behind with our dad.

Vale also knows from Hudson's father that some men just don't take the honor of fatherhood as a commitment.

But I don't want to talk about dads.

Today, Stone is barbequing like he's done for almost two decades. He wasn't much of a cook when we were kids, but he could grill. Vale quickly learned some skills and I used my baking tricks, restored after Dad was gone. Although most of the time, baking was an excuse to feed my munchies since I was high most of my teenage years.

"Gonna stick around for the game?" Stone asks.

My brother Ford is a centerfielder for the Chicago Anchors. Despite being in his late thirties, he's still a starter with a good arm and a great swing.

"Yeah, I wouldn't miss it." While Ford is just above me in birth order, we didn't always get along the best. Out of self-preservation, we stuck together when we were younger, looking out for Vale, but Ford always had one foot out the door, ready for something bigger and better. And he had the damn athletic ability to get himself somewhere.

I hated living in his shadow. However, as I've aged, I appreciate the work Ford had to put in to be the athlete he is and have the lifestyle he's earned. It still doesn't stop me from being envious, but I also know if I had that kind of fame and fortune, I'd only have been in bigger trouble and probably dead. Because with money comes means, and that can lead to almost too much access to costly things like drugs.

In answer to Stone's question, I hadn't planned on sticking around for the game, hoping that once I put in a presence and grabbed a quick burger, I could skip out on family time and maybe meet up with Enya at the hospital. I needed an Adara fix. Almost more importantly, I needed to see Enya. Since our near-kiss at midnight, we've slipped by one another without crossing paths despite the close proximity of my apartment and the bakery. We need to talk and I can't believe I'm thinking such a thing.

Now, I was roped into an entire afternoon with my family, taking their razzing about a woman living in my apartment and my fake-daddy status.

"So," Knox nudges me while we stand near the grill watching Stone flip burgers. "Bag the babe yet?"

"Dude," Clay groans.

"There are so many things wrong with that question. First, the nineties called and want their language back." I wrinkle my nose. "Next, I'm not bagging anyone." And last, how does he know Enya is a babe?

Knox shrugs. "Saw her at the Seed and Soil a few times. She's hot."

"Oh yeah, speaking of S and S." I turn on Clay. "Why didn't you ever mention you were being audited?" And had a hot as fuck accountant working for you.

Clay chuckles. "That was months ago, and I sent you the quarterly reports."

Which I typically don't read. I don't care how the Seed and Soil is doing. I accept my dividends but don't pay them much attention as they drop directly into my account.

"That report might have forgotten a detail or two." I tip up my non-alcoholic beer eyeing my brother over the lip of the bottle.

Clay laughs again, flashing his dimples. "Didn't know I was supposed to state a smokeshow was working for us."

Enya is hot, but I'm kind of irritated that Clay noticed. "Did you hit on her?"

Knox chokes on his beer. Clay smacks our brother's back while answering me. "No, we had a professional relationship. She worked more closely with Judd."

"Speaking of Judd, where is he today?" Vale asks, coming up to Stone with a plate of hot dogs.

Stone shakes his head while Knox groans. "He's with Heather."

Heather Remington is a real socialite, as far as small towns have them. Her daddy owns a set of car dealerships throughout Milton County and somehow Judd has gotten tangled up with Remington Automotive's princess. Little did her daddy know that what sold him cars might not be what's beneath the hood but his daughter laying herself out on top of them.

My family is not a fan and surprised that Old Man Remington allows his daughter near a Sylver. We are definitely not royalty around here. Of the bunch, Judd might be considered the smartest, though.

"God, I hope he doesn't ask her to marry him," Knox mutters.

"That's not nice," Vale scolds.

"*She* isn't exactly nice," Clay grumbles.

"Still, if Judd likes her, we need to accept her." Vale's fierce statement has me wondering if my family would like Enya. I nearly laugh at the thought. They'd eat her and Adara up.

"Speaking of acceptance, I'm real disappointed that you didn't bring Enya with you today," Vale turns on me. "Heard you two are becoming quite the friends."

Not only did Vale bring Enya clothes, but she had visited the hospital again to drop off a baby gift. She couldn't see the baby, but she met Enya in the family waiting area where extended family can hang out and support moms and dads who visit their newborns.

Each time I pass through the room I'm reminded that Enya doesn't have anyone. Her parents haven't come to the hospital. I don't even know if they talk. I kind of can't wait for Enya's sister, Cadence, to arrive so Enya has someone in her corner.

Well, someone besides me, but I'd happily fill all her corners if she needed me.

"Heard you were spreading gossip about us," I quip, reminded that Knox called Enya my baby mama and he'd *heard* things from our sister.

"Not gossip." Vale shrugs. "I like her. And I know how hard it is to be a single mom." My sister was married for a short time. Her husband wasn't great, and he relinquished all rights as a father when he moved away to work on an oil rig.

Stone's head pops up at Vale's words. "You aren't alone, though." Our eldest brother came through again, taking care of our sister when she was young, newly divorced, *and* a new mother.

Serving time when Hudson was born, I'd been MIA when she needed me.

"I know, which makes me feel even more compassion for Enya." Vale squints at me. "Her parents haven't even called to check on the baby."

Dammit. Why hasn't she told me? Seeing as Vale is buddy-buddy with my roommate, I ask, "Did she happen to mention the father?"

Clay's brows lift. Stone watches me.

"No. And even if she did, I wouldn't betray her trust unless she's already mentioned him to you." Vale eyes me, searching for an answer. The truth is, Enya is tightlipped about him, other than he hadn't been kind to her.

You're kind to both of us. And frankly, it's refreshing.

How could anyone not care about Enya? Then I consider her parents and whoever Adara's father is, and I don't want to think about any of them.

Enya has me. And Vale, apparently.

"Thanks for looking out for her." The gratitude I just gave could come from anyone, but my family is reading me. I'm thankful Vale has extended herself to Enya and my appreciation suggests I care about Enya.

"When you goin' to make an honest woman out of her?" Clay questions, lifting his beer and pointing at me.

"Enya already is an honest woman and I'm not the father. I'm just her roommate. For now."

"Why?" Vale stares at me, eyes widening. "What do you mean *for now*?"

"Didn't Enya tell you? She owns the old Wallace farmhouse." Stone continues studying me.

"Fuck," Clay mutters blunt and low. His eyes shift toward Hudson making sure he's out of hearing range. Our nephew has been busy digging in the dirt along the side of the yard.

"I heard that," he calls out without even lifting his head or looking in our direction. "That's one dollar, Uncle Clay."

"A dollar?" Clay huffs. "What happened to a quarter?"

"Inflation." Hudson still doesn't glance upward.

Vale smiles at her son before looking back at us. "Trudy Wallace mentioned the place had sold and the owner was doing extensive renovations to the house. I hadn't realized it was Enya, though," Vale explains. Concern fills her face. "When does she move in?"

"A few days." And I'm not counting down like I can't wait. Her move will be bittersweet. Plus, I don't like to think of Enya living in that house. Alone. And with a baby.

"Are you helping her move again?" Vale watches me, searching for something.

I shake my head. "She says she has movers lined up."

"I'm not convinced her contractor is doing his best by her. He wasn't local and I've seen some of his work." Knox's statement reminds me he's been out to the place, doing some brickwork there.

"Like what?" I'm instantly on alert that Enya's contractor took advantage of her.

"Just little things. Like the tile job in her bathroom is shit. The sink in the powder room is off-center. Thankfully, her kitchen cabinets were an independent crew and they installed them for her."

"I don't like how any of that sounds," I admit. Enya hadn't told me about any issues with her new home, only that the contractor pushed for another week. However, Enya held firm on her move in date. Two weeks with me was her limit.

Knox slaps his hand on my shoulder. "When she moves into her new place, not going to be your problem, though, is it?"

"Maybe another man will move in," Clay adds.

"What the fuck? What other man?" I snap.

"Whoever the baby-daddy is," Knox continues.

"Or a new guy who wants to be the baby's daddy," Clay arches a brow at me.

Fuck that. And fuck them.

"I doubt there is any rush to find a man," Vale states, watching me. "Enya isn't in an emotional place for another addition to her life. Adara is going to take all her time and energy."

That's right. Enya is only focused on her baby. She isn't looking for a man in her life. She doesn't need one. She has me.

For now.

Chapter 14

[Enya]

While Sebastian was at his family dinner, I took time before heading to the hospital to do some laundry and restock his refrigerator. He hadn't accepted any money for the previous groceries he'd bought and after two weeks of staying with him, items had dwindled enough that his fridge resembled my former one. I wasn't much of a cook and being out on the road for work, I'd often skip a meal or order something quick from any place local. Having homecooked meals has been a treat.

Sebastian truly spoils me. He's unintentionally burrowing into my heart with all he's done for me. But a woman can only handle so much rejection before she takes the hint. After blatantly asking him to kiss me the other night, and his refusal, it couldn't be more obvious how Sebastian feels about me. I need to leave sooner rather than later for self-preservation.

I know me. I'll grow attached and complacent, and I don't want either to happen. Actually, I appreciate that he didn't kiss me, admitting he couldn't handle it, if it didn't lead to more. That makes him honest that he's only interested in sex. He's a virile man, and my body wasn't ready yet. My heart isn't either. He'd spared us both.

The curtain to Adara's pod whips open and Sebastian freezes, eyes lowered to my chest where I'm nursing her. "Sorry, I—" His voice cracks.

I've been alternating between nursing and bottle feeding, although the nurses told me not to be discouraged if Adara rejects nursing completely. My little wonder is already in a confused state, having left my body early. My only concern is she get the nutrients she needs to help her grow. Thankfully, we're balancing between both methods, at least for a little while.

Breast feeding is one of nature's greatest gifts and a miracle of the female body. We can feed our young. I'm not ashamed.

Still, Sebastian's cheeks are bright red when he turns his face to the side. His Adam's apple bobs along his throat. He has a sexy throat which is a weird thought, but one I can't neglect.

"Just let me . . ." I struggle to reach a blanket draped over the side of Adara's bassinet. With the movement, she pops off me and Sebastian has a clear view of my swollen breast and wet nipple, if he was looking. Which he isn't. Instead, he's still as a rock, clutching the edge of the curtain like he's ready to tear it down, or the flimsy material is holding him upright.

I fix my bra and adjust my shirt, then lift Adara for snuggle time. She needs to be vertical for fifteen minutes to help with her digestion.

"We're covered now."

Sebastian slowly turns his head. His fingers cautiously release the curtain as if he's afraid to let it go. His warm eyes soften when he gazes down at Adara on my chest.

"How was your family day?"

His head snaps upward, eyes meeting mine before he swipes a hand down his face. "Long." He quickly finds a chair to pull up near me. His gaze drops to Adara again. "My brother plays baseball for the Chicago Anchors, and they had a game today. I was talked into staying to watch."

He has a brother who is the sheriff. One who owns Sylver Seed and Soil. Another who is an accountant. Vale is his sister.

"How did I not know this and who am I missing?"

Sebastian looks at me, pulling his gaze from Adara. "What do you mean, who are you missing?"

"You told me there are seven of you and I'm missing someone."

"Stone, Clay, Judd, Knox, Ford, me, and Vale."

"Knox. I haven't heard of him. Is he the baseball player?"

"He's a bricklayer. He was in the military for a bit and now he's a local fireman. He said he laid the patio at your new place."

"Ah."

I can't say I know everyone who worked on my home. I'd given the contractor full liberty, which I've come to regret. A recent inspection told me the shower basin won't drain properly because of the faulty tile work and the sink in the powder room is off-center. The contractor tried to convince me it was an optical illusion. I wasn't convinced and found a new tile installer for assistance.

Mentioning my place gives me the opening I need. "Speaking of my house, it's ready for me to move in." Not completely true, but close enough. All the mechanicals function, but I'm still waiting on my office window, closet organizers, and some trim work. Once I move in, I'm hopeful my daily presence will speed up the final touches. The project has taken long enough. Checks have been written. I'll manage the remaining to-do list on my own.

"Really?"

"I'm moving in on Tuesday." That's in two days and my heart flutters. *I'm moving into my new home.* I'm leaving Sebastian's. Emotions conflict inside me.

Sebastian lowers his gaze, staring at my hand on Adara's little back. "You don't need to rush."

"But I've stayed long enough."

His gaze lifts again, ready to argue with me, but I cut him off. "I accepted an offer on my condo, and it's time to settle into my new home." As I'd been at his place for two weeks, the realtor had free rein to show my place as often as she wished. Minus baby things taking up a corner of the living room, the place had a better selling vantage and sold easier.

Sebastian nods once and reaches out for Adara's back, brushing his fingers against mine as he strokes over her little bottom.

"The movers will make a secondary stop at your place for all my stuff."

He glances up at me. "You don't need to do that. I can take your things to the house." Only he swallows hard as if it pains him to make such a suggestion.

He's already done enough, and I can't ask for more. "It's covered."

I want to sound confident, but my voice cracks at the finality. I'm leaving the comfort of Sebastian's apartment for my new house. I should be a little more elated by the prospect. I am excited, but I'm also strangely anxious. It's been a long time since I've lived in a house, with a yard, slightly remote from others. In apartment dwelling, I can hear my neighbors through the walls. With my new house, I can hardly see my neighbors.

Then again, this is what I wanted. I wanted wide open spaces and fresh air for my little girl. A new beginning outside of city living. With her birth came a new leaf and with summer almost here, I was ready to enjoy a change in season.

A change in my life.

Glancing down at Adara, I have so much to be grateful for. My baby. A home. I look up at Sebastian still focused on Adara. His hand pauses at the base of her back as if he can't remove it from her. As if he doesn't want to stop touching her.

I'm eternally thankful for him, too. A new friend. The thought is bittersweet when it shouldn't be. Who couldn't use more friends? I ignore where I've leaned into wanting more with him. Where I was hopeful of kissing on his couch and being taken on his bakery counter. I'm not in a position to be desirable.

Plus, I'll never be of interest to a man like Sebastian. A good man with a haunted past and no desire for a family.

With a soft sigh, I weakly smile, fight back tears, and glance down at Adara.

She's my reason for everything, as she should be.

Chapter 15

[Sebastian]

Enya moved out and I fucking hated the silence she left behind.

My apartment had always been a sacred refuge, but in the short time Enya had been here, she'd transformed the space into something more. Something more *homey* feeling. Now, it was eerily quiet and almost uncomfortable without her presence.

A week has passed with daily text updates on Adara from Enya. My nightly visits to the hospital continue which I purposely plan later than normal. The decision is for my own sanity because if I saw Enya, I might beg her to move back in with me. Or worse, ask her to let me live with her. And I could never live in the Wallace farmhouse. The thought of that place makes my skin crawl.

I also didn't like thinking about Enya there alone. Just outside of town, off Route 10, the place is within distant eyesight of a neighbor but not close enough to hear or witness issues. It had been the perfect place to hide in, hang out in, and cause trouble in, and ten years ago, trouble happened often there.

I was confident the house was different now. Knox hinted it was a real beauty. Picture perfect, he said. Like straight off a home-improvement show. But I couldn't unsee in my head what the place had once been. What it represented. Dank rooms. Dark nights. Drugs and death.

Located west of town, I almost always went east, and if I needed to head left, I'd take a wide berth to avoid that old country route. However, my thoughts drifted there often over the past seven days.

Removing a hot tray of brownies from the oven, I almost collide with Rena who feels like a shadow lately.

"Rena, watch the fuck out." She's used to my rough voice, so I don't think anything of snapping at her. What I do notice is her hand sweeping over my belly and around my side as she ducks to avoid being hit with the tray. The touch skims around to my spine as she sneaks past me, making me hypersensitive to my employee intimately touching me again. We work in tight proximity. I like to think we have a rhythm, but some days we are just out of sync. Like today. And the last seven.

Rena's attention feels different once again.

"Sorry, boss." Her smile is too bright. She's a pretty woman although a little rough around the edges with tattoos down her arms and vibrant red curls. A real badass baker like me. We've been open with each other about our pasts, sharing our recovery experience, but we aren't what I'd consider close. I've given her a second chance as my family has given me, because people deserve them.

Still, have I been dense like Stone said? Have I not *seen* Rena? She works hard. Stays late. Comes in early, if I need her. But is there more to her that I've been missing? And why are my eyes open now?

My fucking brothers.

I wish I'd been able to rely on Barnett more, but he was still in high school. His availability only covered a few hours late afternoons and some weekends. With the time I'd been taking lately for myself, to see Adara, I could really use another part-time employee. Thank goodness it was almost summer, and Barnett has more time to give me with the break from school.

Because when Enya stayed with me, I needed—*no, wanted*—to skate out early to get to the hospital. Moms and dads had twenty-four-hour access, so there wasn't ever a rush to visit, but by mid-afternoon an itch would creep in. A desire for a fix. An Adara snuggle.

I'd never admit that to anyone.

But Adara's soft skin and baby scent just did something to me. I needed the hit to get me through nights with Enya wandering my apartment and then nights without Enya in my place. I missed the fragrance of her perfume lingering in my bathroom and her extra bottles of shampoo in my shower. I missed knowing she was in her bedroom and even the throbbing hum of her breast pump. I missed her constant appreciation and warm smile when I cooked for her. And the way she tucked into the corner of my couch, sighing to herself as she read.

Dreams danced in her eyes, and I wanted to know every desire and thought when I had no right. She wasn't my wife. She wasn't even my woman, and she wasn't the mother of *my* child. Adara belonged to Enya and Enya belonged to herself.

My brothers' ribbing haunted me. Someday, some other man will move into Enya's place and take over the real role of being Adara's dad. He'll sleep beside Enya and steal all the Adara snuggles. And—

"Fuck," I growl as Rena swipes by me again. *Did her hand just brush my ass?*

"Your phone is buzzing."

"What?" My watch and my phone are linked, and I glance down at the face, where a notification momentarily pops up and then disappears. Some days, I tune out the constant dribble of conversation in the family chat. I don't need to know Clay saw a pretty girl or Vale saw some old friend. Or Ford checks in, demanding reassurance we watched his game or saw his catch, like he's a little boy on a T-ball team instead of a major league baseball player.

Did you see me? Did you see me? Yeah, yeah. We saw him. Envy had no place in me. Ford worked hard but he also had it all and he made it seem so easy. Beautiful wife. Three adorable little girls. A big house. Fancy car. The picture-perfect life.

Something I'll never have, as my past made the frame around images of me hang a little crooked no matter how many times I've tried to straighten it.

"Boss?" Rena quips.

My phone is buzzing in my back pocket and on my wrist again. "Right," I bark, reaching into my jeans for the device.

A notification appears from Enya. **Adara gets to go home.**

My lips curl.

"Is that . . ." Rena makes a disgruntled face as I glance up at her. "Are you . . . smiling?"

"Fuck no." But I can't help the curve of my mouth and the flutter in my chest.

Adara gets to go home. She can leave the hospital and Enya can love on her twenty-four seven.

I'm so happy for you, I instantly text, overwhelmed with relief while strangely saddened that I won't be skipping out early to see the baby at the hospital. She'll be home now. No reason to keep pretending I'm her dad.

My gaze falls to the worn hospital band on my wrist. Adara Violet Calloway is listed right above my name. For half a second the Calloway name fades away and Sylver replaces it.

Quickly, I dismiss the thought. My phone lights up again with an instant response. **You're the first person I thought to tell.**

Shit. My heart is hammering so fast I press my palm to my chest. *She thought of me first?* She means I'm the first person to know this news. Next, she'll text her sister. Maybe her parents. Maybe even Vale. Soon enough my family will know Adara is home. They've already given me shit for Enya living with me. Then moving out. All their jokes and jests can stop now.

Adara and Enya are exiting my life.

This is awesome news. But a sour taste fills my throat.

A reply pops up. **I have a few things to do while she passes a car seat test. Then we can leave the hospital together.**

I continue to smile, preparing to send one last message. Maybe a thumbs up? A smiley face? Fuck, what am I thinking? I don't do emojis.

Three little dots appear, and I hold my breath as they flicker and disappear. Pop up again, and then blink away. They light up one more time before words fill a text bubble.

Would you like to be our welcome home committee? You could meet me at the hospital or be the first to see her at the house.

My breath hitches. I can't do that. I can't go out to the Wallace farmhouse. But Enya thought of me first. She messaged me moments after receiving this good news.

"Rena," I bark, not glancing up at my employee. "I'm going out for a bit."

+ + +

I make a quick stop before heading to the hospital. My palms sweat at the thought of going to the old Wallace place. But that sweaty feeling might be a mixture of elation that Adara gets to go home and fear for the next steps. Despite her premature status, she's perfectly healthy, and she's doing great. Gaining weight every day. Making faces. Opening her eyes. Giving me a smile, even if it's a false pretense. She just has gas.

However, I'm genuinely scared in a way I've never been afraid before. Not that Enya won't be a great mother, but that she'll be alone in that farmhouse with no one looking out for her and the baby.

As I approach the NICU pod, Enya races up to me and wraps her arms around my neck as if she hugs me every day and I shouldn't be surprised by this action, which I am. Slowly, I circle my arms around her and tug her tight to me. Excitement vibrates off her body.

"This is it," she whispers near my ear. "It's really happening." Anticipation exudes in her strained voice. *Is she scared, too?*

Vale told me becoming a mother was the most thrilling and frightening thing she'd ever done. She didn't regret Hudson for a second but there were secondary fears. She hadn't had a mother. Our father had been shit. Vale didn't trust herself. But some maternal instinct to nurture kicked in, and she's been the best mom.

Enya is going to be the same way.

"It's really happening," I whisper back to her, dipping my nose to her neck to selfishly inhale her fresh rain scent. Slowly, she slips from my arms, and I fight the urge to hold on a little longer. Instead, I let her glide away.

"How did this happen so soon?" The doctors wanted to keep Adara until she reached her original due date.

"She just hooked her little fingers around the tube and tugged. It slid out." Enya's tone is full of awe and pride as she imitates what must have happened. Her daughter is a fighter. A survivor, like me.

"You ready?" I ask.

"A photographer is present, and they want to take going-home pictures. It will only be a few minutes while the discharge papers are still being worked up." Her voice rises with each item.

With my hands on her shoulders, I slip them down to her wrists, feeling the stress rippling through her. "Hey. You got this."

"I know." She blows out a breath, and chews at her lower lip. "I'm just a ball of emotion. Excited. Nervous. Relieved. Sad." Her eyes snap up to meet mine.

"Sad?" My brows pinch.

She timidly smiles and waves a hand between us. "It doesn't matter."

But it does. I want to know why she's sad.

"Ms. Calloway?" A woman approaches with a camera around her neck. Enya twists but I don't release her wrists.

"Hi," she greets the photographer.

"If you're ready, I'd like to take a couple pictures by the window. The natural light is perfect. We'll do a few of baby. Baby and Mom. Baby and Dad. And then all three of you."

"Oh, I'm not—"

"That sounds lovely." Enya speaks over me and flips her wrist in a way she's suddenly holding my hands, squeezing my fingers.

Within minutes, I'm watching a woman snap photograph after photograph of Adara. Then Adara and Enya in the sweetest pose as they gaze at each other. Before I know it, a picture is taken of me staring down at Adara. I rapidly blink as she looks up at me, giving me another of those gas-induced smiles that tricks me into thinking she's sharing a special grin. One only meant for me. Like we have a secret.

"Looks just like you, Dad." The photographer has no idea what she's saying. Correcting her is on the tip of my tongue, but I can't seem to form a response.

"Okay. Family ones."

My head snaps up at the instruction, and I'm ready to pass Adara to Enya when the photographer tells Enya to stand at my side and slip her arm around my back. She wraps one arm behind me but the other glides across my waist, and she tucks into my side.

We gaze at each other. We look down at Adara. The camera clicks and clicks.

"You're a beautiful couple," the photographer murmurs. "One more direction. Keep holding her Dad, but turn to face Mom."

I glance up at Enya who offers me a sheepish smile. Something she sees on my face prompts her expression to falter. "I should have asked your permission about all this. I'm a little wrapped up in the moment and I forgot . . ."

Forgot we weren't a family.

"No. It's fine," I lie. Or maybe the lie is I'm a little more okay with this situation than I should be.

Facing each other, with Adara cradled between us, we both gaze down at her. Awe fills me one more time like the day she was born. She's so tiny and sweet and adorable.

Her small fist is wrapped around my heart.

Glancing up one more time at Adara's mom, I realize Enya holds the same position.

My heart is in her hands, and I don't know how to feel about this.

Finally, the photographs are finished. "I'll text proofs to you in about fifteen minutes. They'll be watermarked but you can share the link with anyone you wish. Buy as many or as few as you want. No obligation." She's professional, and without a pushy sales job, because she knows whatever images she sends to new parents, they'll purchase all of them.

My credit card is already buzzing in my wallet. Even sight unseen, I'll be buying every one of them.

Unfortunately, another half-hour passes before Adara is placed in her car seat and allowed to go home.

Enya's home.

I trail behind Enya's Honda Passport in my truck where my palms sweat on the steering wheel. As we get closer to Route 10 and the farmhouse, nausea hits. I can't believe I'm headed in this direction, returning to this keeper of bad memories.

Only, when Enya turns onto the gravel drive, and I follow her, the house before me is one I hardly recognize. The roof is black tin. The exterior is bright white with wide vertical siding. The windows are replaced, and wider than I remember, with black trim around the glass. The once broken-down porch is completely rebuilt and widened as well, like a welcoming smile. Nothing is the same on the outside but the general outline hints at the original place.

The harder part will be entering the house, but first I help Enya with Adara in the infant car seat. Following Enya, my breathing shallows. A bead of sweat forms along my temple. Enya unlocks her home by a keypad and struggles a bit with the sticky latch that eventually gives, and she pops open the front door. Once inside, a freshly painted, hardwood staircase is before us. With a quick glance right to left, I take in the living room and dining room on either side of the staircase. The open concept is so different from the original layout that included small, divided rooms.

Enya keeps walking and I blindly follow, blinking at the bright white interior and the overstuffed furniture.

"Is that new?" I nod at a couch that I don't recall seeing in her apartment.

"My condo was kind of cold and a remnant of a past life." She shivers. "This is a home. I wanted softer colors and comfy furniture you can sink into. Live in."

The light gray sectional is certainly inviting. As we round through the living room, I stop short at the sight of her kitchen which runs the entire length of the back of the house. I love my apartment kitchen. I put in high end appliances for small spaces and it's perfect for me. But Enya's place is professional grade with a six-burner range, a double oven, and an extra-large refrigerator.

The space is a foodie wet-dream, and she doesn't even like to cook.

"I don't plan on leaving here anytime soon, but for resale value, I might have splurged on the kitchen." Sheepishly, she looks at me.

"It's fucking gorgeous." My throat is thick with awe, and I'm not certain if I'm talking about the damn kitchen or the woman looking at me with coffee-colored eyes, that draw me in like the bean-loving addict I am.

"Where do you want me to put her?" I nod toward Adara's car seat in my hand and Enya chuckles.

"Just set her down anywhere."

Gently, I place the seat on the floor beside the couch. "I have a few things for you. I'll be right back." I duck out to my truck and quickly return with my gifts.

"For me?" Enya blushes at the large bouquet of flowers, similar to what I brought her when she had Adara.

"Welcome home." The words are bittersweet. I'm happy for her. She's practically glowing in this space. Her home. Her new life. But I'm not going to remain, and I already feel myself retreating. If I don't step away soon, I'm going to want something I can't have. I'm going to ask for something I can't do, like stay.

After setting a paper shopping bag on the large island countertop, I pull out the items, naming them each. "Bread, wine, and salt."

Enya tilts her head, giving me a puzzled smile.

"Oh, come on. You had to have seen *It's A Wonderful Life*?"

She stares at me, still questioning the reference to a holiday classic.

"Bread." I lift the loaf I made this morning. "So this house will never know hunger."

Next, I reach for the saltshaker. "Salt. So this house will always have flavor."

Lastly, I hold up a bottle of wine. "And wine. For joy and prosperity. Or something like that." I might not have gotten the quote one hundred percent correct but the point is, I want Enya to be happy and healthy here.

"And for your sweet tooth." I reach inside the bag and pull out a small bakery container.

"If that's a lemon cake, I love you, Sebastian Sylver." The words rush out like the icing drizzled over the top of this miniature Bundt. Thick and gooey, and full of meaning I shouldn't misinterpret. She doesn't actually love me. She loves my cake. She's appreciative, like she is of everything I do for her.

I could quip back: *Guess you love me then*. But I hold my tongue.

Enya doesn't even acknowledge what she's said. How it sounded or the fact she didn't mean it. "And what does lemon cake represent?"

That I could fall in love with you, too.

I shrug. "This one is a new tradition, I guess. Sugar, for the sweet things in life. Tangy citrus, to keep life interesting."

She smiles as if she approves of my off-the-cuff explanation. "You're too good to me."

"I'll never be good enough, sugar," I say before I can stop myself. I want to bite off my tongue for admitting so much.

Enya stills. Her gaze falls to my face, brows pinching, questioning. She looks at me long and hard, until I'm nearly crawling out of my skin from the intensity. Then her warm eyes soften to liquid chocolate. "I disagree."

Her argument is like a gentle caress as if she's cupped my cheek and held my chin, forcing me to face her, accept her simple, cryptic reasoning.

My skin heats. Heart hammering.

Before things get too awkward, she turns toward an upper cabinet. "Share the cake with me."

"I shouldn't. This is your first day for you and Adara in your new home."

Enya glances at me over her shoulder. "There isn't anyone else I'd want to share this day with. We need to celebrate."

"I only brought one cake." The single dessert is just for her. A private celebration. Like when she found out she was pregnant. She bought the mini cake then to celebrate.

"Then we'll share." She doesn't even hesitate, turning with one plate in hand. She opens a drawer in her kitchen island and she pulls out two forks.

"What about Adara?"

"Maybe you could take her out of the car seat," Enya suggests as she pops the lid on the bakery box and sets the baby-Bundt on the plate.

I squat and remove a blanket covering Adara's legs, then unbuckle the restraints. Adara does a cat-like stretch, arching her back and tipping back her head but her eyes remain closed. Lifting her, her position remains tight and tucked until I rest her in the crease of my elbow. She settles in, completely undisturbed.

"God, I wish I could sleep so heavily."

Enya watches me as I stand on the opposite side of the island. "You aren't sleeping? I'd thought with me gone and no more middle of the night alarms ringing, you'd be sleeping as deep as her." She nods at Adara.

"Your alarms never bothered me." I glance at Enya across the counter. She looks small in this open space, almost dwarfed by the magnitude of this island. For a fleeting moment, I imagine spreading her out on it. Her entire body would be my buffet and I'd join her on top of this masterpiece to please her.

Quickly, I shake the image.

"Still, I thought you'd be relieved," Enya adds.

With Adara in my arms, I round the island desiring to be closer to Enya. Needing her to look me in the eye as I plead with her. "Please stop acting like you're an inconvenience in my life. I asked you to move in with me. I wanted you there." I breathe out. "And I'm . . . out of sorts . . . with you gone."

Her head tilts. She gives a quick glance at Adara before looking up at me again. "What do you mean out of sorts?"

Lonely. Empty. Not as comfortable in my own skin without you near me.

"It's just an adjustment. You've grown on me." I wink.

"You've grown on me, too." She slowly smiles. "Which is why I want us to still be friends. Please. Come see Adara whenever you want." Enya glances down at the baby and swipes a hand over her tiny head. "She loves you."

"Sugar," I whisper as my breath catches. There's no doubt Adara and I share a bond. I brought her into this world, quite literally. She's nestled into my arms, like she belongs there. Like she wants a piece of my heart, and she has it. She's everything to me, but one day she's going to be everything to some other man.

I don't like the thought, but I have to accept it. Enya and Adara deserve better than me.

"Cake," she whispers as softly as I called her sugar. For a second, I think she's calling me cake and then I chuckle when I realize she means the lemon Bundt, sitting on a plate, waiting to be eaten in celebration.

Adara is home.

Enya lives in her new house.

There is much to be commemorated.

I only wish I could explain why I don't feel very festive on either count.

Chapter 16

[Enya]

Sebastian appeared almost skittish when he entered my home. Like he was impressed but he also couldn't wait to leave. I didn't know how to read him. I'd taken a big gamble asking him if he'd like to be present when I brought Adara home with me. After all he'd done for me, my heart told me his presence was important. Like he should be here with me, with us.

However, for a week, I'd been sending text updates about Adara, and it felt like he was avoiding me. His responses were minimal. Maybe he didn't want progress reports on Adara, but if that were true then I didn't know why he still showed up to see her at the hospital. The nurses kept me informed that Adara's *dad* visited in the evenings, after I'd left. If any of them thought it strange that we no longer visited at the same time, no one mentioned it.

When Adara yanked the feeding tube from herself, signaling she was ready to feed on her own, I got the good news that she could come home. The sudden adrenaline coursing through my body was a mix of conflicting emotions. Elation. Anxiety. But ready.

I'd called Sebastian on a whim. Along with hormone mayhem from the early delivery, issues with nursing, and a lack of sleep, I was all twisted up about him. If he rejected the invitation to bring Adara home with me, I told myself I wouldn't hold it against him. He had things to do. A bakery to run. A life to live outside of me and my baby. But I was also hopeful he might want to share in this moment.

My baby was finally home.

Once again, I was grateful for Sebastian. His quiet patience. His wish to celebrate. We shared the miniature cake like we did the day I told him I was pregnant—one bite at a time. I watched his mouth suck at the fork, smearing icing along the tines, and then taking another turn at the utensil to swipe it clean. Observing him eat shouldn't be a turn-on, but it was a hint that my libido wasn't completely non-existent. I still had weeks before I could consider doing anything sexual, but it didn't mean the fantasies of him kissing or holding me had lessened. There was relief in knowing I *could* be attracted to a man.

However, I was solidly in the friend-zone with Sebastian. He was a good friend, too, although he didn't stick around long after we finished his dreamy lemon cake.

Why would he? He had a life. Not that I didn't think I had a life as well. Mine was only vastly different than his. I was a single mother with a newborn baby as my sole priority. He was a single man who could do as he pleased. I hated the thought, and not because he had freedoms I didn't.

Because I didn't want him to be with another woman.

Selfishly, I wanted him all to myself. For Adara and me.

"Congratulations on bringing Adara home," Sebastian had finally said to me, leaning in to innocently kiss my cheek before pressing a kiss to Adara's head. Then, he couldn't seem to run fast enough down my porch steps and across the drive to his truck.

Watching him leave, I took a deep breath. He didn't sign up for this parenting gig. I did. I wanted this little bundle in my arms.

"Just you and me, Cookie," I murmured to her sweet head.

That's my reality.

+ + +

Within days of Adara's homecoming, my younger sister arrives, and I'm so grateful for another adult presence. Cadence is three years younger than me, with dyed-blonde waves and blue eyes. We hardly look like siblings. Where I'm all business casual, she's artistic chic. I followed the plan my parents wanted for me. Cadence lives my dream. However, my path was also a conscious choice on my part. I wasn't ever a risk taker. Not until now. Not until Adara.

After hours of pacing and trying to interpret what a crying baby needs, Adara finally sleeps, and Cadence and I collapse on my couch.

"Here." She hands me her glass of wine.

"Maybe one sip," I whimper, exhaustion heavy in my limbs while I'm too keyed up to sleep. I take the glass from her and sip the sweet rosé. God, I've missed wine, but for Adara's sake I'll continue to abstain for a while. Adara and I have compromised on this complicated feeding routine, where half the time she nurses and the other half she takes a bottle of expressed breast milk, causing me double duty. The NICU nurses told me this is normal for preemie babies.

My sister and I broke into the wine Sebastian gave me. Selfishly, I wanted to keep it sealed a little longer, hoping one day I'd drink it with him. We'd celebrate something else momentous for Adara. However, that was a fantasy, and Cadence convinced me to open the bottle now.

I hand the glass back to her and we quietly sit in silence, marveling at the pureness of no sound. Sinking deeper into the couch, I close my eyes but know that sleep will elude me for a while longer.

"Do you think I made a mistake?" I whisper.

"Little late to ask that question. It's not like you can return her," Cadence jokes. Her voice is as lyrical as her name.

"I don't want to return her." Exasperation fills my lowered voice. "But Mom and Dad still think I made a mistake."

"I thought you stopped listening to them." Cadence scoffs, rolling her head on the cushions and pinning me with a glare.

"I have." I sigh. "Dad called when I first moved here. Mom is still refusing to acknowledge she's a grandmother."

Cadence makes an eek-face. "They suck."

They didn't always suck, though, and that's what hurts the most. In so many ways, I need my mother. I need to learn how to *be* a mother from her, but I don't want to be a mother *like* her. One that pushes her child in a direction she doesn't really want to go. One who convinces her child it's better to stay unhappy than to leave an unhealthy relationship. One who judges her child's decision-making, calling it a mistake . . . when it was not.

For my mental well-being, I had to block out the negativity of my parents and do one thing I wanted without their approval. As I neared forty, I had to stand up to them and make a decision. I didn't need their toxicity in my life.

"But I'm still asking. Am I in over my head?" When I made the decision to have Adara, I was thinking with sound body and mind. And heart. I wanted a baby. I wanted *this* baby. Her. But there had been moments in the past month when I'd questioned myself. Will I be enough? Will I even be a good mom? Will she love me like I love her?

"Do you feel like you're in over your head?" Cadence shifts so she faces me better.

"A little bit."

She lifts the wineglass, snorting into it before muttering, "That's shocking."

"Why?" I stare at my sister, who is easygoing and laidback. Not that her life as a country singer has been easy but her carefree attitude allows her to skate through life.

"Because you're the most put together person I know. You're an accountant for heaven's sake. You thrive on order." She moves her hands, improvising boxes in the air, like a flow chart in the making. The wine dangerously jostles in her glass.

"You know I didn't want to be an accountant."

"I know," she whispers.

I don't fault Cadence. I'm so stinking proud of her for following her dream. For standing up to our parents and telling them where they could stick their ideals. But I also saw my parents' perspective. They were frightened of the future. They wanted Cadence and I to take every opportunity that Seamus didn't. They wanted us safe, secure, and employed as a means to stay out of trouble. Cadence is employed, even if they don't believe singing on a stage is a worthy job. She makes more money than they've ever seen, but they still don't understand her. It wasn't the money Cadence chased. It was the freedom to be her own person.

While I had the same desire, it took me a lot longer to do my own thing.

I really do like accounting. I just had other aspirations when I was younger. And now I have Adara, a dream I didn't think I wanted until time felt like it was running away.

"Have you heard from Lance?" Cadence's question surprises me.

I scoff. "No." Watching her, I narrow my eyes. "Why would we speak?" My ex and I have nothing to say to one another. When he broke us off, he easily walked away. Me, not so much. I'd given eleven years to the man who promised forever and dreams of a family. I'd been such a fool.

"Just thought he might have reached out."

"You know we aren't like that." Last summer, we had a drunk I-miss-you moment, and it was a disaster. After that slip in judgement, I severed ties with Lance for my own self-preservation.

"He knows about the baby." The questioning statement from Cadence holds the answer.

Lance knows. Adara isn't his concern. He thought I was crazy to have her, just like my parents.

"So, tell me more about the hottie playing daddy? When am I going to meet him?" Cadence wiggles her brows. She's seen the professional proofs from the hospital photographer of Sebastian holding Adara.

That's fake-daddy? Her mouth had dropped. *He can bake my cake.*

I'd laughed until I realized that she might not be joking. Cadence was vibrant, famous, and very single. While she didn't have staying power in a relationship, she did have knock-out looks and a killer body, and a penchant for one-night stands. In comparison, my body now includes swollen breasts and a pocket of skin bulging at my waistline. My belly looks like a Mack truck rolled over my flesh.

Being envious of Cadence feels pointless, but I'd be all kinds of jealous if Sebastian met her and fell for her. She'd use him up and spit him out, leaving crumbs in her wake.

Sometimes I worry Sebastian thinks I used him. As much as I've apologized, and thanked him, and offered money to supplement his groceries or his mortgage, he's never accepted anything in return for what he's done for me.

"I don't know that you'll get the chance." Sebastian has been absent the entire week my sister has been present. Other than a mysterious drop-off, which included a mixture of Bundt cakes and cookies, along with another bouquet of flowers, I haven't seen him.

When I messaged him that my sister was arriving, his immediate response was *have fun*, as if she is here for a vacation instead of baby support. When I thanked him for the bouquet and baked goods, he simply replied with a thumb's up emoji. I still send him updates on Adara and a picture or two a day, but I'm starting to think I'm bothering him more than sharing information.

I don't like the sensation of abandonment I feel from his absence. It isn't his responsibility to be here for me or Adara. He has free will to go about his business. Still, I miss him. And I hate that I might have brought this feeling on myself. I tried to please my parents and it was all for nothing as they stepped away from me when I made one of the most important decisions of my life. Then Lance rejected the idea of marriage and family after years of promising a future together. I fault myself for involving Sebastian in my current circumstances. I reeled him in, so it shouldn't hurt that he's pulled back.

"It was all pretend anyway," I whisper, reminding my sister and myself. Originally, she *ooh-ed* and *ahh-ed* about Sebastian's acting ability. A total stranger, suddenly starring in the role of my baby's father, so I could see Adara during those days I wasn't allowed to leave my hospital room.

Too bad there were so many moments when the acting looked realistic. When it appeared like he might actually love Adara.

When I told Sebastian Adara loved him, he looked like he might get sick.

When I joked that I loved him, he looked worse.

The idea of us loving Sebastian makes him ill. Which is too bad because he is my only friend around here and there is no faking my emotions.

I'm pretty certain I love Sebastian Sylver.

"There's a part two to my mistake question. Did I make a mistake moving to Sterling Falls? I have one friend and no acquaintances here. I hardly have neighbors." The decision to move hadn't been rash. I'd been wanting a house and a yard for a while, and I bought this farmhouse shortly after I found out I was pregnant.

"Brutal honesty?" Cadence pauses, watching me, and I nod. "You didn't have many friends left in Huntington because of Lance. Clients don't count as acquaintances. And you didn't know your neighbors there, either."

"I knew Mrs. Bertsch."

"The cat lady living next door to you?" Cadence wrinkles her nose. "She doesn't count."

"Why not? She was my neighbor."

"And a strange odor was coming from her place." Cadence lifts her arm high and exaggeratedly pinches her nose as if she smells something bad.

"I think she was smoking pot over there."

Cadence chuckles. "Well, then I wish I'd known her better."

We both laugh.

"My point is you were ready to leave Huntington. Anywhere you moved, you wouldn't have had what you had there, but that's what you wanted. A fresh start."

"But now I have Adara." And I'm alone out here. I wasn't frightened of my surroundings, but there was an adjustment to the space in a large house with open land. I'd been an apartment dweller most of my adult life. This was different and I accepted it for me, but had I done right for Adara?

"She's another layer of the freshness." Cadence shifts so her side presses into the back of the couch. Her head rests against the top of the cushion. "Where are all the questions coming from? It's not like you to doubt yourself."

I snort. "I doubted myself for eleven years." My entire relationship with Lance had been one questioning moment after another. Did he really love me? Why hadn't he asked me to marry him? When would we have children? Why wasn't I enough for him?

"And you stopped doubting yourself once you let Lance go," she reminds me. "You've made all the smart decisions for *you*."

She was right. I finally did what I wanted to do. I quit the firm and went independent. I left Lance in my rearview mirror. I bought a house. I had a baby.

"You're going to be a great mother," my sister whispers, heartfelt and reassuring.

My eyes well with tears and I blink through the haze of emotion and exhaustion. "You think so."

"I know so."

And on that note, Adara starts crying and I'm on call again.

Chapter 17

[Sebastian]

"What's with the sour puss, sour puss?" Knox teases me as we sit in Milton's Roadhouse.

"It's nothing," I lie.

"You seem grumpier than usual," Clay adds, lifting his beer and eyeing me as he drinks.

"More curmudgeon than your typical curmudgeon." Knox wiggles a brow.

"What? Are you a fucking poet tonight or something?"

"Not sure how that rhymes," Clay mutters, setting down his beer.

Knox squeezes my shoulder with his thick hand. "I have a way with words." He winks. For a man who acts like he's a ladies' man, he isn't. He's a flirt, but I can't remember the last time he got laid. Not that I need to know when my brothers do such a thing, but Knox hasn't had a consistent woman in his life for a long, long time.

For that fact, I can't remember the last time I got laid and maybe that's what I need to rid my head of one brunette, single mom living in a house that haunts me.

I'll give the place credit. It hardly looks the same, but ghosts lingered within the updates. I don't like Enya living so far outside of town and without neighbors who can keep watch over her home a little better. However, none of it should be my concern.

"Seriously, what's weighing heavy in that big head, little brother?" Clay's tone isn't patronizing. As second in command after Stone, he took up where Stone left off. As in, Clay played the role of older brother more than father-substitute like Stone did.

I shrug, lifting my non-alcoholic beer and taking a deep pull from the bottle.

"Trouble with the missus?" Knox arches a brow, but Clay watches me, apprehension in his expression.

"Enya moved out." They both know this. "My home is now blissfully quiet and free of disruption."

"Was she really a disruption?" Clay studies me.

"I'm back to doing what I want, when I want," I continue, avoiding a direct answer.

"Didn't know you'd ever stopped," Knox mumbles, tipping his head in greeting to someone across the bar.

"Knox," Clay hisses, low and disappointed.

If anyone should know about being a free-spirit, or at least strong-willed, it would be Knox. He left for the military, practically sprinting to get out of this town and leaving behind his high school sweetheart when we all thought they'd get married.

"Fuck off," I mumble to Knox.

"There he is." Knox perks up, smiling too wide, and egging me on. "Heard you were getting friendly with the nurses at the hospital. Ever play doctor with one of them? Show her your stethoscope?"

Knox is such a nosy fucker.

"No." I huff. After my run in with Sedona and Trinity Haven, I kept to myself. Plus, I was there for Adara, not picking up dates.

"Heard Halle Reynolds is back in town." Clay's teasing puts the attention back on Knox.

His head whips so fast, he could clear the table with the jet-stream left behind. "Halle?"

Speaking of that high school sweetheart.

"Although, I guess it's not Reynolds anymore." Clay tips up his beer again and drinks.

Did Knox just growl? My eyes widen as Knox's narrow at Clay. Clay only chuckles, knowing Halle is a sore spot for Knox. He doesn't like to talk about her. Then again, their puppy-love was almost twenty years ago. And for a nosy man, how did he not know this nugget of information?

"Look who's a bear now." I poke his arm. *Jab. Jab. Jab.* Like he does to me.

"Can never breach the Brick," Clay jokes of Knox's nickname. He's impenetrable, or so he thinks.

Knox swats at my hand and I chuckle deep at his failed attempt to swish me away. Clay gives me a smile and I feel myself relaxing for the first time in weeks.

"Rena's over there." Knox tips his head in the direction of my employee.

Already knowing where his comment is leading, I cut him off. "Rena does not have a crush on me."

I will not be telling my brothers about the flour incident, or the liberty Rena took to frost my body before I cut her off. Or how she inappropriately swiped at my ass. I really need to talk to her about boundaries.

"Really?" Knox's brows lift. He mimics chef's kiss with his fingers before stating, "You're a bagel, and she wants to *schmear* on you."

"*Ew*," Clay groans.

"Watch yourself." I point a finger at my brother, who captures it, and holds hard, like those finger traps we had when we were kids.

"Her soufflé wants to be topped by your crème." Knox pulls my finger toward his mouth but I'm strong enough to tug free.

"That's enough," I bark, causing Knox to burst into laughter. He got me where he wanted. All riled back up.

I try to be sly as I glance at Rena who is watching my brothers and me. She catches my gaze and smiles, but I look away. I don't think of her like that. I don't want her thinking of me period.

"She's my employee." I don't dare call her a friend. We aren't. We make baked goods together. She's getting a second chance at life at the bakery, like me.

"Maybe you should sign her check."

I'm off my stool so fast, Knox's arms flare as I push him off his. Clay is quick, catching my brother before he hits the ground while cursing at him. "What the fuck?"

My heart hammers. My fists tighten. Maybe a fight is what I need to dispel this energy I can't seem to control. Knox is asking to be whupped, even if he is my brother.

"Do you need to head to the stable?" Clay's question recalls when we were kids, and the testosterone grew thick in our home. A punching bag hung in one of the stalls in the old stable. Unfortunately, our father preferred to use his children instead of the bag. The stable became off limits to Dad once our mother died. She'd been the one who loved horses and we didn't keep any after her death.

The stable became a place I both loathed and loved.

Eventually, I found something else to take the edge off, but I'll never be going back to drugs.

Maggie is suddenly at our table. "I don't want no trouble in here." As the owner of Milton's Roadhouse, she scowls like a disgruntled mother. Hands on her hips, her tone is firm. "Do I need to kick the lot of you out of here?"

She tips her head toward the entrance.

"We'd never cause you trouble, Maggie." Knox flirts, wrapping his arm around my shoulders and pulling me against his side a little too tightly.

"You better not." She huffs before spinning on her cowboy boot-clad feet and strutting away from us across the hardwood floor.

Knox slides his arm to my neck, putting me in a choke hold. I swat at the back of his head to release me.

Clay admonishes both of us. "Can you two act like you're nearly forty, and not behave like fourteen-year-olds?"

"Okay, *Dad*," Knox teases, releasing me at the same time I push at his belly.

"Fuck," I grumble, running a hand over my hair and feeling my phone vibrate in my pocket. Without a thought, I pull it free from my back pocket and check the caller ID.

"Sugar?" I'm out of breath as I answer.

Glancing at Knox and Clay is a mistake as they both raise brows and stare at me with wide eyes. I give them a single-finger salute.

"Sebastian, am I interrupting something?"

I heavily exhale and rub a hand through my hair again. "No. What's up?" I'm going for casual disinterest, but the truth is, this is the first time I've heard her voice in almost two weeks, and I'm far from cool.

"I'm sorry I called you, but I don't know who else to call."

"Enya." I groan, already irritated by another apology. "What's wrong?"

"I heard a noise, but now that I have you on the phone, it's probably nothing and I'm being silly."

"What noise?" I jostle the phone between my chin and shoulder, reach for my wallet and pull out a twenty. Slapping it on the table, I turn away from my brothers and head for the exit.

"It's probably just an animal. I'm so tired, I'm just imagining things." Her quiet huff does not disguise the trace of fear in her voice.

"Where's Adara?"

"In my arms."

"Where are you?"

"In my living room."

With the open concept, and lights illuminating the first level of her house, she's a guppy in a fishbowl.

"What about your sister?"

"Cadence left days ago."

What? "Baby, I want you to go upstairs. Stay on the phone with me and lock yourself in the bathroom."

"Sebastian, like I said. I'm probably being silly. Just hearing your voice, I feel calmer."

Fuck, I should not like the way that sounds. I want her to hang up and dial 9-1-1 but I'm also afraid to let her off the phone.

I've made it to my truck and have the engine started. My phone clicks over to hands-free and I'm reversing like I'm a NASCAR pro. "I'm on my way."

"I didn't mean to interrupt your night."

"You can always interrupt me. Just stay on the phone with me. Tell me something about Adara. Anything. How is she doing?"

Within seconds, Enya's voice softens as she tells me about the baby. How much weight she's gained. How she scoots around until she's comfortable on Enya's chest. How she lifts her head.

I'm pulling into Enya's drive faster than I should be and the gravel kicks up underneath my tires. "That's just me," I tell her as I climb out of the truck and slam the door. "I'm going to take a look around. If I'm not at your front door in three minutes, you call 9-1-1."

"Now *you're* scaring me."

"Sugar, do as I say. Please."

I circle the perimeter of her house, not even trying to be stealth-like as I'm itching for a fight. Forget the stable. Forget Knox and his jabbing jests. The sensation rippling up my arms and causing my heart to hammer reminds me of the last time I was here when everything went to hell.

That fucker had messed with my sister, and in return he had someone bigger, stronger, faster messing with him.

But anyone thinking they can meddle with this woman—with Enya—will have more than hell to worry about.

After a rapid circle around Enya's house, I stare in the direction of the distant woods, knowing well the path that leads through the trees. A roughly two-acre meadow surrounds this place before the woods begin. Within the forest is an open space, protected by the heavy trees. Parties were held there. Deals were done, too.

When I was arrested, I came clean and the local sheriff's department was able to take down a dealer or two before others wised up and moved to another location. Which means Stone was able to chase off suppliers and buyers, pushing them into another town, another set of woods.

Rounding back to the front of the house, I climb the porch stairs, thumping up them like a warning. Enya opens the door and I'm slipping my arms around her before I can catch myself. With a gentle kick, I close the door behind me and hold her tight to my chest. Adara is at Enya's shoulder, and I press my nose into her baby-sweet neck.

"I told you to wait for me upstairs," I whisper, lifting my head and staring into Enya's wide brown eyes.

"I heard you in the yard." With her still in my arms, I catch a whiff of her as well. Rain-sweet and a bit of baby scent blend together.

Pulling back, I notice she's wearing my T-shirt and possibly nothing else. Looking her in the eye again, purple smudges darken the skin beneath her warm irises. "Are you getting any sleep?"

Her shoulder lifts and lowers. "Some." She presses a kiss to Adara's head.

"When did your sister leave?"

"Three days ago."

"I thought she'd be staying for two weeks."

"So did I." Enya looks away, lips returning to Adara's head for a lingering kiss. Her avoidance suggests she doesn't want to discuss her sister.

"What did you hear outside? What did it sound like?"

"Honestly." She turns back to me. "It sounded like someone was walking across the porch."

Fuck, I do not like the sound of that. I spin toward the front door and glance out the side window at the porch. Someone could easily walk along the decking and peer directly through the living room window.

"Maybe this place really is haunted," Enya teases.

Sharply turning back to her, I say, "Don't even joke about that."

The smile on her face disappears and I step toward her, brushing her hair back from her cheeks and scooping it behind her ears. "I'm going to stay tonight."

The suggestion—no, demand—that I stay should surprise me. It's like when I volunteered to be Adara's dad. But my immediate request isn't random. Unease at spending time in a place that holds so many bad memories is outweighed by the need to keep Enya and Adara safe.

Enya's forehead crinkles in shock. "What about your plans?"

"What plans?"

"It was loud when I called you. Were you out with friends? Or maybe on—" She cuts herself off and pulls back from my hands on her neck. Turning away from me, giving me her back, she mumbles, "Never mind."

A slow grin curls my lips. Did she think I was on a date? Would that upset her? I don't want her thinking such a thing and I cover her shoulders with my hands, swiping them down her arm to her elbows and tugging her back to me. I inhale at her neck once more. "I wasn't on a date, baby. So don't be like this."

She spins toward me, a little fire in those dark eyes. "Be like what?"

Jealous. Envious. Worried.

"There's nobody in my life." I tip up her chin while I silently wish *she* was the someone in my life.

"There doesn't always need to be someone *actively* in your life. Just one night and . . ." Her eyes shift, and she kisses Adara's head. Is that how Adara came to be? Was it a one-night stand that led to this precious baby?

Now I'm the one jealous, envious even, that a man had his hands on Enya for one night and fuck him for not standing by her side for all the rest of her days.

Then again, I'm here because someone else isn't, and I'm not leaving tonight.

"Let's get you to bed." With a hand on her lower back, I guide her toward the staircase. Following her up the stairs, I ignore the thump in my chest, reminding me of things that happened in this old house. Maybe that thud is from something different, though. Like the vision of climbing these stairs every night, following this woman to a bedroom we share, and lying next to her like she belongs to me.

Quickly, I shake those thoughts from my head and follow her to a large bedroom at the end of the hallway. I don't remember such a room being here.

"Did you combine rooms or something?"

"I did. This space was two small bedrooms and I made it into the primary bedroom. I converted another bedroom into a nursery and added a closet. The last bedroom is my office slash guestroom." She pauses as she nears a bassinet and sets Adara down. The infant crib is beside a queen-sized bed with rumpled sheets on one half of the mattress and a plethora of pillows.

Images of Enya in that bed, tossing and turning with some other man fill my head, causing my adrenaline to rise again.

Leaning forward, I run a hand over Adara's belly, worried I'll disturb her but also needing to touch her. To remind myself she's safe with me here. I'll never let anyone get to her.

Standing straighter, I look at Enya. Our eyes catch for a second before I lean forward, kissing her forehead and lingering for a second. "Get some sleep. I'll be downstairs on the couch."

As I pull back, Enya grips my wrist. "Stay. Please." Her voice is a smoky whisper in the room illuminated by only a nightlight plugged into an outlet.

I can't. *I shouldn't.*

Her hand lowers for my palm before her fingers slip along mine as if she's ready to let me go. Swiftly, I catch her hand and lift it to my lips.

"Are you sure?" I question against her knuckles.

"Please."

Fuck, I can't deny her.

Nodding at her, giving into her, she cups my cheek. "Thank you. Just let me brush my teeth."

I release her and watch as she enters the bathroom off her room. Glancing back at her bed, I sigh, before toeing off my boots and removing my socks. I tug my belt free and set it on her dresser.

"Need a t-shirt to sleep in?" Her voice is all tease and a bit too seductive when I turn around to find her smile aimed at me. "I'd offer you mine, which is really yours, but it's taken."

God, she undoes me. Keep my shirt. *Keep me.* "I'm good."

"Won't you be uncomfortable in your jeans?"

Fuck, yeah, I will be. I already am, feeling the tightness in my balls and the stiffness behind my zipper. My body is already reacting to being in a bed with her and we haven't even laid down.

"I'll be fine." I step up to the side she clearly sleeps on, which is closest to the bassinet, and hold up the sheets. "Get in, Sugar."

Watching me, she folds down to the mattress and then lays on her side. Her hand catches mine again. "You're not leaving, right?"

I want to believe there's something more in her plea. Like she's no longer scared, just wants reassurance I'll be here through the night. Leaning down, I kiss her forehead again before rounding the bed. With a tug, I pull back the sheets that are made up tight to the top and catch a whiff of Enya as the blanket unfolds. I slip onto the mattress, laying on my back, and stare straight up at the ceiling.

I can't remember the last time I slept in a bed with a woman. *Just slept.*

Beside me, Enya rolls, and I sense her looking at me. Taking a second to calm my breathing, I turn only my head toward her.

"Thank you, Sebastian. You're always so good to me. And I don't want you to think I've taken advantage of you. Before. Or tonight."

"I don't." Slowly, I shift to mirror her position.

"I've missed you," she whispers, eyes scanning my face.

"I've missed you, too, sugar."

Her mouth opens like she wants to say something else, but then she slams those delicious lips shut, and rolls to her back. She tosses an arm over her eyes, and I wait her out, wanting to know what's going through her head. A tear slips from her eye to her hairline but she's quick to catch it with the hand over her face.

"Enya?" I scoot closer to her and slide my arm over her waist. "What's wrong?" *What did I do?*

"You're so sweet, Sebastian. And I know you didn't mean it the same way as me, but it was just nice to hear that you've missed me." She brushes away another tear. "I don't understand why you've stayed away, but I can't fault you for keeping your distance." She wipes her entire hand over her face and peers at me with watery eyes. "From the day we've met, I've been a hot mess."

"I like messy things."

My response only seems to make her cry harder, and she rolls toward me, where I tuck her into my chest and press my lips to her head. The blankets form a wall between us, keeping my body from hers, which is best, because the way this woman is feeling, the last thing she needs is my hard dick pressed up against her soft center.

Still, I want to assure her, I'm here for her. "I'm sorry I've stayed away. I was giving you space to adjust with Adara. And visit with your sister."

She nods into my chest as I lie to her. I stayed away for my own self-preservation. Because if I hadn't, I'd end up right where I am now, wishing and hoping for things I don't deserve.

Like listening to Adara softly snore in her bassinet.

Like holding Enya in my arms all night.

Chapter 18

[Enya]

When my alarm goes off, Sebastian sits upright beside me, swiping a hand down his face as if disoriented and confused.

"Go back to sleep," I whisper, hesitating before I swipe my hand up his back. Shifting to sit up myself, I add, "I just need to feed Adara."

He falls back to the pillow and scrubs both hands down his face. "What time is it?" His sleep-filled voice is sexy as hell.

"Midnight."

With my back to him, I change Adara's diaper and lift her from the bassinet. She stiffly stretches, tucking up all her limbs, as if I'm disrupting her dreams. Her feeding schedule is every three hours to help her gain weight.

"Mind if I do this here? I don't really want to go downstairs." The request feels selfish, but my bed is cozy and I'm drowsy.

Rigidly, Sebastian shakes his head and I prop up a pillow. He reaches over to help, fluffing a second one against the headboard.

Once seated, I tuck Adara into position and lift up my tee. She latches on and I watch her as she softly sucks. Her eagerness echoes loudly in the quiet room, or maybe I'm just suddenly hyperaware of Sebastian's presence beside me.

Hesitantly, I glance over at him. "I guess I didn't think this one through." He can't really see my breast but there's no doubt what Adara is doing.

His gaze shifts from where Adara is tucked into my arm and lifts to my eyes. "No. It's so amazing. Life really is a mystery and a miracle."

"I'm so fortunate." I gaze back down at Adara a second before looking over at him. "Not only for her, but for you, too."

"Sugar," he groans like he does when he's exasperated by me and my gratitude.

"I mean it. Can you just take the compliment for once? You're an incredible man, Sebastian. And I truly feel lucky you came into my life when you did. You've been by my side through a lot, and I don't deserve all you've done for us, but I'm so thankful. You're an angel."

Sebastian swallows hard as his focus stays on my face. Maybe he sees that I really need him to read my sincerity and take my gratitude.

"Thank you," he whispers. "I'm not typically called an angel. More like the devil."

"Why?"

Propping up on an elbow, he keeps his eyes on me. "When I was fourteen, I wanted to sell drugs to help my family."

His gaze drops to Adara's feet tucked beneath my other arm.

"My dad had died when I was twelve and Stone came home, giving up a lot to take care of Ford, Vale, and me. He was suddenly responsible for three, almost four other people. Knox already had one foot out the door, but he wasn't eighteen yet when Stone stepped in. Stone was only twenty-two."

I remain quiet, watching him wrestle with his memories.

"We were struggling financially. I just wanted to help. The Seed and Soil had been almost run into the ground. Clay was doing all he could to build a better reputation, reassure creditors, and restore some faith in the community that we *were* a decent family."

Sebastian sighs and falls to his back, staring up at the ceiling. "Vale wanted to take dance lessons. And Ford needed new baseball equipment. Even Stone deserved the nice things he was denying himself. And I wanted a guitar. I was going to be a bad ass rock star."

He looks up at me with a smirk that certainly would have had teenage girls screaming and a few moms removing bras and tossing them onto a stage.

"I didn't know you could sing or play an instrument."

He snorts. "I can't. I just wanted to own a guitar." Exhaling, his body relaxes. "Anyway, we were poor. Poorer than when our dad had been around. I'd been approached by a senior at the high school to sell pot at the middle school."

Sebastian peers at me. "I'd asked Knox if he thought it was a good idea. If he thought, it would help the family."

When silence falls between us and Sebastian looks away, I prompt him. "What did Knox say?"

"He said he'd kick my ass if I went anywhere near Josh Geary." He chews at the corner of his lip. "I didn't listen."

His gaze lowers for his chest and he swipes a hand over his firm pecs. "Got hooked myself. Sold on the side. Became *real* popular." Mockery fills his voice.

"Then I started getting in trouble. Issues at school. Stone had to intervene." Bitterness joins the mix in his tone. "I would have dropped out if Stone hadn't taken me to school every day. Even walked me to class a few times." His laughter is sour. "It was so fucking embarrassing."

Another deep pause falls between us, and I switch Adara to my other side. Swiping a thumb over her cheek, I hope I can be strong as she ages and keep her out of trouble. I don't want to turn a dismissive eye like my parents did. And I never want to fret like Stone Sylver must have done over his siblings. I don't want Adara to worry she won't be provided for or loved.

"I didn't go to college, Enya." There's shame in his admission. "I worked at Seed and Soil, sinking deeper and deeper into the drugs, thinking that place would be my entire life. Slinging mud, like my name suggests."

Only his name doesn't mean mud and I'm about to correct him when he continues.

"Then shit got heavy. I'd been in trouble for breaking and entering, but I wasn't a fucking thief." His voice drops lower. "Then someone tricked Vale." He shifts his head, and an intense gaze meets mine. "He promised her things he couldn't give her, and he wanted to do things to her a brother should never hear. He'd brought her to a party she shouldn't have been at. Thankfully, she got away from him. He didn't get away from me, though. He ran to this abandoned farmhouse and . . ."

He swipes both hands over his face again and jackknives upright, startling me with the sudden movement. "I should go."

Reaching for his forearm, I squeeze his warm skin. My touch is cool from the story he just told and the fear inside me that someone intended to hurt Vale, violate her.

"But you don't have to." I don't want him to leave, and I don't want him to feel his confession changes how I view him. He's still a hero, despite his past. Maybe even his past is the reason he's heroic now.

"Don't romanticize me," he warns, his tone sharp and surprising, as he watches me, reading me. "I've done terrible things. I hurt my family. I got kids hooked on drugs. I killed a man," he reminds me, and I make my own connection between his admission and what I've just learned. My home was the abandoned farmhouse. Only it isn't abandoned now. It isn't even the same blueprint.

"Is it difficult to be here?" Can he not enter this place without thinking about what happened here once upon a time?

Slowly, I release my hold on his forearm and adjust Adara. She's fallen back to sleep, and I swipe at her languid mouth with my finger. Shifting her to my shoulder, I gently pat her back, hopeful for a burp to prevent gas.

Sebastian doesn't answer my question. He also doesn't make a move to leave the bed.

Once Adara gives a little belch, I gingerly rise from the mattress and set her back in the bassinet. Then I turn to face Sebastian.

"I don't want you to be uncomfortable here. The house's footprint is very different than its original layout, but I understand if you feel like ghosts are still present." I don't mean literally that spirits haunt my home, but if the memories disturb him, I'll have to accept he won't want to visit me. "I don't want you to feel bound to stay."

I won't be an obligation to him. He doesn't owe me anything. If anything, I'm indebted to him.

But it's more than feeling beholden to Sebastian. His kind heart drew me in. The chemistry between us makes me want to keep him.

He's been nothing but a genuine gentleman, offering up his home, playing Adara's dad, and now this, staying the night to keep us safe.

The part I need to keep in check is how insanely attracted I am to him. His settling presence. His strong embrace. His silent comfort.

The way he looks at me makes me feel like I'm a puzzle he wants to piece together. Or maybe a craving he won't allow himself to taste. But I've already made a fool of myself over him. *Twice.* I kissed him months ago in momentary celebration and instant attraction. Then I asked him to kiss me again, and he refused.

He'd done the honorable thing. He wants to be friends and I'll take him any way I can. If that means holding at bay the yearning I have to be touched by him, the longing I harbor to experience him, then I can do that.

Because I don't want to lose Sebastian.

My fear is bigger than my attraction. I'm afraid he'll walk out of my life because he's sick of playing hero to my hot mess. He'll leave behind a gaping hole in my heart.

Turning toward the bathroom, I need a minute to collect myself. But the sudden rustling of the bed and then strong arms around my middle stops me in my tracks.

Sebastian's nose presses into the side of my neck. "It isn't you, Enya. It's all me."

My eyes close, recalling similar words rearranged and said by another man.

You're just too much, Enya. And it just isn't in me to give you what you want.

What I'd wanted was my boyfriend of eleven years to love me. To propose to me. To give us a family.

How had I been so blind? Why was I doing it again? Clinging to someone who has been open about what he can and cannot handle.

"I need to use the bathroom," I awkwardly state to break this weird tension between us. Plus, I don't know how to respond to his statement. It isn't him. Sebastian is the one who has done nothing wrong. He's been open from the start on how he felt about fatherhood and family. He's also been here for me in ways no one else has. Even Cadence had to leave early. I'm the one left feeling like it's always *me* who wants too much, too soon, too fast.

Although I wouldn't call eleven years of waiting too much, too soon, or too fast.

Now, I'm the one wanting things, wishing on spent dandelions, for a seed of hope that Sebastian won't walk out of my life.

When he releases me, I take a moment to gather my thoughts and pee. When I return to my room, I don't expect to find him still in my house, let alone in my bed. But he's sitting on the edge of the mattress, waiting for me.

"I'd like to stay." His voice is gravelly and rough, like when he first woke from the alarm. "When is Adara's next feeding?"

"At three a.m."

He sits up straighter. "I'll get her then." In the NICU, Sebastian bottle fed Adara on occasion. "I have to be awake by four anyway for the bakery. You can get some extra sleep."

See? Just when he thinks he isn't being my personal knight in shining armor, he gleams brighter.

Chapter 19

[Sebastian]

The last thing I want to do on Sunday is tackle a family dinner. With Knox and Clay still blowing up my phone, wondering what happened to me on Friday night, and asking if Enya and the baby were okay, I just need a day off.

I was hoping to convince my brother Judd to skip dinner and take a ride with me. His secret passion is his Harley and I'd acquired one a year ago. With the weather warm and the early summer sunshine, the day is perfect for hitting the highway.

Unfortunately, Judd is committed to another dinner with Heather's family. Honestly, I don't know what he sees in the high maintenance woman. Judd is smarter than all of us. He deserves someone who loves him, and who he loves in return. And no one in my family is convinced my brother loves Miss January in Remington Automotive's yearly calendar.

When I round the old house for the backyard, I stop short. "Enya?"

"Hey," she sheepishly glances up at me from a seat at the picnic table. Her smile is weak while her eyes are bright, almost hopeful.

Was she wanting to see me? Then again, why is she here? Stone and Vale have a strict family-only policy. This was to prevent a revolving door of my brothers' female friends. I've never brought a woman to meet my family.

"What are you doing here?" I swallow back the harshness of my tone. The sharpness of my question is unwarranted, especially when Enya's face blanches.

It's not that I don't want her present, it's just— *I don't know what it is.* I didn't sleep well last night, tossing and turning as my nose tickled with her lingering scent although it had been twenty-four hours since I spent the night in her bed. I purposefully stayed away last night.

But I hadn't gotten much sleep the other night when I stayed either, although the shuteye I did get was deep. Her bed was comfortable. Or maybe it was just Enya's nearness and the soft sounds of Adara that brought me comfort.

A quick glance at my brothers does nothing to ease my sudden tension. Clay stares at me from his seat opposite Enya at the picnic table. Knox stops short of the table, holding a beer in each hand. His brows furrow like I'm an idiot. Stone watches me from his position near the grill, eyes pinched as they often are when he looks at me.

I glance back at Enya, but she avoids looking at me. With her head lowered, she quietly answers my question, "Vale invited me."

Hastily, she stands, bumping her knee against the underside of the wooden table and righting Adara in her arms.

Adara looks at me instead. Her eyes are open and alert while I'm not certain anything is in focus for her yet. According to what I'd read, she can only see blurry shapes and shades of black and white. Sometimes when she peers at me, like when I was feeding her a bottle the other morning, I swear she saw me. Saw me for the phony that I am. Giving me a look, like *who did I think I was pretending to be a dad?* Pretending to be *her* dad. While I was growing more attached to her every time I hold her.

I've missed our feeding sessions at the hospital and snuggling with her there as well.

"But I don't need to stay." Enya's terse tone interrupts my stare down with Adara.

"You're staying." Turning at the sound of Vale's warning, I'm met with a glare that could rival a scolding schoolteacher. Stepping up to my sister, I take the large bowl of potato chips from her hands.

"Be nice," she mumbles, eyes shifting from me to Enya and back.

I'm not being intentionally mean, it's just— *I don't know what I am.* This woman has me all out of sorts and everywhere I turn I'm getting texts about her, and calls from her, and soft smiles and a warm night in her bed. And I want things I shouldn't want.

Like peeling off that flowing dress she is wearing which hits just above her knees and accentuates her plump breasts. Then I want to lay her down on the picnic table and have my way with her beneath the bright sunshine.

She's such an anomaly to me. The other night, I told her what happened to me. How my life has been, and she didn't bat an eye.

Why was that? Why was she so easy to confide in? So accepting of my past? She didn't give me a disgruntled flinch or a disapproving glare. She took what I told her and then asked me to stay. Hell, she even gave me an out if I didn't want to stick around, leaving the choice in my hands because she clearly wasn't kicking me out.

Did she want to keep me?

It was one of the stupidest questions I've asked myself. And I've done some dumb things in my life.

When I glance at Enya, she has the diaper bag hitched over one shoulder and Adara tucked against her chest. "I should go."

Of course, she doesn't want to keep me. I'm being an ass.

She steps up to Vale and awkwardly hugs my sister. "Thanks for the invitation. Maybe I'll take you up on that book club invite, even though I haven't gotten much reading done lately."

Vale gives Enya a concerned glance before she scowls at me again. Then she peers back at Enya, softening her expression. "I don't want you to leave."

Vale gives me another disapproving frown, side-eyeing Enya with an unspoken warning. *Fix this.*

Enya doesn't offer me a glance. "Today is about family." Her statement feels abrupt, like she's left the sentence unfinished.

Today is about family, and she isn't part of ours.

Today is about family, and she doesn't have any present.

Today is about family, and I want her to be mine.

And I'm such a shit for reacting stone cold at her appearance in the yard. I'm just a little surprised. Maybe shocked is the word. Maybe I'm just being an asshole because I should have invited Enya myself, but I've had my reasons for keeping her away from my family.

When she brushes past Vale and brusquely crosses the yard, it hits me how much I want her here. I don't want her to leave, and I especially don't want her to run off because of me. Because I've made her feel unwelcome when that's the last thing I intended. I want her present. *With me.*

Taking off after her, I near the corner of the house and catch her by the elbow.

"Wait. Just wait." I'm breathing hard like I've run the perimeter of our property not taken a few generous steps across the grass.

Enya swings to face me. The diaper bag falls from her shoulder, catching in the crook of her elbow. Adara fusses in Enya's arms.

"I'm sorry," I blurt before she can offer me an apology. I don't want her damn forgiveness when she's done nothing wrong. "It's just—"

What is it?

"It's just . . . I should have invited you myself." Suddenly, I feel anxious, like something is buzzing just beneath my skin. The truth is I've wanted her to meet my family, but I've also wanted to keep Enya to myself a little longer, as someone special just for me. Stone might be kind of a stickler about people outside the family but that's on him. And Vale might be doing her thing, asking Enya to join us because that's just Vale, including her new friend. But Enya belonged to me first, and I should be the one introducing her to my family.

"You don't need to say that."

"I'm not—"

Her quickly raised hand stops me. She adjusts Adara again. "Vale is becoming my friend, and I don't have many here. I wanted to get out of the house for a little bit, but I should have cleared it with you first. This *is* your family."

"It isn't that I don't want you here." I don't know how to fully explain myself without revealing too much about my feelings. How much I want her, and not just as a friend. I'm struggling to keep my attraction to her in check. That mouth. The curve of her hips. The shape of her breasts. I could hardly keep my hands off her the other night.

"It's more about them, than you," I explain. They're going to think things about us that aren't true. They're going to ship us together when that vessel can never sail. They're going to love her when I can't keep her.

"I don't even know what that means."

"They're going to tease me." I sound like a five-year-old, worried about being bullied. I can hold my own, but Enya is important to me, and I don't want them belittling her by trying to link us together, like a couple. That isn't what Enya wants, and it isn't what she deserves.

Enya juts her hip and presses her lips together, twisting them to the side. I can't tell if she's fighting laughter at my whining or finally seeing the real me. The one who leaves disappointment in my wake.

Finally, she says, "Do you need me to protect you from your big, bad brothers? Need me to flex some muscle at them?" She lifts her arm, dangling the diaper bag at her elbow still, and weakly attempts to pump her bicep.

I bitterly scoff and shake my head. *Why am I acting this way?* Like I'm a snarling dog when I feel more like a lovesick pup.

Because I'm scared. Because eventually she will get sick of me and find a better man, and my family is going to blame me when she walks away.

It will be one more bad decision on my part.

"Please," I whisper. "Stay."

Enya stares at me until I grow uncomfortable with her gaze. The intensity of her looking at me, like she could scorch me, embedding a permanent scar when she leaves. Or like she could be my everything if I'd only let her a little closer.

Dismissing the thought, I hold out my hands, no longer giving Enya a choice about staying or leaving. "Give her to me."

The spell of Enya's gaze is broken, and she steps closer, shifting Adara into my arms. With the baby secure in one arm, I reach for the diaper bag on Enya's elbow and hitch it over my shoulder.

"I made it awkward," Enya mutters about the little scene we just gave my family.

"Trust me, they're going to forgive this and forget it." Because they're going to love her.

When I turn around, all eyes are on me, like a firing squad, only they don't know whether to shoot, laugh, or shit themselves. Etched in each of my family member's faces is doubt and confusion. They can't believe what's before them.

Me . . . holding a baby.

However, Stone has the faintest hint of a smile. Just the corner of his mouth curling upward.

I take a deep breath and step forward with Adara as my shield.

"Looks good on you," Stone mutters as I near him.

"What does?" I snap.

"Fatherhood."

"I'm not—" I start but halt when Adara's little hand swipes at my chin. She doesn't really have the capability to reach but it still felt like a tender touch. Like she purposely wanted to draw my attention before I said something I shouldn't.

Like I'm not her father.

When I'd really like to be.

+ + +

I'm not certain who is more of a hit with my family—Enya or Adara. For men who don't have children, Stone, Clay, and Knox coo over the baby like she's a princess.

Vale takes a turn, too. Nostalgia fills her eyes. "One minute she's eight weeks old, then you blink, and eight years have passed," Vale says, staring down at Adara in her arms.

"Mom," Hudson whines from a hammock set up in the yard where he's playing a handheld video game. "I'm nine."

"Eight. Nine. Nineteen. Thirty. You're still going to be my baby," Vale gushes at her son.

"You're so embarrassing," he groans while fighting a smile. His eyes never leave the handheld screen.

Vale and Hudson are close. She's a good mom. Without ever knowing our mother, I'm certain Violet Sylver is proud of the daughter she wanted so badly. I like to believe Vale behaves how our mother would have, had she lived to finish raising her children.

"Adara will probably feel the same way about me one day." Enya chuckles as she addresses Hudson.

"It's a parent's right to embarrass their child," Knox teases.

Stone, Clay, and I exchanged a look. Our father certainly embarrassed all of us, but his attention wasn't the good-natured teasing that happens between Vale and Hudson. The embarrassment he offered was late night calls from the local bar and the bruises on our skin.

Needing to touch Enya after my brother's comment, I run my hand up her spine and squeeze her nape. With Enya present, blending so easily into this afternoon with my family, I've taken liberties I probably shouldn't have, but can't seem to help. Like sitting close to her on the picnic table bench where I straddle the seat and close her in with one leg behind her backside and the other bracketing her knees.

At my touch, Enya turns her head and gives me a soft smile.

"Can we have dessert now?" Hudson whines, proving that his nine years still mark him as a child.

Vale gazes over at Hudson. "Say please. Uncle Sebastian was supposed to bring a variety of baby-Bundt cakes and—"

"Did you bring a lemon one?" Enya interjects, eyes widening with excitement as she shifts to face me. Her hands clasped together at her chest, like a child begging for a treat. She's so fucking cute.

"Ah yes, the lemon baby-Bundt cake queen." Clay strokes his barely-there scruff, teasingly narrowing his eyes as he examines Enya. "Care to explain how you met my brother and never told me."

"I told you," Enya defends. "I went into the bakery once and fell in love with the lemon cake."

At first, I only hear *fell in love* and then the echo of *with the lemon cake*. Of course, she meant my cake, not me.

"Yes, but you actually met him." Clay nods toward me. "The curmudgeon baker himself."

"Was he supposed to be in hiding?" Enya teases. She hesitantly glances at me, like I might have told my brother our secret. We more than met. We shared a moment. A kiss that rocked my world, curled my toes, and did at least five other cliché things to me.

Squeezing the back of her neck again is my signal our secret is still safe inside me.

"And you actually like him?" With a sharp turn of my head, I glare at Clay who gives me a wink.

"He's okay." Enya bites her lower lip while watching me.

"You ever get sick of him, you come back to me, baby." Clay winks at Enya.

"Hey!" I snap.

With a deep chuckle, Clay continues, knowing he's gotten to me. "This is what I mean. This guy went all ape-shit when he learned you'd been coming to the Seed and Soil for months, and he hadn't known."

"Really?" Enya arches a brow, while a sweet smile curls her lips. Her gaze remains on me while she questions Clay. "And why did he care that I'd been around for months, and he hadn't seen me?"

She probably shouldn't poke me—the bear—because the revelation would include our kiss and how I'm still pissed that she'd been this close without me knowing. I could have met her sooner. I could have been there for her through her pregnancy. The thought doesn't startle me as much as it should. I wouldn't have let her out of my sight if I'd known she was available and nearby.

"That's a good question. Why did you lose your shit, Seb?" Knox drones, playfully wiggling his eyebrows.

"That's a dollar each," Hudson interjects.

"I didn't say a bad word. I said ape . . . *doo-caca*," Clay protests.

"Nope. The S-H-word was in there and it counts. Pay up." Hudson lugs himself from the hammock and strolls over to my brothers, rolling open his hand like a professional bill collector.

Knox and Clay each reach in their pockets. Knox slaps a five-dollar bill into Hudson's palm. "Count it as a deposit. I'm owed four more swear words today."

Vale rolls her eyes. "How about if you tame the language?"

"But I like language. All language. I don't want to discriminate," Knox jokes.

Enya laughs at the antics around us. The sound of her being so carefree with my family is doing funny things to my chest. I'm more relaxed than I've been around my family in a long, long time. Plus, the pleasant guffawing is nice to hear. With Adara's birth, there have been lots of tears and tension. For once, Enya is all humor and smiles.

Needing to touch her again, I place my hand just above her knee beneath the table. Her skin is soft where her dress rides up her thigh. My fingers squeeze at her inner leg while my thumb coasts over her summer-warm flesh.

"I'm going to have to give her back to you so I can get those cakes," Vale says to Enya, offering up Adara.

"Let Sebastian get the cakes," Stone admonishes. He's been his typical quiet self today. Just observing our family. Taking in the brood he raised.

"Give her to me," I interject, holding out my hands for Adara. It's not like my family hasn't seen me carrying her, but everything goes quiet again when Vale passes Adara to me. Enya watches me over her shoulder, her side still to my chest where I cage her in on the picnic bench.

"Your brother was right earlier." Her voice is lowered for only me to hear.

"Oh yeah. Which brother and what did he say?" I jostle Adara a little and press a kiss to her head.

Enya smiles, slow and sweet. "Fatherhood looks good on you." Her grin deepens before realization hits. "Although I don't mean you are . . . That is, I didn't mean to imply you were . . . well, I'm not saying you're—"

"I get it." I tip up my chin, before holding my cheek to Adara's downy head. "And if I ever considered being a dad, well . . . no one would top this pretty girl." I kiss Adara's head again. "But I'll never be a dad. Fatherhood isn't meant to be for me."

Slowly, the wide grin on Enya's face fades. "Yeah. I know. You've been pretty clear on how you feel about it."

She doesn't flinch; however, she swings her legs free from beneath the table and rises off the bench. Smoothing down her dress, she says, "I think I'll help Vale with the cakes."

With her back to me, I check out her ass as her hips sway a bit and her dress floats just above the backs of her knees. That's a damn sexy spot on her.

"That's a whole lot of sugar," Knox hums and I catch him watching Enya.

"Fuck you," I mutter over Adara's head.

"You can deduct his swear word from my tab," Knox hollers to Hudson who is headed toward the house as well.

"You know, typically, I'm the damsel in distress guy." Clay reminds us of all the strays he'd taken in as a kid, until our dad would give them the boot. Sometimes literally.

"She isn't in distress." Enya is one of the most levelheaded people I've ever met. She doesn't need rescuing in anyway.

Stone clears his throat. "Bit of advice…"

Oh, boy. Here we go.

"Don't fuck this up." He tips his chin in the direction of the house. "She's someone you're only going to get one shot with. And regret it if she walks away."

Wisdom fills Stone's voice. He had that once in a lifetime woman, but he's never acted like he regretted losing her.

"Like a one-hit wonder," Knox teases, attempting to break the sudden tension around the picnic table.

Clay backhands Knox's chest. "Dude."

Stone doesn't respond to their shenanigans. He only keeps his eyes on me. "Do the right thing."

He means let them go before I do something stupid like hurt all of us. And yes, I'm including myself in the list because the moment I walk away is the moment I'll be turned to ashes, burned by the loss of both my flames.

Enya and Adara.

Chapter 20

[Sebastian]

Because I'm a glutton for punishment, I follow Enya home that night, using the excuse that I want to make sure she gets back to her house safely. I'm still unsettled by the noise she heard the other night. Although she's brushed it off as nothing more than a wandering animal, I don't believe animals make stomping sounds.

While I didn't return to her home on Saturday, after staying over the night before, I can't seem to stay away now that she's met my family. With Adara on Enya's chest, we sit side by side on her couch. The television on low volume.

"Why didn't you tell me your sister had left?"

Enya shrugs and narrows her eyes at the television screen. "It wasn't like you could do anything about it. She just . . . left. She's like that."

Still, I would have been here for her sooner had I known. "What do you mean *left*?"

"Cadence is . . . flighty. She's also famous and that means at times she can only think of herself." An edge roughens her voice.

I shift and rest my arm on the back of the couch. However, my fingers have a mind of their own and I touch the side of her neck with the back of my knuckles, needing to feel her skin, needing to comfort her.

"Tell me more about her."

"She's an amazing singer." Enya cranes her neck to look at me. Her voice drops. "She made my dream *her* reality."

Continuing the need to touch her, I brush her hair over her ear, running my knuckles down the column of her throat again. "What dream, baby?"

"I wanted to sing." Enya sighs and looks away from me, gazing at the television again. "Every little girl dreams of being famous one day, right? Or maybe that was just me. Bright lights. Big city. I wanted to be on stage and sing my songs, breaking hearts, and healing souls." She chuckles.

I can see her on a stage, lighting up a stadium, entertaining a crowd. "I didn't know you could sing."

Enya shrugs again. "I'm not bad."

Shifting again, I lean into the cushions. "Sing something for me."

"No." She laughs harder and Adara jerks on her chest. Her little arm jolts upward. Her fingers splay outward. Enya softens her voice. "No."

"If you wanted to be on stage, you'd have to sing before an audience."

"That's different. I could sing in a room full of people but one on one . . . it's just different."

"Please." I clasp my hands together and do my best imitation of my nephew when he wants something from Vale.

Enya chews her lip while she shakes her head.

A failure at begging, I acquiesce. "Okay." I drop my hands and return my arm to the back of the couch, and pick up a strand of her hair, wrapping it around my finger. "Why *did* you give up your dream?"

"I was the peacemaker in our family. Between my brother and his drug issues, and my younger sister, who was a bit of a wild child, I felt like I had to make up for each of their shortcomings. And I wanted to please my parents." Enya takes a deep breath. "So, when I went to college, I went into accounting instead of majoring in music like I wanted."

Looking at me, she adds. "It's kind of silly because most famous musicians don't even go to college. They go from choir risers to dingy bars to discovery. And I was just simply someone who liked to sing."

"I don't think you're simply anything, sugar." I playfully tug at the hairs wrapped around my finger. She's more complex and beautiful than anyone I've ever known. Her sister might be famous, but Enya is so much more.

"I'm not jealous of Cadence. I'm really not," she continues. "As her big sister, I'm super proud of her. She went on to find fame, using her passion to get there. It's just that she's so busy, I hardly see her. And sometimes, I think she wants to run away from me when I've been her biggest cheerleader."

"Why would she run away from you?" The idea shocks me. Enya is perfect.

"I'm a reminder of how messed up our family is. My parents' lack of support. My brother's death."

I nod with compassion. "I get that. Ford is the baseball star in our family. He's the brother above me in birth order and it sucked to be in his shadow. He's uber talented, don't get me wrong, but it's difficult to be the next in line when he is so successful. My failures seem even greater in comparison. And Ford couldn't get out of here fast enough. Our family was too fucked up for him."

Our entire family was too fucked up at one point.

"Families are *so* messy, sometimes." Enya gives me an understanding smile, and I cup the back of her warm neck.

"It's why I don't think I'll ever have one."

Enya's eyes lose their spark. Her smile melts away.

While I have my beliefs, my timing in making such a statement feels off. Maybe unwarranted even. Sometimes, I'm not certain I even feel the same way I once did about families and fatherhood. "I didn't mean—"

"It's okay. You're pretty clear on how you feel about families, and I respect that. Fatherhood isn't for everyone. At least you can admit it."

Yeah, but admitting it feels like I've put my foot in my mouth. Or worse, I'm telling a lie. For all my denial, I can admit I love my family. Vale is still my best friend. And I've grown to appreciate Stone despite his continued disapproval. Fatherhood wasn't something he wanted either, or at least, didn't deserve to have thrust upon him at such a young age.

"Is that what happened with Adara's father? He hadn't admitted he wanted to be a dad until it was too late." Was Enya already pregnant before he told her he didn't want children?

Enya shakes her head and adjusts Adara in her arms. "No father. Just wanted to be a mother." She presses a kiss to Adara's head. "I wanted my own family. Maybe that's how *I've* run away from mine."

I stare at her, absentmindedly stroking my thumb along her neck. My gaze drops to Adara whose eyes are opened and looking up at her mother. I'm reminded of the hospital pictures on Adara's discharge day. The love between them is so pure, so unconditional. It's the rawest of emotions. So visible, so present, in every glance between them. Every touch.

Enya softly hums and I vaguely recognize the tune. Then she sings and I realize the song is "Thank God" by Kane Brown and his wife, Katelyn. The duet is about forgiveness and gratitude.

Enya's voice is fucking beautiful.

As she sings, I slide my hand over hers, until our fingers intwine. Like the song, her hand fits perfectly in mine. We seamlessly blend like cookies and cream.

I'm not what I would consider a tactile man, other than formerly using my fists as a resolution. After being in jail, I'm even less of a touchy guy. But with Enya, there's a physical need to be close to her. A pull I can no longer deny. I don't want to send out mixed messages, confuse our friendship, give her hope where there is none, but when she's near . . . I can't seem to keep my hands away. The draw to her flame is too strong. She gives warmth to my bones and heat to my heart.

Maybe I'm the one confused. I'm the one afraid to hope.

What would it be like to come home to her every night? To share moments on the couch like this, talking, holding hands, watching our baby? I mean, Adara. Enya's baby.

On the final verse, Enya fixes on my eyes on mine as she finishes. The last lines linger between us, softly drifting off until silence surrounds us.

"I don't really believe in God." Roughly spoken, I'm overwhelmed by her voice and the lyrics.

God? What kind of god takes away my mother and leaves behind a father who hates my existence? What god forces Stone to give up his life and me to flip mine to drugs? Then again, those were human choices. Some bad decisions. Some reckless actions.

Lifting Enya's hand, I kiss her knuckles and let my lips linger against them. She's made decisions as well. Gave up a dream. Tried to please her parents. Had Adara on her own. She's a goddess, and I only wish I were worthy enough to worship at her temple.

"At the very least, you should believe in the power of gratitude and forgiveness." With her hand still against my lips, I close my eyes. Could a woman like her forgive my past? I'd told her some scary shit and once again she didn't even flinch. She just took my truth and didn't judge me.

"You didn't say anything the other night when I told you about my past. About selling drugs and being in jail. Beating a man. Aren't you afraid of me? Or repulsed by me?" I keep my focus on her hand, tracing over her firm knuckles with my thumb, truly confused by this angel in my life. "Don't you find me unforgivable?"

"Unforgivable?" She chokes while she blinks rapidly three times. Her hand squeezes mine in return. "Honey, everyone is forgivable. As for being frightened, you've never given me a reason to be afraid of you. Not physically."

I lift my head, prepared to question her meaning. *Not physically?*

Dawning strikes. She means emotionally. We are so wrong for each other.

She wants a family. I don't.

She's perfect. I'm broken.

"I'd never be repulsed by you." A spark flickers in her eyes as she meets mine.

There's something undeniably pulling us together. Like a twisted moth to a brilliant flame, there's an attraction that we both ignore but the struggle is real. Her brightness is too intense.

Enya releases her hand from my fingers and stands, setting Adara down in a portable bassinet in the living room. The baby has fallen back asleep to her mother's voice. When Enya returns to the couch, she presses at my shoulder, forcing me to my side on the couch. Wedging herself onto the cushions, I shift until we face one another. Wrapping an arm over her, she tucks her arms between us, but clutches at my shirt.

"I believe in God, Sebastian. Or at least, Fate. And there's a reason we're here. Right now. On my couch. Together." Enya ducks her head and rests her cheek against my sternum.

I'm hanging on every word, thinking she has more to say. Is this Fate? Is this forgiveness? Is she some strange form of redemption? The thought is too much. The hope a reckless risk.

I remove the elastic band holding her hair and comb my fingers through the long length, watching as the shiny dark strands slip through my roughened fingers. I'll never let her slip away.

"Sugar?" Tilting my head, I glance down and see her eyes are closed, her fingers still tight in my shirt, like she isn't willing to let me go. A soft snore tells me she's fallen asleep.

I press a kiss to her forehead and settle in. Looks like I'm spending the night again in a house I thought I'd never visit, with a woman I don't deserve, because of a baby who holds my heart.

Both my flames have ignited something in me and I'm not ready to give up the warmth.

+ + +

After giving Adara a bottle at the three a.m. feeding, I leave. Sneaking out like I didn't spend most of the night. Pretending to myself that leaving by four means it wasn't an overnighter.

I was only sharing time with my girls.

I'm such a liar.

Because the following night, I made an excuse to return. I'd noticed some bookshelves still in a box waiting to be assembled, so I build them, help Enya place items on the shelves, and then linger until we pass out on the couch again.

The next night, I had another excuse. The toilet in her first-floor powder room had been rattling in the morning. A little adjustment fixes it, and then I offer to make Enya dinner. We watch three episodes of *Ted*

Lasso. With Adara on Enya's chest, we sit side by side until both my girls are sleeping. It's another night on the couch.

And each night, Enya and I share tender touches. My knuckles along her neck. Her fingers tracing over mine. We're friends, I remind myself, but every stroke stokes the heat between us. The something more I keep denying. I wish I could ignore it, but I can't.

Because Enya, my flame, burns too bright.

Earlier today, she went to Huntington to see her doctor. Gone most of the day, she returned to Sterling Falls much later than I expected her.

I've been waiting on her porch as the evening started to grow dark, and when she finally pulls into her driveway, I am ready to implode with comments about calling me and letting me know she is safe. The other night—the one when she thought someone was on her porch—still has me rattled. I don't like the idea of her and the baby out here alone even with the security alarm she's installed.

However, the vibe coming off Enya when she exits her SUV tells me to hold my tongue from any scolding. For now.

Once I help her carry Adara into the house, Enya commences cabinet slamming and restless pacing.

"What's wrong?" I demand.

"I'm hungry and I forgot to stop at the store."

Forgot? I don't believe it. She's Miss Efficient but I can see that *hanger* has set in, so I step over to her cabinets, hunting through them for anything I can toss together.

Pasta. Some milk and cheese in the fridge. It won't be my best meal, but I can wing it here.

I'm helping myself to a pot and filling it with water when Enya stops aimlessly moving around.

"What are you doing?" Her tone is sharper than she's ever used toward me.

"I'm making you dinner." Typically, I'd snap back at a person speaking to me like she did, but I keep calm, acting like she isn't ready to lop off my head.

I proceed to turn on the stove and set the pot on the burner. Enya takes Adara from her car seat and gets situated on the couch to nurse her. Tension fills the air in the open concept room, and there's a lot of space to fill. Still, it's thickening like the cheese and butter I'm melting together in a separate pan while the pasta boils. I check Enya's cabinets for additional spices and mastermind a combination that will add a little flavor to the cheese mixture.

When Enya's finished nursing, our dinner is almost ready to be served. She sets Adara in the portable bassinet and stalks directly to a wine bottle next to her refrigerator.

"Ready to tell me what's going on?" I ask as Enya pours the last dregs of wine into a glass and then slams the bottle onto the counter after finding only a thin layer remains in the container. She picks up the glass and downs the skimpy amount in one gulp.

"I saw my ex today."

Fuck! "I didn't know there was an ex." My forehead creases tight as I scowl at her. This is bad. This is so bad. He's going to want Enya back. He's going to want Adara. "You've been so tight-lipped about Adara's father."

"He's of no concern to Adara. He's just my ex." Enya huffs and twists to rest her backside against the counter. Her fingers curl around the edge of the top, and she stares toward the living room where Adara sleeps. "We were together for eleven years."

Whoa. Eleven years? That's longer than I was incarcerated. That's a . . . commitment.

She cranes her neck to face me standing near the stove, where I'm ready to light myself on fire. Because he can't have her back.

"Eleven years and not a single proposal of marriage. *He didn't want to get married,* he'd eventually told me. Never been his plan to be a husband or a father."

The admission hits me like a sucker punch in the gut. It's an echo of all I've been saying to her. But I'm not him.

Enya turns her head toward the living room again and squints. "He's met someone. She has two little girls and he's getting married."

Fuck.

Attempting to tamp down the dueling vibration of my fear of losing her and desire to pummel him for hurting her, I gruffly ask, "When did you break up?"

"Three years ago, although we had one of these stupid moments last summer. A night at a party with mutual friends where a few margaritas turned into I-miss-you and a shared bed." Enya shakes her head, lowering it like she's ashamed or embarrassed. "I was such an idiot."

I knew it. I knew Adara had a father. And it's him. Her ex.

Instantly envious, I want to vomit, right after I throat punch him for getting in Enya's head and then slipping into her vagina and gifting her Adara. He doesn't deserve to be anywhere near Enya or the baby.

Because I'm here.

The thought hits me upside the head. *I'm here.*

I'm a greedy, selfish bastard, who has never been stopped from doing what I want to do. Never shied away from what I wanted, and I don't know why I've been making an exception for Enya and how I really feel about her.

I want her. All of her.

Suddenly lifting her head, she glances at me. "But." She exhales. "I'm over him. The second time around it was me who said I couldn't be with him. I couldn't have a casual fling with someone whom I'd once lived with, once thought I loved. We'd shared an apartment. We'd shared a life. I wasn't going to be some piece on the side. And I'm so much better without him."

She should never be someone's side-piece. Enya is the full package. Looks. Brains. Motherhood. He's the fucking idiot. But I'm thankful for his stupidity because I'm the lucky man standing in her kitchen, making her dinner.

I'm here.

"If you're over him, I don't understand why you're so worked up."

She shakes her head again, like she isn't going to tell me, but I can be relentless when I want something. And I've made up my mind I want her. I don't know where the future leads but that's never been how I work. I react first. Ask questions later.

I turn off the stove and step closer to her. Her gaze remains pointed toward the floor, where she draws on the hardwood with her big toe. Her hands still clutch at the countertop behind her. Tugging on her chin with my finger and thumb, I prompt her to look up at me. "Talk to me."

Her eyes narrow. "I went to the doctor today and I'm cleared for sex, but seeing him, seeing him *move on*, makes me feel like I never will. Not that I won't move on from him. I *am* over him. But it's the having sex part. Like I'm never going to have sex again. Have someone touch me. Someone taste—"

"Enya," I growl, cutting her off because the images invading my head are too much. My fingers on her skin. My mouth on her pussy. Her legs wrapped around my waist as I drive into her.

Abruptly, her hand covers her mouth, and she mutters into her palm. "Oh God. I don't know why I said all that to you."

With our gazes locked on each other, I swallow hard. Further visions arise. Spreading her thighs and burying my head between them, getting drunk on her as she coats my tongue and eventually allows my dick inside her.

Fighting down the vivid fantasy, I say, "We're friends. You can tell me anything."

"Yes, well . . ." She shakes her head again, brushing loose hair over one ear as she avoids looking at me. "You've made it clear how little you're interested in me other than friendship and I shouldn't have—"

Sliding my hand into her hair, I fist the soft tresses at the back of her neck while I lean my lower body against hers pinning her against the countertop.

"You want to repeat that last part to me again." My throat is as thick as the butter and cheese combo in the pot. I can't believe what she just said.

"I shouldn't have said all that to you?" Her voice lilts, choking on the higher octaves as she questions herself.

"No, the part before that." My jaw clenches. My teeth grind. How does she not know how I feel about her? How hard I've been fighting myself?

"You're not interested—"

"Do not complete that sentence." I tighten my fingers in her hair, gently tugging so I have her attention. "What gave you the impression I'm not interested? I'm here every night."

I'm sleeping beside her, torturing myself with how much I want her.

"Because we're friends." She clarifies with a dash of bitterness.

"It's not because we're friends." My tone is too sharp, and her eyes widen, hurt filling them. "Fuck. We are friends, it's just . . . you have no idea how much I want you. I want to touch you, and taste you, and—" Dammit, I want everything with her. More than tasting and touching. I want to breathe the air she breathes. Smell her scent on my clothes, *my* flesh. I want to hear her laugh and swallow her cries. I want to see her before bed and wake up with her in the morning.

And no other man is going to receive her laughter or sooth her tears, or her taste her lips.

"Sugar." I tug at her hair and then lower my mouth to hers.

The second our lips connect I'm transported back to that first kiss. This is so much more. The warmth of her mouth. The scorch of her tongue. The flame of desire roars inside me. Being with her will burn me to the ground, but I'm willing to go up in the blaze because I can't resist her anymore.

"Please don't pity me," she mumbles against my mouth before leaping into another kiss, tugging on my lips, and rushing her tongue to meet mine.

"Pity you?" I murmur against her mouth, swiping my tongue against hers before explaining. "I'm mesmerized by you. Enthralled by you." I lean into her, kissing her harder, stroking over her tongue again. My dick strains behind my zipper, and I grind into her, emphasizing that pity is the last thing I feel for her. I've never been so hard, so hungry for someone in my life. She's my new addiction.

"Let me touch you." I press my forehead to hers with my desperate plea. My hands cup the sides of her neck while my breathing is ragged and rough. I need to be closer to her, to feel her around me.

Taking her hand, I step back, prepared to take her to her bedroom, and show her exactly how *interested* I am in her.

"Wait."

"Why?" The greedy bastard in me doesn't want to wait any longer. I can't keep denying myself, stalling through friendship, and ignoring the attraction. Another man, any man, would be eager to step in and take my place. Be with Enya. Father Adara. And I can't let that happen. I won't.

I'm here. Call it fate or redemption or some mysterious being intervening in my life, but I'm making the choice. I want to *try* with her.

"I'm not sure . . . I mean, I tried on my own . . . but it wasn't happening." She looks away, embarrassed by the admission before glancing back at me. "I'm a scared, and if it doesn't happen for me, I don't want to hurt your feelings."

Giving her a confident smirk, I say, "Baby, it's going to happen. We'll take our time. There's no rush. It doesn't all have to be tonight. Just let me kiss you. Touch you."

Fuck, my patience is unraveling. I don't know if I can go slow, but for her, I'll try.

Hell, now I'm anxious but I lead her to the couch and take a seat. Spreading my legs, I guide her to sit before me, between my thighs with her back to my chest.

I scoop all her hair over one shoulder and kiss along her neck. Her head tilts to the side, allowing me more access to her soft skin. Inhaling, she smells rain fresh like the day we met.

"Do you have any idea how long I've wanted you? How much I think about you?" I murmur to her flesh. Warn myself to be patient, I'm hasty when I sip harder at her neck and scrape my teeth along the column of her throat.

"How long?" She stammers before I nip her harder, sucking at the juncture of her shoulder and neck. Her breath catches. Her pulse skips. She hitches up her shoulder while leaning into me.

"Since that first moment in my bakery. No, before that. When you fell outside of it."

"So embarrassing," she whispers, struggling as I continue to suck at her skin, pushing the loose collar of her dress aside and open mouth kissing her shoulder. Her breath catches again and her shoulder flinches up toward her ear.

"What?" I murmur, moving on to her nape.

"That tickles, but it feels so good." Her voice is low, throaty and strained.

I squeeze at her shoulders, digging my thumbs into the muscles behind them, wanting her to relax. "Do you trust me?"

"Always." Her breathless response has me eager to please her. Eager to *deserve* her confidence.

Massaging her shoulders, while sipping at her neck, she turns her head, so our mouths meet again. Kissing her is better than perfectly frosted lemon cake or chasing a high.

Her mouth is a new drug for me.

One I knew I'd be addicted to if I ever got a second taste. She's the perfect blend of sweet and fresh, melting on my tongue and making me hungry for more.

Her, and Adara, wrapped up in one pretty package. A gift for only me.

Chapter 21

[Enya]

I'm kissing Sebastian Sylver.

Holy shit. I'm kissing *Sebastian Sylver*, and I've never been kissed like this. It's all lips and tongue and teeth.

His teeth are just incredible. Every nip. Every tease.

Gradually, his hands move from my shoulders down my back and around my sides. As his fingers lightly brush the outer edge of my breasts, I stiffen.

"What?" Sebastian hums into my neck, stilling his hands.

Oh my God, his teeth in that spot. I can't think for a second.

"It's just . . . those are still Adara's." If I started leaking, it would be so embarrassing.

Sebastian murmurs against my skin, his nose tickling my neck. "She's a damn lucky girl." The vibration of his words slithers between the valley of my breasts and straight down to my lower belly.

No, I'm the lucky one because this amazing man is kissing me, touching me. Giving of himself once again to prove to me I can do this. I can orgasm. I can be touched.

I clench my thighs. A spark developed down there, where I'd thought the flame had flickered out. But I'm still young, and I'm still eager for intimacy. It just didn't seem like an immediate possibility.

As I said to Sebastian, I didn't want his pity, but my conscience has stepped out the door, and I'll take whatever he gives me as long as he gives me something.

His teeth have been an amazing start.

"This okay?" His hands coast over my belly, swiping below my breasts, and trussing them up a bit. They tingle as he spreads his fingers, causing his thumb and forefinger to form a perfect cup to lift my breasts, pressing them together without actually covering them with his warm palms. "I'll be back to pay you homage another day, you beautiful tits."

The words zing down my midsection, like a shot of something spicy and strong, warming my insides.

He lazily drags his palms down my sides and over my stomach, which I suck in as I sit straighter.

"Why'd you do that?" He rubs his nose along my neck and around the shell of my ear.

"It's just . . . Adara again. My belly isn't what it once was." Firm. Trim. Flat.

"Since I've only known you as you are, I love what I feel"—he squeezes at the fleshy pooch—"You're sexy as hell, sugar."

He continues moving down my body, slipping both his hands between my legs, and forcing me to spread my legs wider, like a burlesque dancer on a thin chair. His hands cover where I'm warm and damp. Then Sebastian is fisting the skirt portion of my dress and lazily scrunching up the material, like the rising curtain on a Broadway show. I'm the main attraction and when his hand brushes over my underwear, wet with desire, it's like the spotlight flipped on. I'm center stage.

"Getting eager, baby?" he teases, smiling against my neck while I squirm against the heat of his palm covering me.

When his fingers skitter over my soaked underwear, I flinch. Like when the first spark of rock against rock sparks, a crackle, a hint of flame, a tease that warmth is coming.

I sharply inhale, relieved by the sensation while eager for the full effect of fire.

"Still okay?" Sebastian wraps one arm around my middle, locking me in place while he peppers my neck with kisses. His other hand skims down my thigh to my knee before slowly gliding back along my inner leg. He squeezes at tight muscles, tugging my legs open a little wider.

My breathing is ragged. My heart hammers. I don't know what to do with my hands, so I clasp his thighs and relax into his chest. Tilting my head against one of his shoulders, I turn my face toward his.

"What do you want, sugar?" His voice is all seduction and promises of pleasure.

"Touch me," I beg.

He rushes his finger to my center, tickling over my panties once more before pushing them aside and delicately stroking over sensitive folds and slick skin.

"Pure fire," he exhales into my neck. "My flame." Praise fills his voice as his fingers lightly caress, tenderly teasing. It's like stage lights narrowing in, following the curves and twirls of a dancer.

I'm breathless.

"Did you think about me when you tried on your own?"

"I did." My answer is one long exhale of admission.

"But it didn't work." His voice is strong, confirming. Almost emphasizing, of course it didn't work on my own. He completes me. "Our imagination is never as good as the real thing."

He hums near my ear. "Because I've imagined touching you a million times, but nothing I dreamed up compared to how this feels. How *you* feel, soaked and needy against my fingers."

"Oh God," I whimper, as he brushes over the sensitive nub, triggering me to curl forward and clench at his thighs.

"Ah," he groans. The sly bastard knows exactly what he's touched, and the intensity of his fingers increases, circling and flicking. Picking up the pace and deepening the pressure.

"More," I beg.

"I'm trying to be patient, sugar. Tender." He peppers my neck with whisper soft kisses. "But it's so fucking hard, Enya. *I'm* fucking hard."

I shift so my backside rubs the firm wedge in his jeans. I hadn't considered how much I might turn him on. We've been playing cat and mouse with our attraction, and he's repeatedly rejected me. But there's no missing the hard, firm length in his pants, trapped but eager to be released.

"Sugar," he warns as I swipe my backside against him, seeking friction there as well.

"I need you." With my fingertips digging into his thighs, I shamelessly lay myself bare to him. *I need him.*

His fingers work their magic, taking me higher, making me wired. In a frenzy of desire, my hips thrust. His fingers dance. I'm out of control. My insides have gone from a fluttering stir to an arousing spiral.

"Sebastian," I moan, arching my back, seeking his hard shaft at my backside and rocking against his fingers. He dips one inside me, and we both moan. When he pulls back, the echo of my excitement whispers around us. This is the crescendo. A singer gearing up for that long vibrato, holding a tune and projecting outward.

Sebastian circles my clit once and then rushes inward with two fingers this time.

My throat rumbles. A low moan escapes, as my channel clenches around them, gripping them, milking them. With my hands on his thighs, I roll forward, pulling his fingers deeper into me.

"Baby," he groans over my shoulder. "Look at you."

His seductive praise has me glancing down to where he's touching me, watching where his fingers slide into me. With my legs spread wide and my dress draped over my hips, the stage is set. I'm going to release the biggest orgasm I've ever had. I can already feel it building.

"That's right. This pretty pussy wants me. *Me*," he growls.

"You. All of you." I whimper, knowing I've never been this turned on, this desperate for anyone.

But it's not just anyone. It's Sebastian, a man who has been nothing but kindness and comfort. He's my hero again, in a new way, in a way where I shouldn't confuse physical attraction with emotional connection.

Still, I am connected to him, drawn to him, and what he's doing to me is blurring the lines he's tried too hard to set between us.

"That's it, baby. Look at that pretty pussy taking my fingers." He groans before nipping my neck.

I'm lost in the bliss of his encouragement. My lower half rocks, taking his fingers, giving him a show.

When his thumb swipes over my clit, my legs threaten to snap together but Sebastian has a firm hold on my thigh, keeping my legs spread.

The resonance of my excitement sings before me.

My breath hitches as he presses over my clit with his thumb. Again and again, he strums, finding the rhythm that will push me over the edge. He moves as if he knows my body. He's as familiar with me as I am with myself. He's even better.

Clutching his denim-clad thighs, I tip back my head, thrust my hips forward, and let go. A strained wail floats up my throat and out my open mouth as I come with my legs wide open, my center dripping.

I'm a rain shower, sprinkling down to the stage as the singer hits her final note.

Spent, I sag backward into Sebastian's chest. My head drops to his shoulder, and he peppers me with more kisses, up and down the column of my throat. I drift downward from the high, slowly loosening my hold on his legs. My breathing restores to a slower tempo.

But I'm ready for an encore.

I want one more song. One more performance.

I want more of Sebastian.

We're a flame that's only starting to flicker. I want the inferno that will burn us to the ground.

Sebastian tenderly withdraws his fingers and lifts them to his mouth, sucking them between his lips. He hums near my ear. "Fuck, baby, I knew you'd taste like pure sugar."

His words inspire me, and I slide off the couch, boneless as I lower to my knees. Then I spin to face him.

"Enya?" His brows lift, his eyes widening in surprise. I grip the waist band of his jeans and tug him forward, wanting him to lean back into the cushions and let me have my way with him.

I need to taste him. Is he sweet? Or tangy. Or salty and fresh.

I have the button undone and my fingers on the tab of his zipper when Adara lets out a squawk.

No. *No, no, no, no* . . . I need to reciprocate. For all this man has done, I want to make him feel good, special, important to me. Worthy. He deserves my gratitude. He deserves love.

He needs to be the highlight of tonight's show.

"Please," I cry.

"Baby." Sebastian cups the side of my face. "Tonight was all about you."

He claims he's been mesmerized by me. He's enthralled with me, but I'm the one trapped under Sebastian's spell. I'm the one desperate to show him how good we could be . . . together.

I'll never be the same. I'll never want anyone like I want him.

"But I want to—" I tug at the waist band of his jeans.

Adara makes another squeak, the recognizable sound hints she's winding up for a full-blown cry.

Sebastian softly chuckles and bows his head. "She needs you, baby."

I need him.

Not just for sexual healing but for everything else I know he could offer me. Offer us. He'd be a wonderful life partner and a perfect father.

The thought has me loosening my hold on his pants and falling back on my heels. These aren't new musings. Sebastian has been here for me, here for us.

I want him to know I'm here for him.

Leaning forward, his kiss is deep with a strong thrust of his tongue and a sharp nip of my lower lip before Adara's cry steals the show.

Sebastian rests his forehead against mine. "You get her. I need a minute and then I'll finish making dinner."

Dinner. One more positive checkmark on the list of all things Sebastian. With my measly kitchen offerings, he's making me a meal because I'd been hungry and crabby. And then he did this. He took care of me again, when I was afraid I might be broken.

When I thought I'd never feel desired again.

And I very much want to share my blooming desire with Sebastian Sylver.

I'd also like to steal a sliver of his heart.

Chapter 22

[Enya]

After taking care of Adara, I lead Sebastian to my bedroom where we'll be a little more comfortable than pressed together on my couch. However, we curl around one another through hours of broken sleep, just breathing each other in, and remaining silent about the line we've breached.

He takes the three a.m. feeding like he's done for the past few days and then slips out for the bakery.

His kiss was incredible. His touch out of this world. The unleashed attraction between us burned like wildfire, like I knew it would. But I still can't get a few things out of my head, like how Sebastian thinks he doesn't deserve love. He doesn't want a family. And I shouldn't push either on him.

Love and family are my dreams. Still, I can't help wanting Sebastian to be part of my fantasy and that's just stupid. He's been very clear on his stance.

I've convinced myself he touched me because he felt sorry for me. He did what a friend might do, only the thought of being friends with benefits with Sebastian sours my stomach. I'm not cut out for casual relationships. Lance and I were together for eleven years because I'm a commitment kind of girl. I want forever, not just-for-tonight.

With these thoughts in mind, I need to get out of the house.

Vale is my savior today with her invitation to the women-only, bi-monthly book club. She told me no one would mind if I brought a baby, especially as little ears won't understand naughty words. She also told me few people will have read the assigned book for this month's meeting. With a wink, she said wine and womanhood would be the main topic. I'd feel guilty attending if I wasn't so eager to be away from my house for a few hours.

Late afternoon, the summer sun is still high in the sky. I park in the public lot before moseying down Corner Street with Adara in her stroller.

The streets of Corner and Main are no longer a driving thru-way, but a bricked passage intersecting the two roads. We wander into the clothing store, check out the furniture place, and step into a mercantile with local fare promoting Sterling Falls. I've yet to visit the famous waterfall but plan to make a trip when Adara is a bit older.

After exhausting all the stores, I second-guess myself before deciding a trip to the bakery is in order. I could use some lemon cake goodness after dinner. I'm treating myself to dinner at the diner before book club.

The soft jingle of the bell announces our arrival and I struggle with the door before someone seated near the front window jumps up to assist me.

"Thank you, kind sir," I tease the rugged man who nearly fills the space. Our eyes catch for a second. With sandy brown hair and a thick beard, he's strikingly handsome, but the polite smile he offers in return doesn't reach his dark eyes, and a strange chill runs down my spine. I dismiss the tremor as a shift from the heated afternoon to the air-conditioned bakery.

Once inside, I press the stroller forward, watching Rena slam the cash drawer beneath the countertop shut. She quickly buries her hand in the pocket of her folded-over apron before smoothing down the pouch, as if securing something inside.

At my approach, her head snaps upward and a clenched-teeth grin hardens her expression. "Hey. Enya, right?"

I tilt my head. She knows darn well what my name is. I lived above this bakery for weeks after Adara's birth.

"Rena, right?" I joke while playfully pointing at her in hopes to soften the edgy vibe she gives off.

She offers a sharp chuckle before asking, "What can I get for you?" After a short pause, she adds. "Sebastian isn't here." Her eyes narrow, like she's telling me the one item on the menu she can't offer me is him, but I ignore the ridge of hostility around her. I have no doubt she's infatuated with her boss. *Who wouldn't?* Lemon cake and Sebastian Sylver all day? The fantasies I'd have if I worked here . . . Then again, my imagination works overtime without being an employee, especially since I've had Sebastian's touch.

The nip of his teeth along my neck. The suction of his mouth against my skin. The tease of his fingers and then the pleasurable tension of their full length. I shiver again at the memory.

"I'm only here to spoil my appetite before dinner. I'll take two lemon baby-Bundt cakes, please." Might as well stock up.

Rena swiftly moves to the glass display case and tugs the tray toward her to remove two mini cakes. If I weren't watching her, I'd lay money on her dropping drool or spitting on them. However, she can't seem to move fast enough. The cakes are boxed and rung up with nimble fingers. Then she shoves the container into a bag while I tap my credit card against the payment machine.

"Have a nice day." The salutation is said through gritted teeth.

Puzzled, I take the bag she offers and spin for the door. As I press the stroller forward, the man near the window hops up again and opens the door for me. I'm almost to the exit when the rumble of feet descending wooden stairs whispers through the bakery and then the door to Sebastian's apartment opens.

"Enya?"

Rena said he was out, but he was upstairs? With my fingers clenching the stroller and my back to him, I close my eyes a second to level my composure, still my voice is too high when I twist my upper body and say, "Hey."

Sebastian's gaze drifts between me and the man standing close to my side, holding open the door. He takes quick steps toward us before stopping and glancing down at Adara who is wide-eyed and fixated on the soft lights overhead.

"Were you going to sneak out before saying hello?" He lifts his gaze to me, brows pinched, side-eyeing the man beside me again.

"Rena said you were out." She was clearly covering for him because seconds after Sebastian entered the bakery, a woman exits the privacy door of his apartment. She's dressed in sleek business attire, with a dark pink pencil skirt and a black blouse that accentuates her breasts, crossing low between them. Her arms are on full display as the shirt cuts off at the shoulders.

Sebastian glances back at her and tips up his chin in a non-verbal sign for her to give him a second. Then he turns back to me. "So, you ladies out for a walk?" His voice holds not a drop of strain or shame that I'm witnessing a woman leaving his apartment.

After last night with him.

The reminder is further confirmation that he did what he did because he feels sorry for me. I'm a single mother concerned I'll never have sex again, or at the very least an orgasm. He proved I could. With him. But apparently, his skills are being used on others, and suddenly, I can't get out of the bakery fast enough.

"Just stopping in for lemon cake." False lightness continues to fill my voice as my gaze catches on the woman waiting near Sebastian's apartment door, obviously needing his attention. "And you're busy."

Pushing the stroller forward, I realize the poor customer has been standing here, holding the door, as well as being a witness to this awkward interaction. Too embarrassed to meet his eyes, I mutter, "Thank you."

Sebastian catches my forearm. "Wait," he grumbles while his eyes search my face.

"You're . . . busy," I repeat. And I don't have time for games.

Lance led me through a guessing game most of our relationship. *When will I be first for him? When will we marry? When will we have kids?* He made it clear none of those things were ever going to happen. At least, not between us.

Sebastian owed me nothing.

I was the foolish one. Again.

Moving forward, I nod at the gentleman still holding the door and tip the stroller to aid it over the threshold. Once on the sidewalk, I take a deep breath. Another shiver ripples down my back as I sense I'm being watched, but I'm uncertain if it's the kind customer or the curmudgeon baker. Either way, I don't look back.

Almost to the corner, the door to the bakery opens with a tinkle of its distinctive bell and heavy footfalls thud along the sidewalk behind me. Sebastian rounds the stroller, firmly planting himself in my path.

"Sugar." He pauses and nods toward the bakery. "What was that about?"

"You tell me? Rena said you were out when you were obviously in . . . and clearly occupied upstairs." It's not my business if he's with someone else. I'd be with someone else, too, if I were him.

Still, I'm hurt. And confused. His actions today prove how much of an idiot I am to think I am anyone special to him.

Sebastian leans forward, stretching his arms over Adara's seat and placing his hands on the stroller handle over mine. "That woman is Judd's assistant. My books aren't adding up. You've seen my office. I keep everything but I have a messy filing system. Sometimes Judd and I argue about my bookkeeping skills, and we clash. He sent Sarah in his place today. I'd taken a file box upstairs. She wanted to look through the receipts in it."

"Oh." Suddenly, I feel foolish for overreacting but still . . . "She's very pretty."

Sebastian pushes off the stroller to stand straighter and crosses his arms. "She's also fucking smart, like you."

With my head still bowed forward, I press my fingernail into the soft cover of the stroller handle. I can feel Sebastian focused on me, but I refuse to look up at him. I'm botching up whatever this is between us by overthinking everything.

He bends his knees and dips his head. "Enya, you're my number one."

My head snaps upward. "Why?" I blink, glance left, then look back at him, searching his face for answers. "Why are we friends?" The question echoes, drawing attention from people on the opposite side of the street. Lowering my voice, I add, "You can stop feeling sorry for me."

"I don't feel sorry for you." Sebastian drops his arms, stretching out his fingers near his thighs. "What did I say last night?"

He said a lot of things, calling sacred body parts pretty and me baby. "I told you I'm interested."

"Interested in what, Sebastian? Hanging out with the single mom who doesn't have any friends? Playing dad when you don't want to be a father?" I sound pathetic. I am pathetic. I've made so many mistakes. Put my faith in so many misguided directions. Then I glance down at Adara and remind myself I've done one thing right. Her. The two of us.

Sterling Falls is the promise of a new chapter where I write the storyline, and falling for a man who doesn't want commitment is not part of my plot again.

"Never mind," I murmur, angling the stroller to walk around him. "I'm taking myself to dinner."

"Yes," he blurts.

I stumble to a stop causing him to stand beside the stroller. He sets his hand on the side bar, holding the stroller in place, but he's gripping it like it might be holding him up.

"Yes. I want to hang out with the single mom. Not because she has no friends but because she's *my* friend. And hopefully, more." His voice drops rougher, raspy. "*I* don't have many friends. And she's . . . you're . . . one of the best people I know. One of the best I've ever known."

"Sebastian," I whisper.

"You're always thanking me, but I should be thanking you. For whatever reason, you fell in front of my bakery."

An embarrassed chuckle bursts from me.

"Fate. God. A UFO. I don't care how you got there." He nods behind me, where feet away from where we stand, I stumbled on my heels and fell on my backside that rainy fall day. "I'm just thankful you're here."

He exhales heavily. "And yes, that means I also want to share in Adara's life."

He licks his lips, closes his eyes a second and turns his head side to side, cracking his neck. "I don't know what that looks like. How to label it." He swallows hard, like he can't find an alternative word for father or dad. "But I want to be here for her. For both of you, in any way you'll have me."

My shoulders relax while my grip on the stroller tightens. I don't want to focus on what he's *not* saying, but what he is. "So what does this mean? For all of us?" Because Adara and I are a package deal.

"I'd like to try." He pauses again. "I want to try *us*. Together." He gives a quick glance toward Adara before looking up at me. A thousand words flicker through his blue eyes, filled with desire for me to understand their meaning when I can't read as fast as the emotions shift through his gaze.

I want to be here for him, too. We can take it one emotion at a time.

"Okay," I whisper, still uncertain what this means for my heart or my future. Or for Adara. Trying isn't rejection, though. And Sebastian and I both have felt stepped out on enough to know trying means so much more than walking away.

"Okay," Sebastian sighs. Relief is the final emotion filling his face. He steps closer to me, brushing at a loose hair and running the back of his knuckles along the column of my throat. "Permission to kiss you in public?"

I chuckle at the reminder of me asking him if I could enter his private domain behind the customer counter.

"Permission granted." My throat fills with giddy anticipation but I'm still unprepared for the intensity of his kiss. His hand cups the side of my neck as his mouth meets my lips. Then his other hand slips into the hair at my nape. While his mouth moves over mine, he holds me like I'm fragile, precious, important to him.

I'm his number one.

He's tied with Adara for first place with me.

The kiss is tender but demanding, imparting on me the effort he's willing to put into us.

When he finally draws back, my eyes remain closed a second and he runs his nose along the side of mine. "Now, you mentioned dinner." He slips his hand around the back of my neck and squeezes. "Where are we going?"

"*I* was going to the diner." I chuckle.

"Then the diner it is." Sebastian releases my neck and turns for the stroller, nudging me out of the way with a light hip check. He straightens his arms and holds his head high as he proudly pushes the stroller with me at his side.

"Sugar?"

"Yeah," I say as we cross the street.

"I can't push this one handed and hold your hand, so could you do me a favor?"

"Sure."

"Slip your arm around me."

Yeah, he's trying to make a statement.

We're together, for everyone to see.

+ + +

During dinner, we discuss Sebastian's accounting issues.

"Over the past six weeks, I've been off in my nightly closeout. Five dollars here. Ten dollars there. None of it is making sense but it's adding up to quite a bit."

"Is there something you'd like me to look at?" Accounting is my field while basic bookkeeping is a different beast. Still, I'm good with numbers and need to get back into the groove. I've given myself twelve-weeks of maternity leave, but I'm torn between how much I love being home with Adara and the desire to stretch my mind a little bit. Most days, I've been in too much of a fog to concentrate on anything heavy like spread sheets, but I'll need to return to work eventually. I'm halfway through my time off.

"Nah. I'll let Judd tackle it. That's what I pay him the big bucks for. And by big bucks, I mean a stock of his favorite cookies and an occasional drink."

"Speaking of drinks, I'm headed to Vale's book club tonight." I check the time on my watch. Adara has been great throughout our meal, but I'm worried she'll gear up for a break down during the book club. I

192

don't want to distract others with her crying. I'm also hesitant to play pass the baby with a bunch of women I'm meeting for the first time.

"Do you have a babysitter?"

"I'm taking her with me." From my position across the table from Adara, I give her a loving gaze. Sebastian set the car seat beside him on the booth bench during dinner, but he took her out of the carrier to hold her.

"Why don't you let me take her?"

"Oh, I can't ask you to do that."

"You didn't ask. I asked you. I can take her to my place." He pauses as we both run through a mental check list of all the items he doesn't have at his place to accommodate a baby. "Or I could take her to yours. You take your time and come home when you're ready."

"I don't know . . ." I chew my lower lip.

"I get it, if you don't trust me." Hurt fills his eyes while he tries to keep his voice level.

I snort. "Don't trust you? Are you kidding? You've done more for me than anyone I know. Of course, I trust you with Adara. It's just . . . are you sure you want to keep doing this? Always stepping up and helping us out?"

Sebastian presses a kiss to Adara's head. Offering one of those sweet moments he doesn't realize he takes with her. "Did I not just announce to the town that you're with me?" His blue eyes light up again.

"Yeah, but . . ."

"No but." He tips his head to address Adara. "We're going to let your mommy head to the book club where she hopefully won't be too unholy."

I laugh. "How am I going to be unholy at a book club?"

"You know where the club is held, right?"

"I have an address. Vale told me it's above The Knitting Shed."

Sebastian huffs. "The She Shed," he corrects. "It once said Sheep Shed but the -ep was removed and now reads She Shed."

"Vale told me it's a knit shop."

"It's a front." Sebastian wiggles his brows.

"What?" I laugh.

"You'll see." He presses his lips to Adara's head but watches me. There's a playful gleam in his eyes that causes me to shiver in a new way. A better way. Because Sebastian's attention is fully on me and I'm trying to accept he might mean it.

I'm with him.

My gaze lowers to Adara.

We're both his.

Chapter 23

[Enya]

Hours later I've learned what Sebastian meant about the local book club. The She Shed sells yarn and knitting supplies downstairs, but the store is a front for another money maker on the second floor. Out of her home, Meredith Mulligan, a sixty-nine-year-old woman, sells a variety of adult toys and lingerie.

"A woman cannot live off yarn alone," Meredith teased before explaining the titillating benefits of a new item she'd received.

Vale told me that the book club rotated to keep things interesting, and tonight was Meredith's turn. A book might have been assigned, but nothing literary was discussed. Wine and women's intimate apparel was the topic of conversation, along with the line of vibrators and stimulators up for purchase.

"You're officially a Sterlet," Vale toasts me.

"A what?" I laugh.

"A member of the book club. It's a play-off the word starlet. For *Ster*ling Falls."

My chest warms from wine and a night out with this silly woman who has quickly become a friend.

"What happens here, stays here." Vale winks before someone bumps into me.

"Trinity?" I'm pleased to recognize the curvy blonde nurse who was once assigned to Adara in the NICU.

"Well, this is awkward." She lifts a dark purple dildo in her hand.

"I'm so happy to see you again," I say, trying to ignore the eggplant-looking item. "Thank you one more time for all your help with Adara."

Trinity waves the sex toy to dismiss my gratitude. "How is that sweet baby? Better question is, how is her daddy? He treating both his girls right?" She wiggles her brows, giving me a knowing grin. As in, she might know Sebastian is not Adara's father.

Vale wraps her arm around me and with false sternness admonishes Trinity. "Trin, you know my brothers are off the table."

Trinity shakes her head. "Men are so stupid." Holding up the purple fake phallus, she shakes it again. "Thus, the need for these things."

I chuckle and reach for her wrist. "It was so great to see you."

"Welcome to the Sterlets. One day we might actually read a book." A teasing smile brightens her face but also suggests she's kidding. This book club doesn't read. When she walks away, I turn to Vale.

"Why are your brothers a touchy subject, other than most of them are hot, and single."

Vale exaggerates a full body shiver. "Hot-headed is more like it, but there's a cold war between the Sylvers and the Havens. It's just stupid, small town, long-time ago stuff. Stuff that should rest in the past where it belongs. Our two families were once best friends. Now . . ." Vale gets a faraway look in her eyes for a second before lifting her glass of wine and emptying it in one long drink.

She shrugs. "In public, Trinity and I don't acknowledge one another, but during book club, we hold a truce."

Vale winks like the dirty book club is a secret society and not a bunch of small-town women looking for an excuse to get out of the house every other week.

"Want more wine?" She nods at my empty hand. I shake my head. One glass was enough.

I'm curious what the cold war involves and if it has anything to do with Sebastian, but I don't ask. Anything I need to know I want to come from him. He has suggested the abuse from his father and explained his poor decisions as a teen. He even admitted how he killed someone, but I'm not afraid of him. Like I told him the other night, physical damage isn't a concern. My heart is the organ that's in danger.

When I finally return home, I'm on a high from that glass of wine and time among women who were friendly and funny. My cheeks hurt from laughing.

Once again, I remind myself I made the right decision in moving to Sterling Falls and I have more than one Sylver to thank.

Vale is welcoming and sweet. "Don't take any shit from my brother," she'd warned me before I left. "He's a good guy at heart, he just doesn't want to believe it. Stay strong." She raises her fist in solidarity. She acts as if her brother and I are an item. As if we have a future, when right now, we're more like an exploration mission.

I don't dwell on these thoughts, though, as I walk up my front porch. Once inside the house, I find Sebastian stretched out on my couch with Adara snuggled on his chest. A mental snapshot clicks, stashing this moment where his big hands are spread over her tiny tush, and her legs are tucked up to her belly, her head sideways, listening to his heartbeat. Her eyes are sweetly closed, mouth slightly agape. I'll store this memory like so many others and wish for things I have no right wishing for with this man.

He said he's willing to try but I still don't know what that would look like. What that means for any of us. Will Adara call him uncle one day? The term doesn't feel special enough for who he is in our lives. Will he continue to be our friend as she grows? He said he wants to be here.

The questions are too heavy for the lightened mood I'm in, and I'm not willing to let momentary melancholy trample the good time I've had tonight.

Instead, I step forward and attempt to scoop Adara off Sebastian. Instantly, he awakens and tightens his hold on her.

"Hey," I whisper as he stares up at me all blurry-eyed and sleepy as I lean over him.

"I didn't mean to fall asleep." His head tips downward as he double-checks that Adara is still securely on his chest.

"You must be exhausted from waking up at three each morning and then heading to the bakery so early."

"It's no big deal. I don't mind." His voice is groggy while it's evident his mind is still in a fog.

"Let me take her," I gently suggest.

He leans toward her head, kissing it like he does. "Sweet dreams, pretty girl."

He's sweet and my heart can't take it.

I lift Adara and step toward the staircase. Glancing back, Sebastian remains on the couch, body stretched down the length. His eyes are still dazed, but he's watching my retreat. He looks comfortable, and I should leave him where he is. He needs sleep.

But I can't seem to help myself.

"Joining us?" I nod toward the staircase, implying my room which I currently share with Adara.

He continues to stare at me, maybe not fully awake. Maybe not wanting to move.

Then he scrubs his hands down his face and hitches himself upright. He presses off the couch and wordlessly crosses the room toward us. He places his hand on my lower back and kisses my temple.

I secretly smile that he'll stay a while.

If only it were forever.

+ + +

Once upstairs, Sebastian collapses face first on the bed, and I prepare myself for another sleep-deprived night. He fed Adara a bottle while I was gone so it isn't time to nurse her yet.

Slipping underneath the covers, I'm careful not to disturb Sebastian who has fallen on top of the blankets, fully dressed. His feet hang off the end of the bed and his arms are tucked underneath a pillow as he lays on his stomach. His head is turned so he faces the window, not my pillow.

For a moment, the scent of vanilla and man wafts through my nose. My fingers itch to trace down his back and slip beneath his shirt but I don't want to disturb him.

"Sweet dreams, Sebastian," I whisper, certain he's already inside his nightly imagination.

Startling me, he turns his head on the pillow, so he faces me. "I *was* having the sweetest dream." His voice is rugged and sexy, causing my lady bits to vibrate.

"Really?" I keep my voice low. "What were you dreaming about?"

He hums as his body shifts to mirror mine. "How was your night?"

Nice topic change. "Very . . . stimulating."

Sebastian chuckles. "You're officially a Sterling Falls citizen once you've learned our dirty little secret."

"Vale told me I'm officially a Sterlet." Pride fills my voice. I haven't been part of a club since college. I'm pretty certain the accounting club does not compare to this small-town book club.

"I don't think you're supposed to tell me that." His husky voice teases me.

"Oops. Well, I'm honored to be included."

His gaze falls to my mouth. "Buy anything?"

My face heats and I'm grateful for the dim light in my room. "Maybe."

Sebastian props up on his elbow, startling me with the sudden movement. "Oh yeah? Tell me about it." His voice suggests he's suddenly awake.

"Tell me about your dream," I counter.

"How about if I show you instead?" The seduction in his voice dissolves all playfulness. The air suddenly crackles.

Sebastian's fingertips tenderly flirt with the cleavage peeking above the tank top I'm wearing over my nursing bra. He traces over the heavy swells, not fully palming them, though, and my nipples tighten.

Quickly, he lowers his hand for my belly and brushes the fitted shirt upward exposing my flesh. With my hand, I cover the subtle roll still present.

"Don't do that," he whispers, leaning closer to run his nose along mine.

"I look like a truck ran over my belly."

"You had a baby, and that's beautiful. *You're* beautiful."

Goodness. This man.

With silent swiftness, he crawls over my lower body, gently forcing me to my back, and tugs at the waistband of my pajama shorts. Taking my underwear with it, he undresses me with care, like someone taking their time to unwrap a present so they don't rip the wrapping paper. Slowly, he unveils my thighs and knees, ankles and feet.

"You're so fucking gorgeous," he mutters in awe as his hands cover the tops of my feet and he slides his palms upward, rubbing over my shins and cupping the back of my knees. My legs are quickly spread apart.

Sebastian continues, skimming my inner thighs, kneading my flesh. A tender press pushes my thighs even wider, exposing me to him. The blue in his eyes ignites to bright flames.

"Tell me about tonight, sugar. What did you purchase? What did you learn?"

Completely under his spell while his hands massage my inner thighs, moving closer to my center but not quite touching me where I want him most, I struggle to speak. "I bought . . . this thing . . . that finds my G-spot."

"Like this?" Two fingers enter me with a gentle shove, exploring, discovering, until I gasp.

Sweet lemon cakes, that feels amazing.

Too soon, he withdraws his fingers but stares down at where they exited my body. "Keep talking."

"It has a rabbit ear, that touches my—" I suck in air as his two fingers return inside me like a tender exam while his thumb presses on my clit.

"Like this?" He's teasing me now, knowing full well where the device can reach and what it does. Withdrawing his fingers once more and releasing my trigger point sets off another whimper from me.

"Want me to use that toy on you tonight, baby?"

Yes. But I also want him. His skin meeting mine. His fingers touching me. The connection is more intimate.

"Or can I use my mouth instead."

Groaning, I swallow, incapable of forming coherent words. I can't remember the last time someone kissed me down there.

"Think your new toy can do this?" Sebastian lowers his head between my thighs and with one thick lap of his tongue, swipes up my slit. My hips buck upward, chasing his mouth.

He chuckles before blowing on sensitive folds. "Tell me my mouth is better."

"Your mouth is better," I moan as my hands splay over my belly, fingers tickling my flesh as I glide them closer to my core.

Sebastian claps a hand over mine, trapping them in place so I can't touch myself. "Tell me you're mine."

"Yours," I groan as his tongue licks over me once more. *I always want to be his.*

Sebastian holds still a second at the strength in my voice. The conviction. I belong to him, but he belongs to me.

"Tell me you trust me." His voice drops, ragged, raw.

"I trust you. Always."

Tension vibrates off his body, ricocheting between my thighs.

"I can't promise to go slow tonight but I promise I'll never hurt you." His mouth is suddenly moving, sipping tender folds, and tonguing sensitive creases. He nips at my clit before sucking at the nub. Then his tongue returns, kissing me, caressing me, driving me mad.

I chew at my lips, holding back mews and moans of pleasure, so I don't disturb Adara.

Sebastian removes his hand from where it covered mine and pins my thighs to the bed instead. I dig my fingers into his hair. My thumbs swipe around the shell of his earlobes while his tongue draws along my slit. He shifts and two fingers easily enter me as his tongue moves to my clit, twirling in such a way, I'm frozen in bliss.

With an intensity I didn't think could surpass last night, a ripple rushes through my middle, like water falling over a ledge, pummeling to a pool below. The crash bubbles. The roar suppressed by my teeth digging into my lower lip. I don't know if I can hold back the scream. Like a dam collecting water, the pressure is too great. I'm breaking.

Sebastian is relentless, pulling the sensitive nub toward him, tugging at me, drawing out the pleasure. His hands cup the back of my thighs, lifting my legs, as he starts savoring me, slurping at me like a treasured dish. A man thirsting for something he's never drank before.

His. Trust. Love.

"Again," he commands at soaked flesh and dripping folds. His mouth moves with ease as his fingers toy with me. "Tell me again, I'm—"

"You're mine." I quietly cry, needing him to know if I'm his, he's mine. "No one has ever touched me like you. Made me feel like you do."

The words sound like praise talk during sexy times, but the truth is laced within them.

Sebastian Sylver is ruining me. There will be no other man after him. I only want him.

Now. Later. Forever.

His tongue continues ferociously feasting, like a beast unleashed and allowed to eat after a famine. Sebastian's entire life has been a dry-spell, and I want to feed his soul, warm his heart, prove to him he's so much more than he thinks he is.

He sucks at my core. *My God, his tongue.* I'm a slippery mess. A blend of fingers and lips, and that glorious tongue. Quickly, I'm cresting again. That river about to barrel over the edge and fall into a canyon, slowing filling with crystal clear water. Because at the heart of this rush is love.

I see it. I feel it. I love Sebastian. And I know he could love me.

Fuck, I silently cry in my head as my body curls forward and my thighs clamp together, caging in his head. The second crest equals the intensity of the first, and after a long, hard rush and then a slow drifting sensation, I float back to the bed, replete and spent.

Sebastian slowly relents, pressing kisses to my core before moving to my inner thighs and brushing his moist lips over my skin.

I take a moment to catch my breath because tonight I will not retreat from pleasuring him.

Chapter 24

[Sebastian]

With strength I wouldn't have expected from her, Enya sits upright and presses on my shoulders, forcing me to my back. Quickly, she scrambles over me, unbuckling my jeans and tugging them downward. She doesn't fully remove them, and I'm relieved she doesn't take the time. I'm so fucking hard, her breath is going to set me off.

When her hand wraps around my dick, my hips buck off the bed. I bite my tongue to prevent crying out and waking Adara. Thoughts of her have me turning my head in the direction of the bassinet. I have some strong feelings about that little munchkin, but if she wakes up right now, I'm going to lose it.

Enya's mouth is a sudden distraction. She kisses the tip of my stiff shaft, which leaks, almost crying for more attention. She swipes her tongue over the slit at the same time she squeezes at the hard length in her hand.

"Fuck, that feels so good," I groan, tipping back my head while reaching for Enya's hair. Scooping the silky length around my fist, I tug the rough twist to the back of her neck. While I would not mind her hair cascading over me, draping over my thighs and curtaining my belly I want to see her taking me between her lips.

Opening wide and drawing me to the back of her throat, she doesn't disappoint. Not that I thought she ever would. From the moment I met her, she's been a wet dream. A fantasy filling my nights while I clutched myself in my own fist.

Enya shifts, swallowing my length before dragging her mouth to the crown. Teasing. Tempting. She's a siren. A playful vixen who is going to wreck me in the best way.

"Sugar," I quietly growl, tightening my hold on her hair. With my head tipping forward, I watch her bob up and down, drawing me into the cavern of her mouth. This is going to be embarrassing because I'm not going to last long.

Months of only memories since that first kiss. Weeks of her nearness but not touching her. Only twenty-four hours since that reuniting kiss. Another few hours from promising I'd try at us.

Us. Her and me.

My balls draw up, distracting me. My back tightens as the pressure builds faster, weighs heavier. I can't stop the spiral.

"Enya," I warn, tugging at her hair to pull her back, afraid I'm going to be too much, too soon.

Only she claps one hand underneath my ass, squeezing at the flexed globe and holding me firmly in place as she sucks me until I have no choice but to release down her throat.

My head falls back, eyes wide but unfocused on the ceiling. My body drains of pent-up desire.

I'm floating in this rush. Swimming in this abyss. Willing to drown in whatever is happening to me.

Is this love? I refuse to believe it's only lust.

Slowly, Enya pulls up my spent dick, swirling her tongue around the crown once more before tenderly kissing the tip. She shifts, and kisses the crook of my leg, where it meets my balls. Then she skims her nose along the V of my hip. I'm going to get a tattoo there to remember this moment.

Her movements are almost as invigorating as her tasting me. The action feels intimate, worshipful.

Could she love me?

My head screams to push her away. I'm not someone she should love.

My heart, however, hammers, begging me to ask her to *never* stop. I want to feel like this forever.

I'm blissed out, I argue. The euphoria of an orgasm. The argument doesn't hold, though.

Enya is better than any dopamine high. She's like some rare, unique drug, specific only to her. The way she looks at me, like I could be her everything. The way she thanks me all the fucking time, but she's genuine. The way her body works with mine, making me feel like a man reborn.

I lift both my hands and rub the heels against my eyes.

What is this woman doing to me?

A tiny squawk reminds us we aren't alone. Adara holds a special place in my heart as well.

Love is too much to hope for and I'm relieved when Enya sits back, eyeing the bassinet. Her hair is wild over her shoulders. Her lips swollen. While I can't touch those tits, they look plump and delicious. Seeing her straddle my body has my dick twitching to life again.

Then her head hangs, hair cascading forward to curtain her face. "So much for post-coital cuddling." The terms are so formal for someone only moments ago talking about her G-spot and sucking at my dick.

Still, I chuckle and drape an arm over my eyes, closing them in the bend of my elbow. I don't know if I can move. I'm wiped out.

Enya climbs over me and exits the bed, cooing at Adara. Removing my arm and turning my head, I see Enya has slipped on her pajama shorts. I should pull up my pants. Instead, I stand and remove all my clothes minus my boxer briefs.

"Need to clean up?" I don't know about cuddles, but I'm a caretaker after sex.

"I could use a second, but she looks ready to fuss."

"Give her to me," I say, reaching out for Adara while I circle the bed. "We'll take a walk downstairs. I need some water. Take your time."

Enya looks at me with dark eyes swirling with questions. I wish I had answers. I wish I could predict the future, instead of this living-in-the-moment attitude. She wants promises and I want to give them to her, but I don't know if I can.

For now, I promised I'd try. And I'd never hurt her.

That means I need to keep my feelings in check. My doubts aren't about her. They're about me.

And now isn't the time to tackle questions or fears. I'll be cuddling in a few minutes, which is another first. Then again, we have been snuggled up on her couch most nights this week.

I've liked it a little too much. I've become damn addicted to it, just like I'm addicted to her.

After a too-quick kiss to Enya, I tiptoe through the dark, quietly carrying Adara down to the kitchen. One handed, I reach for a glass then turn on the tap. Glancing out the window above the sink as the water from the faucet cools, I narrow my eyes and lean forward.

A light flickers in the distance. My perception can't distinguish if it's near the woods or closer to the house. Either way, whatever it is— *whomever* it is—is too close.

"Fuck," I mutter despite Adara in my arms.

I fill the glass and chug back the contents, never looking away from the beam of light sweeping side to side before disappearing.

Was that a flashlight? Was it headlights? What's going on out there? Or rather, *who* is out there?

Those woods and what once went down in them is all too familiar to me. An icy chill rolls down my spine, but Adara squeaks, returning my attention to her.

"I'll never let anything happen to you. Not to you, or your mom," I vow. Promises I intend to keep.

Kissing her head, I stare out the window another second, before turning back toward the stairs.

Even with the light no longer apparent, my confidence staggers. Old fears return.

There's trouble lingering in the darkness.

+ + +

When I wake before the three a.m. feeding, Enya is wrapped around me. I'm a stomach sleeper, so she's pressed into my side, one leg over mine and her arm securely over my lower back like I'm a giant body pillow. With Adara's nursing and me crashing in Enya's too-comfortable bed, we didn't officially post-coital cuddle last night.

The night rushes back to me. Falling asleep with Adara on my chest. Following Enya to her bedroom. I hadn't intended for a second round with her so soon after our first, but everyone knows about the Sterlets and that non-book club book club. I had to know if Enya made any purchases. Then I had to prove I was better than any plaything.

I want to be better in many ways.

Adara gurgles and coos from her bassinet, and Enya shifts, but I'm quick to catch her hand dangling over my side.

"Not yet," I mumble to the pillow, liking a little too much how right this woman feels against me, holding onto me.

Enya chuckles at my shoulder and I roll my head to face her. Her deep brown eyes hit me like sunshine on a cloudy day, lit only by the glow of a plug-in nightlight.

"Good morning," she whispers.

The sound of her voice makes me hard, and I'd love for it to be the best morning by greeting her body with mine. We aren't there yet, though, and I'm surprisingly okay with waiting. I've never taken my time with a woman like I've been doing with Enya. Never spent so much time with a woman, either. The slower pace is refreshing while frustrating. There's no doubt I want to fuck her. Take her rough and fast. Make both our heart rates rise and bodies sweat. However, I also want to feel every touch and whisper.

Her fingertips imprinted on my skin. Her kisses melting against my mouth. Her voice singing in my head.

I might be in over my head with her . . . and her baby girl.

Adara squawks louder and Enya groans. She'll move away from me in a second, so I take her in. Hair wild. Smile timid. Eyes bright despite the darkness. I drink her in, like a morning dose of caffeine to get me through the day.

After a quick kiss to my shoulder, she tugs her arm and I reluctantly release her, watching her roll away from me to pick up Adara.

I need to get out of this bed. I really need to stop spending the night. I shouldn't be here so much, but I can't seem to stay away. Being here feels strangely right.

After last night—both what we did and then what I saw out the window—I won't be staying away until I know Enya and Adara are safe living in this house.

Quit pretending, my heart pesters. I'd be here, danger or not.

Once I leave Enya's, I run through my morning ritual in my apartment, open the bakery, and rush through the early half of the day. Around lunchtime, I call Stone from my office.

"What's wrong?" The directness in answering tells me he read his caller I.D. and immediately assumed there's trouble if I'm calling him.

"Nothing's wrong." My defensiveness isn't going to help me get information, so I take a deep breath and try again. "As you know, I've been spending a lot of time with Enya."

"At the Wallace farmhouse."

"I think it might be time we switch ownership and call it Enya's place."

"So Enya's place . . ." Stone's pause encourages me to continue.

"About a week ago, Enya claimed she heard someone walking across her porch."

"Which people do on porches."

"Dammit, Stone. It was late and dark when that happened. That's the reason I'd left the bar when I was hanging out with Knox and Clay last Friday."

Stone's silence allows me to carry on.

"Then last night, I saw lights out toward the woods just after midnight. I couldn't tell if it was a flashlight or maybe a four-wheeler or a parked car." I lean back in my desk chair and stare up at the ceiling. "But I don't like it, and I wondered if you've heard anything, seen anything out there."

"What are you worried about? What might I find, Sebastian?"

That trouble isn't following me but found me again.

Slamming forward, I brace my elbows on my desk. "I don't know, Stone. You're the sheriff and that's why I'm calling you. If deals are going down out there again, it's a little too close to home."

"That home being Enya's place?" A slight tease fills my brother's voice.

"I'm fucking serious here," I snap, failing to find any humor in a potential situation.

A heavy silence fills the line and I swipe a hand down my face in frustration. "Just forget it."

I'm ready to click off the phone and chuck the device across my office when Stone hollers. "Wait."

My eyes close in relief.

"I'll check it out. Send Andy out there. Could just be kids parking but we'll want to make sure it's nothing more."

Thank you. My throat is too thick to form the phrase. And as Stone knows I'm shit at expressing gratitude, he changes subjects.

"Bringing Enya to the Fourth of July parade in town?"

I hadn't thought about it, but we take the parade seriously in this town because of the friends we've lost in the military. Hell, my own brother is a local hero. *A true hero.* Not like the term Enya keeps labeling me.

"Yeah, I'll probably be there."

"See that you are. And bring your family." With that, Stone hangs up on me before he realizes what he's said.

My family.

Chapter 25

[Enya]

When the Fourth of July arrives, the downtown area is packed with parade watchers. Lining the length of Corner Street with collapsible chairs and homemade quilts, families sit close together to watch first responders, veterans, public school teachers and local sports' teams plus a slew of businesses march along the main road to be celebrated by their community.

Adara is decked out in her first official holiday outfit, complete with red and white stripes and little stars on a blue background. We wait outside the Curmudgeon Bakery for Sebastian who said he'd close promptly at eleven when the parade begins.

Barnett exits the bakery first, and I swear the poor boy's face is beat red when he looks at me.

"Hi Barnett. Happy Fourth of July."

"Hi . . . Enya." He stammers, slipping his hands into his front pockets. "July happy you to fourth."

I bite my lower lip. He's a handsome young man, and I'm flattered that I fluster him a bit. But he's way too young for my liking. Sebastian has told me he's a good kid, living with his aunt, and possibly getting a football scholarship if he keeps his head on straight.

I give Barnett a wave and he holds up his palm before rushing off, swiping a hand through his longish hair.

Sebastian exits the bakery next. He greets me by running his hand up my back before squeezing my neck and then planting a kiss on me that might be a little too much for public. When he pulls back, I'm stunned, but he wiggles his hands for Adara like he didn't just kiss the breath out of me.

We've spent a glorious week exploring each other, learning our likes, and discovering new ones, with tongues and teeth and lips. However, we haven't crossed the line to sex, and admittedly, I'm getting anxious it won't ever happen. Not that what we have been doing isn't pleasant, but it feels like Sebastian is still holding himself back. He said he'd try at us. The effort is present, but something is in the way of taking us to the next level.

When the parade starts, I expect everyone's attention to be on the people marching past us, but I can't ignore the stares of people I don't know, whispering and wondering about Sebastian and me. Holding Adara, he looks like a proud new father. He no longer needs to pretend she is his. However, his actions contradict that he's *not* her father, as he's pointing out things she can't even see and cooing to her like she understands big words like firefighter, schoolteacher, and baseball player.

"My, my, my, isn't this a sight?" A short, trim woman walks up and stands beside Sebastian. She's wearing a suit despite the heat and her blond hair is perfectly coiffed like a helmet on her head. A crooked smirk curls her lips, and I can't decide if she's scowling or smiling.

"Emory Milton, you just mind your own business," a woman next to her *tsks*.

Instantly, I recognize the person who sold me the farmhouse. "Miss Wallace, so good to see you again." It took some sleuthing to find out who owned the ramshackle home outside of town and even more investigating before learning she was interested in selling it. I'm surprised I haven't seen the sturdy woman around town. Then again, I haven't gotten out much and I need to do better.

"Just Trudy," she admonishes, reminding me how she's already told me to call her by her first name. "And girl, it is a pleasure to see you again. I'd heard you had an angel."

She takes Adara's leg between her dark fingers and jiggles the tiny limb.

"This is Adara," Sebastian proudly answers before I can.

"And Sebastian Sylver, just what are you doing holding that baby?" Emory Milton asks, giving him the stink eye like she already knows what we played out. And knows the truth. Sebastian is not Adara's dad.

"Emory," Trudy grits, sternly side-eyeing her friend.

"I have a right to know what's going on in my town." Emory fiercely nods. Surprisingly, her perfect shade of blonde hair doesn't even move with the terse motion.

"This ain't your town." Trudy stands taller, planting her hands on her wide hips while she glares at the woman beside her. "And ain't nothing that says you need to know everybody's personal business, either."

"Well, my daughter is the mayor." Pride effuses from Emory's declaration.

"How is Emerson?" Sebastian asks.

The older blonde gives him a tight smile. "That's Mayor Milton to you, and she's doing just fine. If only that brother of yours would get his head out of his ass."

"Emory Milton!" Trudy chides between a snort and a chuckle.

"Well, it's the truth," she drawls, narrowing her eyes at Adara, and cooing at her in a high-pitched falsetto. "They'd make beautiful babies. Yes, they would."

Sebastian grunts and jiggles Adara. Trudy shakes her head.

"Ignore her." Trudy waves a hand with bright red nails between us. "But you two certainly made a beautiful baby," she coos, jostling Adara's leg again.

I don't want to burden Sebastian with the rumors, which circulated during book club, where Vale was on hand and quick to remind people her brothers were not a discussable topic.

"Oh, we didn't—"

"Thank you." Sebastian lifts Adara to kiss her head before blinding the women with a proud grin. Both women appear stunned at first, but Trudy slowly melts, warmly smiling at Adara.

Then Sebastian shifts his body and aims Adara toward the street. "Look, there's Uncle Knox."

I glance up to see Sebastian's brother in full military dress looking miserable as he walks down the street, subtly waving at people who all stand and applaud him.

"Such a hero," Emory Milton sighs. "Just like his daddy once was."

A disagreeing hum from Trudy accompanies Sebastian sudden choking fit.

"Well, we need to be on our way." Emory's voice is too high as she snaps out of some memory triggered by watching Knox march down the street. "Nice to finally meet you, Enya."

"You, too."

Emory moves along but Trudy lingers a second, timidly grinning before addressing Adara with a final shake of her leg. "We don't pay that woman any mind in this town." She straightens and looks directly at Sebastian. "And you know better than to pay any attention to her either."

Trudy's words are a combination of tough love and gentle reminder. The look she gives Sebastian isn't pity but compassion, like she's familiar with him and his family. She knows his past.

"You need anything, you still have my number, right?" Trudy says to me.

"Yes, ma'am." I can't imagine what I'd need from her, but you never know. As Trudy catches up to her friend, I realize I never introduced myself to Emory, and yet she knew my name. She really does make it her business to know who lives here.

When they are out of earshot, I turn to Sebastian who keeps his gaze on the parade. However, his eyes look distant, haunted even. "How do you know Trudy?"

"Small town." He answers in a snap, thick with snark. Then he squints, still avoiding a glance at me. "She was my mother's best friend, from what I'm told. My dad didn't let her come around once our mother was gone."

There's a story there but I don't press. Instead, I ask a different question. "Why did you do that? Why did you play into them thinking you were Adara's dad?"

Sebastian glances down at Adara, studying her face near his shoulder. "Didn't even think twice, I guess. Plus, our story . . . or *your* story isn't any of their business. Emory Milton is just a nosy, bitter bitch, and she's been trying to ship Stone and Emerson for years. It's not going to happen."

"Why not?"

"Because Stone isn't into town politics, even if he sleeps with the mayor on the regular." Sebastian speaks toward Adara, like he's imparting wisdom to her. "There's a reason my daddy didn't end up with her mama when they were young."

Definitely a story for another day.

"Still . . . Back to you claiming *we* made Adara. You don't need to do that. I can fight my own battles. I'll right the rumors."

"And tell people what?" Sebastian glares at me. "Half this town thinks she's mine, and that half doesn't even matter. As for the other half, I don't care what those people think either." He pauses, watching me. "Unless you do. Unless you'd rather people didn't think I was her dad."

The whiplash happening with this man sometimes is worse than being in a car crash. He doesn't want to be a dad but he's willing to pretend he's one. It's too confusing, and dangerous, for both Adara and me.

"Don't be silly. If you *were* Adara's father, I'd be very proud of that fact." Prouder than the truth, which my parents found unforgivable.

Sebastian gazes down at Adara, who is scooting against him, making her way into a particular position she likes to be held against him, which involves dangling her head and an arm over the crook of his elbow. She's settling in for a nap when it's almost feeding time.

"I just thought maybe you wouldn't like to be called her father. It cramps your—"

Sebastian glares so hard at me, I stop short of accusing his style of being cramped by the daddy rumors.

"Let's get something straight. The only *style* I have . . . the only one I want . . . is this." He jostles Adara in his arms, emphasizing his stance.

For a man who doesn't want to be a father, he's fallen for my baby.

But has he fallen for me?

+ + +

Once the parade is over, people filter into a green space near the downtown area with their foldable chairs and large blankets. Food trucks line the street along one edge of the square and the community gathers for a giant, public picnic.

I hadn't planned ahead, but Sebastian has us covered with a bag of fresh bread, cheese and cold meats, plus fruit and a lemon cake with frosting that's melting in the heat.

He fights a smile every time people come up to him, making faces at Adara and saying how cute she is. No one questions if Sebastian is the father. Gossip is accepted as gospel, I guess, and I only worry for when the truth comes out. That truth being that Sebastian isn't Adara's dad.

He hasn't pressed me for the truth, but there's an accusation in his eyes when he's asked about her father. At this point, I'm certain he thinks Lance is the dad when I've told Sebastian he isn't.

My parents suggested I say Lance was Adara's father. It would make sense after being together so long and having a momentary relapse last summer. They even went so far as to hint I could get child support from my ex if I made such a claim. However, Lance isn't Adara's father, and I would never feel right stating he was. Not only because I don't want his money, but because I wouldn't want his name associated with my sweet baby.

Now, if a certain someone suggested Sylver be her last name . . . But that's wishful thinking and like always, I'm getting ahead of myself. I'm taking Sebastian's kindness, friendship, good orgasms, and a promise to try, and turning that combination into a complex layered cake.

Similar to Lance, Sebastian is not suggesting we are anything other than friends, even if he says he's interested and I'm his number one. Like when younger people say they are talking to someone, but they aren't officially dating. If anything, *I* should be upset that Sebastian isn't dispelling the paternity rumors because the gossip assumes I've slept with a man whom I'm not living with, not engaged to, and not going to marry. A mystery woman who suddenly appeared . . . *with Sebastian Sylver's child*. I'm *his* baby mama.

I shiver at the derogatory suggestion.

Suddenly, the cheese in my mouth tastes moldy and the chunk of bread along with it tastes like chalk. I set down the remaining piece of bread and swipe my hands together.

"I'm going to get a lemonade. Want one?" A group of high school kids are making the refreshing drink from scratch with a full lemon, a cup of sugar, and a container of ice, and that lemony goodness has my name all over it.

"You love your lemons," Sebastian teases. He's lying on his side across a blanket while Adara sleeps in the stroller with a lightweight baby blanket draped over it to prevent the sun from hitting her.

With a tight nod, I hum and stand. As I near the canopied stand, someone bumps into my side.

"I'm so sorry," a masculine voice says at the same time I apologize. His hand lands on my hip while I catch his bicep to steady myself.

Glancing up, I recognize the man who held the door for me the other day at the bakery.

"We meet again." His smile is warmer this time. His eyes are lighter in the sunlight. He squints and glances around. "No baby?"

"She's sleeping in her stroller over there." I point in the general direction of Sebastian, who I notice sits upright, looking like a jeans model with one knee bend and an arm crooked over it, while the other stretches down the length of the blanket. He's perched up on his other hand, watching me.

"Too bad. I could hold another door for you."

Turning back to the stranger and his flirtatious tone, I look at him with pinched brows. "No doors around." I twist to indicate the open space around us.

"I'll just need to find a place that has one. Maybe Milton's Roadhouse, where I can open the door for you, and we could share a drink inside."

My mouth slightly opens. *Is he asking me out?* "Need to escape the heat?"

"Trying to ask you to meet me for a drink." His smile grows larger. His dark eyes twinkle beneath the sun.

I'm flattered by his attention, but I'm not attracted to him. There's something about him that suggests I should be on my guard, although the judgement feels unfair. He's been nothing but polite. Maybe it's just that a certain someone takes up all my headspace and my heart.

"I'm kind of in a tough spot," I cautiously admit. "With the baby. Not much of a social life." I wave a hand, brushing off the rejection, by making Adara my excuse, hoping not to hurt his feelings.

"But you'll be sticking around tonight for the fireworks, right?"

I hadn't decided yet, as the timing depends on Adara and her fussiness. "Still on the fence."

"Well, if you decide to get off the fence, I'd be willing to open a gate for you. Or ready to open a door for you at Milton's." He winks.

My face heats. He's rather charming, and again, I'm flattered. The prospect of a date, when only a week ago I didn't think I'd ever be attractive to any man, is a compliment. However, I already have a man giving me mind-blowing orgasms and mind-puzzling whiplash with his words and actions sometimes in conflict.

"Thank you. Maybe I'll see you there." It isn't fair to lead him on, but his good-natured smile suggests he won't be holding his breath waiting on me.

"At least let me buy you a lemonade." We step up to the table as it's finally my turn and he pulls a twenty from his pocket. Holding it out to the teen, he says, "Make it two."

"You don't need to do that." He probably shouldn't do it. Allowing him to buy me even a simple lemonade sends the wrong message. Before I can protest, though, he's handing me the sugary drink in a large plastic cup. When he's offered his change, he sets the full amount in the transparent jar labeled: College Fund.

"That was very generous of you." I nod toward the tip jar.

He lifts his lemonade and takes a sip, puckering his lips at the sweet-tart flavor. "Gotta go to college. Stay off the streets and away from drugs."

My head swims as déjà vu wraps around me. I've heard those words before, but the voice in my head isn't this man's. The sound is fleetingly familiar. *Who said that before?*

"Well, thank you for the lemonade . . ." I lift my lemonade in salute and pause, not knowing his name.

He winks at me again without offering it. "See you around, Enya." He's quick to walk away before I can question how he knows *my* name. Then again, it's a small town like Sebastian said. As the new person around here, I guess I'm a bit of a novelty, especially since Sebastian isn't dispelling any rumors.

Taking a sip of the sweet lemonade, I head back to our picnic blanket where the man pretending to be my baby's *daddy* is glaring at me.

He stands as I approach. "Who the hell was that?" He snaps a little too gruffly.

"I don't actually know." I sip my lemonade again and gaze at Sebastian with the straw between my lips. If this situation had been with Lance, there would be accusations. *I* was flirting. *I* was leading someone on. *I* was doing something wrong. In hindsight, the behavior was a coverup for his own wandering eye. And Sebastian's upset is a little more . . . complimentary.

"Are you jealous?" I tip my head, with my teeth nibbling the tip of the straw, poking at him.

With hands on his hips, he isn't falling for my ploy to forget the man. "What did he want?"

"He asked me to join him for a drink later and when I said I wouldn't, he insisted on buying me a lemonade instead." I lift the plastic cup.

"Fucking hell. Yes, I'm jealous." With his hands still on his hips, his stance is imposing. Like a toy wound tight and ready to spring. His eyes narrow. "Why did you turn him down?"

I laugh. "Come on. You know why." My smile emphasizes how tickled I am by his display of confusion. Stepping closer to him, I place my hand on his chest, where his heart races beneath his T-shirt warmed by the sun. "I'll pick you *every time*, Sebastian."

His eyes widen. He glances to the side and then back at me. He groans, "Sugar."

"You, Sebastian." I tap a finger to his chest while I take a sip of my lemonade, again attempting to flirt with him and distract him from thoughts of anyone else in my life.

How does he not see how wrapped up in him I am? He's the only man I want which is dangerous for my heart. For Adara's heart, too. Because we're both a little in love with this man who might be strongly infatuated with us but doesn't want a long-term future.

The thought should make me sad, but I don't have a second to think before Sebastian has his fingers in my hair, cupping the back of my neck, and tugging me to him. He kisses me deep and hard as we stand in the middle of a crowded picnic.

Just as swiftly as the kiss starts, Sebastian pulls back. "You taste lemony sweet." He hums, the sound sending new shivers down my spine. "Let's get out of here for a while."

Stunned by the rapid shift in his mood and the heat in his eyes, I nod to agree.

I'll go wherever he leads.

Chapter 26

[Sebastian]

In the coolness of the bakery apartment, Enya feeds Adara who falls into another nap, allowing Enya and me to doze on the couch. With a late-afternoon baseball game on the television, the volume is low. Enya and I lie on our sides with her back pressed to my chest. My arm drapes over her waist and I drift into a foggy sleep. In my daze, I'm punching the man talking to Enya, who'd offered to buy her a drink and then purchased her lemonade.

Lemons are my thing with her.

I'm not certain how long we're quiet, letting the air conditioning cool us from the heat of July, but eventually, Enya turns to face me. Her lush body lines up against mine.

I brush my fingers through her hair. She nuzzles into my chest.

I swipe my hand down her back. She hitches a leg over my hip.

The position opens her up and I rock forward, pressing at her center. Enya loops her leg tighter across my ass, tugging me to her, and I nudge the stiffness in my jeans at the heat of her seam. She's wearing white shorts today with a blue shirt speckled with silver stars. She's a real all-American woman. And she's so much more than I ever expected to have in my life.

I'll pick you every time.

Jesus. She undid me right in the middle of town.

With thoughts of the kiss I'd given her then, and her body squirming against mine now, I roll my hips again. Our mouths meet and I savor the tart taste of lemonade on her tongue. The firmness behind my zipper catches at the soft spot between her thighs and Enya hums. The vibration ripples down my throat like a refreshing drink. Her fingers grip the back of my T-shirt, holding me to her.

Rolling her onto her back, her legs cradle my hips. I curve into her center once more, hissing as my dick weeps to be closer to her. Skin-to-skin. Hard to soft. Stiff to wet. My imagination takes over, knowing how pliable Enya's body would be. How easily I'd slip inside her. How warm she'd feel surrounding me.

I rock harder and Enya's legs wrap around my lower back. My hips move, simulating how it would be if we were naked and bare to each other.

"Sebastian." Enya is breathless. "I want you."

God, I want her, too. "This is awkward as fuck, but I need you to know I'm clean. I haven't been with anyone in months, and I've been to the doctor since then." Staying free of drugs and checking my health regularly is important to me. I don't want any surprises from something stupid that happened a long time ago.

"I trust you." Her breath is soft while strained. She's eager for more and the shift of her body, dancing beneath mine, tells me she's getting close. Through my jeans and her shorts, she's going to come and I'm a proud man that she's so turned on by me.

Thump. Thump. Thump.

"What the—" The sharp rapping of a fist on my door has Enya and I both stilling. I stare down at her, holding my breath, hoping whoever it is will go away.

My girl is about to come, and I want to please her.

"Sebastian? Seb? I know you're in there."

"Are you kidding me?" I groan, lowering my head to Enya's.

She chuckles beneath me. The vibration rattles her body, emphasizing our position. My dick is ready to bust through my zipper and the seam of her shorts. I'm so fucking hard.

"You better get that," Enya whispers teasingly as another fierce hammering happens against my door.

"I'm going to kill him," I mutter, quickly kissing Enya before pressing off her to my knees and offering her a hand to sit upright. Her face is flushed. Her lips swollen from our kissing. "I'll get rid of him."

"It's fine." She waves before I climb off her and stalk toward the door that leads directly out of my apartment to the fire escape.

"What?" I growl as I hastily open the barrier and glare at Knox.

He sways a bit on his feet. "I need a place to hide."

My brows crease. Knox is not a coward. He's a decorated war hero. He's braver than anyone I know and tucks all that bravado into jokes and jests.

"Are you drunk?"

"No."

It might be a lie, but I won't kick him out. Knox isn't one to overindulge. He knows what our father turned into when he did.

"What's going on?"

"Just let me in." He takes a step to pass me, but I place a hand on his chest. He sways like he's about to face-plant to the floor.

"Are you alright?"

"Being alright is relative." He hiccups. "I mean, subjective." He isn't exactly slurring his words, but he isn't steady either.

I step back, allowing my brother to pass, and lock the door behind him before following him.

He stumbles over his own feet. "Fuck."

I could tease him that he owes Hudson a dollar, but this isn't typical Knox behavior. The parade always messes him up a bit and later he'll avoid the fireworks.

Maybe he faltered at seeing Enya because he stops feet away from the couch where she's sitting with her arms crossed over the back of it and eyeing both of us.

"Aw, damn." Knox turns to me, swaying again on his feet. "Why didn't you tell me you were busy?"

Yeah, I was busy and about to get busier, but it's rare a brother needs me, and Knox said he wanted a place to hide.

"Who are *we* avoiding?" I question, because, again, Knox isn't chickenshit. He's dodging something. Or someone. "Is this about Halle?"

"Who's Halle?" Enya asks.

"It's not Halle." However, the grit in Knox's voice and the clench of his teeth tells me his current condition is very much about his high school sweetheart, freshly returned to town. She's the one that got away. It was all his fault, too.

"Let me hang out with you guys."

I glance at Enya who shrugs when I want her to tell my brother *fuck no*. Knox stumbles to the couch and collapses on the long portion. Enya scoots to her official corner. The one she claimed when she stayed here those two weeks. The spot I've commissioned as hers, staring at it too often, missing her in my place.

Settling in beside her, I say, "I want to take you to the fireworks later."

"I hate fireworks," Knox mumbles to no one. He lays on his back, an arm over his face, nose buried into the crook of his elbow.

"I'm not certain Adara will appreciate the loud boom of fireworks and I didn't bring the baby headphones I have with me."

"They make headphones for babies?" Knox asks, lifting his arm and turning his head.

Enya offers him a compassionate smile. "They do."

While Knox and Enya banter over me about baby products, an idea forms and I interrupt, speaking to Knox. "If you want to hang out, maybe you could do me a favor later?"

"Oh boy. The last time you asked me for a favor, you stole Dad's old truck, when you weren't old enough to legally drive."

I scoff at the reminder of hot wiring my old man's beat up pickup one night when he was passed out drunk. Knox was old enough to drive but not willing to take me to meet a girl. I took the initiative on my own. That was shortly before Dad died.

"What's the favor?" Knox asks. His eyelids are already lowering. He'll need to sober up first. Good thing there are still hours before darkness.

I glance at Enya. "With your permission, I'd like Knox to babysit. He can nap now, and I'll make dinner for all of us later. Then he can watch Adara for an hour or so after dark."

Her brows lift, questioning me, before her eyes drift to Knox. In Knox's current state, I doubt she trusts him, but I want her to trust me. I wouldn't be requesting this favor from my brother if I didn't think he was capable of watching a baby for an hour or two.

Still addressing her, I explain, "I'd like to take you some place special we can watch the fireworks. We won't be far from here."

"Where will we be?" she asks.

With his eyes closed, Knox makes a goofy grin. "Damn romantic, little brother."

Fuck him for reading my thoughts. He knows the perfect spot to enjoy fireworks without leaving this building.

"Can you let me surprise you?" I want to do this for her.

Her gaze shifts to Knox again. Lowering her voice, she says, "If you're sure he'll be okay."

"A little shut eye and I'll be right as rain, sweetheart," Knox grumbles groggily.

I take her hand and lift it to my lips. With my mouth on her knuckles, I vow, "I'd never do anything to put you or Adara in harm's way. I trust Knox. He'll be fine in a few hours."

Enya chews her lower lip but gives me a soft smile. Her eyes tell me she trusts *me* and that look does something to me. Giving me a slight nod, she agrees to my plan, and we have a date.

I can't remember the last time I'd been on one, or if I ever officially have been. During my drug days, I didn't date. I fucked around. Since I've been back home, I've shared rare nights with a woman. Strangely, I'm excited, and nervous, for this evening. I want everything to be perfect.

+ + +

Hours later, Knox has napped and sobered.

I feed him and Enya, who easily gets along with my brother, as he regales her with stories about me as a wily kid and reckless teen. My chest expands when I hear her deep laughter. The sound satisfying like smothering frosting over a three-layer cake. The texture rich. The sensation smooth. The final perfection.

While Enya feeds Adara a little earlier than normal in hopes to tide her over, I set up for the fireworks display.

A sleeping Adara is set in a portable bassinet Enya brought with her in my living area. I've placed it next to the couch, so Knox will actively be able to watch the baby. Then, I lead Enya inside my bedroom to a door.

"What's this?" She hesitates as I pop the lock and open the door that exposes a metal ladder and a narrow shaft that leads upward.

"Access to my roof." I wink before holding out my hand. "After you."

"Rooftop viewing of the fireworks?"

I don't respond, anxious once again, but her expression softens while her gaze fixes on my face. "You really are romantic, *little brother*."

She laughs quietly but just as pleasantly as she'd been doing all night with Knox and me. She almost glows from a good night that I hope gets even better.

"Up you go," I joke, swatting her ass.

She jolts forward, glaring at me without an ounce of irritation. Then I'm watching her climb up the roof access ladder and licking my lips at her long legs and short shorts disappearing above me. I'm quick to follow her, only she stops short as she breaches the roof.

"Sebastian." Her voice cracks as she stares at the spread on the rooftop. Blankets and pillows, and a few candles that will soon flicker in the evening breeze.

Maybe the setup is romantic. Maybe it's cheesy. But the tenderness in Enya's expression when she looks at me is exactly what I was hoping for. I'd build a thousand nests just like this to see her look at me the way she is right now. With awe. And gratitude. But something deeper. Something I'm risking to hope for.

Love.

"Shall we?" I nod at the setting, and Enya leads the way. As she folds down to the blankets, I light the candles, then I join her. The night is still warm, but Enya pulls a sheet over her legs. She rests on her hands, as she tips back her head and stares at the stars.

"It's so beautiful here. That's one reason I fell in love with Sterling Falls."

"Yeah." I glance upward. "Sometimes I forget how beautiful it can be." Then, I look at her. Her hair hangs back like a delicate scarf, blowing in the breeze. Her face is illuminated by the candles, but her eyes are the main attraction. Firelight dances in those dark orbs. She's the beauty in this town.

She turns to face me and cups my face. "Thank you for this." The first kiss is gentle—sweet appreciation—but quickly, the meeting of our mouth turns to the passion of our earlier interrupted moment. Enya pushes me to my back and climbs over me. Straddling my hips, she breaks free of my mouth and sits upright. Her palms coast over my chest before she reaches for the hem of her tee and tugs it over her head.

"Sugar," I growl, desperate for her while enjoying the show. This woman is taking over and I'm not about to stop her.

"I'm not ready to remove this." She waves before her bra. "But soon."

"Soon," I groan, rubbing my hands up her belly and cupping the bottom of each heavy swell in the crook of my thumb and forefinger. "God, Enya, I want to fuck you right here." I press her breasts together, plumping them up and emphasizing her cleavage. I can't wait for the day these luscious swells become mine. For now, there are other parts of her to explore.

Quickly, I sit upright and tug at my own shirt, pulling it over my head from the back of my collar.

Seated on my lap, Enya sighs. "Why is that so freakin' hot?"

"Removing my shirt is hot?" I give her a smirk.

"You know damn well you're sexy, Sebastian Sylver."

I shrug. "Still nice to hear from an equally sexy woman." I tip my head to kiss her again, savoring the sweetness of her tongue and warmth of her lips. Then, I flip her to her back, and she lets out a little squeal.

With our eyes locked, we say unspoken things. *Tonight is the night.* Scooting back to my heels, I unbutton her shorts and tug both her underwear and shorts off her legs. Undressing her is like unwrapping a present. A present I never expected to receive, but I'm so excited this gift is for me.

"You're so beautiful." My voice cracks, awed by her beauty and how she's letting me get her naked, exposing all her stunning glory to me.

With all barriers gone, I lower between her thighs and taste where she's sweet and musky. The perfect combination gets me high on her every time. With my tongue swirling around her sacred spot, her body quenches a thirst I didn't know I had. Soon, she's panting, whimpering for me to give her more. When I pull away, she cries out. However, I want to feel her release around me. I want her to unleash and let go with me buried inside her.

With shaky fingers, I remove my belt and lower my jeans. It's not like I haven't slept with women, but I've never slept with an Enya. And that makes this moment special, holy, like it's a first-time thing.

She *is* a first for me.

Naked, I stand over her and roll on a condom. Watching me, she drinks me in, just as thirsty for me. When I lower down to the blankets, her legs spread, and I nestle between her thighs.

The hardness of my shaft hits the softness of her wet heat, and we both hiss at the sensation. I could die right here, a happy man.

"I'm nervous," she anxiously giggles, and I brush back her hair, cupping her face as I brace on my elbows.

Timidly, I chuckle. "Me too." My voice is rough, husky even. "I don't want to hurt you. I promise I won't hurt you. I'll go slow."

She nods, trusting me, and that alone undoes me. My body itches to surge, but my head says take it easy, Sebastian. Be gentle.

With my tip at her entrance, my dick weeps to drive into her, but I hold back the beast. Gliding forward, inch-by-excruciating inch, her body takes me in, gloriously accepting me. Enya shifts, widening her legs, as I move with patience I didn't think I could master. Time stands still as her heat surrounds me, comforts me, warms me to my bones. Taking me into her body is the biggest act of trust she could give me. It's also a connection I've never felt before. A soul-shattering honesty. We fit so well together. She's perfect for me.

Reaching for her hand, I bring it over her head and spread my fingers between hers until she's clutching at mine.

"This okay?" I strain, willing myself to continue the slow pace.

With her hand gripping mine, she sighs. "You feel so good." Her channel clenches around me, drawing me into her.

"Dammit, Enya." My resolve breaks and I thrust the final inches inward. Pausing, I'm seated to the hilt. With my heart racing and my thoughts scattering, I'm the one who needs a minute to collect myself.

Nothing has ever felt like this before. *Nothing.*

She's a flame but doesn't burn. She's heat that doesn't scorch. She's a light in a life that's been too dark.

As if she senses I need time, she lifts her head and kisses me, sweet and soothing. My dick twitches within her, and she falls back with another nervous laugh. I reach for her other hand, pulling it above her head as well and stare down at her.

"You're the most incredible person, sugar. I've never known anyone like you. So trusting. So giving. God, I don't deserve you." Her purity has no place touching the dirt in me, but a tornado couldn't drag me off this rooftop.

"I'm nothing special," she whispers as we stare at one another. "But you deserve anything and everything. You're the best man I've ever known."

It's too much, so I kiss her to stop her from speaking. Or maybe it's in hopes to swallow her words and trap them inside me.

As we kiss, her hips flex upward and I dig deeper into her. Releasing her mouth, I rest my forehead against hers and pull back, dragging my dick from her depths. Not eager to leave her body, I'll only get to the tip before the desire to fill her will pull me forward again.

Back and forth, I move at this measured pace of near escape before seeking refuge inside her again. Enya matches the rhythm, chasing my retreats before catching me and reeling me back in.

We're making love when I don't think I've ever understood the meaning of the words.

Tender. Patience. Every movement is pleasant torture. Every motion is teasing passion. I'm almost giddy while my body electrifies, crackling, coming alive from the lazy dance.

"Sebastian," Enya moans, tipping back her head and exposing her pretty neck to me. "Yes."

It's an answer to an unasked question. She's so close and I'll be right behind her. Releasing one hand, I slip my fingers between us, eager to tip her over the edge. Her legs lift, wrapping around my lower back, trapping my arm in a way I never want to be freed.

Enya moves faster, drawing me deeper.

"Baby," I strain, holding back while keeping pace. My skin prickles. My muscles are coming untethered, about to unleash the restraint.

Patience, man.

The warning does nothing to sooth me. The intensity is too much. Enya is too much, and yet, she's everything. She's sunshine peeking through heavy clouds. And laughter for a sad soul. And the brightness of fireworks across a dark sky.

Just then, the first one explodes in the distance. Not close enough that we feel the force of the boom but near enough the sky lights in speckles of red and white. Beneath me, Enya's face reflects the trickle of fire illuminated behind me before cascading down a black canvas.

Again and again, the fireworks blast. Red for passion. White means innocence. Blue is comfort.

Our pace quickens. My hips thrust, forcing me deeper. Enya surges, taking me harder. Eventually, we're our own explosive celebration of bursting color and booming sound. Enya cries out my name, shattering around me and setting me off, like a personal rocket blaster.

Spent, I collapse over her before rolling to my side, taking her with me as we're still attached. Her leg remains around my hip, and I hold her to my chest, kissing her forehead, her eyelids, her nose.

Another flash of fireworks implodes above of us and three little words I've never said threaten to detonate, scattering across this rooftop, and highlighting something I'm certain I'll never feel again.

I love her. I love Enya.

Afraid she might disappear, like the spent fireworks, I tug her tighter to my chest.

Knowing a finale is inevitable, I can't seem to regulate my breathing.

Because all things bright and beautiful eventually end, fading to darkness again.

Chapter 27

[Enya]

Sebastian Sylver is unlike any man I've ever known. Any man I've dreamed of knowing. He's patient and kind, the very definition of love. And he'd made love to me amid candlelight and fireworks in one of the most romantic settings I've ever been in.

Eleven years in a committed relationship, and not once did I share a moment like I had with Sebastian on his rooftop. Everything was perfection, from the way Sebastian looked at me, to the way he touched me, to the pace he kept in an effort to put me at ease. I wasn't afraid of sex. I was simply anxious about the first time after having a baby. Or maybe it was the first time in over a year. With someone new. Someone different. Someone exceptional.

I was in so much trouble with Sebastian.

When the firework finale finally lights up the sky and the night turns back to black, we kiss once more before Sebastian suggests we get to Adara. He isn't in a rush to roll over and give me his back. He isn't opposed to cuddling. He simply understands that his brother is babysitting, and we are on a time limit.

If only that timeframe meant forever, with more nights like this, and never having to say goodbye at the end of a day.

After we redress, Sebastian collects the blankets, tossing them down the ladder shoot while I blow out the candles.

"Just leave them behind. I'll collect them tomorrow once they've cooled."

He climbs down first, and I follow, saddened as the romantic moment's end blends with the elation still coursing through my limbs. Once Sebastian closes the door, locking it again, I start for the living room, but he catches my arm.

"Wait." The command is quiet, desperate even.

I spin to face him, and he digs his fingers into my hair, combing the strands back to the nape of my neck before kissing me one more time in a long, languid way that has me wishing we could tumble to his bed next and start touching one another all over again.

When he pulls back, he rests his forehead against mine.

"I'm finally able to give gratitude to you." He lifts his head so he can look me directly in the eye. "Thank you."

I coyly smile. "For what?"

"For that." He tips his head toward the ceiling. "I've never experienced anything like that and I'm certain I never will again."

I want to tell him he can have moments like that again and again . . . with me.

The magical moment felt like a fairytale, complete with fireworks while kissing. The setting was romantic. The man a true prince. My fate is sealed.

I am in love with Sebastian Sylver.

But a squeak in the other room draws our attention toward the open bedroom door. Adara calls.

With a quiet sigh before an exasperated chuckle, I break free from Sebastian and head into his living room only to pause at what I see.

The lights are dimmed. A black and white video featuring a heavy metal rock band projects from Sebastian's television. Knox is gently swaying back and forth with Adara balancing on his arm, her head in his palm. When he spins, Adara squawks again, clearly not liking to be removed from her view of the video.

Knox spins, giving us his back and quietly speaks over his shoulder. "She was a little fussy."

"No worries." Dreamily, I glance from Knox to Sebastian and back. Sebastian rubs a hand up my spine and squeezes the back of my neck.

"Is that Guns N' Roses playing "Sweet Child O' Mine"? Sebastian asks.

Knox nods, rocking side to side with Adara stretched out on her arm. "Uncle Knox is introducing her to the good stuff."

Suddenly, my eyes well with tears. *Uncle Knox?* My thoughts momentarily drift to my brother who will never be an uncle. My brother, who Adara will never know. Even my parents, who deny her as a grandchild.

My heart aches for family. A large one with all the quirks Sebastian claims to dislike, but secretly adores, about his.

His stoic eldest brother.

His sister's loving approval.

His brother's constant teasing.

Stumbling, I crash into Sebastian as he tugs me to his side and presses a kiss to my head.

"You're dancing with my girl," he teases his brother.

"You got your own girl." Knox sways his hips and turns only enough to give us his side. Adara rolls her head to keep her eyes focused on the screen. "This girl is going to love Uncle Knox the most. Aren't you, sweet child?"

"Hey now," Sebastian calls out, humor in his warning. My little one already has grown men vying for her love.

With me at his side, he turns to face me, lifts my hand, and drapes my other arm over his shoulder. Then he sways, spinning us in a slow circle behind his couch. The Guns N' Roses anthem isn't exactly a dance tune, but Sebastian holds me close like it's a love ballad. We gently rock as the heavy metal plays out.

When the song ends, I smile up at him despite what I suggest. "I should probably go. It's late and Adara has had a long day out." The last diaper in her bag is reason enough to leave but I don't want to go. Still, it's probably for the best.

"You aren't running, are you?" Sebastian presses his lips to my head, lingering there with his question.

"Running?" I pull back to meet his eyes.

He watches me, asking a thousand questions while not saying a thing. I'm not a runner. If anything, I want to stay in his arms all night and every night after that, but Sebastian is the one who doesn't want the same things as me and I've learned my lesson. Never push where intentions are clear.

"Uh-oh. Sounds like a diaper bomb just went off and that's where Uncle Knox clocks out." He balances Adara before him, bringing her to me and passing her off.

I laugh as I bring her to my chest, needing her to ground myself, remind myself what my goals are in life.

Her. She's my reason.

"And there goes the last diaper," I give as further reason to leave. Plus, the clock is ticking closer to her midnight feed. I could use a shower, and I'm suddenly exhausted.

Sebastian watches as I pack up Adara's things, double checking I have everything. He folds up her portable bassinet and carries it down the staircase. He doesn't ask me to stay, but he does surprise me when he walks me out to my car and says, "I'll be right behind you. Just let me get Knox settled."

You don't have to do that. The rejection rests on the tip of my tongue, but I bite it hard, knowing I want Sebastian to follow me. I want him in my house where I can *post-coital* cuddle him.

He kisses me once more, waiting in the parking lot while I drive off. In the quiet of my Honda Passport, I take a moment to process the day, the night, the rooftop. Coming together with Sebastian was intense. Candles. Blankets. Warm summer air. Everything intensified the atmosphere as our bodies joined, broke apart and came together over and over again.

Only once did I see Sebastian falter. Panic filled his eyes. I represent everything he doesn't want but he's drawn to me for some reason, just not the same reasons I'm attracted to him.

I see stability in Sebastian that he doesn't see in himself. I see love, trust, and a partnership.

If only . . .

As I pull into my driveway, I glance at the house and my hands clutch harder on the steering wheel.

A light flashes across the living room window. From the inside.

Rolling to a stop, I haven't even set my car in park before I press the phone button on the dash. My heart hammers while my blood flow slows. I'm caught between common sense that screams leave, and a faulty belief nothing is wrong. Nothing would happen to me. I'm nobody.

Still, with a shaky finger, I press favorites on the phone tab, and press Sebastian's number at the top of the list.

"Hey, sugar." His tone is light, easygoing.

"I think someone's in my house."

"What?" His voice instantly tightens. "Where are you?"

"I'm in the driveway and a light flashed across the front window . . . from the inside."

"Enya, get out of there. Just reverse out of the drive and pull down the road. I'm almost there." He hangs up but as I click the hang up button, Sebastian pulls into my driveway behind me. He hops out of his truck, not bothering to turn off the engine or shut off the headlights. Racing to the front door, he quickly enters the code and disappears inside.

I don't like this. He's my hero but he isn't a superhero, and I don't want him to get hurt. Pressing at the phone button again, I dial 9-1-1. While the phone rings and rings, I worry every first responder has the night off, being honored on this patriotic day.

Finally, a woman answers. "9-1-1. What's your emergency?"

I explain myself and give my address. Then add, "Sebastian Sylver went into the house alone and I'm concerned for his safety." My hope is Stone might respond to the call because of his brother.

Who's in my house? What are they doing in there? What could they possibly want?

And more importantly, what's taking Sebastian so long?

Chapter 28

[Sebastian]

When I entered Enya's home, the intruder had exited, leaving the back door wide open. I didn't have a clear view of him, other than a dark figure racing across the land behind her home. The open meadow wouldn't hide someone in broad daylight, but the night was pitch black with nothing more than faint moonlight illuminating shadows in the yard.

My reactive nature told me to run . . . toward the offender.

I've only made it halfway across the yard, blindly chasing someone when I hear a call behind me.

"Put your hands up where I can see 'em." I recognize Andy Whitehall's voice.

"Don't shoot." I holler, skittering to a stop before bending forward to catch my breath. Knowing how adrenaline can make a strong man weak and trigger happy, I yell again. "Do. Not. Shoot."

Dammit, I'd lost him. With no lights, not to mention the difficult terrain in nothing more than athletic slides on my feet, I'd lost whoever was in Enya's home.

"Put your hands up," I hear as the thudding of heavy feet draws closer to me.

What the fuck? Slowly, I hold up my hands. "Andy. It's fucking Sebastian. Sebastian Sylver." Hoping he recognizes my voice or at least thinks twice before pulling the trigger on his gun, I cautiously turn around. Somewhere shots ring out and I'm not certain if it's coming from before me or behind. Either way, I drop to the ground, flattening myself.

Thundering feet still rush toward me, and I glance up to see Andy approaching, gun forward and aimed at me.

"Andy," I bark again. "It's Sebastian."

On a good day, Andy's an idiot. I don't have time to think twice about what kind of day it might be for him today before he closes the distance between us, gun wobbling in his hand, but still pointed at me.

With my arms stretched out in front of me where he can see them, body prone on my belly on the dirt, the position is reminiscent of the night I was arrested.

I ran from this same house then, too.

That night, the new sheriff was in hot pursuit. Surprisingly, Stone could run, and he'd tackled me, pinning me to this very field. He'd flipped me over, surprised and disappointed when he saw it was me.

"Don't do it," I'd begged, knowing he didn't have a choice.

"Don't make me choose," he'd responded, knowing he had no other option. He patted down my pockets and pulled out a package. Handcuffs captured my wrists. "Sebastian Sylver, you're under arrest for possession of drugs with the intent to sell . . ."

It was only later that they found a body, beaten to death. My bloody swollen knuckles confessed my guilt.

"What did you do?" Stone had whispered, admitting defeat as we sat separated by jail cell bars. He couldn't get me out of this new hole I'd dug. The resolution would be more than community service picking up trash at the local park.

"I was trying to defend Vale," I'd explained in lockup. My brother had done something similar once upon a time.

"There are other ways," Stone reprimanded.

He was such a hypocrite and I'd hated him that night.

"Andy," Stone hollers, feet rumbling closer to us. "Stand down."

"I got him," Andy states, not giving a care to the truth. Some people still don't forgive me for what happened here. Some won't ever forget, like Andy. "I got the guy."

The clip on his gun clicks and I close my eyes, knowing this is it. Like oil and water, ignorance does not mix with empathy.

My final thoughts are of Enya and Adara. How I love them both and I haven't told either of them how I feel.

"Andy," Stone yells, drawing closer. "Put the fucking gun down now."

"I got him," Andy shouts again. His voice is too high, adrenaline too strong. He remains over me. I don't bother looking up again. Instead,

I close my eyes, willing myself to only focus on Enya. Her sweet kiss. Her soft eyes.

I'll pick you every time.

Suddenly, a body hits the ground hard a few feet from me. A gun goes off again, and I cover my head with my hands, holding my breath.

Inhale. Exhale. Inhale. Exhale.

A quick mental assessment tells me I'm not hurt. I'm still alive. I roll my head to see one large body lying over another.

"Stone?" My voice croaks. A new fear takes over. "Stone!" I scramble to my knees and crawl to my brother.

"I'm alright," he mutters, breathing heavily, words strangled. He rolls off Andy. Both men lay on their backs, facing upward.

"What the fuck, Andy?" I yell, finally upright and stepping over Stone who catches my shin and forces me downward, falling on top of Andy. With a sharp elbow, I slam him in the gut.

"*Umph,*" Andy chokes.

"You idiot," I snap, pressing off him and scrambling back crab-walk style like I can't get away from him fast enough.

"I thought you were him," Andy grumbles.

"Well, I wasn't," I bark, childishly giving him a strong kick in the upper thigh. *Dickhead.* "I lost him."

"What did you see?" Stone asks.

"Not much. Just the back of a shirt. Something draping, maybe a flannel. A hood was over his head, like it was part of the shirt or maybe a sweatshirt underneath. Person wasn't very tall." Maybe my height or shorter, but I couldn't be certain. I'm a terrible witness because I wasn't taking measurements or making out colors. I only saw red and ran.

"You should not have pursued," Stone scolds me.

He's right, but still I snap. "Well, I had to do something." I couldn't let whoever it was get away. He was in Enya's house. What if she'd been home? What if she and the baby had been sleeping? What if I hadn't gotten here?

"Fuck," I growl, pressing up off the ground to stand. Panic strikes. "Where's Enya? Adara?"

"They're both safely in her car."

"But how do you know, if you're out here?"

I race back toward the house, fear pushing me forward. Powering onward, I round the house, and see Enya exiting her SUV.

Nearly knocking each other over, we collide in her yard, holding onto one another like if one or the other releases, we'll melt into the gravel.

She's kissing my neck and my jaw before I'm holding her head and kissing her forehead and her nose. Our mouths finally meet, and I kiss her hard with all the adrenaline and anxiety rushing through my veins.

I need her.

I need to feel her everywhere to convince myself she's safe.

Within minutes, we're interrupted by a throat clearing and then the sharp bark of my name.

"Sebastian." Stone's tone reminds me of the time he caught me on the couch with Rachel Eickelmann when I was sixteen.

Enya and I break apart, but I don't release her. With my arms around her back, I tug her to my chest and place my head on hers, blanketing her with my body, before looking at my brother.

"I need to take a statement," Stone says.

"I already told you what I saw."

"Not from you. From Enya." Stone nods at her.

Andy slowly limps around the house, rubbing at his thigh. "Sir, with all due respect, I should press charges."

"For what?" I bark. "I should press charges on you for holding a gun on me."

"I heard the gunshots," Enya's breath is heavy with fear. "I thought . . ." She shudders against me, and I hold her tighter, pressing my lips to her head again. She buries her face against my chest, wrapping her arms as tightly around me.

"You have a history of breaking and entering," Andy continues. "How do we know it wasn't you?"

What a fucker. "Breaking and entering would be pretty hard to do considering I was *with* Enya when it was happening." We weren't in her car together, but I couldn't possibly beat her to her place. Nor would I have any reason to break into her house. I have the fucking code. Not to mention, there isn't anything in there I'd want to steal. Everything important to me is in my arms.

"Where's Adara?" I whisper to Enya.

"She's in the car, sleeping."

"But your truck is here, separate from hers," Andy continues.

"Right. Because I parked in the front driveway to break into the back door of the house." How is this man even on the force?

"Alright." Stone holds up a hand. "Andy, that's enough of this nonsense." He turns to me. "Sebastian, I'm certain you have a perfectly good alibi."

"Are you kidding me, right now?" I glare at my brother. *Un-fucking-believable.*

"He was with me," Enya interjects. "We'd just left his apartment. Your brother Knox is there now and can attest we've all been at Sebastian's for hours. Plus, I got here first. Sebastian arrived less than five minutes *after* me."

She glares at Andy who takes the dressing down by lowering his eyes.

"I saw lights flash across the living room window from the inside and called Sebastian first."

"Why didn't you call 9-1-1?" Andy admonishes.

"Andy, shut the fuck up," I growl.

"Sebastian," Stone warns.

"I called 9-1-1 after Sebastian entered the house to see who was inside."

"Is anything missing?" Stone asks.

"I haven't been inside yet. Sebastian told me to wait in the car. Then you arrived and said the same thing."

"So he was in your house a few minutes before us?" Andy asks, implication in his voice. "Knowing you have a history here—"

"That's enough, Deputy Sheriff Whitehall. You can head back to your vehicle now."

Andy glances up at Stone, staring at his superior with both shock and hurt before he hobbles toward his car.

"Why the fuck do you let men like him work for you?" I demand of Stone, squeezing Enya tighter.

"Enya," he addresses her, ignoring me. "Let's take a look inside."

"Is there anyone else in there?" Her voice is weak, trembling even.

Fuck. "I didn't look around," I explain to Stone. "I only chased one person out the back door. I have no idea if there was more than one."

Stone nods and speaks into his walkie. Andy returns with an exaggerated hobble and both men enter the house, taking a few minutes to turn on lights and inspect the place.

Enya and I move as one closer to her Honda where Adara is still sleeping.

"I was so scared for you," Enya whispers with a shaky voice.

"Nothing can touch me." I grip her face. "Nothing will touch you or Adara either. Not ever."

When Stone returns to the front porch, waving for us to enter, I remove Adara from the SUV.

Entering her house, Enya begins to visibly shake, shock settling in. I set Adara's car seat down near the couch where I tell Enya to sit. I take a seat beside her and wrap my arm around her as her body continues to tremble. "Sugar?"

"Someone was in my house," she mutters, the reality catching up to her. "I thought you'd been shot." Her face turns white. Her hands visibly tremble. I tug her onto my lap, not getting her close enough. I want her to feel the heat still coming off me from the chase. Use my warmth to comfort her and settle her.

"I'm okay," I whisper to her. "I'm right here." And I'm not going anywhere. No one is going to get near her or Adara, like I promised.

"The bad news is, there was no forced entry." Stone states, standing a few feet from us on the couch.

"What?" I snap.

"The back door might have been open when you chased but there's no sign of forced entry anywhere."

"Are you saying someone just walked into my house?" Enya stiffens on my lap.

Stone doesn't answer but his hard face does. How is that possible? Enya has codes on her entryways and an alarm system. I'm not liking this. Not one bit.

"I'm sorry to do this, but I need Enya to walk around. See if anything is missing,"

Enya nods, and hesitantly lifts from my legs. "Of course."

Immediately, she points at an open door. "I never leave the cellar door open. It's always closed. I hardly go down there." The open door leads to a staircase beneath the main staircase. The space contains boxes and storage items. Despite Enya's renovations, the original cellar remains intact with low ceilings. A portion of the floor is still dirt.

Enya explains how the foundation of the house was repaired but not reconstructed when she bought the place. She hadn't intended to put a full basement in this house. Still, Stone asks Enya to show him around down there. I already know Enya doesn't like to go in the cellar because it's dark and a little damp.

When they reappear, Stone vaguely points around the first floor. "And this is all new construction?"

"There wasn't much salvageable from the original house other than the blueprint," Enya explains. "Most of the layout is not the same as the original."

Stone meets my eyes a second before addressing Enya again. "Let's look around this level."

Enya leads Stone around the open concept while I watch from my perch near Adara. Eventually, Enya leads Stone upstairs.

As my body begins to settle down from the adrenaline rush, wild thoughts build up.

Who was in here? What did they want? Was it a simple break-in?

Or have ghosts revived to haunt me?

Worse yet, am I putting Enya and Adara in danger?

+ + +

"Nothing's missing," Enya tells me as returns to the first floor with Stone behind her. She crosses the space to the couch, and I immediately stand, pulling her to my chest.

The fact nothing was taken confirms this was not a random break-in. Someone was looking for something.

Enya asks the same question I have. "What would they have been looking for?"

"Rumor has it money was buried here," Andy states, glaring at me like I know anything about said rumors.

I'd heard them, but the myth is almost ten years old.

"That's speculation," Stone counters, narrowing his eyes at his deputy. "And we don't work off hearsay."

"Money?" Enya chokes. "Even if someone buried money here, the house was vacant for years. Wouldn't they have come back for it?"

My mind swirls. Was the guy who ran from me at the party in the woods running toward something? Other than hiding out. Other than cowering. Was he here to uncover buried treasure? Maybe something that belonged to him. Or something that wasn't his to begin with.

Guys got greedy. Some skimmed off the top. Took side deals. Stole from their bosses.

I'd never been like that. I wasn't a thief even if I once had breaking and entering charges pressed against me.

"You mentioned the cellar hadn't been renovated," Stone clarifies.

"If someone buried something downstairs, wouldn't that involve a trap door or a secret chamber?" Enya scoffs. "Even a loose brick or a fake one would have been found when the foundation was repaired. The soil in the dirt flooring was disturbed by the foundation rebuild. If something had been buried, wouldn't it have been found? Nothing suspicious was discovered. And, if the old furnace or hot water heater were hiding places, they were both scrapped during demolition. There isn't anywhere to hide something. The rest of the house is all new."

Stone and I exchange a look. Did someone plant something in the new construction?

Andy continues to glare at me, like he knows I know something about this mystery money when I don't.

Enya shifts, placing her back to my chest. With my hands on her upper arms, I can't see her face, but her words are firm. "I know what happened here. What he did."

Andy glances over her head at me but Enya snaps her fingers, getting his attention.

"If you're going to investigate what happened here tonight, with preconceived notions, I'm going to respectfully request of your superior that you aren't assigned on this case." Enya swivels to face Stone. "Do you hear me, Sheriff? That's my official statement. He's not allowed to work on his investigation."

Stone's mouth does this weird twisting thing as he clamps his lips shut. He's getting scolded by this woman . . . who is defending me.

Is he fighting a smile?

I should interject. Say I can speak for myself or fight my own battles, but I'm too tongue-tied. No one has ever stood up for me. No one has spoken in my favor before.

"I will not have Sebastian Sylver implicated in anyway in this investigation, and anyone who speaks ill of him in my home, let alone out in the community"—Enya points toward the front door—"Well, that person is not welcome in my house and should be ashamed of himself, if he represents equality and justice for all."

"Ma'am." Andy swallows, lowering his head.

"Stone, is there anything else you need tonight?" she asks.

"We should check for fingerprints and take some pictures." He glances at me. "Could you go home with Sebastian tonight?"

Absolutely, I want to shout but Enya answers for me. "I just need to grab a few things."

"The less you touch the better," Stone warns.

"I need diapers and formula." She peers down at Adara, still sleeping in her car seat through the commotion. "And a change of clothes for her and me, and then the bottle heater and—"

Stone lifts a hand and roughly chuckles. "I'll walk around with you and point out the best way to pick up what you need."

Enya's shoulders relax and I give them a squeeze. It's been a very long day . . . and night.

But I'm taking both my girls home with me.

Chapter 29

[Enya]

Sebastian drives my car back to the bakery. When we enter his place, the second bedroom door is closed, signaling Knox is inside asleep.

"Would you mind if we put Adara in your room with us?"

"Of course not." Sebastian steps up to me, giving me a kiss before taking the car seat into his room first. Within minutes he has the portable bassinet set up and I'm nursing Adara for a final feed.

Once she's down, I turn to Sebastian who had been lying face down on his bed. "Would you mind if I took a shower?" I'm exhausted, but I need to wash off the bad parts of this night.

"Enya, baby. You stayed here for weeks. You don't need to ask me for a thing." His smile is weak, cautious even. The adrenaline rush from him chasing the intruder has crashed and I suspect he'll be asleep before I close the bathroom door.

Inside the bathroom, everything races back to me.

Someone shot at Sebastian. He still isn't certain if the shot came from the person running away from my place or Andy, the deputy, but—

Someone. Shot. At. Him.

For ten full minutes, I couldn't breathe after that deafening sound and before I spied Sebastian rounding the house. My heart might have even stopped because the thought of losing him nearly killed me.

I turn the hot water handle, allowing the water to heat while the rushing sound muffles the tears I can't contain.

I could have lost Sebastian tonight. In an instant, he could have been gone from my life. From Adara's and mine. Before we truly began, we'd be over.

I turn on the cold water to balance the hot and cup both hands over my mouth to mute the next wave of tears.

Someone broke into my house. No, someone walked into my house. Someone looking for buried treasure, which seems ridiculous. Surely, if someone hid money in that house, it had been found, claimed, or moved by now. As I'd told Stone, nothing from the original home remained other than the foundation and even that had been repaired in several places. Still, someone had invaded the privacy of my house tonight. The home I intended to raise Adara in.

Nothing of importance was damaged or taken, but I feel violated. A creepy-crawly sensation ripples over my skin like I've been touched by someone I didn't want to touch me. Or something unpleasant and gross has rubbed against my flesh. I'm not even certain soap can rid me of the dirty feeling. My shoulders shudder and my spine tingles as if I'm arching away from an phantom hand, a hidden presence, the unseen person who entered my home uninvited.

Stepping into the shower, I close the door like the space can hide me or keep me safe from the invisible intruder. My legs are no longer able to hold me upright, and I fold down to the floor. Like a giant flushing of my system, my limbs have given out. My body trembles once again in shock.

With my forehead tucked to my knees, I don't hear the bathroom door open, but the soft click of the shower stall has me lifting my head.

"Sugar," Sebastian whispers as he squats and stares at me seated against the tiled wall.

Tears slither down my face mixing with the spray of the shower.

"What did they want? I don't have anything."

"I know, baby. I know." Sebastian wears only boxer briefs, and he steps into the shower. In one swift motion, I'm up in his arms, clinging to his chest, wrapping my legs around his middle. My back is braced against the tile wall while the shower pummels Sebastian's side.

"You're okay, baby. You're safe. Adara's safe, too. I'm never going to let anyone get to you. You believe me, right?"

I nod into the crook of his neck and shoulder, but he presses my face back, forcing me to look at him. His eyes tell me he needs the words.

"I trust you," I remind him before my mouth crashes against his, needing to confirm he's alive. *He's* safe. I'm safe. Adara is, too.

Our mouths move, hungry and desperate, like the kiss we shared in my yard. Relief hit me then, as well. I'd been eager to remove his clothes and take him on my lawn in an effort to remind myself he was whole.

Now, nothing holds us back. "I need you," I whimper against his mouth, sipping at his lower lip, then thrusting my tongue over his. Tightening my arms around his neck, I hitch myself higher, dragging my center along his hardness.

"Sebastian, please," I beg.

"Baby, what about earlier?"

Earlier, we had a romantic hour on the rooftop, blanketed in fireworks, and surrounded by the scent of us coming together. I need that again and more.

"What about it?" I murmur, keeping my mouth attached to his.

"Are you sore?"

I shake my head, lips still pressed to his lips.

Sebastian lowers my legs and steps back, removing his soaked boxers. We didn't see enough of each other on the rooftop. I hadn't removed my bra. A blanket covered our legs. But here we stand, revealed to one another, naked and raw. Our eyes roam before I turn around, giving him my back.

"Please," I whine, tipping my forehead to the tile while my palms flatten against the steam-drenched wall.

Sebastian runs his hand up my spine before cupping the back of my neck. He tugs me toward him and sips at my shoulder. Then he's sliding his hands up and down my sides while nipping at my neck. His teeth drag over my flesh. His lips suck hard. His tongue draws lines along the column of my throat. His palms skim up my middle and cup my breasts.

Instantly, the let-down sensation tingles across my nipples. "Shit."

"What?" Sebastian stills. His hands pause on my breasts.

"I'm . . ." This is so embarrassing. "I'm leaking."

Sebastian only hums along my neck in understanding before lowering his hands and gripping my waist. "I want to make you weep elsewhere."

He drives one hand between my thighs while the other clutches on my hip. Rocking my body, he easily slips a finger inside me. Almost immediately, a second joins the first and then he retreats, rubbing at my clit, until I'm panting against the tile.

"Fuck me," I whisper, desperate, wanting him closer. I don't need the orgasm as much as I need the connection. Him inside me. Us joined as one.

However, Sebastian continues stroking the sensitive nub, winding me tighter and tighter.

"Sebastian," I groan.

"I don't have a condom in here and I'm not stopping until you come." He bites the juncture of my neck and shoulder hard, and my knees buckle. My palms squeak against the moist tile, unable to catch on anything for support.

"I trust you," I tell him. We had the clean talk. He knows I haven't been with anyone since last summer.

"Enya—" He pauses. "I've *never* been without."

Having tipped my head forward, I close my eyes and roll my forehead against a grout line. *Of course*. Why am I pressuring him? "I understand."

Then, I gasp. His smooth tip is at my entrance while his fingers work my clit. I spread my legs a little more, shamelessly enjoying the tease. He draws his solid length back and forth along my slit, massaging against my tipping point. I'm so close.

"Sugar? Are you sure?"

My lids flip open. Craning my neck so I can meet his eyes, I say, "I'm sure." I've never been more certain of anything in my life. I want Sebastian Sylver inside me, raw and deep, and losing his mind over me like I lose mine over him.

With a swift thrust, he fills me. My breath catches at the sudden intrusion.

"Did I hurt you?"

"Never." He'd never hurt me. I believe that wholeheartedly.

With his hand back at my hip, he tugs so my backside tips toward him. His fingers work magic at my clit while he hammers into me.

"I can't . . ." He grunts. "It's never . . ." He snorts. "I'm not going to last."

I'm right there. Pressing my cheek to the tile, I bite the inside and hold back a groan as best I can, but sound still echoes around the room.

"Fuck," Sebastian cries out. "Yes."

He's deliciously sliding in and out of me. Filling me. Teasing me. Quickly, a familiar sensation flutters inside me, but I question it. "Sebastian?"

"Gonna come on me, baby."

I moan. "Oh God, please don't stop." He's hitting me somewhere unseen and tapping my clit, and I'm lost in the abyss of Sebastian in me, around me. Us together.

"Yes," he demands, driving faster. I'm nearly bent in half, my body begging him to take everything from me.

"Sugar?" he strains, so close but holding back waiting on me. Like in everything else he does, he's considerate of me first.

"Come," I command.

Buried to the hilt, he halts. Then abruptly he pulls out, leaving me empty from the loss of him.

"No," I whimper, but he keeps his fingers rubbing my clit. Circling, vibrating, driving me to the edge. I make a fist against the tile wall as I hear skin jerking skin. His tip is at the top of my backside. He jolts and pumps, releasing against my skin, signing his name on my flesh.

And I shatter as well.

"Jesus," he whispers, lifting my upper half and flattening me against the cool tile. Lowering his forehead to my shoulder, he exhales. "That was incredible."

I shiver while a giggle ripples up my throat. *He's* incredible. "Thank you."

Sebastian chuckles against my neck. "Now what are you thanking me for?"

"You. Just being you." With my cheek to the wall, he seeks my mouth and I spin in his arms, kissing him with everything I have. Everything I am. I never want to lose him.

+ + +

I wake with a sudden jolt and turn my head to find Sebastian still asleep beside me. When we went to bed last night, he apologized for being a stomach sleeper and then situated me.

"Your right leg over my left," he'd said. I did as I was told. "Now, your arm over my back." Once my arm wrapped over his lower back, he wiggled as if settling into the position of me holding him. This was his form of cuddling, and I didn't mind. Not one bit.

When I wake, though, I'm disoriented and catalogue everything.

I'm in Sebastian's apartment.

Based on the brighter light seeping into his bedroom, it's morning.

Then, last night hits me.

The rooftop. The break-in. The shower. What a roller-coaster ride.

Swiping a hand through my hair, I hold back the mess. We showered after everything, and I went to bed with my hair wet which I never do. Rolling my head on the pillow, I seek Adara in her bassinet. Sebastian must have given her the three a.m. bottle and then crawled back into bed.

When I turn my head to face him, he's watching me.

"Good morning," he groggily states.

"Good morning." A weak smile forms.

He's still in bed. While he works early, and that's a reasonable excuse to leave my place in the dark hours of morning, it often feels like he's sneaking out of my house. Like if he doesn't stay the whole night, he isn't really spending the night.

"You're still here." My surprise cannot be contained.

Sebastian rolls and runs both hands over his face. He blinks up at the ceiling. "I texted Rena last night. Told her I needed her to open for me. I can't work on three hours of sleep." He looks at me, wincing.

I only sleep three hours at a time, if that. "I get it." I pat his forearm, but he catches my hand and rolls toward me.

"What time is it?"

My phone is underneath my pillow and I check clock app. "Eight o'clock."

Did Adara sleep and we missed a feeding? How grateful I'll be when we can skip a nightly feed.

I slip from bed, change Adara's diaper and lift her. Her sleepy body twists and curls, but when I sit back on Sebastian's bed, she settles in to nurse. Most times, Sebastian turns away or he's asleep when I do this so close to him. This morning, he watches.

"She's so incredible." His voice is rough. "I meant what I said last night. I'd never let anyone get near either of you. Hurt either of you." His brows pinch. A deep crease forms. "I'm worried that break in has to do with me."

"What? Why would you say that?"

"I don't know. Everything just feels off. That house *is* haunted in so many ways." He tilts his head to look up at me. "What if money *is* still there, somewhere?"

I don't believe buried treasure exists in my house. I don't see how it's possible. "How much money could we even be talking about?"

Sebastian shrugs. "Who knows? A small drug deal could make a couple hundred, maybe a few thousand. Over time, it could lead to a lot. Or maybe someone had a big payout and stashed it there for a while. It's hard to know."

"A few thousand?" I don't see the value in seeking out money from over a decade ago in a house newly rebuilt without much trace of the original footprint.

Sebastian watches me, eyes intense. "To a small-time dealer or an addict, a couple thousand is like millions. Every penny counts to make a dollar."

While Seamus was the bad boy in our family, I worked hard to remain the good girl. I hadn't considered how deeply troubled, or deeply *in* trouble, he might have been until years later, when we were older.

He'd come to me for money. Lance was furious when I gave it to him, arguing I was enabling my brother and his habit. I might have been, but I also wanted my brother to eat, which was often his excuse. I fell for his lies out of guilt. Guilt that I was who I was—educated, successful, goal-driven—while he was who he'd been. A drug addict. Probably homeless. Eventually, my brother was estranged from the family. The authorities finding my parents upon his passing is a wonder. Sebastian and I remain quiet as Adara nurses. When she finishes, I place her between us on the bed. Sebastian rolls to his side to give her more room and I slip down to my side mirroring his position. For a few minutes, we breathe in her sleeping form. Her tiny body. The subtle beat of her heart. Her entire life is ahead of us. Or at least for me, but I so want Sebastian to be part of the journey.

"When you look at her, I don't know how you couldn't be awed, excited even, for all the stages of her future."

Sebastian snorts. "My life was so fucked up as a kid, I can't even imagine what those stages should look like."

"What was messed up?" I already know most of his story, but I still want him to tell me more specifics.

His forehead furrows, like he's thinking. He doesn't look at me but stares at Adara. "My mom died when I was too little to remember her. But there were moments as I grew up that I missed her. The idea of her." He doesn't blink while watching Adara sleep. "I told you how Clint's mom taught me how to bake. She was the only mother figure I'd known. When my dad found out, and I tried to explain how I missed my mother, I cried. He told me I wasn't allowed to cry for her because I didn't know her. He also said I was a pussy for being so weak and learning a girly skill. That's when the first smack happened." He swallows. "After the next few, I toughened up. Knox often intervened."

"I'm so sorry that happened to you."

Sebastian closes his eyes.

"Losing your mother. Losing your friend's mother. Even losing your father, long before he died. I'm so sorry, Sebastian."

I want to cry on Sebastian's behalf. It isn't fair to ask a child not to mourn his mother, whether he knew her or not. The idea of her must have been confusing and disheartening because he hadn't known her. He had no memory of her. And when he'd received the kindness of a friend's mother, he'd been cut off from her kindness. Belittled for it, punished for it.

No child should be smacked. Period.

"You never told me what happened to your father." I keep my voice low, sensing the topic of his dad is very sensitive.

"He killed himself." Anger and spite fill Sebastian's voice. Not a trace of regret, or ounce of sorrow comes with the memory of his father's death. He exhales deeply, watching Adara again. "I'm worried I'll be like him."

"Never." Shock fills my throat, choking me. There is no doubt in my mind. "You'll never be like him, Sebastian. You're the most caring, considerate, patient man I've ever known."

He finally looks up at me, ready to refute my compliments.

"And this right here." I point at Adara. "She is love. And you are meant to be a father, if for no other reason than to prove he didn't break you."

Sebastian stares at me and I want to say more. I want to tell him how my decision to become a mother came about. How I was hurt by Lance and tired of the pity. *She was with a man for eleven years, but they never got married. Not even a proposal.* Screw everyone else. I didn't need a man to have a child. I could parent on my own. I would be a great mother. A supportive, loving, present parent.

Sebastian's phone rings, like the crackling of glass, breaking the serious moment. He shifts to reach for it on his nightstand. "Hello."

Adara stirs and I place a hand on her belly, feeling her little heart beneath my palm. She's my reason for everything.

"I'll be right down." Sebastian hangs up and tosses the blanket off him. He stands, wearing a fresh pair of boxer briefs and turns to me. He's a work of art. A true masterpiece of muscle and skin and tattoos. He's opposite everything I thought I'd be attracted to and yet I've never felt the pull so strongly to another human being.

"I got a delivery. I'll be back in a few minutes."

I nod, unable to find my voice as I drink in his body. Watching him dress is almost as sexy as watching him undress. He comes to my side of his bed and presses a quick kiss to my lips then lays his hand on Adara's head a second. When he's out the door, I take a minute to collect my thoughts.

And still my heart.

Because I'm in love with a man who doesn't want what I have.

+ + +

After I've used the bathroom and tugged my hair into a messy bun, I dress and bring Adara into the living room. The door to the bedroom where Knox slept is ajar giving me a view of the rumbled bed.

Within seconds, the door at the bottom of the stairs opens and I hear two male voices.

"I got the top."

"I got the bottom."

"Go slow."

"Lift a little higher."

There's nothing sexual about the conversation between men straining as they lift something up the staircase and yet I can't get my mind out of the gutter. Knox and Sebastian are a comedy act as they climb upward with an awkward box.

"I like the top."

"I like the bottom."

Someone grunts. "More control on the top."

"Less work on the bottom."

"You're a lazy fucker," Sebastian states with a laugh.

"I definitely heard how hard you work last night."

My mouth falls open as they crest the top of the staircase and set the box on its side.

Knox glances over at me and winks. "No ceilings in this place."

I gaze toward the rooms walled off but with open space between the wall and the twelve-foot ceiling. My face heats. My cheeks must be fire-engine red.

"Don't tease her, asshole," Sebastian barks but the damage is done. I'm so embarrassed. I didn't think we were *that* loud.

Knox gives a good-natured laugh. "At least someone's getting something."

"Oh. My. God," I mutter, and Sebastian smacks his brother's chest.

"So, what's for breakfast?" Knox rubs his hands together, like an eager child ready to start his day.

"Coffee and a Danish on the house. Downstairs." Sebastian pushes his brother who only laughs again.

"You're kicking me out after I helped you?" Knox nods at the box.

"And I helped you last night. Remember you hid here." Sebastian reminds him. "How'd that work out for you?"

Knox lowers his head, shaking it. "Fuck you." His voice is softer. "I didn't think you would be back last night."

Sebastian and I exchange a look before Sebastian explains to Knox what happened.

"Fuck," Knox hisses, running a hand through his hair. "And Stone is on it, right?"

"He is the sheriff," Sebastian reminds him.

Knox narrows his eyes. "You know what I mean. Stone won't let this rest because it's family."

The ferocity of his statement startles me. *I'm not family.*

"And fuck Andy," he continues. "What a tool."

Knox looks over at me. "Okay, I'm out of here." He crosses the room and rubs a hand over Adara's head. "Thanks for being my date last night. Uncle Knox thinks you're the best."

I glance at Sebastian, who opens his mouth as if to refute Knox's claim. He isn't her uncle. Not biologically. But if Adara had five burly uncles, I wouldn't be upset.

Knox surprises me again by leaning in and giving me a kiss on the cheek. "Don't let him go." My gaze follows his retreat. I don't want to lose Sebastian. Staying would be his choice.

Knox walks back to his brother and claps him on the arm. "Call me later." Then he's thundering down the stairs and closing the door behind him.

"What's this?" I finally ask, nodding at the box.

"It's a Pack 'N Play."

My mouth falls open. "A what?" I know what it is, but what I don't understand is why Sebastian bought the portable crib.

"When I babysat for you, I realized I didn't have what Adara would need in order to sleep at my place. When I invited you to the parade, I'd hoped you'd spend the night. With her. I'd ordered this thing a few days ago, but with the holiday, it didn't arrive until this morning." Sebastian runs a hand over the brown container. "I was hoping maybe Adara could hang out with me sometimes. Or maybe if you traveled out of town and needed help, she could stay with me."

I didn't know how to respond. On the one hand, this was an incredibly sweet gesture, and my heart did cartwheels at the thought that Sebastian put into this idea. He wanted to spend time with my baby girl.

On the other hand, it sounded like he was implying some kind of shared responsibility for Adara. Like joint custody, which was ridiculous. Was he hoping for an every-other-weekend arrangement so he could get a baby fix?

I hated that my mind leapt there and roped my thoughts back in to appreciate the considerate gesture.

Sebastian bought a portable baby crib, so Adara had a place to sleep when she was here.

"That's incredibly generous of you." My voice doesn't express the strength of my gratitude. I actually sound off-kilter, even to myself.

His phone rings again and he pulls it from his pocket. With a deep scowl, he answers. "Yeah." Silence. "Okay, I'll be right down."

He clicks off and shakes his head. "I swear. Rena." As if that explains everything. "I've got to get downstairs. I expected a slow day after the fireworks, but everyone is hungover and wants coffee. And Barnett called in sick."

The high school kid who works for him is sweet in a quiet way.

Sebastian steps over to me. "Make yourself at home."

"I should probably get to mine."

Sebastian runs a hand down my arm. "There's no rush. And I don't want you there without me. Let me check in with Stone. They might still be investigating."

I nod and Sebastian leans in to kiss me. The brush of his lips is too soft, too quick, and reminds me too much of the rushed kisses Lance once gave me.

When Sebastian pulls back, his expression questions mine. "What?"

"It's nothing."

"It's something. You have a strange look on your face."

I shake my head and glance away. "Lance would kiss me like that." I turn back to Sebastian. "It's silly. You aren't him. Just go to work." I don't know why I'm suddenly pushing him away. Everything in the last twenty-four hours is just catching up to me, and I need some space. A moment to think or regroup or I don't know what . . .

"Your father is a dick," Sebastian addresses Adara, rubbing a hand over her head before lifting his hands for my face and tugging me too him for a real kiss.

One involving his open mouth and strong tongue. He pulls at my lower lip with his teeth before releasing me and stares into my eyes. "I can't kiss you like that and go to work. It winds me up and now I'll only think about everything I want to do to you all day."

My face heats again.

"Actually, I'll think about you all day anyway."

"Yeah?" I ask, hating that I'm looking for reassurance. Hating that I hope Sebastian isn't a dead end, or a wrong turn, or just on an unfamiliar path *he* wants to travel again and again until he no longer likes the trip.

"Yeah." He leans in to kiss me once more, a little less intense but not too quick. I'm going to think about him all day, too.

When he steps away, I say, "Lance isn't her dad. I already told you that."

Sebastian gives me a disbelieving look. He wants the truth, and I can trust him with it. "I'll tell you the story later, okay?"

"Yeah?" he mimics me, his mouth widening into a playful smile.

"Yeah. Now go to work."

He laughs and turns toward the stairs, rumbling down them as loudly as his brother did, and I hear in my head a house full of feet thumping up and down staircases.

A house filled with laughter and love.

Oh, but a dream.

Chapter 30

[Sebastian]

"Where the hell is Barnett?" I grumble for the second time this morning. It's a rhetorical question.

I'm edgy. My body still hums from kissing Enya goodbye this morning. Hell, everything in me vibrates from our entire night. The ups and downs of yesterday. I'd wanted to linger a little longer in bed. Make her breakfast and then spend the day on my couch, holding her, making love to her.

The rooftop had been insane. The shower completely unexpected. Enya soft and pure. Enya demanding and needy. Just thinking about her either way makes me fucking hard.

"I told you he called in sick," Rena states, startling me.

Sick. *Sure he was.* A seventeen-year-old boy out on the Fourth of July. If he was anything like me, he was hungover as hell, but I needed him here.

"Rena." I snap as we almost collide behind the counter after I finish a customer's coffee order. She's like a shadow today, giving new meaning to riding my ass. *Give me some fucking space.*

What is with her today? She's already asked me three times what I did last night when it's none of her fucking business. Plus, she's so close to me, hovering even, like she'll learn the details of my night from her proximity.

As we circle around one another, the door to my apartment stairwell opens. Enya enters the bakery, juggling Adara in the car seat.

"Sugar," I grunt, setting down a customer's order and pointing at Rena to ring him up. Rushing around the counter, I catch up to Enya as she closes the privacy door. "What are you doing?"

"It's a beautiful day and I need some air. I thought I'd take Adara for a walk."

Shit. I want to take a walk as well. I'm suffocating today under the pressure of work and the weight of the break-in. Add to that the confusion in Enya's eyes when the portable crib was delivered and then her admission that she's ready to tell me how Adara came about . . . and it's been a fucking long day when it isn't even ten o'clock.

"I'll get the stroller. Wait here." Exiting out the back of the bakery, I take the stroller out of Enya's SUV. The difficulty of living in an apartment with a baby hits me. Living on one floor doesn't involve steep stairs to climb with a weighty car seat. A garage provides easy access to a house. Plus, Enya told me she wanted space, including a yard, for Adara to run and play and discover the outdoors.

The idea is a reminder of my home growing up. How we had the empty stables and a large yard to get lost in, especially when Dad was drunk. I didn't want Adara to ever feel the need to escape but just explore outside. I wanted her to always feel safe.

And I was concerned that I might be the danger in her life.

The break-in messed me up. With Andy's reminder of rumors that money might be somewhere in Enya's place, I didn't like the connection between me and that old house.

When I bring the stroller into the bakery for Enya, a man is just walking into the shop. I immediately recognize him as the guy who bought Enya a lemonade.

Cocky confidence exudes around him when he sees Enya, but the moment we catch eyes—mine glaring, his surprised—he backs out of the bakery, like he's changed his mind about entering.

Coward. I'd love to chase him down and tell him to stay the hell away from my girls, but I stay put and help Enya clip the infant seat into the stroller.

"I'd like to go with you," I tell her, feeling vulnerable with the admission.

"I'd like that, too, but we can take another walk later." Her voice doesn't sound convincing that she'd take a second walk with me. "I just need to get out for a bit."

She means get away from me. I can sense it in her general quiet. She's going to walk away because she'll finally accept it's dangerous to associate with me.

That house holds ghosts, and they've come back to haunt.

+ + +

We don't do single order deliveries other than to fellow merchants, so I'm out on a run with afternoon coffees when Enya returns, and my brother has stopped by.

"Your brother said to call him. And that girl is upstairs."

"Rena," I warn. I do not appreciate her tone or her slighting the woman of my dreams.

"Are you two a *thing* now?"

"A thing?" I counter.

"You know, friends with benefits or something."

While I didn't want to see it, I cannot deny the way my employee looks at me. I am not attracted to her despite my awareness she is a good-looking woman in a rough and tumbled sort of way. After a stern look the day she dumped flour on me, and then tried to feel me up, we haven't mentioned the situation again. However, the subtle touches are adding up and her present attitude is too much.

"Rena, you got a problem with Enya?"

"No problem." Her tone suggests otherwise.

"Because if you do, then you and I have a problem." I point between us because there is no Rena and me. I'm her boss and I've been ignoring her getting handsy with me, but that shit needs to stop. And I won't tolerate anyone disrespecting Enya. We're more than friends with benefits but that's none of Rena's business.

"Got it." She nods once and looks away from me, but she's side-eyeing me like she'd like to knife me.

When I enter my apartment, Enya has her things packed up. The portable bassinet is closed and in its travel bag. The diaper backpack sits on the floor beside it. Enya has an additional tote full of things Stone let her take from her house.

"What's going on?" I ask a little too roughly.

"Stone wants me to meet him at the house. He says I'm free to come home."

"But I don't want you there." The admission doesn't surprise me other than I said it out loud.

Enya stops moving and stares at me. Her mouth falls open like she's ready to ask a question but then clamps it shut. She sighs before saying, "I was hoping you'd come with me."

"Of course." But does she mean come with her to meet my brother or come with her to stay the night, because there is no damn way she will be alone in that house until whoever broke in is caught. "Give me ten minutes."

I need a shower to wash off the bakery and collect my thoughts.

When I'm ready, I drive Enya back to her place in her SUV. We pull into her driveway and find Stone already present, waiting in his sheriff's car. He steps out of the vehicle when we park.

"Enya," he greets her, opening the passenger side door while I work on removing Adara from the backseat.

"Let's go inside," Stone suggests.

Enya waits for me and I take her hand, squeezing it as a reminder she's okay. Nobody is going to get to her or Adara.

However, I don't feel half as confident today as I'm trying to portray. I'm on edge about everything. Like a new day has shifted everything off kilter. How did we go from making love on my rooftop to her home being broken into? Then fucking in my shower to her shutting down at a portable crib in my apartment? The past twenty-four hours have been a topsy-turvy ride and I want everything to stop tilting sideways.

Once inside the house, Enya offers Stone something to drink. I don't miss how her voice catches when she looks at the back door. Whoever was in here, it was like he walked right in. Only the coward rushed right out once he was at risk of being caught.

Stone declines a drink and takes a seat at the kitchen island. I set Adara's car seat down and remove her from it. Enya is at my side, and I pass over the baby, assuming she needs to hang onto her daughter, grounding her in whatever Stone has to say.

"First, let me assure you that a sheriff's vehicle is going to be parked out here twenty-four seven."

"Is that necessary?" Enya asks, pressing a kiss to Adara's head. "It won't be that Andy guy, will it?"

I'm honored she thinks so little of Andy, especially since he might have been the one to shoot at me. I still can't believe how she stood up to him last night for me.

"Andy's been put on a leave of absence. It's fortunate he's a poor shot but hot pursuit doesn't mean shoot first, ask questions later, especially if you don't know whether you're shooting at a victim or a perpetrator. Andy knows better. He really does."

I didn't have any faith in Andy Whitehall, but I deferred to Stone as his boss.

"Anyway, it will be a few other people plus myself at times."

"What if I stay?" I ask.

Stone's brows hitch at the suggestion. "What about the bakery?"

Enya answers. "You can't leave work, and I'm home twenty-four seven right now. I won't live in fear. I appreciate the surveillance for a while."

Feeling chastised, I clench my teeth.

"Unfortunately, we didn't find any fingerprints, which we didn't expect we would. I wouldn't say this was a professional job but it's clear they weren't looking to rob your place, just scoop it out, especially the cellar. The only spot that had been tampered with was the original furnace flue."

Enya nods, knowing exactly where Stone is talking about. "When I got a new furnace, the contractor relocated it."

Stone is silent a moment before he asks, "Is there anyone you can think of that might have it out for you?"

I scoff. Enya can't possibly have an enemy in this world.

"Any suspicious behavior you've noticed around your place or people of interest when you go into town."

I immediately picture the guy who asked Enya out for a drink but wait on her to comment.

"The only enemy I might have might be Rena."

"What?" I bark.

"She's always so snippy with me, acting like she doesn't know who I am. I get it since she's infatuated with you. I'm the other woman."

"You're the *only* woman," I grit.

"But it also feels important to mention . . . I think Rena might be your bookkeeping problem."

"You have a bookkeeping issue?" Stone interjects.

"Enya, that's unwarranted." Shifting my eyes to Stone, he gives me a displeased look. He warned me not to hire her despite all his preaching about second chances. He offered to run a background check on her, but I'd told him I believed her story. She'd come forward with her history. She'd done drugs in the past, like me. She didn't have any arrests or convictions, and I didn't feel the need to pry deeper.

"Stone is asking about suspicious activity. I saw her slip her hands into her apron while in front of the cash register a few weeks ago. She caught me watching her. I didn't question it at the time, but that same night you mentioned being short in your daily close outs. I hadn't put anything together until today when I returned from taking a walk. You weren't around and the bakery was relatively empty except for one patron. She'd done the same thing in the same way. Slipped her hand into her apron pocket and then glanced up at me."

"That doesn't mean anything. So, she was putting her hands in her pocket. So what?"

"She'd just closed the cash drawer, both times."

I couldn't believe this. Why were we discussing my employee? What Enya saw happened at the bakery and had nothing to do with her house. Shouldn't there be an investigation into a real criminal? Plus, this was so fucking embarrassing to discuss in front of Stone who already thought I shouldn't have hired her.

"I don't believe it." Confident, I turn to Stone. "Just because she did drugs doesn't mean she's a thief." Although many people hooked on drugs can beg, borrow, and steal for the next hit. Rena was recovering like me.

"I didn't say she was a thief," Enya interjects. "I just think you should look into the shortages and when she works."

"It's not Rena," I snap. Glaring at Enya, I add, "You gave that speech last night to Andy about equality and justice. Be fair. Rena didn't break into your home."

"Speech?" Enya chokes. "I was defending you."

"Well, I don't need defending," I grouse.

Enya blinks, shocked by my outburst. She jiggles Adara in her arms, bouncing her once, maybe holding her tighter because of my rising tone.

Stone hisses, "Sebastian."

"What? This is total bullshit. Move on. Any *real* suspects?" I stay focused on my brother.

"Unfortunately, there is the possibility the break in could be tied to you."

I knew it. I fucking knew it.

"Like who?" I ask, knowing the list could be long. I'd killed a man. The web of drugs never ended with the removal of one person. There were streams of fingers and hands involved in the system. I'd turned over one guy when I was arrested.

"Seamus Randall?" Stone asks.

"Stone," I growl at the familiar name. My teeth clack together.

"Seamus?" Enya's brows lift. Her cheek brushes against Adara's head. "What does Seamus have to do with Sebastian?"

What? My heart hammers faster at her calm, questioning voice.

Stone sits up straighter, surprise in his solid face. "Do *you* know Seamus Randall?"

Enya glances at me before looking back at Stone again. "He's not a person of interest. He's dead."

"How did you know him?" Stone asks again, focusing on Enya. He's gone into full sheriff mode.

"He was my brother."

The earth falls out from beneath me. I rock back on the stool where I sit. My feet barely catch me and the stool clatters to the floor. Adara starts and lets out a sharp cry. I stare at Enya before glaring at Stone.

"What the fuck?" I whisper. My voice sounds like I'm underwater. I'm drowning from the ringing in my ears.

Her brother? No. Impossible. Her last name is Calloway.

"He was my half-brother," Enya clarifies. "My mother was married before she married my dad. Seamus had a different last name."

Seamus. It wasn't a common name. Had she ever told me her brother's name? We didn't discuss him. She hardly mentioned him other than to tell me he'd done drugs and he was dead.

Her brother was dead . . . because of me.

Chapter 31

[Enya]

"I—" Pure terror fills Sebastian's blue eyes, choking off his voice. The brightness is nearly blacked out with fright and then anger sets in. A shield wraps around him, closing him off. Turning him cold and distant. "I can't be here."

"Sebastian," Stone calls out as Sebastian backs up and bumps into the couch.

Stone stands, holding out his hands like he's approaching a caged animal. I hold Adara tighter, worried about Sebastian.

What is happening here?

Sebastian glares at his brother before looking over Stone's broad shoulder at me. His eyes soften for the blink of only a second. "I warned you I was dangerous."

"What are you talking about?" I have never felt safer than when I am with Sebastian.

But suddenly, I am uncertain about several things. The way he spoke to me. The way he defended Rena.

"How did you know Seamus?" Surely, their familiarity was a coincidence. They'd both been addicts. Not that one thing meant another, but Seamus had disappeared from our lives. He'd been physically close enough to contact me occasionally for money, but we didn't really know where he was, where he lived.

"Sebastian," Stone warns again while Sebastian grips the back of my couch.

"I-I didn't mean to do it." Sebastian stares at Stone.

Do what?

"I know you didn't." Stone's voice drops, sympathetic, compassionate even.

"He died because of me," Sebastian states. Anguish fills his voice and I stare at him. Grief and remorse are etched into his cheeks, marring his features. There's no trace of his smile in lips that are almost white and tightly seamed.

My head aches as the words finally penetrate my skull, reverberating around my brain, like my heart didn't want to process any of this.

He died because of me.

The man Sebastian killed was Seamus.

"You killed my brother." I don't understand. This had to be a bad dream.

I wasn't close to Seamus when we were younger. He was five years older than me, but he was still my brother. I was still saddened by the torture he'd put my parents through and the failure they'd been to him. Sad for him, that he felt the need to turn to drugs to compensate for what was missing in his life.

"We don't know that for certain," Stone states.

"Well, my record says otherwise," Sebastian spits, glaring at his brother. "You were there. You arrested me."

I've never heard Sebastian so angry, so full of venom.

"You know why that was," Stone adds. Still calm. Still holding firm with his brother while keeping his hands spread wide as if to ease Sebastian or capture him.

Sebastian shakes his head.

I'm so confused. There are so many pieces I can't clink together.

Seamus. Sebastian.

He told me he killed someone in this house. He told me he was defending Vale.

His sister. My brother.

I might be sick.

Where did it happen? How? The blueprint of this house is different than ten years ago. The layout rearranged. I glance toward the dining room on the other side of the staircase. Then gaze toward the living room where Sebastian still clutches the couch, ready to use the furniture as a hurdle and sprint out of my home.

My home. Did I feel haunted here? Trudy Wallace told me the rumors about a ghost were unfounded. I'd never felt uncertain. I didn't feel unsafe. A dead man did not break into my house.

"Sebastian?" The question in my voice has him glancing at me.

His eyes look glassy and his lips quiver. "I'm so sorry, sugar."

Then he leaps over the couch and races to my front door. Stone takes a few steps but doesn't actively chase his brother.

Instead, he stalls at the front door, staring out the screen as tires kick up gravel and peel onto the street.

"He just stole your car."

Being that his truck is parked in front of my car in the driveway, and that he was in such a hurry to leave, it makes sense that he took my SUV.

I shrug. "I'm letting him borrow it."

Just like he borrowed my heart for a little while.

+ + +

Adara has been an angel through most of this scene but she's suddenly fussy. I prepare a bottle, so I don't nurse in front of Stone. He makes us each a cup of tea and joins me on the couch when they are ready.

"When my sister had Hudson, I was kind of weirded out by the whole nursing thing. But it's as natural as having a baby."

Stone Sylver is a quiet man. Not shy but stiff, reserved. He's had a lot on his plate, raising younger siblings who had been hurt by their father and missed out on their mother.

"I always had faith in him," Stone begins, referring to Sebastian. "He was just lost. We all were a little lost." A sad smile curls only one side of his mouth. "Sebastian just wanted to help. He wanted to ease my burden when I didn't see it as a burden. I was destined to protect them."

"Appropriate being a sheriff," I offer, mustering a warm smile for him.

"Never planned to be sheriff. Thought I'd go into the military. I played college football and planned to enter the service after I graduated because I just didn't know what I wanted to do with my life. Then I was recruited by the NFL and decided the money would help my family. My dad . . ." Stone pauses. "He'd been in trouble for a while."

I nod, knowing some of the story, but only from Sebastian's perspective. Their father might have been a different man to Stone.

"Anyway, Dad died and here I was, raising my siblings like I was their father, not their brother. I couldn't be both and be tough. The brother said hell yes. Raise some trouble. The responsible adult said get your shit together. It didn't work either way, really."

Stone beats himself up just as much as Sebastian and my heart aches for both men. "You did the best you could."

"Too bad my best wasn't enough for him." He nods toward the door and lifts his cup of tea.

"I'm certain you were more than enough. Sebastian made his own choices."

"And I made mine." Stone glances at me. "I arrested him, for his own good."

In many ways, I understand why Stone did what he had done. He didn't know how else to stop his brother and the downward spiral he might have been on. My parents hadn't stepped up for Seamus. They let him go. If he wanted to do what he was doing, he wasn't their son. They turned their backs on him. Kicked him out. Never looked back. And now, he is gone.

"Will you tell me what happened"—I swallow—"with Seamus."

Stone watches me for signs of distress, but the truth is I don't really know how to feel. My brother has been dead for a decade. He was cremated. There was no funeral. No memorial. My parents didn't want to discuss the circumstances of his death. I don't recall any news coverage of a trial or proceedings. He was just some guy dying from drugs. Nothing newsworthy.

"We'd gotten the call that there might be an issue at the house. We'd received so many calls about this place. Flashlights and suspicious activity. Kicked out squatters a few times. Knew drug deals went down here." Stone stares at the mug in his hand. "I remember wanting to ignore the call, but then Vale called me. Told me Sebastian was in trouble. We came into the house and found a body that was black and blue and bloody. Shortly after I arrived, I heard noises. Someone was running out of the house. I pursued and when I caught up to the person, it was Sebastian."

With one hand, Stone scrubs over his graying beard. "I arrested Sebastian on drug possession with intent to sell. Figured the guy he beat up might press charges and I could get my brother on aggravated assault. Some time in jail might actually enlighten him. I don't know." Stone sighs, leaning forward. "But then, a man . . . your brother . . . was dead. The local judge wanted to make an example of Sebastian. He was my brother, but guilt was on his hands. I convinced Sebastian to plead guilty to manslaughter."

"But you weren't certain, were you?" Stone doesn't sound convinced his brother had hurt mine.

"It's possible your brother had a heart attack during the beating. Didn't look like he fought back based on how clean Sebastian's body was of bruises. And the toxicology report on Seamus was high."

Was Seamus scared? Was he numb? Did he know what was happening to him? Did he just give up? My head is processing too many questions at once.

Stone sighs. "As for Sebastian, I wanted my brother off the market. And he gave us one name. Because of his prior arrest for breaking and entering, plus known drug possession and intent to sell, the judge set the sentence at seven years."

I remain quiet.

"When Sebastian got out of jail, he was clean. He was also a different man. And the bakery was his redemption."

Stone glances up at me. "I don't think Rena is our culprit, but I'll be looking into her. I don't want to rule out anyone from Sebastian's past."

"He said he didn't know her then."

"He didn't, but you never know how tangled the drug web is." Stone gives me a compassionate gaze. "I'm sorry about your brother."

"I'm sorry about yours." Stone had to make some tough decisions about Sebastian. Maybe my parents made a tough choice, too, even if I didn't agree with it.

I tug Adara tighter, hoping I never have to make choices like these about her.

Stone sits a few more minutes, staring at his tea mug. "You're the best thing to happen to him. You and that pretty baby." He nods. "And I don't want him to lose you."

"Right now, I don't know what to think or do. But Sebastian might be the one lost, not me. He doesn't want to be a father or believe in having a family, and I don't think his opinion is going to change."

Heartbroken, I stare down at Adara.

If anything, this current situation has solidified how much he doesn't want those things . . . with me.

Chapter 32

[Enya]

It is after midnight when the soft snap of a car door closing pulls me from bed. I hadn't been sleeping although I was exhausted. A patrol vehicle is parked before the house on the route's shoulder, making a bold statement of protection. The vehicle that made the noise, however, is the one I'd been waiting on.

Racing down the stairs, I open the front door just as Sebastian drops my keys in the mailbox.

We stare at one another through the screen before I press the door outward holding it open for him. The choice to enter, or not, is his, but I have things I want to say to him.

Sebastian glances over his shoulder at the county sheriff's car before turning back to me and taking a step inside.

"How is Adara?" he asks, running his hands along the sides of his jeans.

"She's sleeping." *She already misses you.* And she'll be heartbroken when her three a.m. bottle time arrives and he isn't here.

"Why aren't you?" He glances at me but quickly looks away.

I could ask him the same thing. Instead, I walk to the kitchen and get myself a glass of water. Sebastian surprisingly follows but he keeps the island between us. I don't bother with turning on lights. A natural glow filters in through the window over the sink. A nightlight plugged in near the staircase offers dull illumination.

"How are you doing?" I ask.

"How are you?" he counters.

A lot has happened in forty-eight hours. It's more than I can compute, and I don't want to think anymore. I set the glass in the sink and round the island, stopping directly in front of Sebastian.

"I owe you the truth," I start. "You wanted to know who the father of Adara is."

"Enya." Sebastian turns his head and rubs a hand over his hair. Then he looks back at me. "You don't owe me anything."

He's right. I don't. I don't know *his* truth. If he killed my brother or not. The facts are simple, though. My brother is dead, and nothing can bring him back. It's been ten years, but I lost Seamus long before that time, and he isn't who I want to talk about right now.

"I'd told you Lance never proposed to me in all that time we were together. He never wanted a wife or children. He didn't want a family." I stare at Sebastian who lowers his eyes. The similarity in both men ends there. "But I wanted motherhood, and decided I would get it in any way I could."

Sebastian slowly lifts his gaze.

"Adara's father is sperm donor number 0437."

His brows rise.

"I only know that he was an educated man. He'd gone to college and graduate school. He had brown hair and blue eyes and was over six feet, which tells me Adara might have those same features. Or not. She might be tall, or not. He has no known history of cancer, heart disease, or stroke, but that doesn't rule out that one day she might. Because she's made of two sets of chromosomes but she's still her own person."

Sebastian continues staring at me.

"My parents didn't agree with my decision. They thought I should find a man. A partner. A husband. And admitting I'd slept with Lance last summer, my mother thought I should claim him as Adara's father and ask for child support."

"Fuck," Sebastian groans under his breath.

"But I'm not like them. I didn't need their permission or support. They'd made it clear how they felt, calling Adara my test-tube baby, instead of the wonderful, beautiful miracle she is."

"Damn right," Sebastian mutters.

"I'm giving you my secret, because I trust you." I pause. "According to my parents, this is also my shame. But I'm not ashamed. Love isn't shameful. Love is beautiful and kind. Love is just . . . love. Unconditional. Your past. Your present. Your future."

I've accepted his past. I'll never know if Sebastian was a catalyst in my brother's death, or if drugs won out in the end. And it doesn't matter to me. Seamus is gone. Sebastian is alive, but he hasn't been living.

What I want is a future with Sebastian, but he isn't looking forward. He can hardly get through this moment. Here. Now. And like anyone with an addictive trait, only Sebastian can make the decision to stop the cycle. He has a choice whether to love or not.

"I didn't set out to meet a new man. I didn't plan on tripping in front of your bakery on the day I found out I was pregnant or falling for you after you delivered Adara."

"Enya," he warns.

"But it's you, in my head, in my heart, who is Adara's father. Her dad. You're who *we* want. Love. Unconditional." A tear leaks from the corner of my eye and I brusquely swipe at it. "And nothing is going to change that. Nothing."

Vulnerable and real, I've opened my heart to him. I'm not afraid to love him.

He's afraid. He's in denial of things, of people, that could enrich his life. He's convinced himself of his inability to be a father. And he's been adamant he doesn't want a family.

I'm the one who hasn't listened, living off hope-filled dreams.

"But." I hesitate. "I fault myself."

His head lifts. His shoulders stiffen.

"You've been perfectly honest since the start. And I did this." I point at myself, moving around the island and coming closer to him. "You delivered Adara. I mean, wow, what a connection. Then you pretended to be her dad and offered me your apartment. You stayed with me and slept with me. And I got all wrapped up in everything. I took advantage of you."

He gives me that irritated look, that I once considered cute. The scowl is too hard now. His eyes are like blue daggers. "That is not how things happened."

I don't question him because I'm on a roll. "I get in my head sometimes, and I've doubted myself. Doubted I could do this alone, be a mother on my own. But that isn't really the question. I am doing it. Me and Adara. *I* want a family, Sebastian." I tap at my chest. "And I want you to be part of ours."

Suddenly, his hands are in my hair and his mouth is on mine, hard at first. Taking and teasing with his tongue and his teeth, those marvelous teeth that sting, but then his mouth softens.

"Fuck, Enya. Just fucking fuck." His kisses continue, deepening, desperate.

His hands drop to my hips, and he lifts me onto the island, pressing me back with his upper body as he kisses me, hungry and eager. Then he slides to my chin and scrapes his teeth over my jaw. It hurts while it heightens my libido. A surge of desire rushes to my middle, and as if his mouth is chasing that rush, he sucks on my neck before moving to my chest and down my center.

Hastily, he presses my sleep tee upward and lowers his face to my belly, nipping at my skin as he moves down to my underwear. With one fierce tug, the material is pulled to my knees and then falls off my feet. Sebastian is between my thighs, spreading me with his tongue before sucking at that sensitive nub. Every movement is hurried, and my brain doesn't have a second to catch up. My body takes over, responding to every swipe, every lap.

I just want to get lost in him.

Sebastian's hands cup my backside, and he lifts me upward, like a man might raise a bowl of soup, before slurping at it, drinking it in. I'm pinned in this position with no other choice than to give into his attention. Quickly my body reacts, boiling over, and I come hard and fast, crying out in pleasure. My hands seek purchase on the countertop, but the granite is too smooth.

Suddenly, I'm spun on my back, so my body lays the length of the island, not the width. Sebastian swiftly undoes his jeans and climbs up on the island, pushing me backward.

"What are you doing?" I watch in wonder as he prowls over me. His eyes suggest he's ready to devour me when I've already been his feast.

"From the moment I saw this countertop, I had visions of fucking you on it. Claiming you as mine."

"I am yours."

"Dammit, sugar." Stress mars his face while he lines himself up at my entrance. "I'd never deserve you. Not after what I've done. Not after who I've been."

"You aren't him anymore. You're just . . . you." My voice falters as he swipes the smooth tip of his hard length through my slick folds.

"I shouldn't be here."

"You should." Whether he means in my house or about to enter me, he should be exactly where he is.

"Fuck." With one powerful thrust, he enters me, and I scoot backward on the countertop with the force. Wrapping my legs around the backs of his, I press at his thighs, holding him inside me.

The kitchen island is like a life raft in a sea of uncertainty. But I'm certain of one thing. I want Sebastian.

"Why do you tempt me so much, Enya?" He pulls back and surges forward, filling me over and over again. "Why am I so drawn to you?"

"Because we're good together." My hands are on his biceps, but I slide them to his shoulder blades, pinning him to me in any way I can. Caging him in as much as he towers over me.

His hips move. Mine respond. Back and forth, we rock, tugging at one another, needing each other.

I can raise Adara alone, but I don't want to. I want Sebastian to be her father. I want him to claim her. Claim both of us as his.

"Make me yours," I demand, clutching at the firm globes of his backside, desperate to keep him inside me.

"I— I can't," he strains, but we both know it's too late. I'm already his. I'm in love with him.

Despite his denial, we still thump against the countertop. I chase his retreat. He's drawn into me. We move as one until the catch happens. My breath hitches. He gasps.

"I can't come inside you," he warns.

But he can. However, I don't say it. I ride out the rush as I fall apart around him, clenching at him, desperate to keep him inside me until he breaks the spell.

With an abrupt jerk, he pulls back and kneels. The slap of skin tugging skin tells me all I need to know, then my lower region is coated in a sticky mess.

"I'm sorry," he mutters as a finger spreads his seed just above my tuft of hair. "I'm so sorry," he winces before lowering and kissing me, just once, with tender apology, where he has left my body and taken my heart.

Sebastian scrambles backward and I turn my head toward the kitchen cabinets, watching him in the reflection of the window above the sink.

He swipes his hand over his hair and hangs his head a second. Then scrubs down his face almost as if washing away all thoughts of me. Of Adara. Of who we could be to him.

With shaky fingers, he tugs up his jeans and rights the button.

In the window's reflection, I see him offer me a hand. "Let me help you up."

For some reason, I'm reminded of when I tripped before his bakery, and he held out his hand to help me stand in the rain. If only I'd never touched him then because I now know where we'd end.

"Just go," I whisper, my voice is hoarse although I've hardly used it. "I need space to think."

"Enya." He stares at me for the single beat of a heart.

I see myself in the window's reflection, spread out on my island. Limbs weak. Body sated. Heart shattered.

I only need an apple in my mouth, and I'd look like a depleted feast, carved to the ribs and hollow of any substance.

I swore I'd never be in this position again, and yet, I've done it to myself. I was with a man who was honest from the start. At least, he didn't wait eleven years to tell me the truth. He told me within days he didn't want to have a family. It was all pretend.

When the soft whirl of the electronic lock on my front door suggests he's left and the door is secure, I finally roll from the island, no longer able to face myself in the window.

I've seen enough of me.

Chapter 33

[Sebastian]

For twenty-four hours, I beat myself up for what we did on Enya's kitchen island. A sacred spot in her home where I took the body of a woman I consider a goddess and treated her like a sacrificial lamb.

You should be with me.

I shouldn't. Like the disappointment that I am, I couldn't get around the facts. I'd killed her brother. Or at least brought him close enough to the edge that death took over. It didn't matter. Her brother was gone, and someone was scoping out Enya's home.

She was in danger because of me.

She'd asked me to give her time to think which was code for *get the hell out of my life*, and I should do just that. But I can't. Even with a patrol car outside her place, I'd been by on my bike and looped around to the woods out back to keep my eyes on her house. I haven't slept. I'm exhausted, angry, and hollow inside.

I don't want to lose her or Adara. But I don't know how to keep them, either.

With my head in my hands, and elbows bent on my desk, my office door opens. "What?" I snap, lifting my gaze and glaring at Barnett.

He's young but he's big and he can hold his own against my rough moods. However, I can't deal with him today.

"I realize there's never a good time with you." Sarcasm has no place here today. "But—"

"Then get out," I snap, my anger at full scale, as I straighten.

"I need to tell you something." Barnett isn't a nervous kid. He never gives me pause other than calling in sick the other day, so when he closes the door behind him, I'm the anxious one.

"Are you going to quit?" *Shit.* I can't lose him.

I haven't decided how to handle Enya's suspicions about Rena, and I'm going to lose Rena once I question her. You can't accuse someone of something without proof, and I don't have any. If I value trust between

Rena and me, I'm going to blow that trust by calling her out about the money.

Then again, if I trust Enya, which I do implicitly, her word is gold. And something inside me tells me Enya isn't wrong. Rena is the link to the cash-drawer shortages.

And all of this isn't something I can think about right now, if my number two employee is about to quit.

"Uhm. No, but this is important."

Fuck. I turn my head then glance back at the teen. "Out with it."

He rolls his ankles, flipping his feet so he stands on the sides of them and then curls them back. "So remember when I asked for a raise last summer."

Not this again. My jaw clenches. "Yes." He'd asked for a raise, but I hadn't given it to him. I'd hired Rena instead, needing a full-time employee because he was only summer help and part-time during the school year.

"I needed the money for Bernadette."

His aunt? "For what?"

"She needed medication which her insurance wouldn't cover."

I stare at him, slowly seeing myself in him. Young, eager to help family. "And?"

"Rena felt sorry for me."

Fuck.

"She gave me money. Said it was tips from the tip jar."

We don't collect many cash tips. Most people pay by credit card and post tips electronically.

Okay, it's fine if Rena gave him the small change we don't document. "So?"

"She's been doing it for a while now and I never questioned it. Just figured you must have approved it since she was the manager."

"*I'm* the manager." I sit up straighter. The owner and sole member of the corporation Judd had me form when I opened the bakery.

Barnett nods. "Anyway, I overheard her talking to a customer about a big score."

My eyes narrow at Barnett while my heart catches in my throat. "And?"

Barnett hangs his head. "She caught me listening and told me she'd cut me in if I didn't tell anyone about it. Then she pulled a twenty from the cash drawer. Told me there was more where that came from if I kept quiet."

"She what?" My hands slam on the top of my desk.

"Watching her take money from the drawer had me thinking, maybe the money wasn't really coming from the tip jar, but you. The bakery." He waves around my office. "And now I see I made a huge mistake in taking anything from her in the first place."

Barnett reaches into his pocket and lays the twenty on my desk. "I swear I'll pay back the rest. And if you fire me, I understand." He hangs his head and swipes a finger underneath his nose.

Shit. *Is he crying?* Slowly, I reach for the twenty and place it in my desk drawer. "How much did she give you over time? Do you know? Did you add it up?"

"She gave me small stuff at first and then when she caught me listening, she promised me five-hundred dollars to keep my mouth shut."

"Five-hundred—" I recall telling Enya how hundreds and thousands made every penny for a dollar if someone was poor, or . . . "Are you doing drugs?"

Barnett's hairline rises as he lifts his head. "No. And you know why."

Yeah, I did. His mom had done them and then left him with his aunt.

"I'll get the money back to you somehow. I've decided not to go to college in the fall and—."

"The fuck you aren't." I point at him. "You're going to college. And you're getting that raise for telling me what you heard."

His shoulders relax and a sigh of relief covers his face.

"But." I hold up a finger. "Your pay will be docked until my money is recovered."

His brows pinch, sensing the disconnect in my offer. I'm going to pay him to pay me, but he'll be working more hours, giving me his time instead of the cash. Because I have a different employee to fire.

"What was this big score for Rena?" My heart hammers as I clutch the edge of my desk.

He licks his lips. "She was going to scope out a house. Looking for buried treasure."

"She what?" I stand, forcing my desk chair back and into the wall behind me.

He holds up both hands. "She said no one would get hurt. She'd just get in and get out."

"How?" I swallow back the bile in my throat as Enya's home had been broken into, but nothing had been broken. As Stone pointed out, it's like the perpetrator walked right in.

"Rena had the code."

"Did she now?" How the fuck did Rena know the code?

"She said it was probably the kids' birthday or something . . ." Slowly, realization hits Barnett. "I can't go to jail, man. I have Bernadette to think about."

I scowl. "Why would you go to jail?"

"Rena said if I told you, she'd say it was me who went into the house."

She was fucking blackmailing a kid? *Fuck!*

I pick up my phone and send a text to Enya. **Change the lock code on your house. Immediately.**

The command seems silly. After she kicked me out the other night, she probably changed the code instantly, as she should.

The big, bad wolf had no place in her home.

Next, I dial my brother.

"Stone. I have something you should hear." Then I hand the phone to Barnett.

+ + +

Once Barnett's confession is given, I send him home with sixty-five dollars in his pocket—the money needed for Bernadette's monthly prescription—through the back exit. I'll be closing the bakery myself today. When I step into the main area, Rena gives me a warm smile. Her weird, shadow-like behavior now makes sense.

I walk to the front door and flip the sign to *Closed*. Then I lock the entrance and turn to face Rena. Crossing my arms, I glare at her. I'd trusted her. I'd even stood up for her with Enya, the very person she betrayed, when my girl has been innocent in everything.

"I'm giving you one chance to be straight with me about the cash and Barnett." I don't need to further explain myself. She knows what she's done.

"He needed the money, and you hadn't given him a raise." She's right on that count and the responsibility falls on me. Just because he's a kid doesn't mean his value is any less than any other worker. I'd simply needed someone who could work more hours during the day, and I put that financial business investment on the one person I shouldn't have trusted.

"You stole from me to pay him."

Rena shrugs, not betraying a hint of remorse. "It was only the tips."

"Stop lying to me," I bark, stalking closer to her. "You took money right from the drawer."

Her head pops up and she stares me right in the eyes. "Just once."

"Funny, I don't believe you." Coming closer to the display case, I pause at the entrance to the counter area, caging Rena in the space. "And you're still lying."

"I didn't—"

"Stop," I snap, smacking my palm on top of the display case.

"Sebastian. Boss, you know I wouldn't ever betray you."

"But you did. You stole from me and then blackmailed a fucking kid."

Just like someone once took advantage of me. Knowing I needed the money, and I was eager to help my family, someone reached out a poisoned apple, and I took a bite. I ate the entire promise of money to assist my family and it all backfired. I'd hurt them. I'd killed someone. I'd been in jail. And I was fucking ashamed of myself for those decisions.

We glare at one another. Her face goes hard. She knows I know what she's done.

"How could you do that to Barnett? And how dare you go after Enya? What did she do to you?" Our stare down continues. "How could you think it was okay to go into her house without her permission? That's breaking and entering."

"You've done it."

"That doesn't make it right," I argue, my voice rising enough to shake the overhead hanging lights.

Rena scoffs and crosses her arms. She hitches her hip and turns her head a second. "You don't care about Enya. You just like the attention she gives you. *You're her hero,*" Rena mocks. "You'll never be anything to someone like her."

Fuck that hurts, but I won't let Rena see the stab wound. "You know nothing about Enya."

"She has money and built that new house. What could she possibly want with a reformed addict?"

Stunned again, I don't give Rena the satisfaction of knowing I've asked myself the same question a thousand times. "So, you decided to case her joint. For what?"

"You've heard the rumors, boss. Buried treasure."

"So you broke into her house on some bullshit myth?" *Un-fucking-believable.* But I'm no longer surprised by anything this woman does. This trusted employee who has turned out to be deceitful, manipulative, and sick in the head with her reasoning.

"Technically, I didn't break in." Rena glares, giving me a cocky smile while tilting her head. "Maybe you're just upset because I might find it first."

The wind comes out of my sails, and I rock back before forming a fist on my display case. "You're lucky you're a fucking woman or you wouldn't see tomorrow. And you're not getting anywhere near Enya, or her house again."

"Oh yeah. I heard about that, too. Killed the guy who stashed the money in that house, right?"

What?

"Maybe you do know where the money is and you're keeping the secret to yourself." Rena looks around the bakery. "Or did you use it for this place."

I have loans up the wazoo for the bakery but that's none of Rena's business.

"I offered you a second chance," I remind her, disgusted with myself for trusting her so fucking easily.

Rena glares back at me.

"You're fired."

"Boss." Rena drops her arms.

How can she be surprised? "You're not getting your last paycheck as recompense for what you stole from the till."

"You can't do that." Rena stands taller. As tall as her short stature allows. The tough woman with red hair and tattoos flares.

"Oh, I can. Now leave the key and get out."

Reaching into her pocket, she pulls out her key and slams it on the counter. Next, she takes off her apron and dramatically drops it on the floor. Walking over it, showing her immaturity, she brushes past me.

My entire body vibrates. I want to throttle her, but I've never ever hit a woman, and she won't be my first. I just want her gone.

Rena stalks toward the back door and opens it with force. My eyes close and my head lowers as I hear a familiar voice.

"Rena Gomez, you're under arrest for the unlawful entry of a private residence. You have the right to remain silent . . ."

The rest drifts away as Stone's voice drones on and I reach into my pocket, removing my phone and turning off the recording app that captured Rena's confession.

With no prior felonies or convictions, Rena will have a record now.

+ + +

While Enya's place is under sheriff surveillance, it doesn't prevent me from driving by again tonight. Even with Rena in custody, Stone told me she probably won't be detained long, and that just makes the timeclock on Enya's safety speed up.

Barnett wasn't able to identify the customer Rena was talking to when he overheard her, and this makes me extra itchy. Someone else is still out there, watching Enya's house.

Enya said she needed space to think, and I don't know how to respond to that other than giving it to her. Like a coward, which I've never been, I've kept my distance. No calls. No texts. No impromptu visits.

It's a taste of what life would be like without her and I fucking hate it.

It's also a reminder of my life before I met her, and it's lonely.

Tonight, the weather is warm, but the mountain air is cooling as darkness spreads slowly over the sky. I take my bike for this nightly ride. Funny how I used to avoid Route 10. Now, I'm constantly drawn to it.

As I breeze along the route, I try to wrap my head around all that I've learned.

Barnett. He's just a kid and I'm giving him credit for coming forward with what he heard. His honesty reminds me so much of myself when I was younger than him, asking my brother Knox if selling drugs would help the family. I failed Barnett because I didn't know anything about Bernadette's condition or her struggles with her health insurance.

Rena, on the other hand, is a total conundrum to me. How did I so easily trust her? Our connection was born from our similar pasts. I thought I was doing right by giving her a second chance. Failure again, as I trusted the wrong person. Then again, it's exactly what I did as a kid, believing in Josh Geary when he told me I'd be helping my family, making money, if I sold drugs.

Then I consider Enya, who trusted *me* blindly, unconditionally. I didn't judge her decision to have Adara the way she had. I'm honored she's told me the truth. Trusted me with it.

And even after all she'd learned about my past and her brother, she gave herself to me willingly and still wanted a little more of me.

She wants us. *Because we're good together*. She wants herself and Adara to be mine, and me to be part of them.

Two flames. One candle. A family.

I didn't want to believe in it, but it had been hard to ignore. The way I'm drawn to her. The way I feel about her little girl. From the moment Enya entered my life, she'd been impossible to forget. I was sucked in, willingly following without her even bidding me to do so. Pretending to be Adara's dad. Giving Enya a place to stay. Falling more in love with both of them with every second spent together and missing them with every moment apart.

There is no denying my heart aches with their absence. The separation is something I knew would eventually happen when Enya learned everything about me.

What could she possibly want with a reformed addict? Rena said it best.

I had nothing to offer Enya. But I loved her. I loved Adara. I wanted to be part of their lives.

Blindly, I drive along the route, only slowing as I pass Enya's house, noticing the sheriff's vehicle on the shoulder just off from her driveway. I loop around, heading for the woods again, where I'll perch myself for the night, keeping vigil over the backside of Enya's home.

The siren whirl of a squad car goes off behind me, and red and blue lights reflect in my handlebar mirrors catches me off guard.

What the fuck?

I pull off to the shoulder as the sheriff's car slows to park behind me. A large man exits the vehicle and I hang my head. Removing my helmet as he approaches, snide fills my question. "Is there a problem, officer?"

"I've been trying to find you," Stone says, his voice hard like his name.

"Why? What did I do now?" I keep my head high, shoulders tight, but my voice gives me away. It's always my fault.

Stone tips his head, before removing his dark-shaded aviators that he doesn't need to wear in the late evening light. "Why do you think you did something?"

"Because I always do. And you're always there to point it out."

His bushy brows lift, furrowing his forehead.

"You told me not to employ Rena. Or at least run a full background check on her, and I didn't."

"Even if you had, it didn't matter. She didn't have anything on file but a misdemeanor for public intoxication."

"Then you told me not to invite Enya to live with me, and I still did it anyway."

Stone's eyes widen. "When did I say that?"

"And now you're going to lecture me about how I don't listen. I react first and ask questions later. And look how that's turned out for me." I stare down at the helmet I hold between my hands. There's no reflection in the dark covering with the heaviness of night closing in over us. I don't want to look at myself anyway.

I've fucked up again.

Stone heavily exhales and squints at the road before us.

Here we go.

"You do react, but that doesn't mean you aren't listening."

My head lifts and I narrow my eyes at him.

He looks back at me. "You listen to your heart."

What? My eyes, mirroring the color of his, widen. His still have moments of softness in them, while I'm certain mine are perpetually hard. We've both seen our fair share of fucked up in this life.

"What do you mean?"

"Sebastian, ever since you were a kid, you've been led by your heart. You thought selling drugs would *help* the family, in a fucked up sort of way, and you did it because you love us."

I stare at him, not certain what to say.

"You think I don't know how Ford magically got new baseball equipment? Or Vale got to take those dance lessons?" He stares at me, like an all-knowing father. "Even for me. You got me those overpriced aviator glasses, so I'd look like a bad-ass sheriff when I made the force."

I remember handing him the reflective sunglasses before his graduation. I was high when I told him he'd look bad ass.

Stone holds up the glasses he'd been wearing by their frame. *Those can't possibly be the same ones.* They'd be twenty years old.

But reading my mind, Stone shakes the frames. "These are some high-quality sunglasses."

He's . . . been wearing them since I gifted them to him?

"Look, I know I've been hard on you. You've broken the law, and I'm the law around here."

I huff. He certainly is.

"But you're my brother. I love you."

Who is this man? I tip to the side, my knees buckling. Thank goodness I'm sitting on my motorcycle because if I wasn't, I'd fall over. Never, not once in my life, has Stone said such a thing to me.

"What?" I choke. It's not the best response one could have to hearing such a phrase. It's not even the response I should give him in return. I don't think *I've* ever said those three words to anyone, other than playfully, snarky love you's to Vale.

Stone sighs, lowering his head and hooking his thumbs in his sheriff's belt. "I know it's been tough." His head snaps up. "Life has been incredibly unfair."

My mouth pops open but he holds up a hand. "But you've been given a second chance. Take advantage of it."

"With the bakery." I clarify. "You think I'd fuck that up? It's been three years. I've been working my ass off for my business, and hiring Rena was one mis—"

"I mean with Enya," Stone cuts me off.

I snort. "I never had a first chance with her. I don't have a prayer with someone like her. And you and I both know it."

"What I know" —Stone pauses—"Is Enya is your one and only."

Staring at him, I can't figure out who this man is and what he's done with my brother. He looks like Stone. He sounds like Stone. But the words coming out of his mouth are *not* the brother I know.

"Like you had with Bailey?" My brother doesn't even flinch at the mention of the last girl he officially dated. The one who ripped out his heart and divided two families.

"Not like Bailey." If I expected his voice to be cold mentioning her name, it's not. "That wasn't love."

He lowers his head, staring down at the gravel edge of the road. Then he lifts his big head so fast I almost flinch.

"Love is having a woman who wants you. And Enya wants you. Love is having a woman trust you, and we both know she trusts you. With her life. With her kid's life. Love is family, and Enya and Adara are yours, Sebastian. Do not let them go." He lifts his hand, clenching his fist. "When you have family, you hold on with everything you have to love them. Protect them. Keep them."

For half a second, Stone's voice cracks before he clears his throat with a thick cough. He's done exactly what he's telling me to do. He has loved us. He protected us when he could. And he kept us together, especially Ford, Vale, and me, when he could have walked away. He could have taken that NFL deal and left. Lived for himself. But he didn't. He lived for our family.

When Stone speaks again, his voice is calm, almost encouraging. "For once, trust in yourself, Sebastian. Where is your heart leading you?"

Love is family. And I love Enya and Adara. I love us.

The radio on Stone's shoulder squawks at the same time my phone rings before I verbalize an answer for him. I don't have hands-free wiring on my older model bike, so I pull my phone from my pocket.

As I lift the device for my ear, I hear the dispatcher loud and clear on Stone's radio.

"Suspicious activity." The address is Enya's house.

"Vale?" I choke as I answer my sister's call.

"Seb," Vale's voice quivers. "It's Enya. Something's wrong."

That's all I need to hear before I kick my bike into gear and speed off to save my family.

Chapter 34

[Enya]

It was a beautiful summer evening and a motorcycle had just sped down the highway before the house. The same bike has made a drive-by for two nights in a row, and I'm curious if the rider is a neighbor. I really need to meet them even if I can hardly see their homes.

With Adara strapped to my chest in a baby sack, I take a stroll around the yard which is two square acres. As we near the woods on the backside of the lot, a man steps forward and I stumble to a stop. My hands protectively cover Adara's back and head.

"Hey." The man holds up both hands in greeting. I instantly recognize him but that doesn't prevent my heart from racing.

"Goodness. You scared me." Still clutching Adara to me, I keep my distance despite my vague familiarity with the person who kindly held a door and bought me a lemonade during the Fourth of July festivities.

"I'm sorry." He lowers his hands and gives me a pouty look, expressing his chagrin. "Did you know there's a lot on the other side of the trees?"

My brows crease. My understanding is the woods belong to someone living in another state who has a forester manage the land, keeping vagrants off it and preventing local property owners from encroaching. I don't know why you'd want to own woods in another state, but I didn't question it when I purchased the farmhouse from Trudy.

"Really?" My voice shakes. I don't want to feel uneasy around this stranger who has been nothing but kind. However, it's unnerving that he walked out of the woods on the edge of my property.

"Do you live around here?" he asks, glancing around when the only home in sight is mine.

The urge to get safely back to the house arises, and I don't know how to word a polite escape.

"I do. My baby and I were just taking an evening stroll, but it's almost time for another feeding for her."

He gives Adara a quick glance before offering me a tight smile. "I missed you at Milton's Roadhouse the other night."

"Oh." I anxiously chuckle, pointing at Adara like she was my excuse. "I didn't make it."

"Maybe we could have that drink now?" He hitches his thumb toward the woods, but the last place I'll be venturing with a stranger is into the trees.

The racing of my heart tells me to run, only I can't sprint with Adara strapped against my chest. Logic warns me if I trip or fall, I'll crush her, and I blink back the sudden burn of tears. It was so stupid to travel this far, even on my own property. I'm equally upset that I *can't* freely traipse over my land. Not after someone *walked* into my home.

Stone called me earlier, but I'd been in the shower, and I hadn't called him back yet. I wanted to give Adara and myself some fresh air, but I suddenly regret my decision to take a walk, and not tell anyone about it. Even though the deputy sheriff's car is parked outside my house, I made a rash decision because my current position is blocked from the car's view.

Twisting toward the house, I say, "Maybe you'd like to come to my place for that drink. We could sit on the porch." The porch will put us in sight of the sheriff's vehicle and might even deter my visitor from accepting the invitation. At the least, the situation would limit his visit.

He shrugs and slips his hands into his back pockets. "Sure." He steps closer to me, but I try to keep some distance between us.

"So, you apparently know my name and I assume that's because I'm the new girl in town. I feel awful, but I don't remember yours." He hadn't told me his name but I'm trying to be cautiously polite.

"My friends call me *Rodg*er Neil."

I tightly smile at the emphasis in his name. What a strange way to quantify his name? If his friends call him one name, what's his real name?

"Are you from around here?"

He squints and looks off in the distance. "Used to be. It's been a while since I've been back, though."

"Oh. Did you grow up here?"

Rodger peers at the house. "Not exactly."

This doesn't make sense. Either he grew up here, or he didn't, which negates him saying he's from around here.

As we near the house, I head for the front yard, but Rodger catches my elbow. The touch isn't hard but firm. He fixes his gaze on me.

"Maybe we should go inside. The heat. It's not good for the baby." He nods, acknowledging Adara for the first time.

"But it's so pleasant outside and she's comfortable against me." Thankfully, she's fallen asleep although I can't believe the thumping of my heart hasn't kept her awake. The rhythm pulses in my ears. "The front porch is a great spot to enjoy the night."

His fingers tighten at my elbow. He tips his head forward as if he can see around the house. As if he knows the sheriff's car is out front. "I just want to talk."

"And we can do that on the front porch." My voice betrays my discomfort.

His eyes drift to Adara. "I don't want to hurt you."

"Then don't." The retort is too quick, too sharp. I'm not in a position to poke a bear, and his fingers digging into the flesh above my elbow suggests he's containing himself, but thinly.

"Take me inside."

No is on the tip of my tongue. I could run. I could scr—

"Don't think about it." His gaze falls to Adara again. "Like I said. I just want to talk. Inside. Now." His demeanor shifts from the charming man who'd asked me out for a drink and donated to a college fund into someone else. Someone who exudes trouble and I'm about to let him into my house. No breaking and entering necessary.

He leads me to the back door where the blinds have been drawn shut. Pressing at the lock box, like he's been here before, he chuckles. "See you got smart and changed the code."

I'd read Sebastian's text earlier. First words in almost two full days and all he had to say is *change the lock*, like he doesn't want to be tempted to enter my home again.

Upon Stone's advice, I'd already changed it to a date only two people would know. Sebastian and me.

"Open it," Rodger demands.

With shaking fingers, I press the new four digits and the lock whirls open. Rodger presses the latch to open the door. With one hand on the handle and the other on my elbow, he nudges me forward. If it were only me, I might think twice. I might run or step inside and head straight for a kitchen knife. But with Adara at my chest, I'm at this man's mercy.

I'm so angry, fear hasn't set in. There are no tears. At least, not yet. Talking, I can do. It buys me time, I hope.

Once we enter the house, I pretend he hasn't just coerced me into letting him inside. I walk straight for a cabinet and open the door for a glass. "Drink?"

He chuckles, the sound bitter and tight. He stands in a spot where the staircase leading to the second floor obstructs him from the view from the front door. The spot also contains the door that leads to the cellar. His position also hides him from direct view through the front window. From the sheriff's vehicle out front.

He points at the kitchen island. "Take a seat."

I glance in the direction of the front window.

"Don't do anything stupid."

My attention snaps back to him. His eyes narrow before he offers me a lopsided smile. One I thought might be endearing but I now see is all for show. Reel in the innocent. Hook them with those white teeth and a little charm. The big, bad wolf has come into my farmhouse and he's ready to blow this place down.

True panic sets in and my body begins to tremble. Once seated, I'm grateful because my legs wobble and I'm certain they wouldn't hold me upright much longer. I cross my knees, which allows one leg to uncontrollably bounce.

Rodger scans the open concept room from his awkward position. "Nice place you have here." It isn't a compliment.

I don't respond to him.

"Pick up your phone. Hold it like you're talking to someone."

With a shaky hand, I do as he says, holding the phone to my ear.

"Don't do anything rash."

Like dial 9-1-1? Press my ICE number? Tap the emergency button? I'm trembling so hard I can't control my fingers.

"Now, we're going to chat." Rodger tips his head again, cautiously peering around the barrier toward the front window before looking back at me. "Just tell me where the money is."

"What money?"

"Don't play coy with me. He had the money and I want to know where he put it. Now." His tone is so sharp, like he smacked his hand on the granite.

I flinch. "Seamus?"

"You're a very smart woman, so you know who I'm talking about."

Gotta go to college. Stay off the streets and away from drugs. The statement whispers through my head in my brother's voice.

"My brother." I'm simply making a statement, but his eyes narrow. His smile washes away. "Seamus is dead."

"I know." His forehead creases. "And I want to know where he stashed the money."

"What money?"

His glare tells me not to be a fool, but my head says keep talking, keep stalling.

"How would I know about any money? I'd been estranged from my brother for years."

"Strange then that you bought this place. The very place where your brother was last seen." Rodger casually leans into the door that leads to the cellar. He tilts his head. On second inspection, I don't know how I ever thought this man was handsome. His eyes look wild. His beard raggedy. His hair stands up like he's repeatedly run his fingers through it.

"You knew the money was here all along, didn't you? Did you use it to fix this place up?" His head lifts, and he presses off the door as if the second thought is a new conclusion for him. That I might have spent this mysterious money I didn't know existed.

Glaring back at him, I state, "I've worked very hard to *earn* this place." I'd saved for years before Lance and I broke up, thinking the funds would go toward our future home. When we broke up, I bought out his half of the condo, dipping into that savings, but not destroying my goal. Selling the condo aided in my investment in this house.

"Right. You're the accountant sister. Good with money. The other one is the famous singer." He stares at me, puzzling through my family tree. I fear for Cadence. He knows so much about us, and I've never seen him in my life. "Maybe you took the money and hid it elsewhere." He crosses his arms. "Stocks? Bonds? Savings? No worries. Just tell me where and I can make a deal for you."

"A deal? I'm telling you I don't know what you're talking about. I don't know about any money."

"Maybe your boyfriend took the money after all."

Sebastian? Slowly it occurs to me that the break-in at my house had nothing to do with him and everything to do with me. This man is after *me* because he thinks I know the whereabouts of money my brother had.

"Sebastian didn't have anything to do with Seamus."

"He killed your brother," Rodger bluntly reminds me. "Maybe he was using you to find the money in this old house."

I don't believe it. Sebastian explained his history with drugs. He told me what happened because of his sister that night. He might have beat my brother, but Sebastian did not have an ulterior motive. He was not a thief. He was not greedy. And after the various ways he has treated me with his generous, sweet spirit, I will not believe he had malicious intentions toward me. He might have been malevolent in the past, but he wasn't that man in the present. He couldn't be that excellent of an actor to fake all he's expressed toward me.

Sebastian loved me. He loved Adara. I felt that truth in my soul.

It wasn't that he didn't believe in love, it was that he loved too hard. That's what scared him. He didn't trust love. He didn't trust himself.

He'd been a stupid kid with good intentions. He'd wanted to help his family. Provide for them. He'd been a wayward adult, lost and hotheaded. His final act had been in defense of his sister. For a man who claims he doesn't want a family, he's put them first in every warped decision he's made, time and time again.

Oh, Sebastian.

My doorbell rings and I glance at the small monitor on the counter near the sink that shows me who is on my front porch. The camera is a new installation from the alarm company, that allows me video footage around the house.

Vale.

"Ignore her. Pretend you aren't home."

"Don't be ridiculous. She can see me sitting here." *Can she see him?* He senses the question and tucks closer to the cellar door, placing his back to it and tipping back his head. He curls his fingers into fists and beats one gently against the barrier at his back. He's hidden from view unless someone were to round the back of the house.

Please let someone do that soon.

However, my position, seated on a kitchen stool, with my back to the front bay, can be seen through the sheer curtains over the window that overlooks the front porch.

"Lose her."

This is my chance. I slowly stand, and Adara squawks. She's hungry but I need to get us out of the house.

As I round the staircase on the right, Rodger rounds on the left through the dining room and catches up to me, stopping me directly behind the front door. "Open it slowly. No funny business."

With his hand on the knob, he turns it and taps at my foot, making it an unconventional doorstop that prevents the door from opening all the way. Half my body is covered by the front door. Something pointed presses at my side. *Does he have a knife?* Glancing downward, I notice the long, sharp object just above my hip. He holds steady while his other hand remains on the doorknob, ready to shut Vale out.

"Vale." Her name is high-pitched in my strained voice. Sweat beads on my forehead. My body suddenly trembles even more so than earlier. With the door only partially open, cutting half of me out of view, Adara is uncomfortably close to the edge. And too close to the knife at my side. My hand covers her back as she begins to cry.

"Hey." Vale's brows pinch at my awkward position. "The Sterlets were missing you, so I thought I'd bring the book club to you." She holds up a bottle of wine. No book in sight.

I'd forgotten tonight was book club.

"It's not really a good time." Adara screams louder, like she's been pinched, or she knows we are in trouble, and because I can't scream for help, she is. I bounce, jiggling Adara up and down. A deep squat of my knees makes me look like I'm doing a poor imitation of the chicken dance. I even flap my elbow which makes no sense as I try to soothe Adara. I'm hoping my discombobulated movements appear highly unusual and thus suspicious to Vale.

"Why? Is my brother in there?" Vale wiggles her brows, scandalously teasing me as she tips on her toes to look over my shoulder.

Subtly, I shake my head, very aware of Rodger's presence hidden behind the door, with a knife at the fleshy part above my hip. His head tips to its side against the door.

Adara cries harder. A full-on wail as if he pinched her.

"Maybe I could help with Adara." Vale's gaze drops to the baby against my chest, jostling up and down as I awkwardly bend my knees and flap an elbow. I'm tempted to hand Adara to Vale and tell her to run with my child.

"She needs Auntie Vale time. I heard Knox is trying to one up all of us."

"I'm not alone," I blurt.

Vale's brows lift. Her eyes wide.

The knife at my side presses harder, poking deeper, but not puncturing my skin. Yet.

"I mean . . . I can do it alone. I got this. I got her." My voice quivers. I'm in over my head and a terrible actor. I don't know how to give Vale a signal that I need help.

Adara wails louder.

"Let me call you tomorrow."

Vale continues staring at me, and I hold her gaze, trying to tell her with my eyes that I'm in trouble.

Her brows pinch. "Maybe call me later."

I nod once. Vale's eyes shift to the opposite edge of the door, where a sliver of light might show through or the outline of a man hopefully. She holds still a second, before slowly bringing her focus back to me. She nods once.

"Okay. Tomorrow." She lifts the bottle of wine and then lowers it to set the container on the porch. She steps back, waiting for me to bend for the item, however, she's placed it outside of my reach. Too bad, the bottle would be a good weapon.

With a knife at my side and Adara at my chest, I don't dare risk it.

Instead, I lean back, and the door closes, shutting off Vale from view. Through the door, I hear her quickly turn and skip down the steps like she didn't notice my strange behavior.

Rodger presses his back to the closed door and tugs me before him. He smells of perspiration and something smoky, skunky even. With Adara at my chest, she's a barrier between us but I don't like her this close to him.

He lifts the knife and points it at my face. "You're a shitty actress." He cranes his neck to look toward the front window where Vale's car is backing out of the driveway. "For your sake, you better hope she doesn't make any calls."

"Who would she call?"

He looks back at me. "We both know you're not that dumb."

"If you mean Sebastian, we broke up the other night," I lie. While I'd asked him for space, I wasn't breaking up with him. We needed some time and a little distance to come to terms with all that had happened. I was hoping space would give him perspective. Maybe it had. He hadn't called or texted, other than a demand to change my lock codes. He didn't spontaneously stop by or even check on Adara and me. He'd made his decision. He wasn't going to be part of my family. "He isn't going to rush to my rescue."

"You don't need saving. Not yet." Rodger narrows his eyes, no longer kind or flirtatious. "But what you do need to do is to find my money. Now where is it?"

Suddenly, it's his money?

"I don't know where it is."

"It's here somewhere. Buried or invested, and I want it back. If I have to burn this place to the ground to find it, I will. Now tell me where it is."

"This place already was torn down and rebuilt. The only place untouched was the cellar but there has been extensive shoring up of the foundation. There's nothing down there but a new furnace, a new hot water heater, and an old dirt—" I catch myself.

Rodger's eyes widen and he tugs at my hips. With his feet spread and his legs tight, I'm caught between his thighs, and I don't like it.

"Then you better get rid of Deputy Doolittle out there so we can get digging."

With my hand on the back of Adara, who is bright red and wailing at ear-piercing decibels, I say, "I can't do any digging."

"You can and you will. Now shut that kid up."

+ + +

It's impossible to reason with a mad man.

But with a screaming child in the mix, and my warning that if he hurt her or me, he'd never see a dime of his money, even when I don't know what money he's referring to, nursing Adara buys me time. I take a seat on my couch in direct view of the street where the sheriff's vehicle hasn't moved. Neither has the person inside who is supposed to inspect the perimeter of the house as the night grows darker.

Rodger paces in small, tight circles behind the staircase as Adara feeds and I lose faith. I'm running out of time.

When my phone rings, a warning glare from Rodger tells me not to answer it. Sebastian's name appears on the screen. It rings three times and goes to voice mail.

Seconds later, it rings again.

In the distance, I hear the dull sound of an approaching car and the powerful roar of a motorcycle. When a second sheriff's vehicle pulls up behind the first, I shift on the couch. Rodger gives me another threatening stare.

"That bitch," he mutters, implying Vale.

"It's only the changing of the guards," I explain, trying to keep my voice steady. The vehicles rotate as one shift ends and another begins. Only, the first vehicle remains, while the second one parks.

My heart hammers in my chest. Sweat trickles down my back. Adara is asleep at my breast, but I don't want to move, giving the impression she's still nursing beneath the baby blanket covering my breast and her.

"Fuck," Rodger mutters, leaning his back against the cellar door with a heavy thud. He tips back his head before turning it toward me with evil in his eyes. "I'm not finished with you. You'll find me that money."

He steps toward the back door where the blinds are shut and tugs it open. Instantly, he falls to the floor with the crack of a fist against his nose. Blood pours from his face as he curls into himself.

With Sebastian over him.

A beast unleashed.

Chapter 35

[Sebastian]

There was nothing in my head but white noise and the crunch of bone on bone as my fist pummeled his face. Red blurred my vision. I only had one intention.

But a familiar feminine cry poked at my concentration.

My name was being called from some place distant. A warning. A plea

It didn't matter. This man would pay for threatening my girl. He'd pay for trapping her in the house and scaring her. He'd never get near her again. If he touched her, he was a dead man.

It'd all been my fault. I wasn't here to protect her.

My fists pummel. My heart hammers. Then I'm being tugged backward while I resist. With my arms pinned, my feet flail forward, kicking air. Next, I kick backward, leading with the heel of my hard-souled boots.

"Dammit, Sebastian." A deep, gruff masculine voice grits out.

"Sebastian." The female voice again, soaked in tears and fear.

I lift my head, though not eager to release my glare from the man on the floor, face dripping, mouth cursing.

"Sebastian, look at me." The feminine command sharpens in my ear. The plea is desperate.

I blink. I blink again.

The room comes into focus. I'm still held in a vise grip, keeping my arms pinned behind me and my body upright and off the man at my feet.

My gaze connects with a vision. "Enya?"

Tears stream down her face. "Sebastian, it's me. Look at only me."

I meet her eyes but quickly look away. I've done what I've done for her, but I can't face whatever that look in her eyes means.

Averting my gaze, I see Vale standing a few feet behind Enya, holding a bundle.

"Adara," I whisper.

I glance back at the man on the floor, the one prone, knees tucked to his chest and covering his face with big hands while blood seeps between his fingers. I struggle again against the hold someone has on me.

I want back at that man. Fuck him. Fuck him for making my girls cry.

"Sebastian, settle down." Stone. Demanding as ever, he tightens his hold on me.

"Baby, please."

I lift my head again at the soft plea, catching on Enya's tear-stained face. Her hands are clasped beneath her chin, praying for me with useless prayers. The gates of hell are open and waiting for me. I don't deserve heaven. I don't deserve her, but I'll defend her. I'll keep her safe.

"Did he touch you?" My voice is rough, gravel-filled and deep. If he touched one precious hair or an inch of her soft skin, nothing is going to be able to restrain me.

She shakes her head. "He only scared me." She swallows, her tone thick.

"Let me see," I snap, eager to see her body and check for myself that he didn't harm her.

"If I let you go, you go to her. Do you hear me?" Stone tugs on my arms, locked within his. No one else could have the power to restrain me.

"I need you." The tears fall harder down Enya's beautiful face as she stares at me, willing me with those eyes to come to her.

"Let me go," I grit, eyes focused on Enya. My body stills.

The color drains from Enya's face. Hurt and rejection fill the bright darkness of her eyes. She's misunderstood and I lurch toward her, but Stone holds me back.

"No." I shake my head. "Stone, let me go." My voice cracks. "I need to get to Enya."

Stone holds me a moment longer, squeezing me for emphasis, before he loosens his hold.

Abruptly, I shrug him off and step toward Enya. With my rushed approach, she steps back.

Fuck. She's afraid of me, too. Raising my hands, I surrender to her. But the sight of my swollen fingers and blood-covered palms is only further proof I'm not good for her.

"Sugar," I whisper, desperate, pleading. "Please." *Please don't be frightened.* "I'd never hurt you. I . . . I love you." The words are coarse and rough, as a phrase I've never said before to anyone.

She nearly knocks me over with the force of her sudden hug. With her arms around my middle and her head tucked into my chest, Enya clings to me and I lower my arms.

"I'm a mess, baby." I don't want to taint her with my dirty hands.

She steps back and grabs my shirt, tugging me toward the sink where she draws my hands beneath the faucet and washes them. Her fingers scour while the soap suds. And her tears still fall.

"I'm sorry." I start, voice tight and hushed near her ear. "I'm so sorry." My throat fills. The words are a tremor. "I'm sorry." I choke before lowering my head to her shoulder while she scrubs at my fingers and flips my hands to rinse my palms. Cleansing me. Renewing me. Taking my apology and giving me her forgiveness. Her love.

Before I know it, her arms are around me again, and she's clinging to me. Or maybe I'm clinging to her, as I wrap her in my arms and tuck my face into her neck.

This woman has reduced me to a frightened child, and an angry teen, and a desperate man.

"I love you, Sebastian. I love you." The phrase is a lullaby on repeat as I hug her to me in her kitchen. The background melody is Stone arresting a man and Vale pacing with Adara. The only thing I focus on, though, are the soft, giving words, the beat of Enya's heart, and the strum of her hand over my lower back, soothing me, loving me.

Slowly, I lift my heavy head. My face is damp.

"It wasn't you," Enya says, meeting my eyes. "It was me. He was after me. He thought I must know something about the money because of Seamus." She cups my jaw, gently squeezing to emphasize her words. "It wasn't you."

Abruptly, I pull back and let my gaze roam over her body. "Did he touch you?" My voice turns hard and cold again. "Did he hurt you?"

My eyes catch on the circle of blood near her hip. Hastily, I'm lifting her dress, needing to see her skin.

"He had a knife at my hip, and he nicked me. It's nothing." Her tender palm comes to my cheek and draws my attention back to her face.

"It's not nothing. It's—" My voice catches as I realize once again, I could have lost her. In a flash, he could have done her extreme harm. I tug her to me again, squeezing her to my chest as I breathe her in.

Fall rainstorm. Lemon cake. Baby scent. Family.

I pull back again and drag my fingers through her hair, fisting it gently at the back of her neck. "You were wrong." My voice is hoarse. "The other night. All that you said about us, how we met and what happened. You were wrong."

"How was I wrong?" Her eyes fill with concern, but I never want her to have doubts again. I don't want her to question me or my intentions with her. *With us.*

"A woman didn't trip before my bakery. An angel fell from heaven in that rainstorm. I took one look at her, and I knew I'd never be the same. I'd never want to let her go."

"Then why were you always pushing me away?"

I lick my lips, the truth salty and thick on them. "I was scared. I was afraid I'd lose you like I've lost everyone else." My mom. Clint's mom. My dad. Even Stone to his disappointment in me.

"I didn't think I was good enough," I admit. "Fuck, I didn't think I'd ever be a dad or a man in love. But there you were, telling me you were pregnant. And that first kiss. Then you came back, and Adara came along. And I just wanted it all. Her. You. Us. But I didn't trust myself."

Enya stares at me, hands on my chest, certainly feeling my heart hammering. "Then I'll trust you for the both of us."

I nod, the movement growing heavier and heavier until I pull her to me again, holding the back of her head and the base of her spine, breathing her in. Grounding myself in her.

I turn only my head in the direction of Vale who has given us space and walked with Adara toward the front window. Outside, red and blue lights whirl, and the roar of a car engine comes to life.

"He's gone," Vale calls out. She twists to face where Enya and I embrace. "It's over."

I stare at my sister, holding Adara. She gives me a wink before lifting Adara and pressing a kiss to her head. My sister loves babies. But more importantly, she already loves this little one as much as me.

I release Enya from my arms but cup her shoulders. "I can't promise there won't be more trouble. Someday." My past is still there, lingering behind me.

Enya is already shaking her head, offering a tender smile but one full of promise. "Then, we'll face it together."

How did I get so fortunate? "Why? Why are you so good to me?"

"Because I love you." Her hand slides to my jaw, tugging at the sharp edge of my face. The strength of her words is in her touch, in her gaze.

"I love you," I say again, the words easier this time.

Her smile grows stronger. Heat warms her eyes. She's everything I denied and all that I ever wanted.

"Say it again," I whisper, lowering my forehead to hers.

"I love you. You're mine. You're ours."

"I'm yours," I whisper before brushing my lips against hers, like that first kiss. When I wanted more and took a risk to sip at such sweetness.

True to her, Enya meets my mouth, and strikes the match, igniting this kiss until only heat and hearts exist.

Love flames between us.

I'm never going to deny her again.

+ + +

Hours later, official statements are made, and the floor is mysteriously cleaned. I want to have the entire house sanitized from that man's presence. But first, I need to shower myself. I want to wash off the grime of a motorcycle ride and the stench of that man on my hands.

Vale explained how she drove down the highway, calling me after she called 9-1-1 immediately upon leaving Enya's. She parked out of sight up the road and waited, knowing I'd appear like a vigilante, but also hopeful Stone would be right behind me. Which he was. My oldest brother is always there for me. My younger sister always looking out for me.

As I stand in Enya's shower, I face the spray and let the water pummel my face, hopeful the pressure washing will cleanse my thoughts.

Who knows what Rodger Neil would have done to either of my flames? I shiver at the thought of both of them being extinguished. Fear consumes me again.

Fear means you care, Vale once told me. If you weren't scared, you've lost feeling.

I'd been scared. For all my denials of fatherhood and family, when both options stared me in the face, I couldn't walk away. I wanted them with a fierceness I hadn't recognized yet.

Love. I cannot live without it. Enya and Adara are love.

Love is family, Stone said. I want to be Adara's dad. I want to be Enya's partner in life. And I want the three of us to be a family. I'm confident Enya will never let me stray from this chosen path.

The soft click of the shower door opening and closing tells me she's heard my thoughts. Through the barrier of a bathroom and bedroom, where she nursed Adara and set her in her bassinet, Enya reads me. She gave me a few minutes to myself but knew I couldn't be trusted with my thoughts for long.

Her arms wrap around me from behind and she presses kisses up and down my spine. While I want to spin and face her, examine every inch of her for signs of fear or distress, I melt beneath her attention.

Just this once, I tell myself. I'll let someone else take care of me.

Enya kisses my back and smooths her hands over my chest. She removes her touch only to grab shampoo. "Lean back."

I do as she says, and she massages my scalp, using her fingertips to lather the shampoo. With a gentle nudge, she spins me so I can rinse my hair myself as I'm taller than her. When my head is free of shampoo, she presses at my sides, turning me so my back is to her. I'm a puppet, and she controls my strings. Taking over my movements, she washes me with a tender massage at my neck and over my shoulders, down my back and along my ass.

Her touch is sensual, but she isn't seducing me. She's caring for me.

Her hands work down the back of my legs and around the front, but she never turns me to face her. Skipping over my dick which has grown hard from the tenderness of her touch, she washes my chest, smoothing up my front and over my pecs. Finally, she scrubs down one arm and then repeats the cleansing on the other.

All that remains is my face and my cock. I reach for face wash and scrub at my own forehead, sliding down to my cheeks, when her arms wrap around me once more and her breasts hit my back. Her hands cup my balls, and then she's stroking my stiff shaft.

I quickly rinse the suds from my face and glance down at her fist tugging at my hard length.

"Sugar," I groan at the sight of her pleasing me. Then I lower my hand and cover hers, squeezing tighter, tugging harder. With my other hand braced on the tile wall, I watch as we stroke my dick together.

Enya kisses my back, allowing me to take over and use her hand gripping my shaft to release the last bits of tension inside me.

After I spill and watch my seed slither down the drain, I spin and face her, taking her head in my hands and kissing her. I lap at her tongue and suck at her mouth. I'm spent but I'll give her anything she wants in this new, relaxed state I'm in. I'm floating, finally free and clear of all thoughts. It's a new kind of high. It's Enya.

"I love you," I mutter to her mouth.

She smiles against my lips, happy to hear the words. "I love you, too."

The phrase imprints on my mouth. Instantly, I drop to my knees and stroke a finger against her core. She cups my jaw, tipping up my head so I meet her eyes.

"That was all for you." Her expression says this shower was a gift.

"I want this all for me, too." I swipe along her slick folds, feeling how much she wants me. I'm still baffled, still stunned, but so grateful. I'm the one who owes her a thousand thank yous.

"It is yours." A teasing smile tugs at her mouth. Her eyes heat to a golden brown.

I lower my face to the apex of her legs and wedge between them, forcing her thighs to spread. Keeping my eyes on her, I watch her response as I take my first taste. My tongue swipes across her center. She's pure sugar.

"Baby," she moans, her eyes drifting shut.

"Watch me." I kiss her pubic bone. "Watch us." Then I'm devouring her, sipping at her sweet honey flavor and slicing through the softness of her flesh until she's rocking on my face. I clutch at her flexed ass cheeks and hold her to me until she comes on my tongue.

"Yes," she whispers, her breath hitching.

I glance up to witness her expression of ecstasy.

She's a candle in a dark house. A fire on a cold night. She's my blazing beacon.

And I'm finally where I belong.

With her. And Adara.

My flames.

Chapter 36

[Sebastian]

We did not make love last night, too exhausted by the evening's unfolding to do anything other than cling to each other in our sleep. I didn't roll to my stomach. She didn't use my body as her pillow. We cuddled face to face the entire night.

And when Adara needed her three a.m. bottle, I was there to snuggle my other girl.

All three of us fell back asleep until late morning when I made breakfast.

"I could fall in love with a man who cooks," Enya teases from the other side of the island, reminding me of when she said something similar the first night she stayed in my apartment.

"Oh yeah? Just any man?" Wearing only boxer briefs, I lean across the island countertop and fight a glance at this fixture where I took her. We need a repeat without all the doubts and denial between us.

"Well, I have had my eye on this curmudgeon baker in town." She winks at me, and I chuckle.

"Still don't know what I did to have you in my life or what I can do to prove myself to you."

"Sebastian, you don't need to prove anything to me. You've already done so much. You're kindness and—"

I snort, before groaning. "*I'm nice.*"

"You do realize that being kind is a gift, right? Not everyone does it so easily. Or often."

My face heats and I lower my head.

"Just take the compliment," she teasingly scolds, tossing a morsel of bacon at me.

I hand-block the crispy meat and meet her eyes. "Still want to prove myself to you. That I'm in this forever."

Her brows lift, surprised at the declaration, but I mean it. I want the rest of my life to be the better half of my life. She'll be the better half of me. The person I've been fighting the most in my thirty-five years is myself, and I'm ready to concede the fight.

Love wins.

"Well . . ." She pauses on my eyes before dropping her gaze to my bare chest and scanning down my middle. "The one thing you could do for me is give Adara a sibling." Her lids lift and she sheepishly gazes at me. "Maybe a brother?"

I stare at her, without blinking, feeling my heart grow three sizes within my chest. She wants another child. *With me?* My chest might explode with the warm tension inside it.

My silence causes her to keep speaking. "I mean, it's okay if you only want Adara. Or . . ."

She cuts off her speech as she watches me round the island and spin her stool, so she faces me.

I lean over her, caging her in with my arms. "You want me to give you another baby?"

"Only if—" Her words stop short as I lower to one knee and cup the backs of her calves.

"Sebastian?" My name is as thick as the pancake batter from breakfast.

"Sugar, I've been a man acting on instinct, reacting first and thinking second, most of my life. But there isn't a doubt in my mind that asking you to be my wife is a flip decision. It's the smartest thing I'll ever do. I want a life with you. And Adara. And another baby. I want *our* family." I exhale. "I've been denying love because I couldn't see it in my future but then you fell into my life."

She softly chuckles at the reminder of her fall in front of the bakery.

"But I'm the one who fell that day. I tumbled hard and fast. So fast I didn't even see what was happening to me. Didn't recognize it, either. I needed you to show me the possibility. And with you came Adara, giving me another gift. I want to be her dad. I want you as my wife. My love for the remainder of this life."

I squeeze the backs of her legs. "Will you marry me? Will you allow me the honor of being Adara's father? Will you let me stand beside you for life?"

Tears softly trickle down her face as her mouth sweetly gapes. "Would you want to adopt Adara?"

"I wouldn't ask if I didn't," I tease, jostling her legs. "But only if you want me to officially be her father and I understand if you—" I'm cut off by her hands on my jaw and then her mouth on mine, kissing me sweet and long until I'm ready to tug her from the stool and lay her out on the floor. We have all the time ahead of us to work out our future.

"Yes," she giggles at my lips. "Yes, to you. Yes, to being Adara's dad. Yes, to being your wife. Yes, yes, yes."

Her eager answer has me laughing. "Do you mean it?"

"I wouldn't say it if I didn't." She mocks my rough voice while her face glows with happiness. My flame burns even brighter.

"I don't have a ring, but I'll get you one. Whatever you want."

"I only want you."

With my arms suddenly around her waist, I stand and tug her upward with me. Her legs wrap around my hips.

"No brothers," I tease, pressing kisses to her lips as I set her on a clear space of the island countertop. "Boys are trouble. Only girls. Lots of girls."

Enya giggles as I press her backward and climb over her. Her hands smooth down my chest. "Girls can be trouble, too."

"So much trouble," I mutter, leaning down to kiss her. But I've never wanted to cause trouble more than with her. "Now, how soon before we start working on that sibling thing?"

She laughs harder, until I've stopped the sound with a kiss. Then we make other noises.

And through it all are whispers of words I never thought would apply to me.

I love her and she loves me.

Epilogue

May – 10 months later

[Sebastian]

The late spring's rainstorms were something fierce, and I was getting worried as Enya was meeting a client. She works hard and I was grateful tax season was over although accounting was never ending.

As I stand inside the bakery, working on custom orders in the quiet of an empty shop, my mind drifts.

Rodger O'Neil spends his days and nights in prison for what he did to Enya. Rena was also caught as an accomplice to his master plan to recover mystery money, but she was released on probation. I don't know where she is. I don't care either.

As for that money. . . Knox, Clay and I spent a weekend digging potholes in the partial dirt flooring of the cellar until I decided it didn't matter if money was buried beneath the house or not. It wasn't mine. It only brought trouble. Then I hired a cement company to pour a full slab floor across the cellar. I can't stand upright down there but it doesn't matter. The space only holds mechanicals and storage.

Suddenly, "Imagine" plays through the overhead speakers forcing me to look up at that old quote on the wall. The one I'm so accustomed to that I hardly pay it any attention.

There are no holes in kindness.

I really thought it meant don't be an asshole, but with Enya in my life, I've learned the value of being kind. Or maybe I've always known the trait, I'd just warped the way it should work. I'd done bad things with good intentions because I loved my family.

And I've come to learn how much they love me.

Vale was ecstatic when I married Enya last fall, but it was Stone who fought back tears when I said I was officially adopting Adara.

No more fake daddy. Let all the rumors say what they want to say. I *am* Adara's father. The birth certificate now states the truth. I'm her dad.

The tinkle of the bell above the door signals someone has entered, and I glance up with relief to see my beautiful wife shaking out an umbrella inside the bakery. She gives me a warm smile that says so many things.

I love you.

You're mine.

Forever.

The giant rock on her finger, sparking in the low light of the bakery says the same thing. We married in a beautiful outdoor setting where it appropriately rained. Enya said it meant good luck.

I am definitely the luckiest man I know.

"Hey, sugar." I wipe my hands on a towel and round the counter. She meets me halfway for a kiss that puts other kisses to shame. Enya loves to kiss me. She doesn't accept a simple swipe of lips, either. She likes my tongue, my lips, and my teeth, and I give her everything in every meeting of our mouths.

When we finally break apart, I ask, "Is Adara still with Vale?" My sister loves to babysit.

Enya swipes a hand down her form fitting dress. I love her professional clothing especially when she lets me strip her out of it.

"Yeah. Vale said she'd keep her for a little bit longer." She shivers when the air conditioning kicks on, mixing with the water droplets on her skin.

"Want some coffee?"

"I'd love some."

I circle behind the counter while Enya takes a seat. It's funny how she always sits in the same spot. The place where we first shared a lemon cake. The seat where Adara was born.

"Got a text from Barnett," I call out from behind the counter. "He aced that economics final. He'll be here in a week." My wife gave him some pointers.

Barnett Matthews turned out to be a dedicated employee, working extra shifts to earn back the money he took from Rena. Then I gifted it back to him as a donation to his college fund. He's finishing up his freshman year at WVU under a football scholarship.

I come back around to the table and set down two sturdy mugs. "I have something for you."

Her brows lift as she picks up the sturdy mug and blows at the hot steam coming from the liquid gold inside. She hums. "A lemon cake?"

Okay, I'll get her that, too but I hold up a finger, signaling I need a minute. I head to my office and then return with a small paper bag. Taking a seat opposite her, I watch as she stares at the bag with intrigue.

"You know I've been cleaning out my office." While I consider myself creatively messy, Enya suggested a better system to organize my *creativity*. She didn't intrude, though, knowing I needed to initiate any system on my own. The bakery is still mine and she understands my need to own something as mine. Something I'm continually proud of that honestly, legitimately, legally belongs to me.

She watches me as I dip my hand into the bag. "And I found a few things."

I pull forth one shoe and then another. A mismatched pair of heels that strangely look right when paired together.

"Oh my gosh." Enya laughs, clapping her hands before her mouth as she falls back in the seat. "Are those my shoes?"

I lift one. "The day we met." I lift the other. "And the day Adara was born."

Enya reaches for the one and draws her forefinger and thumb down the spiky left heel that once went with an opposite shoe which snapped off on the sidewalk during a rainstorm. She picks up the other one and chuckles again. "I don't know what I was thinking when I wore these that day." The second heel is chunkier but still tall.

"And why do you have these?" She peers up at me. "Were you hoping Cinderella would return for her slipper?"

Being a girl dad now, I'm familiar enough with fairytales to know who Cinderella is. "Something like that." I smile. "Or maybe she'd at least return for my lemon baby-Bundt cake."

"Well, my sweet prince. I have something for you, too, but first . . . speaking of a lemon baby-Bundt cake . . ."

I laugh as I press off the table and stand. "Yes, my queen," I mock, but she knows I worship her like royalty.

I set one cake on a plate and grab two forks before returning to the table. The plate sits in the middle, but she knows I'll let her have the first bite. I always do because I love to watch her eat my treats. The way she savors it on her tongue. The way her eyes roll back a little. The seductive hum she gives, easily turning me on.

I hold up my fork. "What are we toasting to?"

Enya lifts hers but doesn't clink it against mine. "I'm pregnant."

Her eyes focus on my face as I take in the words. I swallow around the sudden lump in my throat. A good lump. I'll never be able to get a bite of this cake down.

"Your husband must be excited." That's my line. That's how this went the first time. When a woman entered my bakery during a rainstorm and told me she was here to celebrate her good news.

"Is he?" She watches me, hopeful but hesitant.

"Sugar." I drop my fork and scoop her up from the bench seat, drawing her into a tight hug before deeply kissing her. She melts into the kiss, passing her excitement at this news from her lips to mine.

She's having a baby. And I'm the father. Because I'm her husband.

"When did you find out?" I mutter to her lips, dipping my fingers into her hair to remove the tight bun at the nape of her neck.

"I wasn't sure, so I went to the doctor earlier. I'm almost two months along."

"Enya," I whisper, enthusiastically kissing her before saying, "I want to lay you out on this table to celebrate."

She giggles against my mouth and pulls back. "I had the same thought the first time I told you I was pregnant."

I wasn't Adara's father then. At least, not quite, but I'm her dad in every way and this announcement is almost as exciting as the first time Enya told me she was pregnant.

Although this time, she's already mine. No waiting out months. No questioning who the father is. No doubting myself or what I want in life.

I'll get to experience every stage of this pregnancy and I'm here for it.

My hand falls to her belly and I marvel at the size of my palm over her still flat stomach.

"I think Cookie would make a good name."

Enya laughs harder, though the sound is watery, and I glance up at her. "Why the tears?"

"I'm just so happy."

"Me, too, baby." I've never been happier. "Let's go home."

Because I want to take my time with her, not just spread her on a bakery table. There are other occasions for those moments. For this one, I want to go to the house we share, where we raise our family.

Together.

Thank you for taking the time to read this book.
Please consider writing a review on major sales channels where ebooks
and paperbacks are sold and discussed.

More by L.B. Dunbar

<u>Sterling Falls</u>
Small town big on heart. Seven siblings muddling through love over 40.
Sterling Heat
Sterling Brick
Sterling Streak

<u>*Parentmoon (a standalone)*</u>
When the mother of the groom goes head-to-head with the single father of the bride.

<u>Holiday Hotties</u>
Holiday novellas certain to heat the season.
Naughty-ish
Scrooge-ish

<u>Road Trips & Romance</u>
3 sisters. 3 destinations. A second chance at love over 40.
Hauling Ashe
Merging Wright
Rhode Trip

<u>Lakeside Cottage</u>
Four friends. Four summers. Shenanigans and love happen at the lake.
Living at 40
Loving at 40
Learning at 40
Letting Go at 40

<u>The Silver Foxes of Blue Ridge</u>
More sexy silver foxes in the mountain community of Blue Ridge.
Silver Brewer
Silver Player
Silver Mayor
Silver Biker

<u>Sexy Silver Foxes</u>

When sexy silver foxes meet the feisty vixens of their dreams.
After Care
Midlife Crisis
Restored Dreams
Second Chance
Wine&Dine

Collision novellas
A spin-off from After Care – the younger set/rock stars
Collide
Caught

Rom-com standalone for the over 40
The Sex Education of M.E.

The Heart Collection
Small town, big hearts - stories of family and love.
Speak from the Heart
Read with your Heart
Look with your Heart
Fight from the Heart
View with your Heart

A Heart Collection Spin-off
The Heart Remembers

BOOKS IN OTHER AUTHOR WORLDS
Smartypants Romance (an imprint of Penny Reid)
Tales of the Winters sisters set in Green Valley.
Love in Due Time
Love in Deed
Love in a Pickle

The World of True North (an imprint of Sarina Bowen)
Welcome to Vermont! And the Busy Bean Café.
Cowboy
Studfinder

THE EARLY YEARS
<u>The Legendary Rock Star Series</u>
A classic tale with a modern twist of rock star romance and suspense

325

<u>Paradise Stories</u>
MMA romance. Two brothers. One fight.

<u>The Island Duet</u>
Intrigue and suspense. The island knows what you've done.

<u>Modern Descendants – writing as elda lore</u>
Magical realism. Modern myths of Greek gods.

About the Author

www.lbdunbar.com

L.B. Dunbar loves sexy silver foxes, second chances, and small towns. If you enjoy older characters in your romance reads, including a hero with a little silver in his scruff and a heroine rediscovering her worth, then welcome to romance for those over 40. L.B. Dunbar's signature works include women and men in their prime taking another turn at love and happily ever after. She's a *USA TODAY* Bestseller as well as #1 Bestseller on Amazon in Later in Life Romance with her Lakeside Cottage and Road Trips & Romance series. L.B. lives in Chicago with her own sexy silver fox.

To get all the scoop about the self-proclaimed queen of silver fox romance, join her on Facebook at Loving L.B. or receive her monthly newsletter, Love Notes.

+ + +

Connect with L.B. Dunbar